A HUMAN ELEMENT

The Element Trilogy – Book One

Donna Galanti

A HUMAN ELEMENT
The Element Trilogy – Book One

FOURTH EDITION
www.elementtrilogy.com
ISBN: 978-1-7363162-4-5

Cover designed by Ryan Doan — www.ryandoan.com

Praise for A HUMAN ELEMENT

"*A Human Element* is an elegant and haunting first novel. Unrelenting, devious but full of heart. Highly recommended." —Jonathan Maberry, *New York Times* bestselling author of *Code Zero*

"Be afraid. Be very afraid. And be utterly absorbed by this riveting debut that had me reading till the wee hours of the night. A thriller star is born. Don't miss *A Human Element*." —M.J. Rose, international bestselling author of *The Collector of Dying Breaths*

"Lyrical and creepy, Donna Galanti's *A Human Element* tugs on our heartstrings and plucks the gut-strings of horror. This debut thriller author is a true storyteller, highly reminiscent of Dean Koontz." — Dakota Banks, award-winning author of *Deliverance*

"Donna Galanti has created a thriller with a huge, aching heart. Her main characters, Ben and Laura are conjured in delicious detail, as are their personal trials. Galanti's rich and provocative thriller asks big questions. What makes us human, what makes us monstrous? Is there a love that can transcend the physical and emotional, to the supernatural? Galanti has given us an impressive debut. With her blending of romance, the coming of age quest, and the supernatural, she is a writer to watch, who will surely expand the diameters of the thriller genre." —Catherine Stine, author of *Fireseed One*

"Such a beautiful, yet haunting debut novel by Donna Galanti. *A Human Element* will crawl around in your cranium many days after you have finished the last page of the book." —Michael McCarty, author of *Lost Girl of the Lake*

"A thrilling ride full of believable characters, a terrifying villain, an epic battle for survival, and a love worth killing for. The last third of the novel is a race to the finish, and I was glued to the pages, hoping the characters I'd grown to love would finally find the peace they deserved. A page-turner filled with fascinating twists and turns!" —Marie Lamba, author of *Drawn*

"*A Human Element* is a haunting look at what it means to be human. It's a suspenseful ride through life and love...and death, with a killer so evil you can't help but be afraid. An excellent read." —Janice Gable Bashman, author of *Predator*

For my #1 champion, my mom, Suneil Beckley, whose sunshine may have gone out but without her this book never would have been written.

And for my husband, Michael, the greatest provider of alone time there is.

Acknowledgements

Several friends and peers helped get this book to publication.

My developmental editor, Kathryn Craft, taught me how to "not show my underpants" in my writing. She's an amazing writer, editor, and friend.

Thanks to Randi Sherwood, my first beta reader who provided in depth edits and insight.

And so much gratitude goes to my dear friend, Lisa Green, whose support and infinite encouragement uplifted me through the writing of this book—and still does today.

CHAPTER 1: 1979

Ben Fieldstone jumped over the rotted log at the edge of Coopersville Lake. A short lifetime of summers told him it was there. He could barely see it in the moonlight. He kicked sticks and stones from his path with the toes of his red Pro Keds. He wasn't going back. He'd stay in the dark woods all night if he had to. He wasn't taking clarinet lessons this year. Every summer vacation here his parents pressured him to learn a musical instrument. Not this year.

He didn't understand his parents when it came to many things, and tonight was proof. His mom and dad didn't understand him either.

He swatted at a mosquito. Through the trees, the last hint of orange glazed the surface of the lake. Its smooth surface didn't fool him. The water still rippled at the edge like a giant mouth. It stuck out its tongue over and over for another taste. A heavy darkness layered the woods to his left and he made sure he stuck to the rough trail hugging the water's edge. There were no cabins on this side of the lake, and he walked on looking behind him to see where his cabin was. It appeared so far away. He could barely make out its shape.

Something crackled behind him. He stopped and held his breath, listening, but heard nothing more than laughter skidding across the water from the other side of the lake. The lights of two dozen cabins speckled the edge of the water. They eased his fear. *Jeez, it was freezing.* He pulled his sweatshirt tighter around him. These August nights sure got cool. Would his parents discover that he ran away soon? He hugged himself tighter. Now that he was nine and a half his parents would have to take his opinions more seriously.

He resumed walking and pulled his sweatshirt up over his mouth to get warm, just like he'd do on the soccer bench back home. Avery called it his turtle look. She'd reach out and tap his 'cute nose' then run away with a giggle. She was annoying because she talked all the time, but tonight he missed her chatter. In two more weeks, when school started, he'd see Avery again.

He looked up through the dark silhouette of trees across the lake. They stretched toward the sky. Stars winked back at him. Perhaps it was cold up there, too, in the dark. He bet it would be quiet there too, without parents to boss him or Avery to blather on. Among the stars. That would be a good place to hide away from his parents. They'd never find him there.

He recognized the Big Dipper low in the sky, and followed its stars upward to where it connected to the Little Dipper. Could a boy live in them alone? It would be more fun with a friend. Maybe with Avery, even though she talked a lot. They could jump from star to star on the Big Dipper like stones in a creek. They might explore the sky all night and when the sun rose, they could sleep in the warmth of its light.

A blast of green broke through his dreamy thoughts. It sliced the night in two. A bright streak barreling toward the earth. He stood, mesmerized. A meteorite? He had just learned about them in school. It grew larger and larger. A fiery ball. In his excitement, he forgot he had run away. He couldn't wait to get back to the cabin and tell his parents. He jumped around and trotted back along the shoreline. The green light grew larger. He tripped over a rock and fell sideways into the thick brush.

And then something so frightening happened he decided to stay where he was. The moon disappeared. A green brilliance lit up the lake up like a sunrise switched on too soon. Ben shielded his eyes from the light and staggered up to get a better view. He knew a second of terror before an explosion flattened him unconscious.

He awoke facedown. Faint noises bounced around the lake. The smell of burning wood filled his nose with an acrid, dry smell. Sirens shrieked. He stretched his head up and spat out pebbles and broken sticks jammed into his mouth. He spit and spit again, coughing out dirt.

He pulled himself up in pain. His face and hands bled from being slammed into the earth. The quiet realm of the small lake community roared to life with fire and shouts. Where there should have been dotted cabin lights there spread only blackness.

A burning metal smell struck his burning lungs. It *must* be a meteorite. Smoke obscured everything and he couldn't orient himself. Where was their cabin? It was gone. Ben ran toward where home had been. He fell many times and reached for close branches along the trail for support. As he struggled to make the trek back, a mixture of shouts and fire engine horns echoed around the lake. Cabin fires leaped into the woods, fed by the dry August timber. Tongues of flame stabbed out of cabin windows and licked at the rooftops.

Ben ran on, toward where his cabin should have been. In the middle of the blackness, steam rose like the underground coal fire he'd seen on the news. He met up with the others. Fathers and mothers carried crying children. Their fearful shouts swelled in the air around him. They called out to him but he ignored them and continued his pace.

He reached the black abyss and stopped running. His breath spewed erratic clouds in the cold air. The smell here grew stronger than he could stand and he vomited on some rocks. He straightened up after he had nothing left to retch. Before him, a crater the width of his school's soccer field had eaten everything in its path. Steam rose in shoots from the ravaged earth and small fires around its edge illuminated the area. Between these fires, people held their hands over their mouths as they looked down into its depth.

The fire now engulfed half of the mountaintop in a soaring billow of orange light greedily devouring the earth. When the fire engines stopped, the cries of people who had lost their loved ones or houses rose up like the flames. Where a dozen cabins had been now steamed a black mass. In one dying gasp of hope, Ben sought to re-orient but he was sure—this was where his parents' cabin had been. They could not have survived. This dark thing had crushed them.

Ben kneeled at the edge of the crater by the water and cried. He was just a boy covered in dirt and blood who wanted to tell his parents he was sorry for running away. Someone put a blanket around his shoulders, but he couldn't be comforted.

His world had ended that summer night of 1979.

The night he had daydreamed about jumping from star to star along the Big Dipper.

CHAPTER 2: 1980

The girl screamed in delirium as she lay on the raised bed twisting the stiff, starched sheets under her. A stain of sweat and blood spread below her shaking legs. A musky smell hung in the air. Outside the rain streamed down in a torrential rush, beating a tinny rhythm on the windows of the back room of the small medical office.

Doctor Britton's right hand slid inside the girl up to his wrist as he pushed down on her monstrous belly. She screamed until her strength gave up and then trailed off into ragged whimpers.

"The head is turned. Get me the forceps," he yelled to the nurse. The nurse identified the instrument from the table near her and placed it in Doctor Britton's outstretched hand. In all his years as a doctor, he had never seen a woman work so hard to expel a baby.

He tried not to think about the nameless man who waited outside for this baby. The government man in charge told Doctor Britton he must deliver the child as scheduled and his job would be done. But for now, he must stay in this steaming room filled with sweat and blood and screams. It gnawed into his stomach and burned deep in his head. How he wished he could grab the bottle of whiskey from the next room.

Doctor Britton glanced at the nurse who stood from a distance. He could tell she wanted no connection with this one. He too had heard the rumors about how the girl said she had never been with a man. But who could believe that coming from a runaway that showed up alone in town one day at the Methodist church? As time passed, it became evident why she ran away. It was decent of the Armstrongs, a childless couple in town, to hear of the girl's plight and take her in. The nurse must have read his thoughts as she moved closer.

"You're a lucky child," the nurse said. "Lucky those Armstrongs took you in with open hearts as God had intended. But God's help won't forgive your sins and blasphemy now, will it?"

The nurse shook her head. "Your sin is here. Tonight. Pushing its way out into the world. Isn't it?" She pinched the girl's arm. The girl moaned and tossed her head.

"Stop it," Doctor Britton demanded, disgusted with her religious idiocy.

He steeled himself as another scream wailed from the girl, who whipped her head back and forth on the narrow raised bed. He spread the girl's legs wider as he gently pressed the forceps onto the pulsing head pushing out from her. Blood gushed from the girl's pathetic body as it quaked. Her belly rose above her small frame rippling in an obscene dance like a fat man's beer gut that pushed proudly out. Overhead, the lights flickered as power lines swayed in the storm. Stark shadows rose and fell in a wave of menace from the room's corners.

The doctor prayed the lights would stay on and he harbored on, struggling to loosen the child trapped inside the small body. It was a good thing the girl remained half-unconscious. The girl and child would die if he couldn't pull this baby out soon. He focused on his mission and the birth canal. He blocked out the quivering being before him and the useless nurse standing her distance. Who was she to judge? They had both accepted this mission and the money promised to them in secrecy.

Guilt consumed him as he worked on this girl beneath him in this bloody, hot room. She struggled here, all alone in this world and tortured by her body's need to push out a baby far too large for her frame. He was glad she went into labor after midnight and showed up at his home office door, doubled over in pain. No one knew she came here, the girl had said, not even Fanny and Wesley Armstrong. They had been told a couple waited to adopt the child immediately following the birth. No one could know what really transpired.

He had not anticipated the girl's complications but had no intention of transporting her to Albany Medical Center to save her. He had to maintain possession of the child or he wouldn't be paid. He needed this money. He just hoped her fast labor would make her death more believable. Guilt tugged at him again.

Outside a drowning deluge of May showers beat down on the roof. Tree branches whipped at the room's windows. They scratched the glass over and over as if to claw their way in and entangle him in their punishing snare.

The slippery body inside the girl gave way in his hands. "It's coming!"

With her last bit of strength, the girl clutched Doctor Britton's coat. "Don't let me see it!"

He peeled her fingers from him with gloved hands, leaving her blood on his coat.

She smiled and closed her eyes. "But if it's girl...name her Laura."

"Sarah, you've got to push." Doctor Britton allowed himself to say her name for the first time that night. "Pull your legs up and bear down now." But the girl's eyes remained closed.

"Nurse, push her legs up further. We need to widen the birth canal."

The nurse hesitated. She didn't want to touch the girl.

"Now!"

The nurse pushed up on the girl's legs until Doctor Britton had the baby firm in his grasp. He pulled with care, suddenly wishing the girl would live. The amount of blood gushing between her legs suggested otherwise. The head stretched and ripped the girl with its savage size. In a sliding, silent whoosh, he pulled out the child.

"Oh, my God," the nurse whispered.

They stared at the boy he held in both hands. It must have weighed twelve pounds. Through the blood and mucus covering it, the child gleamed pale as the moon. The pulse throbbed through translucent veins with a life force so strong it had ruptured its way into the world. Its forehead was a bulbous mass protruding from a Neanderthal-like skull. Its nose and mouth spread wide across its deformed face. When Doctor Britton wiped the mucus from the eyes, the nurse gasped. What should have been a pale child's newborn blue was instead a pale yellow.

"It's the Devil himself," the nurse stammered. The lights in the room shone bright and dimmed again as if in agreement. "See, it's a sign!"

"Stop it. There's nothing here but a newborn baby with some abnormalities," Doctor Britton snapped. "Get him cleaned up and make the delivery." He cut the umbilical cord, tied it with deft hands, and passed the child to the shaking nurse. Its forehead shone like alabaster and it wailed as if already mourning the loss of being separated from its mother.

Doctor Britton turned back to his patient. After hours of thrashing about in pain and blood, she rested. He felt for a pulse and found none. Her chest no longer rose and fell. The blood that had pumped from her now dribbled at a slower rate. He would wait until he cleaned up to call the time of death. He got a fresh sheet to pull over her face but before he could do it, his gaze rested on the soft, peaceful face.

Sarah...oh, Sarah, he whispered to himself, while the baby wailed. He allowed himself to say her name again. Her damp hair draped around her young, narrow shoulders. Her slender hand drifted off the bed as if letting go of something precious. If they had only gotten her to a hospital in time for a cesarean operation, she might have had a chance.

But he would never be more than a poor country doctor unless he saw this assignment through. Still, he set his hand on her womb, that organ that time and time again amazed him with its capabilities. He was struck by the fact that this mother had been young enough to be his own daughter.

That's when he felt movement beneath his hand. He pulled it away, in shock, then felt again more purposefully.

"There's another one!" The nurse had just finished cleaning and wrapping the pale, deformed newborn, still showing off the capabilities of overdeveloped lungs. She jerked around at Doctor Britton's voice and almost dropped the child.

He had to work fast to deliver this other child who had remained hidden for so long. With an urgent need to preserve what life remained, he reached both hands inside the birth canal and pulled loose the remaining child. A girl. Small in size, not quite five pounds. Her enormous twin had taken over and hoarded the nourishment for himself. He immediately wanted to protect her. She squirmed in his hands. A perfect, normal baby in every way.

"Welcome, Laura."

She whimpered through her ruddy skin and wrinkled her smooth forehead where tufts of brown hair grew above. He laughed in delight and held her out toward the nurse. Even she looked less arrogant by now.

"Just look," he said. "A perfect girl!" He cut and tied the umbilical cord and handed yet another crying baby to the nurse. "Clean her up quickly. We haven't much time."

As he finished cleaning up the still mother, his mind strayed far from the task at hand. He quickly devised a plan. He would deliver the boy to the man outside. Then, he would tell the Armstrongs Sarah died due to complications and that the adoptive parents changed their minds and weren't taking this baby girl. The Armstrongs need never know about the boy, and may want to keep the baby girl themselves. Being God-loving people, they would accept Sarah's fate. Sarah's daughter would console them.

His generous government benefactor need not know about the girl. One baby was expected, not two.

He smiled again as he finished his work over the young mother. Her vessel rested, now at peace. Her children would each find purpose in life. And he was satisfied God had given him a chance for redemption.

The man in black waited at the facility's back door holding an envelope and a small bundle wrapped in a ragged towel. His long coat kept his muscular girth dry from the storm's deluge. His wide-brimmed hat slung low over his jagged face, as water poured off its edge in a steady stream. This weather did not bother him. He waited patiently in the chilled spring night to deliver his packages and receive one in return. The door opened, spilling fluorescent light onto his feet. A plain-looking nurse held a crying bundle in her arms.

The man could hear the child's bellowing cries coming from underneath the blanket covering it. She pushed the child into his arms as if eager to be rid of it. He reached down and hung his head lower, to shield the bundle from the rain and his own face from the glaring light. He took the bundle and handed the nurse his packages. The nurse grabbed the envelope but quickly placed the lump on the ground as if the contents were distasteful. The nurse began to close the door when he heard another far away cry.

The man wedged his foot in the door.

"What was that?" He had to nearly shout over the din of the rain.

"Nothing." The nurse looked up.

The man risked looking her in the eye.

"The girl is in pain and won't keep quiet." She clutched the envelope and folded her arms across her sagging bosom.

"It sounded like another baby," he said.

"It's just the whimpering slut. Now she's paid double for what she's done."

The nurse took a step back as if aware she had said too much already. She glared at him. "Now go on. You have what you wanted. And so do I." She picked up the lump from the ground and shut the door in his face.

The man in black stood there for a long moment, considering the woman's choice of words. He was sure he had heard another baby. What if another child had been delivered and the frigid woman and country doctor kept it secret? *Fascinating.* He decided to keep this information to himself. He would find the opportune time to use it. He was a patient man.

But first, he had to see for himself.

He peeled back the child's bunting and looked for the first time into its yellow eyes. For that moment, the baby fell silent.

"Welcome to Earth X-10."

The baby resumed its wailing.

The man turned with his noisy package and melted into the darkness satisfied, as the doctor had been, that the night's events had provided him with more than he had asked for.

CHAPTER 3: 1987

Laura Armstrong grabbed onto the moss-covered branch and pulled herself up into a nook in the biggest tree she could find.

At seven years old, she stood compact and full of muscle from hours running through the woods surrounding her hilltop home. At fifteen feet up, the branches of the enormous, old oak bowed open to the Catskill Mountains in the distance, behind the farmhouse she shared with her parents. Its grand leaves folded outward like a green stage curtain beckoning its audience. *Come, sit for a while,* it called. *Forget your worldly worries. Be entranced.* She wanted to forget being worried. She had an anxious feeling that something bad was going to happen that day.

Laura balanced her feet on the branches and spread her arms out wide. Her chestnut hair blew behind her in the warm, July breeze. She owned this piece of the world in the little town of Coopersville, New York. She overlooked the sloped meadows and woods around the farmhouse.

Feeling confident in her footing in the tree, she took a deep breath and sang to the woods. She sang to the ancient craggy mountains before her. She sang to the birds claiming the sky and the creek that tumbled along its way. She sang to the squirrels and chipmunks chattering around her.

Her young voice sprang forth with a melody of beauty and grace surprising for a child so young. But Laura accepted this difference, as she knew she was different in other ways too. She had the ability to sense the thoughts of people. At first those thoughts came through in a jumbled disconnect of words, but as she grew older, they became a clear stream of talking in her head. It happened whenever she stood close to someone. She didn't always understand what she heard.

Sometimes frightening words came to her, often from strangers she stood next to in line at the store with her mother. But her mother and father always flowed with kind thoughts, speckled with worry about Laura or money. She never told her parents about this talent, as she didn't understand it herself. She didn't tell them about the other new talents she had just discovered either. Maybe someday she would.

"Laura, can you help me shell peas?" her mother called from the house.

"I'm coming!"

Fanny Armstrong sat on the covered porch shelling peas. Laura put her arms around her mother's neck first and buried her face in her soft hair. It made the bad feeling inside her soften for a moment. Fanny laughed and squeezed her back, then handed Laura a basket of peas to shell. She grabbed a handful of shelled peas from her mother's basket and stuffed them in her mouth before getting to work. They crunched in her mouth with sweetness.

"No headaches today, honey?" her mother asked as her stocky hands worked fast to pop out the peas beneath her wide apron-covered bosom. Laura tried but couldn't pop them out as fast. Fanny rocked away in her chipped green rocker, whistling cheerily, as her hands slit open peas.

"Nope." Today would be a good day. Some days she had headaches so bad she had to lie down on her bed. Her mother would then place cool washcloths on her forehead and neck. Their town physician, Doctor Anna, said it could be child migraines and she would grow out of it in time.

"Now don't eat all these peas." Her mother shook her finger. "Save some for supper. I'm nearly done. After this, I need your help getting the chicken feed and hay from the barn. Daddy won't be home for a bit."

They didn't have a true working farm, Laura's father would say, but they were self-sufficient enough with chickens, eggs, an apple orchard, and an enormous vegetable garden. Wesley said Fanny could make it so they lived off their garden and orchard all year long with the cellar she stocked. By autumn, it would burst full of canned tomatoes, tomato sauce, pickles, applesauce, fruit preserves, and pickled beans. Laura liked to lift the heavy round lids off the giant pickle crocks, dip her fingers into cool wetness, and pull out a crisp one to munch on.

The sky darkened suddenly. She looked up. Black clouds, thick and angry rolled overhead. Her heart raced faster. The bad feeling screamed again inside her.

"Let's go inside now." Laura tugged on her mother's sleeve. They would be safer in the house.

"But we can't let our chores go." Fanny's fingers flew across the peas. *Slit. Pop. Slit. Pop.* Wind whipped around the corner of the house. It knocked over Laura's basket.

"Mommy, come on. A storm's coming." She picked up her basket and scattered peas.

"Laura, you're being silly now. We have to go feed the chickens."

Her mother put her basket of peas down and Laura took it as an invitation to pull her up and toward the door. The wind became a howl. Her mother's apron and skirt flew up. Thunder cracked. They both jumped.

"Oh my," Fanny said. "A storm is coming. Quick, come help me."

"Maybe a tornado! Let's go inside." Laura tugged at her mother's apron.

"There's hardly ever tornados here in the Catskills." Her mother crinkled her nose and hugged Laura. She had the same pug nose as Laura, but much wider. People said they often looked alike, which Laura thought was funny since she wasn't her real mother.

All she knew about her real mother was she had been a runaway who showed up one day. Laura dreamed up many scenarios about where her mother hailed from. Once her mother was a trapeze artist from a traveling circus who got left behind on a tour, another time a royal princess who ran away to escape marrying an evil prince. And one time she was even an alien transported to Earth on a secret mission to see how humans lived.

Wesley often told Laura it was good luck to have two mommies. Fanny watched over her as her 'Earth mommy' while Sarah was her 'Angel mommy' looking down from Heaven. Wesley and Fanny had taken one photo of Laura's mother when she stayed with them. In it, she sat on a rocking chair with her hands folded over her swollen belly. She looked sad and yet peaceful at the same time. Laura could see she looked like her real mother. She would stare at her image and say her name out loud when she was alone. It made her real.

Laura was afraid some days that her 'Earth mommy' would be taken from her too.

Today felt like one of those days.

Fanny jigged across burnt grass as the wind tugged at them. She pulled Laura with her toward the barn. On clear days, Laura liked sitting in the doorway at dusk, looking at her world from high up. Today the barn was a menacing face. A towering building that threatened to gobble them up.

The sky grew darker. Lightning exploded through the angry clouds.

"Hurry," Laura said.

Fanny nodded and wiped her forehead on her apron from the exertion in the July heat. She then went upstairs to the hayloft. Laura positioned herself outside the barn to drag off the hay bales as Fanny threw them down.

"Stand back." Fanny called down to her as she swung open the loft door. It banged on the barn siding in the wind.

"I know." She stood aside as Fanny threw the first bale down, then Laura pulled it to the side while waiting for the next. The trees creaked and moaned around the barn, bending to the will of the wind. Laura's heart raced faster. The bad thing was coming.

Fanny pushed the next hay bale toward the opening when a gust of hot wind blew the loft door shut.

"Mommy, watch out! The door!"

Fanny pushed the door away with one hand, but then staggered forward, and it was like the hand of an invisible person grabbed her. She tried to stumble back but the hand tugged harder at her dress. Laura watched in horror. Fanny shoved the door hard to open it again. The door pulled her with it. Laura pushed against the wind that held her prisoner in its grasp. Her legs wouldn't move forward. She had to get upstairs and help her mother.

The wind rose in a black funnel around the barn. Laura screamed. The funnel rushed toward her, knocking over a wheelbarrow next to the barn with a pitchfork in it. The pitchfork her mother always warned her to not touch. The vicious wind flung Laura into the barn. Her head slammed into the siding and she collapsed on the ground.

"Laura," Fanny shrieked. Laura looked up just as her mother tumbled out of the loft door. She landed on her back. On the pitchfork that lay, face up. Fanny was quiet and still. Her head hung to one side. Her eyes remained closed.

Laura pulled herself up and ran to her mother's side. Blood seeped through the front of her mother's blouse in a spreading stain. Her large bosom didn't move. Laura touched the growing blood spots. Her tears spotted Fanny's shirt. They mixed in with the blood that slowly spread across it. Laura had to make her better. She had to use her new talent. Would it work though? She slowed down her sobbing so she could think. She needed to calm down to figure this out. *Hurry up, Daddy! We need you!*

But Daddy wasn't here now. She had to help her mother alone.

Laura got her hands under her mother's lower back and leaned all of her seven-year-old weight into her. Grunting and groaning she found the strength to push Fanny over on her side. Her blue shirt shone with wet blood oozing outwards in a ragged oval. The pitchfork sunk deep into her mother.

"Mommy, please wake up, please," Laura pleaded between sobs. The black clouds had disappeared. The air was still again. It was a beautiful day. The sun touched everything with a bright glow. The birds sang overhead. How could her mother be silent on the ground here and everything be still the same?

She put her hands on her mother's side and closed her eyes. She wished her hardest that the pitchfork would come out of her mother's back. Just like when she wished the glass chunk out of her foot after she ran barefoot through the woods last week and stepped on a broken bottle careless teenagers left behind.

As she had sat that day on pine needles and cried, with blood running down her foot, she held her foot and wished for it to be out. Then the jagged glass worked its way out and fell to the ground. The pain and blood stopped, too. When she touched the spot, where the glass had punctured her foot, the cut disappeared. She never told her parents. There was no scab or scar at all.

Laura continued to visualize the fork's tines moving backwards out of her mother. She imagined she pulled them out herself. Drops of sweat rolled down her neck and forehead but she didn't wipe them away. She kept her hands on her mother's side, calm, but the rest of her body shook with fear. She wished and wished. And then she prayed.

"Please, dear God, don't let my mommy die."

A soft thud cut through the summer sounds around her. She opened her eyes. The pitchfork lay on the ground before her. Blood oozed down the metal spikes. Laura let out a huge sigh, having grown dizzy from holding her breath. She shoved the fork away and rolled Fanny on her back again. She laid her head on her mother's chest and put her hand on her arm that sprawled on the dirt where she fell.

"Mommy, please wake up," she whispered. She inhaled her mother's scent as she sniffled into her shirt. She smelled of sunflowers and wet earth after a spring rain. She tried to hear her mother's thoughts but there were no sounds in her head. Just quiet. She didn't know how long she lay across her body. The world disappeared. Fanny and Wesley were her whole world. If they weren't there to take care of her, who would?

"Laura?" Fanny opened her eyes. She turned toward her and half-smiled.

Laura let out a great sob. Her chest could almost burst open with joy. She touched Fanny's face and hugged her close not wanting to let go.

Fanny moaned and patted Laura's hair with a shaky hand. "What happened? I fell and then...nothing."

"Mommy, it's okay. You fell on the pitchfork but I helped you."

Fanny touched her shirt and pulled away blood on her fingers.

"I made the pitchfork move out of you. You were bleeding, but I fixed you and now you're all better."

"You made the pitchfork move? I don't—understand. How—" Fanny stopped mid-sentence as Wesley's truck turned into the driveway. He was hunched over the steering wheel, filling the cab with his bulk. He jumped out of the truck before it rolled to a stop and ran over to them.

"What happened? Are you two all right?" Wesley fell on his knees and put a hand each on Laura and Fanny, his brown bangs flopping low on his tan forehead.

"Daddy!" Laura moved into his chest and squeezed him as hard as she could, burying her face in his warm, safe bigness.

Fanny moaned. Laura and Wesley helped her sit up. "Fanny, you're bleeding! We've got to get you to a hospital." Wesley touched Fanny's blood-soaked shirt and pulled her toward him.

"I-I'm okay, really." Fanny smiled. "I think we had a tornado. Can you believe it? But Laura saved me. Didn't you?"

"Yep." Laura grinned. "Mommy fell from the wind on the pitchfork out the loft door. I was so scared but I just told my thoughts to move the pitchfork out of her and fix up her insides."

Wesley and Fanny looked at her with astonishment. Laura showed them the rake and Fanny unbuttoned the top few buttons of her shirt. Dried blood and a row of dots ran across her skin from where the rake had pierced her. Laura ran her fingers over them.

"See, Mommy? All better now."

Laura moved her hand away and the dots of blood vanished. Wesley and Fanny looked at each other and then at Laura. She smiled, proud of her work. Fanny touched Laura's face and smiled back. Wesley looked afraid, as if he didn't understand what had just happened.

"Come on," he said. He put his arm around Fanny and helped her up. "Let's get you into the house and get Doctor Anna over here. Maybe she can tell us what happened."

"No, no." Fanny shook her head. "I don't need Doctor Anna to tell me I'm all right. Whatever happened is God's will."

Wesley looked at Laura again. "I don't know if it's God's will at work here ...or something else."

Laura hung her head and helped Fanny to the house. She had seen how her father looked at her. She didn't want him to look at her that way. She just wanted to be his normal little girl again and have him toss her up in a tickle hug and sing silly songs and snuggle up with a book. She didn't want their life to change.

As they walked in small steps across the lawn, Laura spotted movement in the woods across the road. A man dressed in black. He stepped out from behind a tree and stared at her. She had never seen him before. He moved closer onto the road and stood motionless under the bright sunlight that created long shadows in the late afternoon.

Even from across the road she could see his bright, green eyes. He crammed his hands into his black jeans as he hunched over. His thick, furrowed eyebrows gave him a menacing look, yet his face held puzzlement too. Laura looked at Fanny and Wesley but they hadn't seen the stranger. She shut her eyes and pinched her forehead, feeling a headache coming on. When she looked back, the man turned and melted into the shadowy woods. She held Fanny's hand harder.

Laura just wanted everything to be the same. But she knew in her young heart her life might never be the same.

CHAPTER 4: 1987

Ben Fieldstone watched the coffin as it was lowered into the earth and fantasized new ways to kill his foster father.

He drags Frank in his drunken daze to the shed, holds up his reeking body, and presses his head in the vise on the workbench. He winds the mechanism...tighter, tighter...Frank mumbles and shrieks...his skin splits and blood oozes down his face.

He didn't know what would happen if you squeezed someone's head in a vise. Would it just pop and bits of brain and blood explode outward or would it be a slow, bloody mess? His heart pulsed quicker just thinking of it. He could never kill Frank, though. Ben was tall, but thin, and no match against Frank's bulky, squat frame.

"Hey, let's go." Frank nudged him. "I need to get outta here." His red-rimmed eyes made him appear forlorn over the passing of his wife, Emma, but Ben knew it was the booze. He nodded and flicked his bangs from his eyes and glanced over at the man who had been standing motionless across the cemetery throughout the service. He stood with his legs far apart, an immense figure clad all in black. Ben couldn't see his face. Who could he be and why was he was there? But Ben had bigger problems to deal with now.

He ripped off his jacket and headed toward the rusty car baking in the blistering August heat. It was as if the world had taken its last breath. Summer had sucked the life out of all things green, leaving the cemetery a burnt landscape. His shirt clung to his chest, and the sweat rolled down his back.

He already missed Emma. His foster mother had been kind to him, when she was sober. But when drunk, she had stared at the TV, ignoring Frank's rages. Those were the nights Frank chased him around the house.

Sometimes he used the belt, the one with the heavy metal buckle on it that could catch him across the tender parts behind his knees. Sometimes Frank just liked to kick and pummel. Ben, at seventeen, was afraid to fight back. He'd weather the beatings until he turned eighteen. He had been in five foster homes over the past eight years. He'd seen worse.

He and Frank drove back in silence.

"You need to take over Emma's place now." Frank pulled up to their small bungalow. "The laundry, dishes, cleaning…grocery shopping, too."

A tear slid down his sagging cheek. He didn't bother to wipe it away. Ben tried to feel sympathy, but staring at Frank's rough hands on the steering wheel, he only felt hatred.

"No problem." Ben jumped out of the car. Up in his room he stretched out on his bed and let his mind wander. If he hadn't run away the night at the lake, he would be dead too, just like his parents. Sometimes he wished it had happened. Dead would be better than this place. Since then he had closed himself off from people. He didn't want to take the chance of loving anyone again. Besides, no one wanted to adopt a sullen teen. If a foster family decided not to keep him, he couldn't be hurt by their rejection. So he shuffled along from family to family, biding his time and keeping his painful memories just beneath the surface. He closed his eyes against them now and dozed off.

When he woke up, dark enveloped him. Banging noises came from downstairs. He jerked upright. What could Frank be doing? He eased out of his room and moved with quiet control down the stairs from his room. He found Frank smoking at the kitchen table. The light hovered dim, the globe full of dead bugs. Ben counted nine empty beer cans scrunched up on the table.

"Want something to eat?" he asked, to gauge Frank's mood. He opened the fridge.

"If I wanted something to eat, don'tcha think I'd be eating it?" Frank spat out. Grimacing, he dropped his head on his arms and started to cry.

Ben stood still. The sobbing bounced off him. He shifted from foot to foot the longer Frank cried. He forced himself to move nearer and placed his hand on Frank's thick shoulder.

"We'll be okay. You'll see." Ben tensed and snatched back his hand in disgust. As he turned back to the fridge, Frank touched his bottom. Ben stopped mid-step. He held his breath. He told himself it was just a light pat. Until the pat became a caress. It lingered. Soft in its want. He darted to his room, not looking back.

He dragged out his backpack from beneath his dusty bed and filled it, keeping one ear cocked for Frank's approach.

And it came.

He shoved the backpack under his bed. The door swung open, and there stood Frank.

"Don't ever walk away from me. You hear?" Frank leaned on the doorframe, his shirt clinging to his gut.

Ben nodded with his head down, hoping Frank would leave. He had a terrifying vision of Frank throwing him on the bed, pulling down his jeans, and mounting him like a pig. He clenched his buttocks together.

"Why don't you answer me?" Frank staggered into the room, his face red and sweaty. He grabbed Ben by the shirt. "Get up!"

Ben shook off Frank's hand. "Leave me alone! You make me sick."

Frank's eyes narrowed. He shoved Ben down. He kicked him in the back, then the head. Ben curled into a fetal position.

"Who do you think—you—are?" Frank delivered a kick with each word.

Fury exploded through Ben's brain. *Enough!* He grabbed Frank's foot mid-kick, throwing him off balance, and punched him hard in the chest as he fell. Frank made a loud *whoomph* as he landed on an elbow. He slowly stood and clutching his elbow, took a shaky step toward Ben. But then Frank's red face suddenly turned pale and he grabbed his left shoulder. He contorted in a twisted dance. With a gruesome grimace, he stumbled out of the room.

Ben touched his forehead. Blood oozed slick. He wasn't sure what just happened. But he was glad it did. His hands trembled. His back knotted with pain. He had to get out.

He pulled out a boot from under his bed and grabbed a roll of money he had been pilfering from Frank's top drawer over time. He had enough for a bus ticket and a cheap room for a few days. He'd find a place where no one could hurt him again. If he was found and brought back to Frank the beating might be more than he could take. But he had to face this fear. If Frank did more than beat him he would want to die anyway.

He swung his backpack over his shoulder and looked back at the bare room. He had never belonged here. He fought off self-pity and pushed open the door to listen. The television's ghostly light poured from Frank's bedroom and murmured old comedy.

Ben tiptoed to the door. Frank sat in bed, his eyes shut. He had passed out, an arm spread out on his leg, newspapers strewn around him. A cigarette hung from his fingers, the ash still glowing. The television flickered, canned laughter filled the room. Ben kept his gaze on the cigarette. The ash grew. Then the cigarette slipped. It quivered. It tumbled in slow motion. Nothing happened. The sheets smoldered. Laughter rang out again. Ben looked at the television. Some character ran around a kitchen. His gaze returned to the fallen cigarette. Minutes passed like hours to him.

He needed to choose. Run, or pick up the cigarette and prevent the certain fire? If he did nothing and Frank died, would he be a murderer? But Frank could have killed him just now. Might still kill him, or worse, if he ever caught him. He continued to stare where the cigarette fell.

The flames burst up from the newspapers and sheets and fanned along the comforter. It framed Frank in a soft glow. They licked with hungry abandon through the old bedspread until Frank's image blurred. Why didn't Frank wake up? But he looked so serene, so harmless. Ben felt free and safe seeing him like that.

And he knew. He had to live. He wanted to live.

He ran.

CHAPTER 5: 1991

Laura pumped her bicycle so fast her legs burned like the rising sun along the empty road. Summer spilled all around her as the sky grew lighter, casting long shadows across her path. She had slipped out of the house just as the birds woke up. They called to her as she sped along. *Hurry, hurry, Laura*! She chugged up and down hills.

She spun down the narrow entrance road to the grassy parking area and bumped along the uneven ruts that had been there as long as she could remember. Once she reached the birch logs that stretched across the grass marking the parking area, she threw her bicycle down and pulled off her backpack.

She unzipped the sagging, worn bag and brought out the knotty old blanket she always carried with her. She never knew when she might need it. She could find herself drawn through thick woods to where a window opened onto a glorious field of soft blowing grasses. Then, she would glide through the golden rushes and rest amongst nature's soft noise to stare at blue skies.

It was magical how a field came to be in the middle of the woods, a bare, open plain encased by uneven and roaming rock walls. Maybe it was a magical meadow that appeared just as she came upon it and disappeared when she left. She loved the movie *Brigadoon* about a town in Scotland appearing one day every one-hundred years. The town stayed the same while the world changed around it in a flash.

She spread out her blanket on the grass and sat cross-legged, facing the lake with her notebook and pen in hand, waiting for the sun to hit the water. She wanted to capture in words the beauty of the summer morning all around her. The sun burst out of the treetops and shot shimmering jewels across the water. Laura shielded her eyes and her heart leaped with a thrill. She had made it just in time.

The cool morning air blew off the water and embraced her. She closed her eyes for just a second to feel the warmth of the sun on her face, but instead a slobbery snout nudged her cheeks and hair.

"Hey," she shouted in surprise and scrambled up to find an old, chocolate Labrador sniffing her legs. He had white whiskers around his jaw and a pleading, sad look. He instantly became her friend. She fell back down on her knees and wiggled his ears.

"Where'd you come from?" Laura scratched his head. "You're so cute!"

She laughed as he tickled her with his nose.

"Scooter," a gruff voice called. "Come here, boy."

Laura looked up to see a trim, old man whacking through the brush in the woods. It had to be the hermit people talked about. She had seen him from afar, with his gray cap, but never up close. The old man twitched, startled to see her there with his dog. He stopped a few feet away from her. He didn't look like a hermit but a nice, normal grandpa dressed in jeans and a green plaid shirt. He leaned on a crooked, black walking stick. He looked in good shape for an old geezer.

"Scooter, come here, boy," he called again, but the dog remained entranced by Laura.

"He's so sweet." She nuzzled the dog's head and smiled at the old man.

He scrunched his eyebrows down as if to get a better look at her. "He took off on me."

"Maybe he knew I would be here and wanted to make friends."

Scooter jumped up with a woof and put his paws on her as if in agreement.

"See?" Laura laughed. "Scooter. What a cool name. Are you fast like a scooter?"

"*Hmph*, not anymore." The old man moved toward her and whistled to get the dog's attention. "Well, come on Scooter, leave the girl alone. Let's get home."

Laura stood up. "But you didn't ask me my name and I don't know yours either."

The old man frowned, taken off guard by her directness. "It's Jim Barrens."

"I'm Laura Armstrong. I'm eleven." She stuck out her hand and smiled. "Nice to meet you."

Jim looked at her hand as if unsure what to do, as if children were a mystery to him. Finally, he shook her hand and nodded.

"Cool sunrise, huh?" Laura pointed at the sky. "I like to come here early when no one is around. It's as if I'm the only person awake in the whole world. But now you're here, too. Did you get up just to see the sunrise?"

"Um, not exactly. Scooter here had to go out."

"Oh yeah, dogs are like that, I guess. I never had one but wanted one. We just have cats but they live in the barn. And chickens, too. I feed them and clean their house. I name them all, too, and can tell them apart. They're feathers are so soft. We got new ones this year to lay more eggs to sell."

"*Hmph.*" Jim nodded. His gaze followed her hands that painted pictures in the air. "You must live close by if you biked here, eh?" Jim moved a little closer and jerked a thumb at her bike.

"I do. I live a couple miles away on top of a hill, on the long windy road going down the mountain."

"I know where it is. I live up there." He pointed up into the woods.

"I know. I've seen you sometimes. You're the only person who still lives year-round above the lake, right? People call you a hermit. Are you?"

"Am I what?"

"A hermit?" She tilted her head at him and raised her eyebrows.

"No." He paused for a moment. "I am a solitudinarian."

Laura giggled and spread her arms out wide. "What the heck is that?"

"A person who chooses to be alone and does it well."

"So what's the difference between that and a hermit?"

Jim looked out over the lake. The sun rose clear of the horizon now. "A hermit is sad and lonely and lives far away from people. I am none of those."

"But you're not near people. You're the only person who lives at the lake now."

"Yes, but not by choice. The government took care of that."

"What do you mean?"

"Well, that's a conversation for another day."

"So we'll meet again?" Laura flicked her hair out of her face and grinned at him.

"I suppose." Jim nodded in a non-committal fashion. "Do your parents know you're here?"

They continued to pet Scooter, who by now leaned his long body into both of them, luxuriating in all the affection.

"They know I take off early in the morning to catch sunrises. It's all part of my journal writing, see?" Laura picked up her book from her blanket and flipped through the pages. "I'm making a sunrise diary. It's a book of all the different sunrises I see in all kinds of weather. Clear skies, snow, rain, mist. Sunrises are like snowflakes you know, each one is special. Today's sunrise is different than any other sunrise you'll see. Neat, huh?"

Jim scratched his cropped, gray hair and gave her a full smile. Minute by minute he seemed less like a hermit to her and more like a friend.

"Definitely," Jim said. "But why not take pictures of the sunrises and have a real visual memory, not just a description?"

Laura's eyes grew wide and she clapped one hand on her journal, startling Scooter. "Aha! Because a picture is so easy to take. Every sunrise I see makes me feel and see different stuff. Mist is a cool one. The sun glows through it and the water drops look like glittery fairies. And my description of each sunrise will also change because of how I feel that day too. That can't be found in a picture, right?"

"Hmm…photographers may argue the point, but I get it." Jim now had a full grin on his face. "Well, time for us to go. Come on, Scooter, you old dog."

Laura knelt down and put her arms around Scooter's neck. "You're so sweet, I love you."

Scooter woofed in agreement.

"You could meet me here again some other sunrise, you know, or anytime? You and Scooter. I'm home-schooled so can come whenever."

Jim looked down at her and nodded. "We just might. Bye now."

Laura waved as they left and turned back to the lake. The sun grew bright overhead. The mist had blown off the water. The day stood open for business. Since she missed writing about the sunrise maybe she would just have to write about her new friends, Mr. B and Scooter. How cool she had met the hermit! He intrigued her and she had to find out more. She sensed he didn't want to get to know her. She sensed his thoughts and his past. *He's afraid, that's all.*

She smiled as she described him in her journal.

Mr. B is a serious, old solitude dude who roams the woods with his loyal chocolate lab, Scooter. He is sad because he lost his wife and pretends to be gruff but has a good heart. Oh, and nice blue eyes too.

It would be her mission to help Mr. B. She pulled out her thesaurus she carried in her backpack. Now what was the opposite of solitude? Social? *Boring.* She looked up another word for social. Convivial. *Great word!* She wrote it down. She would make Mr. B into a chooser of people not aloneness. He would be a convivialtarian. That would be her word for the day, if it existed. She plotted next what she could do to help her new friend become part of her world.

She couldn't wait to share it with him.

Jim woke up the next day at 6:30 a.m. to rain and darkness. It drummed loud on the cabin roof. A sound he liked. Nature talking to him. It made him feel not so alone. He was glad he had the place winterized ten years ago. He could be snug from rain and snow. It wasn't a large place, but just enough for him and Scooter. The place he most enjoyed in the summer was the screened-in porch. He could enjoy the woods without being devoured by mosquitoes.

He saw Laura in his mind sitting at the lake writing about the rainy sunrise. *Today's sunrise is different than any other.* Her words echoed in his head and he smiled thinking about her. He tried to remember the last time he had such a conversation and couldn't. He'd been alone a long time.

He and his wife, Susan, had bought this as a vacation place years before people started building cabins around the lake. Back then the lake appeared at night as a dark void below. Through the years they watched as each cabin lit up below. It looked like a set of Christmas lights strung around one large glass globe.

Then, there were the two agonizing years when Susan battled cancer. Jim could only watch her slip away. The cancer spread to her brain but her loss hadn't been a blessing. He had been filled with rage and couldn't bring himself to speak to people. He sold his tax accounting business and their house in Pennsylvania, said goodbye to three old friends, loaded household items, and drove with Scooter the four hours to the cabin. These days he was surrounded by his own silence and Scooter's snoring, not the chatter of energetic children.

He got the sense with this girl, Laura, the spotlight on the stage he stood on alone would grow to encompass the audience as well. But then the solitary life he had built over the past years would disappear. He wasn't sure he wanted that to happen. He had grown content, at peace.

"Enough ruminating, Jim."

He got up and fed Scooter, then poured himself a mug of strong, Columbian coffee. He cupped his gnarled hands around it to feel warm in the chill and damp of a rainy, July morning. The cold made his arthritic hands stiffer than usual. He stepped out on his covered porch to watch the rain and nearly dropped his coffee cup. There on the small table beside his rocking chair sat a pie. It smelled delicious. Sweet, baked peaches oozed juice over a golden crust. He touched it and found it still warm. A folded note was placed beside it with a sunflower on top.

Dear Mr. B, something from my orchard to you. I hope the sunflower brings you a ray of light on this rainy day. Your new friend, Laura.

He didn't know how she managed to carry a pie in her backpack over bumpy, dirt roads in the rain without smashing it, and then up the overgrown trail to his cabin. She must have been up quite early to bake this for him. She must still be nearby. He grabbed his rain coat and roused Scooter, who was snoozing again after his breakfast.

"Come on, old boy." Jim stroked his ears. "We have to go find Laura and thank her."

Scooter perked up at her name and trotted along beside him down the porch steps and out into the rain. Big, wet splotches plunked down on them as the rain fought to get past the heavy leaf cover. They followed the rough, half-mile long path down to the lake. Small footprints oozed in the mud every few feet. She had been here all right. In the course of one day a young girl befriended him and baked him a pie. He couldn't stop smiling. At seventy-two years old he was actually giddy.

"Come on, Scooter, we don't want to miss her. Keep up, boy."

The old dog and the old man reached the bottom of the trail and the lake spread out before them. Tendrils of mist rose from the water lapping at the shoreline. A gray curtain of rain fell steady and soft. A faint *pling, pling* called out as the raindrops met their end.

Jim stopped and peered through the fog that rolled across the water and filled the woods beyond. The sky hung heavy, descending upon the mountaintop as if it wanted to crush it. He could see the ghostly outlines of several empty cabins surrounding part of the lake. They sank into ruin after the government forced the owners to sell so they could close off the lake area affected by the meteorite all those years ago. The damn government didn't even have the sense to knock the cabins down.

Jim peered through the fog and found a lone figure by the lake wearing a bright yellow and green slicker with a hood hung over her face. She huddled on a boulder that overlooked the lake. He made his way over to her.

"Hello there." The rain slowed to a misty shower.

"Oh, hi!" Laura looked up at him and smiled. Her journal balanced on one knee. Scooter ambled over to her with his tail wagging. She stroked his wet ears. "Did you get your pie? I didn't know if you'd be up, but I wanted to find your cabin."

"Yes, that's why we came down here, to thank you. So…thank you."

"You're welcome. I love your cabin. It's so cozy in the woods. We live in a big, old farmhouse with acres and acres. That's where I picked those peaches from. My mom made the crust but I did all the rest."

Jim beamed and rocked from foot to foot. "Well, we best be going. You too. Go home and get dry. We thought you might be down here writing your sunrise picture and wanted to say thanks."

He turned with Scooter to head back up the trail.

"I have a new name for you, Mr. B."

Jim turned with a puzzled look. "What's that?"

"You're a convivialtarian and don't know it." Laura grinned.

"What on earth is that?"

"Just wait and see." She hopped off her rock and headed for her bike, waving goodbye.

Jim watched her ride away in the rain. He had made a friend and it filled his heart with gladness. For years, Scooter had been all he needed. Now this young, animated girl drew color around him when he didn't even know he'd been colorless.

It felt good to care about someone else again.

CHAPTER 6: 1991

From then on, every few days, Jim would find a present on his porch. One time it was gooey chocolate chip banana bread, another time a homemade card with pressed flowers, and another time a juicy blackberry pie. His favorite was a daisy in a chipped blue bottle with a painted scene of a mountain and lake, and there sat his cabin amidst the trees. He placed it on the kitchen window to let the sun shine through it.

He didn't always head down to the lake on those days he knew she had been there, but more often than not he did. He enjoyed Laura's chatter, spattered with amusing words she found in her ragged thesaurus, even that day when she caught him in a cranky mood and called him a curmudgeon.

"Am not," Jim denied, his eyebrows crinkled down.

"Are too," Laura shot back. "You're vexed. Huffy. Surly. And all of these make you a curmudgeon of the most colossal kind."

"Impudent imp." He shook his walking stick at her. "You don't want a fracas with me, you mischievous moppet."

"Aha," she cried with glee. "You've been reading your thesaurus, haven't you?"

"Never, you wayward whelp." And Jim laughed in spite of a grumpy mood brought on by arthritis and a bad night's sleep. Laura never failed to cheer him up.

One day he woke up to find an invitation to her house for dinner, with a box to check yes or no. He smiled at her childishness and after pausing, checked yes, and left it on his porch for her to pick up. He was curious about these parents who had raised such a charming and mature child.

Jim pulled up to Laura's farmhouse in his old green Jeep Cherokee on a sunny Saturday afternoon. September had crept in and frosty nights had turned some leaves yellow and orange. Laura burst out of the front screen door and skipped over to him.

"Hey, Mr. B!" She hugged him as he stepped out of the car.

He stiffened a bit, but warmed to the hug and patted her on the back. "Hi."

She pulled him along to the house where her parents welcomed him. He could tell that Laura did not come from these stocky, country folks, but her cheery disposition did. Her gracefulness and petite pixie looks stood out next to her parents' big-boned thickness and wide facial features.

Jim shook Wesley's rough hand and thanked him for having him to dinner.

"You're most welcome. A friend of Laura's is a friend of ours. Of course, she just mentioned yesterday that she met you at the lake recently." His gravel voice rumbled in the kitchen and he eased his large bulk into a wide rocking chair by a stone fireplace, motioning for Jim to sit in the one next to him.

"Yes," Jim said. He looked at Laura, unsure of what to say.

"Mr. B and I just met and I thought he'd enjoy a good home-cooked meal since he lives all alone," Laura said, squeezing Fanny's waist. Her eyes pleaded with Jim to go along with it.

"Well, we're certainly glad to meet you and enjoy a meal together." Fanny smiled at Jim then returned to stirring a savory smelling stew over the stove.

Homemade bread baked in the oven and its delicious warmth wafted over him. He sat down and looked around the cozy kitchen. Baskets and pots hung from the beamed ceiling and bunches of herb pots lined the window. A bay window overlooked a pond and the Catskill Mountains in the distance. A worn chopping block held crocks full of end-of-the-season onions and tomatoes just collected from the garden. It all smelled so earthy and homey. This house was so alive. His cabin was empty and lifeless in comparison.

"Laura's been telling us all about you and Scooter," Fanny said.

Laura grinned.

"I hope good things." Jim chuckled as he rocked. "Old Scooter. He's fourteen years old now. Old even by a Lab's standards, but a good match for me. We have the same, slow pace."

"Why didn't you bring Scooter, Mr. B?"

"I wasn't too sure how good of a guest he would be."

Fanny turned to smile at him and wiped her hands on her apron that draped over her large bosom. "You can bring Scooter along any time.

We love animals, right, Laura?"

"Yep, now come on, Mr. B. I want to show you the chickens and apple orchard and barns and everything!" She tugged at him to get up.

"Now, Laura," Fanny admonished. "Perhaps Mr. Barrens wants to sit and relax and have some sweet tea."

"Let the man be," Wesley chimed in.

"Oh, that's quite all right." Jim allowed himself to be pulled through the front door.

"Dinner in twenty minutes or so," Fanny called to them as they headed outside.

Jim tried to keep up with Laura's energetic gait. He admired her chickens and how clean she kept their house. She climbed her favorite tree to show him the view, but he remained firm about staying on the ground himself. He followed her into the apple orchard and listened to her talk about so many things.

"Your mother and father are wonderful people." It was hard for Jim to get a word in with Laura's enthusiastic jabber as he picked his way around bruised and crushed apples.

"I know, but, they aren't my real mother and father."

Jim waited for more.

"But you knew that, didn't you?"

"I guessed it, yes, but how did you know?" He turned to look at her as she skipped around the apple trees, swinging her lithe body from trunk to trunk.

"Because I hear people's thoughts."

Jim's eyes widened. He didn't know if she toyed with him or meant to be serious. She peeked behind a tree and laughed.

"I'm serious. Oh, but that's not all. I can do other things too." Laura closed her eyes and hugged the tree next to her. The limbs shook. Jim stared, confused at first. Was it the wind? But the warm September air hung still. The branches jiggled and jumped, sending ripe apples falling down in a rain of red.

"See? Isn't it neat? No ladder!" Laura laughed. "Now we need to gather these good ones so my mom can make applesauce. She makes the best applesauce, all chunky and cinnamony." She grabbed an empty basket at the base of a tree and filled it with the fallen apples. Jim moved forward to help her, unsure of what just happened. Where did this girl come from?

"I don't know where I come from." Laura bent her head, searching for apples.

"You can read minds," Jim sputtered in disbelief.

"I told you, didn't I?" She looked up with a grin.

Jim moved forward to help pick up apples. "But how did you make the tree move?"

"I just think it and it happens. I don't know how it works."

Jim nodded. He could understand that. Life had its mysteries. Like cancer. There were things you couldn't see or explain.

"You still miss her, don't you?"

"Every day." Jim sighed. He stood up. He had been a lucky man, one time.

"But you're still lucky."

"I am?" He was startled to find how easy it became to follow a conversation with her from his head.

"Sure. You have Scooter and now me as a friend."

Jim smiled as they finished filling the basket then each grasped a handle to walk it back to the house.

"There!" Laura grabbed Jim's arm. She dropped her handle and apples tumbled out. "Do you see him?"

Startled, Jim also dropped his handle and allowed the basket to fall.

"See who?" He looked around the peaceful orchard, the afternoon sun slanted in the waning days of summer. Wasps buzzed around juicy apples rotting at their feet. He held a hand up to shield his eyes from the soft glare. Something dark moved in the trees up the hill.

"It's him." Laura shrunk down. "The man in black. I've got to find out who he is. Come on!" She pulled at Jim's hand. He pulled her back. She let go and took off running.

"Wait, are you sure that's a person? Maybe it's just a deer."

Jim stumbled over apple bumps after her, when something sharp stung his neck and left hand. He slapped his neck and a third sting hit behind his ear. Stingers shot into him, over and over. Laura kept running through the orchard. He tried to call after her but he could only rasp out a whisper. His throat swelled and he couldn't catch his breath. A burning pain spread through his chest. He doubled over and fell sideways onto a tree stump. In the distance a man stepped out from behind a tree toward Laura. She was almost near him.

"Laura." He wheezed. What could be wrong with him?

The woods around him spun and nausea rose and fell in waves. He clutched his chest as the burning grew more intense. Jim watched, unable to get to her, as Laura stopped and faced the man in black. The man stood thirty feet or so from her. He stared at her in silence. His bulk loomed wide amongst the trees. He shimmered as if his body floated in the air.

"Why are you watching me?" Laura's voice cut loud and clear through the woods.

"I need to know what you are."

She flipped her head to look back at Jim. He shook his arm in the air. She hesitated, then turned and ran back toward him. He closed his eyes.

"Mr. B!" Jim fell off the stump and lay on the ground. When Laura reached him he felt barely conscious. His breaths came fast and shallow. He couldn't get enough air in him. She fell on her knees beside him.

"Wasps." Jim wheezed in between breaths. She felt his hands and neck. His skin puffed up in a red swollen mass around each sting site. Behind his ear grew another swollen lump.

"I didn't know you were allergic. I wouldn't have brought you in the orchard!" She placed one hand on his neck and one on his hand and closed her eyes. "Please don't die, Mr. B. You need to get well. You need to stride-the-woods with your walking stick and faithful dog. Please!"

Jim heard her speak, but it was far away down a tunnel. Minutes passed.

"I'm so sorry. It's my fault. I brought you here." Laura cried and shook Jim's hand. Her tears fell on his stung hand and she wiped them away.

"Not your fault," Jim said in a clear voice and opened his eyes.

"Oh, Mr. B! Can you get up?"

Laura helped him up.

"What happened?" He scratched his head as she steadied him with her hands.

"You got stung real bad and I'm so, so sorry. I didn't know you were allergic."

She hid her head in his shirt and sobbed. Jim held her and looked through the woods, but didn't see this mysterious man. "But I'm not allergic, Laura. And I'm fine now but how'd that happen? It's like the stingers' poison just worked its way out of my body."

"I made it come out. I didn't want you to die, like my mom almost did. I saved her once, but I didn't know if I could save you." Laura continued to cry. "I just imagined pulling the wasp stingers out and sucking out their venom. I imagined you being able to breathe."

Jim stood still, his stomach clenched. "Is that one of the other things you can do? Heal people?"

She nodded, her head still buried in his side. He took a deep breath and tilted her head up to look at her. Tears streamed down her face.

"But who was the man, Laura? Did he ever try to hurt you?"

"No, he always watches me from far away. I don't know who he is. Today he looked funny. Like a ghost. All shimmery. I asked him why he watched me. All he said was—" She rubbed her eyes with the sleeve of her shirt.

"He needed to know what you are." Jim stroked her smooth hair. "I heard him."

"So what am I?"

Jim also wanted to know the answer to that question.

"I couldn't read the man's thoughts though," Laura said. "But I sensed a bunch of feelings all jumbled up inside him."

Jim's head tumbled with all that had happened in the course of a short afternoon. He was certain that meeting this young girl would change his life forever. For the first time in years he grew excited to be alive, but he was also exhausted from his near-death encounter and needed a long nap.

"I know what you are. You're one amazing girl. You saved my life. We'll sort this all out later. Come on. Let's go back to your house. I've had enough excitement for one day. And Laura?"

"Yes, Mr. B?"

"Can we find a way around the apple orchard?"

Laura peered behind her into the woods, but the man in black was gone. She turned back and smiled at him. They picked up the fallen apples and basket and followed a different path back to the house.

"I'm assuming your parents know all the things you can do," Jim said.

Laura nodded. "That's why I'm home schooled. They don't understand what I can do, but I guess they want to protect me."

When they had almost reached the house, Fanny called to them from the kitchen window. "Laura, Mr. Barrens. Dinner's ready."

Laura looked at Jim. "Don't tell my parents about this, please. You're okay, right?"

They put the basket down and Jim touched his neck and hand. No swelling or redness remained. He felt fine. "It's amazing, really, amazing." Jim shook his head.

Laura put her hand on his. "Please, Mr. B, promise you won't tell them. They worry enough."

"All right, I promise. But if I find out you're in danger, all promises are off. Agreed?"

"Agreed."

"Come on now. I'm starving." Jim had so many questions, but at seventy-two he had learned patience. He could wait until she told him more in her own time.

They picked up the basket of apples and went inside to have a normal dinner.

From then on, Jim was welcome at their home anytime. Most of the time though he and Laura visited at the lake in the morning. One cool October day Laura had finished writing her sunrise entry when Jim and

Scooter showed up. They stood together in silence and watched the early morning sky turn from burnt orange to a brilliant blue.

"Mr. B, were you there the night the meteorite hit the lake? Did you see it?"

It wasn't the sort of question Jim expected but he answered the best he could. "I sat on my front porch with Scooter when it hit. I saw it coming but was knocked out from the crash and woke up later."

"What did it look like? Did it zoom down really, really fast?"

"It was this streak of light that pierced the sky. It pulsed in a peculiar shade of green. At first I thought it was a plane, but it kept growing in size. The light grew bigger until it blinded me and…then I don't remember what happened."

"Wow."

"But I don't think it was a meteorite." Jim stared out over the lake.

"Really? What then?"

"Whatever crashed that night wasn't all the government said it was."

Laura stared at him. "What do you mean?"

"When the government came in here and took charge, it was like they were covering something up. Too eager to buy up all the cabins. Too eager to get people away from the crash site."

"So what was it?"

"I'm not sure. Something man-made. A secret government project gone wrong, perhaps."

"Maybe it was a spaceship!"

"I don't know about that, but I do know some things are better left alone."

"We should go over there, to where it crashed and look around."

Jim scratched his head and frowned. "The government already came in and cleaned it all up years ago."

Laura jumped up. "I know. But maybe I can sense something about what happened that night."

"I thought you could only read minds?"

"I thought so too but what if I can sense things from the past. Memories and stuff? I never tried." Laura pulled at Jim's sleeve. "Come on!"

Jim gave in and followed her along the overgrown path around the lake to the north end where the crash site spread out. They wound around the decrepit cabins lining part of the lakeshore.

"Wait." Jim called out to her. "It's wetlands in there." But she kept going.

Laura reached the end of the lake where the meteorite fell from the sky all those years ago. Skunk cabbages and cattails now grew in the crater. She made her way to the tall fence surrounding the crash site and ran her hands along it looking for a way in. She pushed her way through an opening and ran forward to the edge of the crater, and then down the hill into the bottom of it. There she reached the small valley floor and knelt down amongst the tall grass to place her hands on the ground. Jim shoved his way through the fence. He held Scooter back who wanted to plunge ahead, eager to reach Laura.

"There was something here, Mr. B. Something—or someone!"

Jim and Scooter reached her side. "It could have been something from yesterday or last month or last year."

"No. Someone was here the night it struck. And it wasn't a meteorite."

Jim shivered in the morning chill and blew out frosty breaths. The day didn't promise to get above fifty-five degrees. "It doesn't matter now. It happened years ago. What if you're reaching for something because you want to believe in it?"

Laura shook her head and closed her eyes, her hands still pressed to the ground. "He crashed here, I feel it. I know him. Not know him as met him…but know of him." She looked up at Jim with tears in her eyes. "So much sadness." She put her face in her hands. "He was here under the ground all alone and dying."

Jim didn't know what to make of all this. He still didn't understand her powers, but believed miracles happened. Scooter nudged Laura, distressed by her anxiety. She threw her arms around his neck and hugged him.

Jim rocked from foot to foot. "Who was here? Who do you know?"

"I don't know. But he came here from far away and was so hurt and alone. He'd lost everything and he needed to do something important. And a girl. There was a girl here. I can't see her face though."

She stood up, looking around the small valley.

"Laura, you said you knew him. What do you mean?"

"I don't know. I can't explain it. But I feel someone else is still out there right now. Someone from that night. Connected to me. But I don't know who."

She turned to look at Jim, tears still shining in her eyes. "What's wrong with me? Why can't I just be normal?"

Jim held her and smoothed her hair. "Honey, there's nothing wrong with you. You have some special gifts. I don't understand them, but maybe God gave them to you for a reason."

As far as her question about being normal, he couldn't answer it. He didn't know if anyone could.

CHAPTER 7: 1991

Ben watched the curvy, tall brunette from across the bar. She flicked her long hair back and laughed with her short friend as she sipped a beer. Her white teeth gleamed against her tan in the red glow of the Chinese lanterns strung above the bar. Ben could tell she was a tourist seeking vacation adventure in Honolulu's rough spots. Hud's Place was no place for a white *wahine* from the mainland to be hanging out after 10:00 p.m.

North of Hotel Street in Chinatown, or NoHo as it was called, carried its distinction as the known spot for prostitute action any time of the week. He swallowed the last of his beer and laughed to himself. SoHo could be a better name for the so-many-ho's that could be had around here.

He knew.

At twenty-one and after three years stationed at Pearl Harbor in the Navy, he had sampled them all. Chinese, Korean, Hawaiian, Philippine, Tahitian. Anything exotic you wanted. If you liked big mamas you could hook up with fat Samoan women, lurking on street corners strutting their expansive goods.

"Hey, let's get outta here and head downtown." Andy Novatoski clapped his big, tan hand on Ben's back. "Some of the other guys from base said they'd meet us down in Waikiki later. There's a new place on Kapiolani. It's supposed to be hopping. Lots of blonde babes from California seeking some sailor lovin'."

"I don't know." Ben's head hurt from too many Hinano beers and he was thinking of switching to vodka to get good and drunk. It could relieve the dull pain throbbing at his temples, until tomorrow. Hud's Place was not a bar that handed out flowery, umbrella Mai Tais. Beer and straight booze only in this dive bar. It sat in Chinatown's red light district where you could get cheap, stiff drinks, and listen to some decent music. That is, if you could get past the prostitutes, drug dealers, and meth addicts begging for money.

Tonight a hump-backed man, reminiscent of Johnny Cash, cranked away songs on the tiny stage. The place only had a maximum capacity of seventy-five and Ben liked that. It was a dirty, dark cubbyhole where he could hide. Sometimes Andy tagged along to humor him.

"Come on, man." Andy persisted. "Enough of the ghetto Chinatown scene. Let's go where the clean action is. I don't want some old cougar winking her gray *punani* at me. I want me a young thang after some hot sailors!"

"Big, blond, Viking sailors you mean." Ben grinned back. Andy was a magnet for all kinds of women, but he could score easy with the young girls on vacation from anywhere-USA. At 6'4" Andy stood larger than life with streaked, white-blond hair, ice-blue eyes, and chiseled features. He looked like a Norse god standing at the helm of his great ship, sailing into harbor from a long voyage at sea.

Women shivered when they saw him, probably envisioning him throwing them over his shoulder to claim them for the night in a romping good time. All Andy needed was a cloak, horned helmet, and axe to complete the look. Unlike himself. Ben appeared as a scowling, rebellious teenager mad at the world with his slouched posture, dark looks, and hands shoved in his pockets.

"Nah, just a dumb Pollack they can have their way with," Andy shot back. "We'll find someone for you, I promise. I'll share. You can be my brooding sidekick Hank, from Texas. The chicks will think you've been hurt by love and want to heal your broken heart. Come on, let's go."

Ben looked over at the dark-haired beauty at the other end of the bar, glad they had arrived early and gotten seats. She smiled at him and then looked away. He could see the top of her breasts pushing up through her white tank top as she leaned over the bar to get another beer. Her friend said something funny and the brunette flung her hair back. Her breasts poked out in enchanting round mounds as she arched her back and laughed. She looked so clean and white and American.

Usually he came to Hud's to be left alone and drink himself into a slow stupor among hip music. He could always count on ending up in a back room on Hotel Street. There he could get quick relief for $50 followed by a dazed cab ride back to the base. In World War II a night here for sailors involved getting 'screwed, stewed, and tattooed'. But tonight he lusted for sweet sex with an all-American girl.

"Nope," Ben decided. "I'm going to stay here and check things out."

Andy caught him staring at the brunette across the bar and laughed.

"Dude, she is so not your type. I thought little Asians wanna-sucky-sucky was more your thing? You know, love 'em and leave 'em in fifteen minutes? That tourist chick won't even give you the time of day. It'd take you fifteen minutes just to get close to her. Forget about it, man."

"Yeah, well, I can dream, can't I? Besides, I'm not feeling the downtown, social scene tonight." He ordered a straight up vodka from the bar and downed half in one chug.

"Okay. But if you keep drinking this fast you won't be able to find a cab to get back to base. You sure you want to stay here?"

Ben smiled at the girl across from him who caught his eye again. She bent down to say something to her friend and looked back up at him. His time here on the island was almost up and he would get ship duty overseas when he re-upped on his next tour. It may be his last chance for a night with an American girl for a while.

"Yeah, I'm sure."

"Okay, but now I don't have my sacrificial friend with me to offer up to the street trash that jacks me up on the way out of town."

"That kung fu grip of yours will ward 'em off. Now get outta here. I'll catch you tomorrow."

"Okay, later, brah. Stay clean." Andy gave him the Hawaiian hand salute and made his way out through a throng of Marines, locals, aged women, and hipsters. It all created a blended, steamy smell of sweat, stale beer, and perfume.

Andy was Ben's only friend. He accepted his moodiness and didn't ask questions. One night on a drinking binge, Ben found out that Andy had been orphaned, too, when he was seven. He lived in an orphanage for two years until he was adopted. They didn't talk about their past, but Ben felt it connected them. From what he guessed Andy had a rough time of it, too. He gave a final wave to his friend as he left the bar.

The Johnny Cash wanna-be left the stage in a spattering of applause and a new band set up for the boisterous, late night crowd. Ben finished his drink and ordered another vodka, a double this time. He'd make sure it went down slow.

He looked up. A tall man stared at him from across the far end of the bar. It wasn't a passing a glance. He had on a black T-shirt that stretched across his muscular arms and chest. Even in the murky bar light his bright, green eyes glowed eerie in the dim light of the bar. He looked familiar to Ben. He'd seen him before but couldn't remember where. The man nodded at him and then disappeared into the crowd, his massive body pushing through the throng of partygoers.

Ben shook his head in puzzlement and wished he hadn't. The room spun a bit. His drink was almost gone already. Too soon. He sipped the ice in his glass and debated whether to get another. It suddenly reminded him of his foster father's drinking, his empty beer cans around the house. He didn't want to think about him. He wasn't like him.

After watching Frank go up in flames four years ago, Ben jumped a bus for Florida. He landed in Orlando, and took on cleaning jobs at resort hotels to live. The day he turned eighteen he walked into the U.S. Navy Recruiting office in Orlando and signed up as an enlisted sailor. He yearned for free education, free food, and a regular paycheck. He had no other options to survive. Besides, he was sick of making minimum wage to sleep in a cockroach-infested room stinking from overflowing trash dumpsters outside his window.

After boot camp, he set off for Navy photography school in Pensacola, which got even better. He enjoyed the white, sand beaches across from his barracks and learning the photography trade. After graduating school and arriving in Pearl Harbor, Ben spent his duty processing Top Secret aerial photos of non-allied military locations around the world. The job was okay.

He enjoyed more getting out of the photo lab and taking photos of command events and experiencing the beautiful island. And not just the natural beauty. He wanted to experience all Oahu had to offer, and in the way of women. A few times a month he would take a bus or cab to Chinatown and spend his paycheck on good music, drink, and a girl. Sometimes a cheap blow, other times the full deal. Tonight he wanted something else though.

If this brunette was a tourist, her time here was short. Maybe she was looking for a one-night stand with a sailor. He had sampled slews of these tourist girls. If she had a hotel room nearby in Waikiki, even better. They could get rid of her short friend for a bit to have a good time. Ben kept several condoms on him just in case. He had tasty ones too for a good blow job. He wanted to keep clean. God knows you could catch any kind of disease from a Hotel Street hooker or even an all-American girl.

Ben downed the last of his vodka as the buzz around him grew louder. The band rocked with Pink Floyd and Santana songs. He had waited too long to make his move when he looked over to see two buff men talking to the brunette and her friend. He knew immediately they were from the Marine base at Kaneohe Bay.

The brunette frowned and shook her head as her short friend grabbed her arm to pull her away from the bar. The Marines were drunk and leering at them. They must have said something obnoxious to the girls. The hard-core looking Marine leaned on the wall with his arm over the pretty girl's head. He loomed over her, a mass of muscle with a razor-sharp buzz cut and a large tattoo of Daffy Duck on his right arm.

The leaner Marine grabbed the arm of the short girl while his muscle friend put his massive hand on the brunette's shoulder. She tried to shrug it off but he gripped her tight.

Ben jumped off his bar stool and leaned into the bar as a wave of dizziness hit him. He was drunk and any move to intervene with these two Marines was stupid, but he didn't care. He still had a slim chance of getting rid of the obnoxious grunts, rescuing the girl, and getting some. Or maybe he was looking for a fight. He pushed his way around to the other side of the bar and put a hand on the big Marine's tattoo.

"Hey, jarhead, why don't you leave them alone?"

The Marine tilted his head to frown down at Ben, but kept his hand on the brunette's shoulder. She looked at Ben in relief.

"Yo, squidy, is it? Why don't you go back over there and keep on looking, 'cause you ain't getting any of this."

"Neither are you, jerk off," the brunette yelled, and shoved the Marine away.

The Marine laughed and sneered down at Ben. "I just told her if a fresh, mainland twat came to NoHo she needs to get banged, and real good. And I'm the one to do it. What's wrong with that?"

The brunette pleaded with her eyes for Ben to help them. The music and chatter roared around them. No one noticed them in the corner.

"Yeah, what's wrong with that?" The lean Marine echoed his friend's sentiment with a grin. "Why don't you go back to swabbing the deck, skinny boy? I bet you bend over and give it to the officers good, don't ya?"

A haze of rage hit Ben and he punched the smaller Marine in the mouth. He got another shot in across the grunt's nose when the big Marine lifted him up and carried him out the door, crushing him against the crowd. Ben forgot about the girls as he landed on hard asphalt and staggered up. The street reeled around him as blow upon blow hit him. He had found that fight.

"Fucking squid, who the fuck do you think you are?" the big Marine roared at him, as his fists smashed into his stomach and face. Ben doubled over and fell to his knees. Blood dripped down. He wiped it away as the crowd that gathered to watch spun around him in a blur. The other Marine kicked him in the side and he fell sideways on the street, hugging his waist.

From his view the brunette mouthed, "I'm sorry" as she ran off with her friend. The two Marines didn't notice. They were too busy beating the shit out of Ben. *So much for being a hero. Or winning a fight.*

"That should teach you Navy fuckers to mess with *Semper Fi.*"

"Yeah, *Semper Fi.* Do or die!"

They gave him one last kick as they laughed their way back into

Hud's. No one helped him up. It was Chinatown. If you weren't dead, you were fine.

Ben stood up slow. His side throbbed and his jaw ached, but the vodka flowing through him numbed much of the pain. Not so bad. He wiped the blood from his face and stumbled down Hotel Street. Out of the corner of his eye the green-eyed man watched him. He had his hands in his pockets and leaned against the window of a cheap gift shop. His black T-shirt and jeans blended into the shadows under the overhang. Ben stumbled on. A vague memory of that man from long ago hung in his head, but it was all jumbled up.

Beat up and with no prospects, he needed to find a 'relaxation parlor' and some company. It didn't take long in Chinatown for him to be approached.

"Howzit, sailor? You hurt? Need some *wahine* to take care of you?"

Under a yellow sign blinking 'live nude shows', a pretty Hawaiian girl smiled at him. On the wall behind her rose a giant mural painted rust red of a Vietnamese girl in traditional garb carrying a machine gun. In his fuzzy state, they looked both part of the mural. He wiped his hair back off his face and squinted at the real girl. She had long, brown hair and wore a white tank top over a mini skirt, reminding him of the girl in the bar.

He should just forget this night and grab a cab back to base to sleep off the booze. Instead, he walked over to her and smiled back. He could fit a quick blow in before heading home. She stood as tall as him in her low heels. He blinked to remove the double vision of her.

"Maybe. You got a back room nearby?"

"Yeah, sure thing, sailor buggah. Da cute! Pretty gray eyes, too." She mixed in the local Pidgin dialect with English. "I'll wash your handsome face for free."

She laughed as he touched his face, remembering the blood. He must be a scary sight. She motioned him to follow her down a side alley. Grabbing his hand she pulled him into a dark room, lit by a dangling bulb over a single bed. She pulled a sheet down over the door and pushed him down on the bed. He'd been in dozens of rooms just like this over the past few years. It was better than getting closer to some girl who might screw you over and leave you anyways. That's what all people do, hookers or not. Screw you and leave you. Life now was about taking what he wanted and not giving any of himself away.

"Kay den, pay up front, honey, if you want the real thing. $50 for ten minutes and a nice slow blow. Or $250 for thirty minutes and the full spread. You're pretty so I'll make it last. I'll go get something to wash your face."

"Just a blow."

Ben pulled the money out of his wallet, and a condom, and fell back on the bed with both in his hand after she left. The room spun. Hud's sure didn't rip you off on watered down drinks. A cool, wet rag moved across his face and he squinted in pain. It smelled like beer and perfume. He opened his eyes and she smiled at him with slanted eyes.

"Are you Hawaiian?"

"I'm a mix, honey. Home-grown Hawaiian with a bit of Chinese. It don't matter here, though, eh?"

He shook his head and closed his eyes again, willing the throbbing throughout his body to go away. "Use a condom please," he whispered in a hoarse voice.

The girl grabbed his money and condom and laughed. "Sure thing, sweetheart, since you ask so nice."

The girl put the rag away and got down to business. She was true to her word and made it last. In his vodka-blurred condition he wasn't getting off so quick anyhow. She used her fingers and tongue everywhere. So good. He sat up half-way and cradled her head in the final moment. He pulled on her hair. It came loose in his hands. Was she wearing a wig? He shuddered and moaned as burning fire flowed through him. Then he passed out.

He woke up to someone shaking his arm.

"Come on, sailor boy, get up. You can't pass out here. You've been out another twenty minutes. You owe me another $200 or my man will kill me. He's waiting outside for me. He follows me and knows how long I been in here. He'll think I gave you the full thing. Okay wit dat?"

Ben sat up and blinked. Why did she wait around? Easy money to swindle, he guessed. The girl stood over him. She was so tall. A dull hangover started in the back of his head. She bent down and shook his arm again.

"Come on, you done here. Now pay up and get out. I've got other tricks to find. I'm sorry you beat up, but not my problem." She tapped her foot and waved her hands at him.

Ben stood up and the room tilted. He steadied himself and stared at the girl's hair, now longer on one side. He pulled at it and her wig came off in his hands. She yelped and grabbed it back. Only she wasn't a she. She was a he. It was clear now. There bobbed his Adam's apple.

"Show me your tits," Ben whispered, enraged.

He had to know for sure. He ripped the prostitute's tank top down on both sides to find a silicone filled bra and a chest as flat as his. He shoved the man away into the wall, who shrieked, clutching at his fake tits and top. Ben shook. Nausea swelled in his throat and he lunged for the door.

"My moke come after you! You don't pay me for the extra time!"

Ben turned around and punched him in the face. The transvestite screeched and fell on the bed, holding his face. He was a pretty, young man. A man who had sucked his cock and slid his fingers in his ass. And Ben paid him to do it. He doubled over and threw up all over the floor, then grabbed the sheet on the door to wipe his mouth and stumbled out.

"You knew! You knew I was *mahu!*" The young man followed him out in the street and yelled at someone. Ben hobbled then mustered the energy to run. He ran in a jerky path down Hotel Street, looking from side to side for a cab to take him back to base, when a kick from behind his knees took him down. He fell on the street and gasped for breath.

A massive local stood over him. "You cheat me, stupid sailor boy? Is dat what you want to do?"

"Yeah, that's him, Koko." The transvestite stood next to his Samoan moke. His wig now back on, but askew. He smiled at Ben and put his hands on his hips. He had blood on his face from where Ben hit him. How could he have ever thought this was a pretty woman? Ben stood up in a torpid daze and shook his head. Before he could speak the giant grabbed his shirt and glared at him.

"You see my girl here? You ruin her pretty face so she can't make tricks and I'll kill you. She's my money-making *mahu*. You want a beef with me, boy?"

Ben shook his head again. He couldn't look at the prostitute. It made him want to throw up again.

"You pay up now. Price just went up. $300. Or you not getting home any time soon, 'kay den?"

This night was going from bad to worse. Ben tilted his head back and laughed. Dizziness spun through him. People in the street spun around him, too. "I'm not paying extra for some homo to suck my cock. That's false advertising."

He laughed at his own words, even as the first punch came. And the next one and the next. The Samoan pummeled him until he couldn't see anymore. Blackness consumed him as he curled up in the street. The hooker laughed at him. "You crazy white boy, gonna get it now, real good!"

Then Ben passed out. He woke up curled up in the same fetal position with breezes blowing around him. He was in a car. Why couldn't he see? He struggled and found his arms and legs tied. He put his hands to his face. A rough bag covered it. He screamed and threw himself around the car.

"Yo, *haole*, keep it down back there," a deep voice called from the front. Two hands shoved him back down on the seat.

"Yeah, sailor buggah. You gonna get big time buggered soon," another voice called. It was the Samoan, Koko. Ben kicked his arms and legs trying to get at his captors.

Then a hard punch to his head sent him back to darkness.

CHAPTER 8: 1991

Ben woke up again to something hard and gritty scratching his face and chest. He wore only his underwear and was bent over a boulder, face down. The bag on his head had disappeared and he adjusted his eyes. The lights of Honolulu blinked below in the far distance. The tropical wind blew across him. He shivered, although it was a warm night. The moon glowed three-quarters full overhead.

He struggled to move, but his hands and feet were tied with rope. It cut into his skin and pulled at the stakes in the ground that held him bent over the rock. He was spread out vulnerable for whatever his tormentors would do to him.

"You awake, sailor boy?" Koko smiled at him and slapped his head. "I picked up my friend here, and we're gonna teach you a lesson real good. Right, Kami?"

Koko's friend, Kami, leaned into Ben's face and leered. Larger and darker than his partner, Kami's teeth gleamed bright against his skin.

"Oh yeah, real good. This is where we take the *haoles* that don't behave, right, Koko?"

"Damn straight. We make nice, friendly boys out of you."

The two Samoans laughed.

Ben turned his head to look at them. "My friends will be looking for me, you know. My base will be looking for me. I know where you are in town. You do anything to me and the Navy will find you."

"No one ain't ever gonna find you, brah." Kami chuckled. "After we done with you we gonna throw you off the cliff, right, Koko?"

"Yep."

Ben knew where he was now. The Pali Lookout. It hung over

Honolulu on the Koolau Mountain Range. They must have parked and carried him down the old Pali road, overgrown and forgotten after the new Pali road had been built. It was hidden in the jungle off the beaten path. He remembered the so-called suicides up here. He understood now some might not have been suicides.

"I'll pay whatever you want," Ben said. "Just let me go now." His body ached everywhere but he could think again.

"Don't give me your stink eye, boy." Koko slapped his head again. Ben turned his face away. "Yeah, we'll take your money, but you owe us more, now."

A sharp *s-n-a-p* cracked the air. Ben screamed when a whip cut across his back. "You motherfuckers." *S-n-a-p*. The whip cracked again across the tender back of his legs. He strained at the ropes. Blood trickled down his legs.

"Motherfuckers? I hold the whip and you curse me?" Koko leaned into him. "Hey, Kami, wanna take a turn?"

"Heck yeah, brah."

S-n-a-p. The whip cracked Ben across his buttocks. Streaks of fire cut into him.

S-n-a-p. Across his back.

"My poor sailor boy," Koko said. "Had enough?"

Ben tried to speak, but he could only nod.

"Kay den, my sweet friend, we do something else more fun, eh? We don't want you passed out and miss the party."

A click popped in Ben's ear. Shiny metal flashed before him. A hand caressed his ass. He clenched his buttocks together, struggling against the ropes that held him over the rock. One of them pulled his head up by his hair and slapped duct tape on his mouth. Ben quivered.

"Got chicken skin there, eh?" Koko caressed his arms. "No one will hear you scream up here. This is a haunted place. Your screams carry away on the wind, right, Kami?"

"Right, brah. People too scared to come up here at night with the ghosts of our ancestors roaming about."

"Yeah, and we like to hear your screams, but just to be safe we shut you up anyways."

A knife tip pushed painfully at Ben's lower back. He tried to shrink into the rock. The rough surface cut into chest and arms and thighs.

"Be still or I'll cut you good," Koko growled in his ear.

The large Samoan sliced down the back of Ben's underwear and ripped it from his body. The jagged rock edges pressed painfully into his private parts. He tried to raise his bottom away from the rock to alleviate the discomfort.

"Ah, my friend, I like that." Koko sighed in Ben's ear. He rubbed

Ben's naked bottom and reached between his legs to massage his balls.

Ben flung himself about on the rock like a crazed animal, pulling at the ropes. They were so taut he had only an inch of leeway. Blood oozed down him as he scraped his naked skin across the rock. But the stakes held fast. He couldn't budge them. Koko laughed deep and long and held his balls tight. Ben stopped his flailing as the pain in his scrotum increased.

Deep anguish surged through him. Had he escaped his foster father's advances only to be gang-raped here by these Samoan monsters and thrown off the cliff to a spiraling death? He heard about one suicidal man who had survived jumping off the Pali lookout. The wind had been so strong it blew him back. It was like the hand of God picked him up and placed the man gently back down. Perhaps Ben would get so lucky and be spared as well. He might not want to live after these two had their way with him though.

He closed his eyes and forced himself to find a dark place with peace and no pain. The two men continued to taunt him, but they echoed far away in a tunnel. He held his breath, willing himself to pass out. The wild wind of the mountaintop raged around him and shrieked in his ears.

One of the men pulled Ben's head toward him. Ben pulled away, squirming to fight him off. "Hey, sailor boy, if you no fight it will be better for you in the long run, eh? Then again, I like the ones that squirm."

"Yeah, keep squirming, man. My big man Kami here is real hung. He'll fill you up real good and then it's my try."

The two men laughed, their voices picked up by the wind and carried off.

Ben was in hell. He didn't know why he had to suffer. But this would be the end of his pitiful life. Here on this Hawaiian mountain it would now be over. Humiliation, repulsion, anger, and pity for himself consumed him as he lay sprawled across the rock. Finally, he wept. The tears burned him as they seeped around the duct tape over his mouth.

"Yeah, you cry, my little *wahine*." Koko leaned his heavy frame onto Ben, crushing him into the biting rock. "You no longer a virgin after I'm done with you."

Two hands held his buttocks open. Ben tucked his head and shoulders in tight to brace against the penetration that would rip him apart. Then two loud cracks shot out over the howling wind. The hands fell away. He let out a huge sigh, dizzy from holding his breath.

Ben opened his eyes and craned his head around to see what had happened. Under the bright moonlight the outline of the two big Samoans rose up from the overgrown road. They didn't move. The wind whipped the giant leaves of the banyan and guava trees about like sails on a great clipper ship. The buzz of traffic from the new Pali road carried up to him from below. He scanned the area. What had happened? Who else hid out there? He pulled at the stakes. His hands shook as he tried to break free.

"Forget it, kid, they're held down in cement," a deep voice said. "These stupid locals make up these playgrounds just to mess with us *haoles*."

Ben swallowed the saliva stuck in his throat and focused on his surroundings. There stood the green-eyed man, hidden in the swaying banyan trees. His black outfit blended into the dark forest. He moved toward Ben and holstered his gun, then popped open a switchblade from his back pocket.

"I am not here to hurt you," the man said when Ben shrunk into the rock. "I'm going to cut the ropes."

In a few swift movements he slit the ropes binding Ben, who staggered back. The man caught him and held him up, then ripped off the duct tape.

"Who are you?" Ben's body trembled from the rush of fear and a fierce headache pounded in his temple.

The man didn't answer. He bent over one of the dead Samoans and pulled out a wallet. He looked inside and threw it at Ben. "It's yours." Then the man led him by the arm down the overgrown road where he handed Ben his clothes from the brush. He tried to put them on but his hands shook so bad the man had to help him. He winced from the whip marks brushing against his jeans and shirt.

"Come on," the man said. Ben looked back at the dead men sprawled face down. They oozed like two fat walruses sunning themselves in the moonlight. "Don't worry about them. I'll dump them later, somewhere they'll never be found."

In a daze, Ben followed his savior up the rough road, stumbling behind him in the dim moonlight. Those men had carried him unconscious down this road.

"I'll take you back to base then you're on your own," the man said once they reached his car, parked off the main road. "Don't speak of this to anyone. Understand?"

Ben nodded and climbed in the car. He looked over at the stranger in black who had saved him. His mammoth biceps flexed as he drove, hunched over the wheel. The man's body looked crushed in the sedan. His square jaw tensed as he clenched his teeth. Ben turned to the window and closed his eyes. He had so many questions jumbled in his head. The wind blew soft on his face as they sped down the mountain curves.

Giddiness rose in him from the pit of his stomach to his throat. He bent over his knees with laughter. He laughed and laughed and then he sobbed with relief. He would live. Just like when he chose to save himself from his foster father. But this time a stranger chose for him to live.

The man looked over at him, both hands gripping the wheel. "Get yourself together," he warned Ben. "I know what those bastards planned to do to you. This island is a cesspool of crap. Tropical paradise, my ass. Occasional good weather doesn't make up for the trash-filled streets, gangs, and homeless. That's what the tourists don't see."

Ben stared at him, fascinated by the man's lengthy dialogue and then a memory flickered. "You were at my foster mother's funeral. Why are you following me? Why save me?"

"I'm an interested party. Leave it at that."

"I can't. I would have died up there for sure."

The man didn't respond.

"Thank you."

The man looked at Ben. His green eyes glowed in the moonlight that filtered into the car.

"Someday you might not thank me. Someday you may not survive."

Ben didn't know what to make of his comment. He started shaking again.

"Just close your eyes and breathe slow."

Ben wanted to throw up again. He remembered being sick in the hooker's room. That seemed like days ago since all this happened. He hugged his waist and closed his eyes.

They reached town and the man whipped in and around Honolulu traffic and stopped the car near the Pearl Harbor base. "You're good from here."

"I don't even know your name. Will I ever see you again?"

The man stared straight ahead and didn't answer. Ben bent his head down and stepped out of the car.

"Tonight was a warning," the man in black said in a low, deep voice. "Make a life for yourself while you have the chance. You can't change the past."

"How do you know about me?" Ben turned back.

The man looked up at him. He squinted as if in pain. "And get out of the Navy. It's not the place for you. The government will only fuck you. Get out now."

The man slammed the door shut and sped off, leaving Ben standing on the curb.

He made his way to his barracks and collapsed on his bed. His roommate was still out somewhere. Ben fell into a deep sleep but couldn't escape the night. In his nightmares the Samoans laughed as they whipped him. His foster father joined them, snapping the whip on his back and cursing him for letting him die. *Murderer!*

Then he fell off a cliff. The wind rocked his body but didn't push him back to safety. He screamed as he fell into the darkness. He tried to grab onto something but it was a black, empty abyss. Then a bright green light appeared above him. It grew larger and larger. He shielded his eyes as he fell, terrified. The green light rushed faster and faster toward him. It came for him. It would crush him just like it crushed his parents.

And he was headed straight to hell.

CHAPTER 9: 1988

Laura faced the lake to say goodbye. She would leave for college in a few days. And her whole world would change. This past week she went back and forth from feeling excited to scared to nervous. After being home schooled she had grown used to being alone in her own world. There had been some kids she hung out with through the home school association, but she never had any desire to see them outside of home school events.

And then of course, there was Mr. B. He had slowed down a bit this summer, as if old age had now decided to settle in. At seventy-nine she had to admit he did look old. It didn't matter. He was her best friend. He hadn't laughed as much since Scooter died many years ago. She suggested he get a new dog but he refused. She understood that Scooter had been one of the few things in his life still connected to his wife, so he had special meaning. Laura also understood you can't replace such a thing.

She stared out at the lake, leaning against her rock by the shore. Her mind raced with all she had to do before leaving for New Paltz University. She thought of all the cool college things she would encounter. Boys, parties and friends. What if she couldn't find her classes on the gigantic campus? What if she hated her roommate? She would have to hide her special powers. She didn't want people to see her as a freak. She just wanted to fit in. Would she?

Mr. B told her not to worry about such things. Worrying is a waste of time, he said. Just jump in and be yourself, he told her, and all will work out. Thank goodness she had gotten a scholarship to pay for most of her tuition. Her parents didn't have much. And it was only an hour away. An hour wasn't so far. But an hour could change her world. She could come home anytime. Right?

She smoothed down her long hair and stood up to stretch her arms out wide. She wasn't a tomboy anymore, but it didn't mean she liked the way she looked. She wished she had a bigger chest, her nose wasn't so turned up, and she wasn't so tall. Laura's long legs helped her tower over Mr. B and her parents. Mr. B told her that wasn't such a great feat as he was shrinking by the inch every year. He said she had become an old-fashioned beauty. When she asked him what he meant, he just said she had grace and style, and that with her big brown eyes and lively wit she could charm anyone.

She might never know where she got her height and looks from. But she hoped to someday. She still had hope a relative would come forward looking for her natural mother, Sarah, and find Laura instead. When she felt alone and unsure of herself she would visit the crater at the end of the lake and place her hands on the earth. Then she would feel connected to this someone who had crashed there all those years ago. In feeling his sadness it made her feel not so alone. To her, they were sad together.

She had covered every foot of the crater over the years hoping to sense new information, but never got more than her initial vision of the strange, sad man and the girl whose face she couldn't see.

She closed her eyes and willed herself to force away the headache coming on. She still hadn't outgrown them and learned to suffer through them. They remained unpredictable and so she accepted them as part of her.

She breathed deep again taking in the smells and sounds of her lake. Even Mr. B called it Laura's Lake. A smooth cacophony rose of cicada saws, crow echoes, rustling leaves, and the tapping of a lonesome woodpecker. It all blended with the smell of sun burnt grass. This would be her last sunrise for a while here.

She picked up her notebook and wrote. She wrote and wrote and not just describing the sunrise, for she had written hundreds of sunrises over the years. She wrote about how the lake came to be her home, her friend, her place to be her true self. It was her goodbye.

A car driving fast down the dirt road toward the lake disrupted her writing. She threw her notebook in her backpack and headed toward the overgrown parking lot. Who could be speeding in here at 6:30 a.m.? Mr. B's rusted Jeep bounced down the rutted road and shuddered to a stop in front of her.

"Laura, come on," he yelled out the window. "Sheriff Barnes just called me. There's a fire at your house."

She ran for the car and jumped in, leaving her bike leaning on the big rock. "Like the fire alarm went off from something burning on the stove?" Laura's lip trembled and she tried to blink back the tears that filled her eyes.

Jim slammed his foot on the accelerator, kicking up dust along the dirt road, and headed toward her house. They both smacked their heads on the roof. "Sorry about that," he said, then cleared his throat. "No, honey, I don't think so."

"Why? What did the Sheriff say?"

Jim's knobby hands gripped the wheel. "He said someone drove by and saw flames shooting out of the top windows and called the fire department. The fire truck is on its way there."

"But my parents...I left them asleep upstairs. Saturday is the one day they sleep in."

Laura looked at the trees flying by as they sped along. Jim put his hand on hers. She looked down and grasped it. His old hand looked like a carved piece of wood an artist had been working on for years and kept etching new lines into it.

"What if they were still asleep?"

She rocked herself as they neared her house.

"For all we know, they could have gotten out of the house."

"You don't believe that," Laura cried. "I know what you're thinking. I am too."

They heard sirens in the distance. Jim sped up as they reached the turn to her house. An acrid smell filled the air and they came around the corner to a fiery scene. Flames shot out of the first and second floors of the farmhouse reaching for the sky. Its angry inferno crackled through blackened wood. The windows glared a jack-o-lantern orange with black, thick smoke pouring out. The wrap-around porch still stood intact but then with a shriek the wood gave way. The porch rails splintered and smashed down.

Two firefighters sprayed the flames with water sucked from the pond to no avail. Their attempts made the fire angrier as the flames grew taller, spouting from every crevice. A second fire truck pulled in the shale driveway behind them, its sirens blaring as it wailed to a stop spewing rocks from its large tires.

Laura leapt from the Jeep, before Jim could roll to a stop, and ran toward the house. The ferocious heat hit her with a blast and a firefighter grabbed her.

"Wait! Stop, Miss!"

"It's my home! My parents are in there. You've got to save them!"

"We're trying but we can't get into the house yet. The fire's too fierce. I've never seen a blaze so explosive. If they're in there, we won't know until we get this more under control. Hang on!"

He held her to his chest and waved over the other firefighters coming from the second truck. Laura clutched his jacket and sensed his goodness, warmth, and sympathy. She wanted to hide in his wet, smoky jacket for a long while and feel everything would be okay.

"Please get in there soon," Laura whispered. The firefighter nodded and patted her back. Jim came to her side. The firefighter released her with a grim face and barked out more orders to the others. Another emergency helper brought them blankets and water.

Jim and Laura watched as the bottom floor windows exploded. The second floor windows had already blown out. Then with a wrenching screech the top of the house caved in. Only black timbers were left behind, pointing toward the sky in jagged spears. Jim pulled Laura back further to the road. The heat seared them in its growing intensity eating through the wood like a hungry savage. Flames engulfed the house. They watched it crumble completely and disappear into smoky rubble.

Jim squeezed her hand. The firefighters still hosed down the house shouting out instructions. Laura turned away. She didn't want to see her parents' burnt bodies through the dissipating smoke. She hoped they weren't in there. Maybe they left early to go to the store and get chicken feed or out to breakfast at the bakery in town...or something.

Cars now lined the road to watch the blaze destroying her home. People leaned through their car windows and stood on the side of the road shaking their heads and pointing. Shock stole over Laura. An hour ago she left here on her bike to say goodbye to her lake while her parents slept in their beds. All she had lived in this house. She believed it would always be here. And now it was all gone in one hour. If she hadn't gone to the lake she would have been here to save them.

"I can go back home and call someone for you, Laura," Jim said. "Who can I call?"

"No one. There is no one."

They had been a family unit of three strong and while they had ties to the community they stayed to themselves. They had been everything to each other, but at least Laura had Mr. B too. She was grateful for him. She wiped her face, streaked with charcoal smudges from ash and tears, and squeezed Mr. B's hand back, trying to draw strength from him.

Then she saw him. The man in black. He stood hidden in the trees behind the gawkers. He wasn't pointing to the house or talking to bystanders. He stared at Laura with his bright green eyes. His hands were shoved into his pockets as he hunched down. His black jeans and T-shirt stood out in comparison to the colorful summer clothes of the onlookers. But something was strange about him too. A pale glow outlined his body and he swayed in waves, as an image being projected on an outdoor movie screen moving in the breeze.

She ran from Mr. B toward the man screaming. "Who are you? Why me? Did you do this?"

The other people stopped talking to stare at her too. Then the man in black vanished. In a blink of her eye he just disappeared. She collapsed on the ground crying. Mr. B picked her up and held her. She broke free and ran over to the Fire Chief who was instructing his crew.

"When are you going in?"

"Just now, Miss. Please, stay back. This fire could re-ignite or cause an explosion."

The firefighters had doused most of the flames and moved toward the house. An acrid, burnt smell poured out of the scorched remains of Laura's childhood home. She hid her head in Jim's jacket and waited. After a while she looked up. The Chief walked toward them. He shook his head.

"We found two people. A man and a woman. I'm so sorry."

Jim hugged her harder. Two other firefighters carried out two long things with sheets over them. Laura doubled over with a cramp and holding her stomach, she stood up.

"I want to see."

Jim nodded. The Chief took her arm and helped her through the broken wood and glass and metal. All the things making up her life lay strewn and twisted in a smoking mass grave. Laura stood over the two sheets and the Chief lifted the top covers. It couldn't be them. She told herself she would never remember them like this. She forced herself to stare. She owed it to them. Tears flowed down her cheeks but she didn't make a sound. Then the stench overcame her and she turned away to gag.

"They may have been asleep and succumbed to the smoke before the fire got to them. We won't know until the coroner sees them."

Laura nodded and stumbled back to Mr. B to fall on her knees. A keening sound came from her like a wild animal. She wailed in grief, hugging her sides and rocked. Mr. B knelt with her. She sensed his love and anguish flow into her. His tears mixed with hers on the ground. With her powers she still couldn't save her parents.

She vowed from then on she would forget her powers and never use them again. And she would find this man in black. In the dark abyss of her grieving mind she also vowed she would leave this place and never come back again.

CHAPTER 10: 1998

Ben stood on the balcony and overlooked Waikiki Beach under the stars, breathing in the tropical air floating around him. It carried the intoxicating warmth of sea air, burning tiki lamps, and floral scents. Mixed together it would make any traveler feel excited to be here in the land of luaus, leis, and lava flows.

To his left stretched the lights of Waikiki leading to Diamond Head, rising in a crooked wave under the moon. To his right stretched a string of hotels filled with tourists and their dreams of Hawaii. And in front of him spread out the Pacific Ocean, sparkling black in the night and lapping at the shore where couples held hands and kissed.

Ben turned back to his room to unpack, feeling cynical in his candy-cane view of this place. He pitied the blinded tourists who came here to capture the romance of the islands. They saw the gloss, not the bile beneath. He almost didn't take this assignment due to the location, but seven years was long enough to try and forget. At twenty-eight, none of it belonged to his life now. He could be a tourist now too. He pushed his bangs aside, and stared at his red-rimmed gray eyes in the mirror. His eyes now matched the gray that had crept into his black hair years ago.

Tiredness hit him in waves. He felt the effects of the long flight here from Florida. But how different it was from his old Florida days. He admired the ornate room and tall vase of flowers on the dresser welcoming him from the Taylor family. He had come a long way from the dumps of Orlando and his discharge from the Navy.

The phone blinked red and he retrieved two messages, one from the Taylor family, wishing him a good night and inviting him to breakfast the next morning. The other came from his old buddy, Andy, inviting him to dinner the next day and threatening to kick his ass if he didn't show up. Andy got sent back here for a second tour of Pearl Harbor after sea duty and Ben wouldn't miss seeing him.

Andy had saved his life years ago when Ben needed a second chance. He went a little crazy after the terrible night up on the Pali Lookout. He wandered around the base the next day. Andy found him later sprawled out on the barracks rooftop with intense sunburn. It was the one place he could hide and see the entire sky spread above. Andy led him to sick bay.

The doctors talked to him but he just stared at them. He felt dead inside. After a series of tests and discussions about his condition, the doctor rubber-stamped his file "Personality Disorder" and the Navy booted him with an RE-4 discharge. It came as a friendly send-off but said loud and clear, "Here son, take an honorable discharge, but by the way you're unfit for re-enlistment. Not military material. Sorry."

Afterwards, he headed back to Florida and lived on his savings, supplementing it with doing package deliveries on bike between local businesses. He re-lived his days in the same dumpy motel before the Navy with Jack Daniels. He still had Andy as a friend but he lived three-thousand miles away, connected by a $2 a minute phone call he couldn't afford. He *could* afford Jack but still couldn't shut out the dreams of the lake. In the dreams he always ran along the shoreline trying to get back to his parents. And sometimes the meteorite chased him wanting to crush him.

He remembered the night he had stumbled out of bed, still half-drunk. The dream that night wasn't about the lake or the meteorite. He saw his parents clear for the first time since the night he ran away at nine years old. His mother played the piano on the front lawn of their house in New Paltz. His father played the flute. They stopped and looked at him and holding hands, they walked toward him smiling.

"It'll be all right, Ben," his mother said in her soft way. "We still love you."

"You've got to live for us," his father said.

"Everything will be all right, if you want to live." His mother nodded.

"Do you want to live, Ben?" His parents stood in front of him and they each took one of his hands. He felt their touch. So warm, so real. He felt an unfamiliar feeling rising in him. He loved and he felt loved. It had been so long.

He then awoke and stood naked at his window overlooking the trash dumpsters. The moon shone down illuminating the scene. He knew this scene well. Drunks sleeping off their booze in the parking lot, rats raiding the garbage, and the poor sloth of life living all around him in an angry haze trying to exist in a depressing world. He fell to his knees and buried his head in the carpet.

"Yes, I want to live. Help me live."

He sat on the floor and stared at the moon. From the floor it was all he could see. It glowed with new hope in his window. When his head cleared and the sun faded the moon to a pale outline in blue, he called his old buddy, Andy. He had kept in touch with him along his drunken route. Andy had become an officer since he last saw him, after being recommended for officer training school. Yeah, Andy had done well.

"Yo, Ben, my man." Andy sounded wide-awake as if the night still ran young on his end, although he was hours behind Ben. "What's going on in the armpit of Florida? Still lazing around?"

"Yeah, well, that's why I'm calling." Ben grinned. It felt good to hear his voice.

"Let me guess, out of money and used up all the chicks there?"

"The first one is right anyways, but I don't need your money." Ben paused. "I actually need a job. I need something." His voice cracked. "I need..."

"I get it," Andy said in a serious voice. "Let me see what I can dig up and call you back. I know some people I can reach out to. Give me a day. You don't care where or what the job is, right?"

Ben laughed. "Hell no, I'd take a job hauling elephant dung from the local zoo right now."

"Well, just 'cause you're in deep shit doesn't mean you have to work in shit or shit where you work or eat shit and die or...hell, never mind." Andy chuckled. "I'll call ya in a couple days, buddy."

Ben laughed again and hung up, glad he had called him. Andy moved in different circles since becoming an officer. Andy called him a few days later with an unusual project. A family he knew planned to head out on a six-week vacation to the Mediterranean. They were a well-off couple with two kids who wanted to take a photographer along to capture their memories. They would pay all expenses and a nice salary. It would be a dream job and the second chance Ben needed to jump back into the world of the living. He also knew Andy took a chance on him.

"You are cleaned up, right?" Andy had to ask.

"I am now," Ben answered. It was true he hadn't drunk since two nights ago. He went through two nights of hell to find his way back between the delirium tremors, the parched mouth thirsting for more, and the paranoia. He had been given a second chance—again.

"But can you stay sober?"

"Not a problem. I promise. Give me this gig, and you'll have no worries."

And that's how he found himself two weeks later dragging his camera equipment, that had been collecting dust, and a duffel bag through the noisy, pungent-smelling Athens International Airport.

From that moment on, Ben grew a business out of traveling with the rich on vacation. It started with one referral and another and another. His clients recognized good candid photos when they saw them and Ben's quiet way put them at ease, often not realizing he was around them capturing their intimate moments.

From the beginning Ben made it professional, but families still remained a mystery beyond his landscape. They vibrated as a package of harmony and discord wrapped up in duty and tied with love. He wasn't part of their unit but he could be a respected partner for a short time and it was good enough for him. He became part of the living again and living good, traveling the world for free. From Paris to Rome to Nepal he lived a dream life. The world had become his home.

And now he was back here in Hawaii. There was something full circle about that. After a day of shooting the Taylors surfing at the North Shore, he showered the sand off and caught a cab to Andy's place in Honolulu. As Ben pulled up and paid the cabby, he knew he wasn't anywhere near Hotel Street. Palm trees lined the streets in perfect alignment gracing white stucco homes with beige trim on low, wide roofs. Quiet and serene. Definitely not NoHo.

He wondered if Hud's Place still cranked out music and drinks in the midst of hooker heaven. He guessed it did. The idea now of paying some hooker to blow him off in a seedy room when he could take care of business himself for free made him queasy. And the transvestite. He wasn't that Ben anymore, but it was hard not to think about it, being back in Hawaii. Memories hid around each corner waiting to suck him down in a monstrous undertow.

"Ben, my man!" Andy grabbed him at the door and picked him up in a bear hug, cracking his back. He looked like the same white-blond, Norse God Ben had left seven years ago. A whisper of wrinkles graced his ice-blue eyes now, but he stood as big and tan as ever.

"Dude, you're breaking me! How ya doin'?"

"Well, glad to not be the same old skinny-ass James Dean wanna-be you are. What the hell have you been living on, Pez and beef jerky?"

Nahhh…Pez is *passé*. It's strictly Skittles and Cheetos. I keep the maids guessing about the colorful ring I leave in the tub after peeing in it."

"Nastier than ever I see." Andy grinned and chucked his hair. "No wonder you still can't get laid with peeing in the tub, and all."

"Actually, the girls love it as I never leave the seat up. They think I'm sooooo polite."

They both laughed, enjoying each other in a return to their old banter. Andy led him into a large foyer. "Seven years. I can't believe it. Way too long."

Ben nodded. He burst with things he wanted to talk about with Andy and looked forward to the evening ahead of hanging out with his old buddy. He was the only one in his life who knew about his past. Except the Pali Lookout. He could never tell Andy about it.

And as time went on he began to think he had created the man in black in his mind to save him. Could a figure conjured up shoot the bad asses that tried to rape you, help you dress, and then drive you home? Andy was cool though and had never pushed him to talk about that night. Andy knew memories could come back to haunt you.

"Well, you've got some nice digs here, Lieutenant. What pirate booty ship did you jump on, sailor?"

"Not a ship, but a world-class cruise." Andy pointed to a woman who walked into the room. Her skin glowed bronze and her black hair hung in a liquid sheath of curls cascading down a rounded body. She glided toward Ben. Perspiration twitched on his upper lip. She smiled at him with sparkling white teeth and held out her slender hand, revealing a glint of diamonds in the foyer light. Her black sloe-eyes captured his gray ones with amusement and welcome.

"Hello, Ben Fieldstone," she said with a lilting accent.

"Ben, this is Likini, her and I, are, well...engaged."

Andy grinned and put an arm around the woman.

"Nice to meet you, and congratulations." Ben shook her hand and raised his eyebrows at Andy.

"I know, I didn't tell you." Andy said. "Well, now I am, so come on in to our place."

They ate a traditional Polynesian feast of steamed pork, yams, and marinated fish in lemon juice and coconut cream. Likini had prepared it with a Tongan twist, reminiscent of the island she came from in the South Pacific. Ben complemented her about it several times. She was a lady and he forced himself to watch his obscene banter with Andy. He wondered if she was a lady in bed too. Knowing Andy, probably not. So he stuck to regaling them with funny travel stories from around the world and ate himself beyond full.

No one had cooked him a meal in their home in years. He tried to remember the last time and recalled glimpses of being with his parents at their friend's house. He remembered how he would stuff himself as fast as he could with dinner and dessert, sitting politely amongst candles, listening to boring talk about the cost of furniture or cars. All the while he would shake his legs back and forth under the table waiting to be excused.

The moment would finally come and with a whoop he'd escape to the back room to watch *Hart to Hart*, *Fantasy Island*, and sometimes, although he wouldn't admit to liking it, *The Love Boat*. Ensconced with popcorn and an old blanket he would pass the evening in front of the knob-controlled television while the grownups played canasta, getting louder with each drink. He liked being alone in his own world just as he liked it now.

"Thank you again," Ben said as he got up to clear the table.

"So many thank you's is not necessary." Likini's stilted English drawl flowed over him like smooth liquor. "But I'm glad you enjoyed it."

Andy rolled his eyes. "He's in love with you pretty lady, plain and simple. Drooling at the mouth. Struck dumb by beauty."

Ben looked down at the dirty dishes he held and cleared his throat.

"It's okay, Ben." Likini smiled up at him. "It's a complement and you don't have to help with the dishes. Please, go enjoy your time with Andy. You have a lot to talk about, I can imagine."

She swirled away in her flowing white halter dress and Ben watched, mesmerized. After he and Andy moved to the back screened in porch he had to ask his friend.

"How did you meet her when she's from Tonga?"

"At a command ceremony dinner," Andy explained and lit up a cigar, offering one to Ben. He puffed at it, after watching Andy do the same. A buzz filled his head mixed with the beer he had. Two became his limit nowadays and no heavy stuff. "It was held off base and she attended with her cousin who is a JAG officer here. I asked her to dance and that was it."

Ben understood. He needed no further explanation.

"This is her place, actually. She visited her family here years ago when she was eighteen and met some older captain. She ended up marrying the guy. He was killed soon after in the Persian Gulf and had a bundle of extra life insurance. So she was pretty well-off to buy a house here."

"You're one lucky guy," Ben said and raised his beer glass. He wondered if settling down was worth it.

"That's for sure. But what about you, man?"

Ben half smiled and flipped his bangs up. "Women? Forget about it. I should thank you for that, again. With the travel I do, I'm never home. I actually don't have a home. When I'm between jobs I usually rent a suite for a month somewhere and relax."

Andy studied him and leaned back, puffing on his cigar, then gazed at the blowing banyan trees silhouetted under the moon off his porch. Ben stared at them too. Banyan trees. The last time he had seen them he was being whipped, bent over a rock. He peered up toward the mountain knowing the Pali Lookout hung there over Honolulu, hiding its dirty secrets. He could see the menacing boulder in his mind waiting for its next victim to cry out on its hard surface, painting it with new blood. He looked back at Andy.

"Listen to me, my friend." Andy leaned forward and eyed Ben. "I don't know what happened to you here, whether it had to do with your childhood or some prostitute you wronged but I think you're still running away from it. You may have cleaned up your act but you're still alone. A loner."

This was not the conversation Ben envisioned. He didn't want to get serious. It hit him Andy had changed as much as he had in seven years.

"So, what's wrong with that? I jet-set with the rich, see the world for free, and get paid for it. Not a bad gig and I have you to thank for it. Maybe I'm not like you."

"You're definitely not like me, but it doesn't mean it can't be great for you too. And I'll tell you why. Because you're missing the big picture. It sounds corny, but love does make the world go 'round. You should stop running from it, and your past, and find it. Likini has changed my life."

"Good for you. But how the hell am I supposed to have a relationship traveling all the time. And I can count on this hand the one-night stands I've had when I'm not traveling."

"So, change your career. Give yourself a home base. You've been doing this for years now. You're smart, make a change."

That hadn't occurred to Ben. He liked his job because he didn't have to make excuses to himself for why he couldn't settle down. He also didn't think about having a home to go to every night as well. It felt safe. Just like getting his bone smooched by hookers rather than a girlfriend had been safe, although it turned out not to be. He still ran from his past and he knew it. It hit him with clarity in an instant.

"Likini knows my past and she's cool." Andy half-smiled at him. "Everyone has a past. It's your future you can change. You can't run forever."

Ben nodded. The two friends sat in silence smoking and finishing their beers.

"Just promise me you won't be heading down to NoHo while you're here." Andy joked to lighten the moment, and winked at him. "I don't want to be pulling your butt out of a jail cell. Some big Samoan might be sweet on your skinny ass and take a closer look when you're bending over to tie your shoe."

Ben couldn't help laughing. If Andy only knew how close to the truth he came. "Yeah, no hookers for me anymore. It's just me and Rosie, all the way."

"Dude, I'm telling you, get a regular woman. At least one you can keep on the back burner while you're traveling." He glanced toward the kitchen. "I found a real tiger in this one. She may act like a lady, but not behind closed doors!"

Andy slapped the table and the talk moved on to lighter topics with funny stories at sea, wedding plans, and raunchy jokes. Ben needed it. Maybe he didn't have a home or a girl, but in a way Andy had become his home. For now it was enough.

That night he dreamed. He stood at the lake on its shore. The stillness covered him in peaceful quiet. The moon shone high overhead painting the wave tops with gold that lapped at the water's edge. Something moved in the distance on the path leading around the lake. It was a girl. She walked toward him as if she knew him. Finally, she stood before him and smiled. He found himself smiling back.

She took his hand and stared at him with her large, brown eyes. She looked so lovely. Her hand was warm in his, her touch sent waves of yearning through his body. She reached up on her toes and kissed him. He squeezed her hand and found himself kissing her back. Their tongues intertwined in a soft, embracing dance. He gave himself to her mouth, falling into her sweet wetness. She put her hand behind his neck and pulled him closer.

"Ben, do you know what I am?" Her eyes held him in a trance.

"*What* you are? What do you mean?"

"Come with me, I'll show you."

He followed her as she led him down the path. Then he looked up. Something green shone in the sky. The meteorite. It would crush them. She was leading them toward the spot where it would crash.

"No!" He pulled her with him to go back.

"Come." Her large eyes drew him into her.

"No, follow me," Ben urged. "Can't you see, it's coming!"

"Come." She caressed his hand. "It's where I belong. We can belong together."

"No!" He dropped her hand and ran. His legs pumped fast over the rocks and fallen logs on the path. He turned once. She still stood there under the moon. The green thing filled the sky behind her as it streaked toward them.

She was smiling.

CHAPTER 11: 2001

Laura woke up to a vicious headache. It involved the kind of pain brought on by a bad mix of tequila and beer. In the dark of her room she remembered dancing on the shuffle board table at P & G's bar with her roommate, Moe, and doing upside down margaritas. She groaned as she also remembered making out with Dennis Matthews from class and letting him feel her up at the bar. *Ughh.* She pulled herself up and staggered to her dresser mirror.

She switched on the light and groaned more. She also remembered she had let him give her hickies all over her neck in the quest to make the coolest shaped one. She didn't even like Dennis. She groaned again. The only two guys she had been with in college weren't memorable. One she lost her virginity to in a walk-in closet at a house party. The other one she dated for a few months, but he went in pursuit of other girls.

Then she remembered that Moe's parents were coming over that night to take them out for dinner to celebrate their college graduation tomorrow. How could she hide these hickies? She couldn't wear a turtleneck because a May heat wave had settled over New Paltz, hanging in the air like a fire-breathing cloud.

Coffee, croissants, and water. Lots of water. And then more coffee. That's what she needed. She pulled on a T-shirt and jean shorts over her trim, and aching body, and inched her way to the kitchen. On the way she peered into Moe's room. The light from the hallway settled on a covered up lump in the darkened room that shifted in bed. Yep, dead to the world. She was better off not feeling this hangover. The microwave light blinked 11:15. They had five hours until Moe's parents hit town.

She chugged down the last two aspirin she could find with a glass of water and sat down on the ragged, brown-plaid sofa in the small living room. She closed her eyes to wait for the throbbing in her head to go away. Then she would force herself to walk to The Bakery down the street to get strong coffee and croissants. It was Laura's favorite food spot in town. She craved a carb-fest of feta-spinach croissant and pesto tortellini. Then she might have the energy to clean their dirty apartment before Moe's parents came.

The place wasn't much, but it was heaven compared to living in the dorms for two years. Her scholarship paid for most of her tuition along with her job at the campus bookstore and small student loans. The money saved from the sale of her parent's property helped pay for her living expenses.

But in three weeks they would be moving out. Laura, to North Jersey for a job in communications with a large corporation, and Moe, to New York City for an advertising job. They would be peons making peon money to start.

Moe and her parents had been her family for the last four years, ever since she met Moe as a roommate on her first day on campus. She had been a couple of days late getting there, still in shock over her parents' death. Then Moe strolled into the room all tall, blonde, and bubbly. She was built like a football player and just as loud.

"Hey, it's the late arrival. You got a fake I.D.? Man, do I need a drink! My brain is already fried from trekking across this dinosaur of learning!"

Laura smiled for the first time in days and found herself chugging down a pitcher of beer at P & G's bar with Moe an hour later, after forging the worst fake I.D. in the history of the school. They became best friends from the beginning.

But on the big campus of New Paltz University Laura found herself having panic attacks getting to class. She felt terrified of crossing the campus amongst thousands of other people. Sitting in large lecture halls freaked her out. She felt trapped. The sweat would trickle down her armpits and the tickle in her throat would rise to a crescendo of spastic coughing attacks.

She would then flee the classroom as hundreds stared at her. Many days she retreated in her dorm room to eat Ramen noodles and watch *Mr. Ed* and *The Addams Family* on Moe's little black and white television all afternoon. It never occurred to her she bore a heavy burden grieving alone. Then the day came Moe yelled at her for not going to class.

"Why don't you go to class? You think you'll get to be the big-time reporter you want to be so bad if you skip class?" Moe glared at her, a backpack slung over her shoulder ready to head to class. "Are you too good to go? Is that it? Too smart for your own good? Because if you don't go they are going to start failing you and then what? Back home to the boonies you say you come from?"

"No." Laura huddled under the blanket with some dumb romance book. It took her mind off serious stuff.

"Well, I know for a fact you have journalism class in twenty minutes and that comforter is stuck to you like a wedgie in the crack of a sweaty, fat kid's ass."

"So what?" Laura tried not to laugh. "What's it to you, okay? Just leave me alone. Go on, get outta here."

"What's it to me? I'll tell you. Because if you get thrown out I get stuck with some nerd roommate who can't attract the hot guys when we go out, like you, that's what. And my whole social scene goes out the window and I never get laid again for the next four years. I'll practically become a virgin again. Technically, after four years of no sex, that's what happens."

"Doesn't sound as if you had too much trouble the other night, slut puppy." Laura threw back without looking up.

"I thought you were asleep." Moe tapped her foot.

"Who can sleep with your loud mouth getting banged?"

"That's it. You're pissing me off now. You better get your shit together because I don't want you to get kicked out and go back home."

The word *home* sent Laura into an emotional spiral. She pulled the comforter up to her forehead and willed the tears to stop. "I don't have a home, okay?"

Then the tears spilled down in a river of release and she let out a great sob. She waited for Moe to shut the door and leave, but she didn't. The comforter was pulled down off her face, and there stood Moe with a crooked smile.

"Okay, spill. Oh, wait, it looks like you are." Moe grinned. "I guess I can skip my class for once."

Laura told her about her parents dying in the fire right before she left for college, about her beloved home where she grew up, about her good friend, Mr. B, and her special lake. She even told her about the mysterious man in black who appeared every few years.

"Most likely he's got it for you bad, man." Moe laughed. "I mean look at you, you're smoking hot with that hair, those eyes, and that body. Has he ever touched you?"

"Well, no. And part of the time I was a kid anyways."

"Hmm, evil pedophile maybe?"

"No, he never came near me. Besides, he looks like somebody's big uncle."

"Yeah, sugar daddy uncle maybe. Did he call out crude comments?"

"No."

"Said, 'Hey, baby, wanna get it on?'"

"No!" Laura laughed.

"So there you go. He's a good guy. A guardian angel who ogles you from afar. Sure, you get a buff guardian angel in black. Me? With my big-boned dorkiness I'd get some fat slob with drool hanging off his mouth tripping over himself in awe to glimpse my Amazon beauty."

"You're not dorky," Laura insisted, but she felt better.

That night they stayed in crying and laughing. Moe hugged her and listened.

They whipped up frothy margaritas in their blender, dug around in their shared closet for tortilla chips and salsa, and spent hours chatting about boys and school like normal freshman girls do. Laura felt like a clean and empty bowl waiting to be filled up again.

But she never told Moe about her special powers. Since then, almost four years ago, she never did. She forced herself to forget about her strange abilities as well, and over time the thoughts of others faded from her mind. She now had a safe harbor with Moe and it helped free her from her past, a little bit.

After her parents died, Mr. B had convinced Laura to leave for college. She had no choice. She had nowhere else to go and she wanted to get as far away from Coopersville as she could. He helped her take care of the details like the cremations, the brief service at the church in town, and listing the land for sale.

She stayed with him those few days before she left for college and huddled in his loft bed, crying much of the time, until he told her it was time to go or she would miss the start of the semester. So Laura left for college in a fog and vowed to forget all she had known and been, except for Mr. B. He stayed the one good thing she could count on.

And now she was moving on again to start a career in communications for a large healthcare company in New Jersey. Moe had tried to persuade Laura to find a job with her in New York. Moe wanted to conquer the big city together, but Laura wouldn't be able to survive in a world of concrete and skyscrapers. She needed trees and space. At least New Jersey had some. She found a cute studio apartment next to a park where she could sit in her kitchen and look at the leaves changing. She wanted to be alone again.

Laura sighed and forced herself to get up from the couch, after concluding the hangover headache would not be cured by aspirin alone. She washed her face, threw her hair under a frayed baseball cap, and brushed her teeth hard to eliminate the metallic taste in her mouth from a night of drinking. Feeling near normal, she drew on sunglasses to hide her puffy eyes and headed out for much needed sustenance at The Bakery. She grabbed a coffee cake and quart of orange juice too, just in case Moe's parents stopped in for breakfast before graduation on Saturday. She felt comforted knowing they were coming in town.

After years of spending holidays and vacations with them, they became the family she lost. From the moment she met them—and Moe embellished them with her tale of woe—they took her in under their wing and granted her daughter status. Moe's mother, in a way, reminded Laura of her own mother. She was a big, bosomy woman, as tall as Moe, who would crush you in a floral-scent filled hug.

Outside of Mr. B they were all she had. She wished he could make the graduation ceremony but he had a bad cold. At eighty-three he had slowed down but his mind was still sharp and witty. As she waited in line at The Bakery to pay, she made a mental note to go visit him this summer.

The sun shone high overhead as she walked back to the apartment. Sweat trickled down her back in an uncomfortable drip. It proved to be another humid, hot day. The headache that had subsided came crashing back in painful waves. She pressed her palm to her forehead and wiped the sweat away.

This wasn't a hangover headache. This was the same headache she had as a child. The familiar pain blinded her and she stumbled down the narrow street back to the apartment. She hung onto the railing heading up the stairs and fumbled with her keys to get in the door. She had to get out of the light and lie down. She needed more aspirin and Moe had to have more in her room.

"Moe," Laura called out but got no answer. She must really be hung over to still be asleep. Through squinted eyes, Laura saw the microwave glowing a fuzzy 12:55 p.m.

She shoved the food into the fridge and shielding her eyes from the bright kitchen light, shuffled to Moe's room and pushed open the door. She opened her eyes wider to the cool, blessed dark. The pain enveloped her head in a stabbing vise. A smell invaded Laura's nose. An overpowering coppery smell. She gagged. Fresh waves of it hit her. She bent over holding her side.

"Moe? Sleepy head, get up. You didn't get sick in here did you?"

Laura stood up. Moe's outline rose from the bed in the dimness. Laura felt herself along the bed with one hand while covering her nose with the other to ward of the stench. The comforter was pulled all the way up over Moe's head.

"Moe?" Laura whispered again, this time fear snaked its way down into the pit of her stomach. She shook the top of the comforter. It felt wet. She pulled it down and shook Moe but felt wet, floppy rags. She pulled away. Both her hands dripped with warm, wetness. She gagged again, afraid she would throw up, and jumped back to the wall.

"Moe!" She shrieked now and scraped her hands along the wall reaching for the light switch. "Where is it? Where is it?"

At last she forced it up and closed her eyes from the glare. When she opened them red ran down her fingers and arms. Her red handprints decorated the wall in a pretty border. It wasn't vomit. Moe hadn't thrown up on herself. Blood spread slowly to stain the comforter. Its crimson circle grew larger. Laura stared at the cover, poked up in clumps hiding Moe's face. She shook off her paralysis and ripped back the comforter with both hands and screamed.

Moe's eyes bulged from her head and her lips were pulled back in a twisted, silent scream. Her hands faced palms to defend off something in her final, terrifying moments. But it was her neck Laura stared at. Those weren't rags she felt in the dark, but the pieces of Moe's neck flapping open. Her neck had been savagely ripped open. Claw marks whipped around her wounds. Blood pumped out of a gaping hole in Moe's neck.

Laura fell to her knees at the bottom of the bed and twisted the end of the comforter over and over. She felt herself falling into a dark pit where no one could follow. It was her parents' death all over again. She punched herself over and over in the gut in anger and grief. She wanted to hurt as those she loved hurt. All the normalcy of the past four years became erased in this room.

"Come get me, you freak!" Laura sobbed into the air. "I'm waiting."

She wiped her bloody hands on the rug. Scrub. Scrub. She couldn't get it all off. She banged her head on the floor and tore at the blanket in a mad craze when something fluttered down off the bed. A piece of paper. She clutched it in her blood-encrusted fingers. Words scattered across it.

One day this will be you. He is toying with those you love but it's you he seeks to destroy in the end. He won't stop coming. Remember your powers and use them. You must survive. Be true to what you are and you can stop him.

A fury grew inside her and she shoved the note into her front shorts pocket.

"Stop who? Who is he? What do you want from me?"

But he was right. She had to try and use her powers. She had forced herself not to use them over the past four years, and the thoughts of others around her became softer until their sounds faded out altogether. She had saved her mother and Mr. B once with her healing powers. Could she save Moe?

The gruesome thought of putting her hands back onto Moe's bloody, ripped open neck forced her to push the vomit back down her throat. But she had to try. She staggered to her knees, and looking up at the ceiling, placed her hands on her friend's body. Her fingers moved over her chest and slid across her shredded neck. Laura forced her hands still.

"Come back, Moe. Please."

She imagined pouring her life energy into Moe through her fingertips. She imagined her neck stitching up and the blood pumping once again through her body. She imagined her alive and laughing. But she felt nothing. Either her powers had truly left her or Moe was too far gone to bring back.

Laura fell back on the rug and crawled out of the room. A bloody trail of handprints followed her. *Red. Blood is so red.* She stared down at her stained hands.

"Come get me, you asshole. Whoever you are. If it's me you want." She cried, as she hobbled on hands and knees.

She was tired of being strong and overcoming tragedy. She didn't want to be strong again. Pain shot through her head like a mechanical arm stabbing her over and over with an ice pick. Dizziness engulfed her. She welcomed blissful darkness to rescue her from this nightmare. She didn't want to remember Moe as a gruesome, shredded thing.

She kept crawling. She had to get to the phone. Then the shaking took over and she rocked on her knees on the musty shag rug. She had to call the police. It was the sane thing to do. But instead, she curled up into herself and just lay on the floor, praying for her own death.

The man in black stood in the parking lot hidden by a bush and watched Laura's apartment. He looked at his watch and decided he had to call the police now. He had seen her go in fifteen minutes ago holding her head. He wondered if she could handle the scene she found. He wished he could protect her from it, but she would survive it and it was the desired outcome.

He walked over to the pay phone on the street corner and dialed 911. He pretended to be jogging when he heard screams and saw a suspicious character in bloody clothes run out of apartment twenty-two. He hung up when the operator asked for his name and address. He sighed and walked away. It was all he could do. He should not get involved. But he already was. If he wanted his kind to go on the girl had to survive.

CHAPTER 12: 2006

Doctor Bjord lived every day knowing he wasn't considered a serious scientist by his peers any longer. As a promising geneticist in the 1960s and 1970s he once had the entire international science community at his ear. When his last triumphant project proved to be a disaster, he was shunned by the government and stuck down in this government facility basement to rot out his existence on animal testing.

The President of the United States did not even know of the work done here in this windowless building in Arlington, Virginia. But Bjord did. He knew too much for them to give him his walking papers. They wanted to keep him safe and imprisoned under their watchful eye, and give him enough menial work and a huge paycheck to keep him satisfied. But most of all they wanted him to keep an eye on the bungled results of his final project.

At seventy-five years old he wouldn't be around much longer to be of any trouble and yet, there was the slim chance he could still create something of value from his pet project. Bjord hadn't given up. If his experiments worked he would be triumphant again. He would be crowned brilliant and brought back to the world on a pedestal for all to hail. He would transform the world with his genius and make America's military unstoppable.

If his experiments worked. *If.* His brain worked over the details of his recent failure and how he could make it work next time. He had to make it work. What was he missing?

A knock at the door halted Bjord from writing in his daily log. He shuffled over to it, passing nattering, caged animals in his path. He unlocked the door with trembling, aged hands and opened it to see Bruce, one of the building's many security guards, standing there with a covered tray in his hands.

"Hi, Doc. Got his meal tonight as usual. Some kind of meat thing."

Bjord took the tray from him. It shook in his weak fingers. "I didn't realize it was time already."

"Hey, you know what they say, time flies when you're having fun." Bruce smiled and turned away. Bjord glared at the security guard's retreating back down the dark hallway. What an idiot. He will go home, eat meat and potatoes, make love to his sagging wife, and have a satisfying night's sleep with no thought in his head but which game is on television this weekend.

Bruce stopped at the elevators and gave Bjord a wave before he stepped through the doors and shot up to a lighted world where people lived in real time. Time for Bjord remained the same. His concept of reality included permanent darkness that enveloped him in these concrete walls as his own clock ticked away, stealing each minute.

Bjord never left these walls. He slept in a cot in an old connecting storage room with a dribbling shower and a fridge stocked once a week with groceries delivered to him. He couldn't stand the building's cafeteria-style mush. He had his paycheck deposited into his bank account that had grown substantially over the years. He couldn't wait to spend it on himself in lavish style when his brilliant project succeeded. Then he could deliver the most amazing weapon the U.S. government would ever possess. He just hoped to succeed soon before age took over his body.

Bjord shambled back to his work area carrying the tray and turned a corner leading to a back area of the expansive basement. The dark cavern that spread outward sat below a large complex of rooms housing five-hundred government employees. Bjord preferred to contain his work in the largest main room. There was one other room and he headed there now.

Bjord reached the back of the dim corridor and placed the tray on the floor. He slid open the viewing window of the iron door before him and seeing nothing disturbing slid it shut. He pulled a set of keys from his pants pocket and fit it in the keyhole. The iron door lay three feet thick, protecting the world from the soundproof room beyond it. Bjord slipped the key in the lock and turned it clockwise. He then removed the keys, placed them on the floor, and proceeded to slide three heavy bolts out of their placement that covered the width of the door. This ritual finished, he picked up the tray and pushed the heavy slab open.

Laura woke in darkness and confusion. The nightmare pulled at her in waves of fear and she sat up, focusing on the streaks of moon filtering through her bedroom. She switched on the bedside lamp and drew her covers up around her shoulders. Her alarm clock blinked a repetitive florescent green and she stared at it as flashes of her nightmare came back.

She had been running through dark woods by her lake back home. An evil man chased her in the silent shadows of trees and moonlight. She could not hear the man chasing her as she dodged around trees and rocks. She did not know who he was, only that he stood taller than the average man. She glimpsed a frozen leer every time she saw him not far behind her in the brush.

Was it a game of cat and mouse and she was the prey? To survive she had to find a hole to hide in. If the tall man found her he would slash her throat open with his monstrous hands, all the while grinning as her lifeblood pumped into the wet earth. He would then carry her drained corpse up the mountain and bury her deep where no wild animal could dig up her remains and feast on her flesh.

She stopped as she came out of the woods to find herself teetering on the edge of an enormous pit. She scrambled down the slope of the hole, scraping herself on dirt and pebbles. She reached the bottom and threw herself on the ground clawing at stubby grass. She flung dirt to the side, tearing her hands and nails. She peered up at the pit's edge to see the man standing above her in a dark silhouette. They were connected. But how? The clouds raced behind the man. He stood with arms crossed, mocking her meager attempt at escape.

She couldn't stop now and resumed her digging when her hands hit something hard. She cleared away the dirt to reveal a small black metal door. She pushed away the moist muck on it and pulled down on the handle.

She looked once again to the top of the pit. The man had stopped grinning. He unfolded his arms and strode down the crater's steep walls. An evil scowl shadowed his face. His descent would be her death.

She tugged down on the handle and with one strong push cracked the door open and squeezed through the opening. She found herself in complete darkness so solid she lost her balance and leaned to feel for something to brace upon. Her hands came in contact with smooth, cold walls. She ran her hands along the walls as she lurched forward through the tunnel.

Her head knocked against the narrow sides as she stumbled along, when her body smacked into a wall of cold metal. Terrified of the blackness surrounding her, she threw herself on the metal wall looking for a way out when she felt a handle. She yanked it down fast and pushed, then shielded her eyes as she entered a room infused with an emerald green glow.

She heard the man behind her rip open the entrance door to the tunnel as easy as a candy wrapper. She shoved the door shut behind her. It would be only a minute before he would reach her. She frantically pushed a panel of lit buttons on the door desperate for one of the buttons to lock it.

The man slammed against the door, throwing her off her feet. Death was here. But then the door handle lit up in a neon yellow glow. She knelt and prayed it stayed locked. The man slammed against the door again and it held. He didn't utter a word in his workings. He just kept pounding over and over in a steady silent mission.

Laura's vision adjusted to the light and she stood and stared in wonder at the colossal oval room pulsating with vibrant aliveness. The light emanated from walls in undulating waves. She pressed her hand onto the moving wall. Supple warmth enveloped her. She became the wall and moved in beat with its timeless rocking energy.

She peered into its elastic smoothness and saw the face of another. It was round with tufts of white hair framing its head. Its eyes gazed at her with a yellow shine. A strange face. She couldn't bear to look at its strangeness yet she couldn't take her hand away. Sadness overwhelmed her. *We are connected.* He had been hurt and was so far away from home. He was the creature that had crashed at the lake all those years ago.

And there stood the girl turned away, facing the creature. He reached out to touch the girl, pod-like fingers stretching wide. Light glowed luminescent from his fingertips. Laura was mesmerized. The girl reached her hand out to meet the creature's pulsing hand in welcome.

But the spell was broken when Laura heard the man pounding in erratic frenzy. She pulled back from the wall. He would break through soon. His strength, animalistic and frenzied, surpassed any human. She rushed around the room seeking a way out. *There!* A tunnel, hidden in the shadows, led out of the room. She ran toward it when the man broke through the door and lunged at her in one swift pounce.

That's when Laura awoke from her enemy. She had been having this nightmare for months now and was powerless from stopping it. It controlled her when the night came and the safety of the waking world disappeared.

The creature-man sat on the concrete floor, his bulbous legs splayed out in front of him. His head sunk on his chest. He appeared to be sleeping. Yet he did not sleep. He reached his brain outward into the night air probing for satisfaction. He had come so close many times. Then the vision always faded away, no longer in his grasp. What he sought either had traveled too far a distance for his mind to grab or his senses were too dull to attack.

The man knew his limitations. His mind probing skills worked within a few hundred miles. He had killed many times in the outside world while his body stayed imprisoned underground. He was not always successful because they kept him drugged and this weakened his powers. It was difficult for him to push through the drugs and use his abilities, but when he succeeded it delivered intense satisfaction. Sweetly orgasmic. And the girl. She had become his top prey.

Bjord taunted him with her and said a monster like him could never have a normal life like her. But the man found ways to punish the girl for living a normal life. One time he created a raging windstorm and pulled her mother out of the barn door to die. But the girl saved her. Another time he found the girl in the orchard with the old man. He sensed he was special to her and sent hundreds of wasps to take him down. But she saved him too. *Bitch.*

But he had succeeded at last when he sent his probing eye into her house. Filled with a crazed fury, he shot out a burning streak from his mind's eye and sent the old house into a crackling display of violent flames. He shivered with pleasure as he watched her mother and father burn. He wanted to make her feel as bad and angry as he did. And someday he would kill her with pain.

The man gloated over the deaths he had invoked, yet he had to be careful in his choosing. They knew when he killed because they recognized his style of murder. He had killed many random people on the streets. They had a researcher for the sole purpose to investigate murders nationwide to see if they resembled his method of murder. Even when he varied it somehow they found out. But not always.

He would wait in fear to see if they discovered his kills. If they did, they would gas him and shoot him up with drugs. Sometimes the doctor would add something special to the cocktail injection to send spiraling waves of pain through his deformed body. It was how they controlled him. The pain was intense and he was not immune to it.

And so he had been reduced to mostly sucking the blood of small animals he came across in the nearby plentiful woods through his mind powers. These creatures gave him a mere flash of pleasure, but their brief squealing ended too soon from his death jaws.

The man placed his hands on his deformed head and soared outside of his prison walls, into the cool night air. Soon he spotted a stray mutt roaming the lamp lit streets. He sent his mind's eye in for a closer look and swooped in to begin the ripping and tearing of canine flesh.

Laura got out of bed and moved toward the window overlooking the street in the New Jersey suburb that sprawled a few miles from New York City. She wondered about this man who chased her at night while she slept. She peered out onto the street as if to see him down there. *I'm looking for a man who doesn't exist. I don't even know what his face looks like.*

At twenty-six, Laura prided herself on practicality and organization of thought. Working in corporate communications for a large New Jersey-based national healthcare organization, she had to be. Her twelve-hour days consisted of writing company newsletters and executive memos, meeting ever-changing deadlines, and catering to executives who could scrap whatever communications project she had just completed. She hated it, but the hectic atmosphere and overtime kept her so busy she didn't have time to think about her life, or the nonexistence of it.

When Moe died four years before, Laura spent a week in the local hotel with Moe's family. They clung to each other to make it through the funeral services. She also had to remain in town as the investigation in Moe's brutal death was conducted. She took the questioning well. Campus officials pushed the police for answers as parents, in town for graduation, demanded answers from them.

Graduation went on the next day but Laura did not attend. In shock, she took refuge with Moe's parents. Investigators were baffled by the attack, as they could find no signs of how it happened. Laura never told anyone about the note she found. It wouldn't lead to answers. No prints, no fibers, no DNA. Just like there had been no cause found for the fire that destroyed her home and killed her parents. Moe's death remained a mystery and families remained uneasy at the idea of a crazed killer out there in their town. Drugs, they whispered, must have been drugs.

In the end, they ruled out Laura as a suspect and told her she could go. Go where? Off to New Jersey to start a career Moe would never have? She returned to the apartment to pack her few belongings as fast as she could. Moe's mom and dad clung to her in their grief, but Laura struggled to comfort them. A deep emptiness overwhelmed her at being abandoned of the only safety she knew, again.

"Honey, come live with us." Moe's mother, Grace, pleaded with her the day they left. "You have no family. You can stay with us as long as you need to." Moe's father, Joe, nodded and smiled at her.

But Laura pulled away from them. She didn't want to be anyone's substitute daughter. Part of her wanted to be taken care of, but another part of her wanted to run. Run far away and forget. "Thank you, but I just can't. I'm starting my job soon and have to move into my apartment in New Jersey. I have to go."

"Are you sure? We've all been through such a terrible time here, are you going to be okay on your own?" Grace held her hand and looked at her with watery eyes.

Laura hugged her and blinked back her own tears. "I'll be okay. I've been on my own a long time. And you know part of me can hear Moe laughing and teasing me, as usual…about getting on with my life after four years here. I feel like she would want me to go."

"Will you call us and come visit? Promise?" Grace hugged her back.

"I will." But Laura couldn't bring herself to say she'd promise. In her heart, she knew she wouldn't see them again.

A few months afterwards, the nightmares began.

Laura sighed and dropped the curtain down over the window shutting out the street scene. She tried to dismiss the dream that gnawed at her. She crawled back in bed and curled around herself for comfort. Sleep finally dragged her away and she dreamt now of meadows and carnivals. This time the grinning man did not appear. He hid in the darkness of her mind, watching her from afar.

Bjord stepped into the small cage that faced another cage positioned in a square room large enough to house one person in studio-style comfort. The creature-man sat naked on the cage floor, cradling his head in his hands. The man sheltered here was not interested in comfort. He was interested in killing. He raised his head to stare at Bjord. Tormented, twisted images on canvas surrounded the man in crooked piles leaning against his prison walls. His works of art embraced his cell. Painting soothed his savage rages.

Doctor Bjord averted his eyes so he wouldn't have to see the sadistic evil fleshed out in oil. People in the throes of being burned, whipped, choked, stabbed, and crushed to death by the hands of beastly things. One woman in particular the creature man painted over and over. His obsession.

Bjord bent down and raised a latch that opened a small window near the cage's floor and placed the tray on the other side, into the large cage where the man sat. "Dinner X-10. It's meat. Just what you like."

X-10 eased himself off the floor and rose to his full height of 6'5''. Bjord felt the twinge of fear he always felt when his prisoner rose to his complete stature. He was a vicious god in his nakedness with muscles bulging out in every direction. His penis hung enormous even flaccid, a fierce protrusion. The man did not wear clothes for his skin was too sensitive to tolerate fabric.

X-10 could twist the cage apart in an instant and kill Bjord with his hands or enter his brain and induce a heart attack. He had killed many guards in such fashion already. Yet Bjord knew he would not harm him. For now. X-10 needed him to exist in the subservient routine created for him.

The scientist enjoyed redirecting X-10's rage away from him to the girl. Bjord didn't know who the girl was, but X-10 had talked about her for years, convinced she waited out there for him to come. Bjord thought it was just a fantasy, created to sustain imprisonment, and he enjoyed creating stories about the girl involving family, love, freedom, and happiness. Experiences X-10 would never have.

And Bjord's stories fueled his prisoner's anger toward the girl on the outside misdirecting X-10's hate for the doctor. Bjord feared X-10's powers and didn't seek death yet. The iron door had been constructed after one killing spree left thirteen men dead, half of their throats ripped open while the other half were found clutching their chests in a frozen grimace. X-10 had been seven years old at the time.

X-10 could not break through the door that now imprisoned him. He had tried many times and failed. If he could reach through the cage and kill him in one swift movement, he would not be able to open the iron slab as only Bjord's voice activated the door to open for his retreat.

Bjord had also devised a way to spray drugs through the ceiling vents and put X-10 to sleep within seconds. This was useful when Bjord needed to take blood for his experiments, although his heart raced when doing so. To be so close to his prisoner was nerve-wracking. But X-10 knew if he killed Bjord that he would starve to death with no witnesses or mourners, only perhaps after dining on Bjord. The scientist could see his prisoner licking his own bones clean after a good meal.

"Hello, Doctor. Have fun playing with the animals today?" X-10's mouth turned upward in a smirk. He ran his gnarled hand through his thick hair as if standing relaxed on a golf course contemplating a shot on the ninth hole. His flattened nose spread across his oval face in a widening mound of flesh and enlarged nostrils. Bjord forced himself to look away from the ugly creature standing before him.

"Now X-10, you know I'm a scientist. I don't play with animals." Bjord turned toward the massive man again. "I use them to further the cause of science. And what I will use your genes for will be brilliant."

X-10 laughed long and then growled. "My name is Charlie, you imbecile."

"Charlie is a name for humans. A name for a likeable fellow. You are neither of those. You will never be a Charlie. Your number is X-10 and that's all you will ever be called by. And let's not forget how I've helped you, X-10."

The creature stopped laughing and his eyes gleamed into Bjord's with an intense hatred. "And how would that be, Doctor?"

"You eat well and spend your time painting and reading. But you'll never have the freedom to do anything you want, like the girl. She isn't a freak, like you. And you need to remember your small freedoms are at my doing. And I can take them away in a heartbeat."

"It would be at the expense of your heartbeat ending, I'm afraid, Doctor—and the girl's. I will find her." X-10 laughed and then grunted. "And if you'd never taken me I wouldn't be here as your experiment. If you'd never imprisoned me I wouldn't be suffering this life of abstinence." His voice rose in a sharp fervor. "If you'd never brought me here to live in this dungeon I'd be out killing all of you stupid pigs!"

X-10 edged nearer to the cage that held Bjord safe. The scientist trembled and stepped back closer to the door ready to activate his escape. He felt a piercing in his brain as X-10 probed him. A stabbing pain enveloped his head.

"And the first one I would rip to pieces would be you, Doctor Bjord!" The monstrous man swung his arms and lunged at the cage, crashing over his civilized dinner, and shrieked in a demon wail while clutching the bars. "*You*, Doctor. I would rip open your throat inch by inch and suck your blood out. Then I'd chew on you for a while and contemplate your worthiness as a meal! Not worthy, I'm guessing, you filthy old man!"

Bjord crouched by the door and screamed out for the door to open. He ran through the opening before it had fully swung out. The last words he heard from his experiment gone awry were, "You'll beg for death soon, Doctor! And my name is Charlie!"

Bjord pushed the door shut behind him with all the strength he could muster. The stench of sour sweat rose up from him. He reached up to slide open again the viewing window, his heart still beating fast. X-10 had resumed his floor position and once again cradled his head. It appeared as if the entire incident had never happened, except for the smashed tray before the cage, dripping ooze of 'some kind of meat thing'.

CHAPTER 13: 2006

Laura's fingers tapped across her keyboard in a race to finish. She had ten minutes to write the executive memo to all employees from the CEO about the company buyout. She sighed and stretched her neck, tired from working fifteen-hour days with the intensity of the buyout going on.

As communications specialist for the corporate communications team, she was on call twenty-four hours during the negotiations and contract phase. Tensions throughout the company ran high. The whisperings around the company strained with fear and guessing which departments would have layoffs and who would be the first to go. Laura would have a job until the end. Someone needed to crank out the word to eighty-thousand employees across the country.

She didn't care. After four years of working for one of the nation's largest healthcare companies, she was burned out at twenty-six and had no desire to climb the corporate ladder. She took the job here after college although she had dreamed of becoming a reporter and communicating the injustices of the world. It sounded so naïve when she thought of it.

The reality, she found out when interviewing for reporter positions during her last semester of college, was that she couldn't live on the pay. Not with student loans, car repairs, insurance, and rent. So when this job came along at a high entry-level salary she grabbed it. And she regretted it.

Since the beginning, unease filled her as she sat in on conference calls and met deadlines under executive orders. She felt as if she appeared on stage every day giving a terrible performance until it hit her—she wasn't meant to do this. She had enough money saved up between bonuses and raises. She could afford to take a pay cut and start over at another job.

When this buyout craze finally came she promised herself she would look to get out. She could go anywhere. She loved being independent and free to make a change, but missed having a family to run to when she needed a shoulder to cry on. She had drifted away from Moe's family over time. It was too hard knowing them. After a while their phone calls stopped and she felt relieved. She just wanted to forget and start over. Would she ever make her own family someday? A family she would want to hold onto no matter what terrible things happened? She hoped.

She forced herself to focus on the work at hand and read the memo again for the third time. It looked good and the clock was ticking. She had to email it to the CEO for approval to send out over mass email.

"Laura, how are you doing on the memo? Need help?" Renee, her boss, leaned over her cubicle. She was the communications manager and on the fast track to director. A rotund woman of thirty, she dressed in attractive garb and asserted herself to compensate. She maneuvered her many rolls of fat in designer clothes and colorful scarves down the hallways into meetings with style and grace. She didn't seem bothered by her large girth or want to change it.

Laura liked her immediately, and even though Renee was only a few years older, she took Laura under her wing. Laura became her first staff member as manager and she took the role as mentor very seriously. Laura respected her and hid the fact she did not take her role as the mentored so seriously.

"All done," Laura called back. Renee came around the cubicle and skimmed the memo.

"Looks good. Send it on its way."

"On its way…now. That was an easy one. Now let's hope he'll approve it right away and we can cross it off the list."

"Yep, but they'll get harder to send as we get down to the wire with the buyout and see who loses their jobs."

"I know." Laura shook her head. "I'm here until the end though."

"Me too." Renee grinned. "Hey, want to hit the café for lunch? On me."

"Sure thing, boss."

Laura grabbed her purse when a loud cracking noise shot from the hallway.

"What the hell was that?" Renee looked at Laura.

More cracks rang out and then screaming.

"Oh my God, someone is shooting!" Laura pulled Renee down with her under her desk in the corner of the cubicle.

Six thousand employees worked at their company headquarters in three buildings. The floor Renee and Laura worked on housed four hundred of them in a sea of cubicles. Laura had always hated cubicles and now found relief hiding in one.

"Can you get under here more?" Laura whispered and pulled the chair toward them as far as it would go. She thanked God she wore her long coat today as it hung from her chair, a curtain hiding them.

"No, I don't think so." Renee let out a tiny sob and bit her lip. "How can this be happening?"

The screams tapered off and silence remained. Laura heard crying from down the hall. Then another gun shot. Then silence again. The phone on her desk rang. Its blaring ring startled them both.

Laura gripped Renee's hand and put her fingers to her lips with her other hand.

"It's not me," a man's voice shouted out. "Someone is making me do it. It's not me!" The man began to sob. His sobbing grew louder. He moved noisily into their area. Laura forced herself to breathe slow and silent. Renee shook as tears ran down her chubby cheeks and dripped onto her silk scarf. Sharp pains shot through Laura's chest, but she had to focus now on surviving.

Renee's leg twitched. "I can't stay like this much longer," she whispered. "Charley horse."

"You've got to," Laura mouthed back.

Renee's twitch got bigger. Her leg shot out and hit the chair with a bang.

The man's sobbing stopped. They heard him crashing alongside cubicle walls toward them. Renee gripped Laura's hand harder. They clung to each other.

"I'm sorry. It's not me!" He pulled out the chair they hid behind, exposing Renee's large body. "Stop it! Let me stop!"

He looked familiar to Laura. She tried to think of his name. He was skinny and about forty. His hair stood up in hand-pulled points and tears ran down his cheeks. Sweat stains spread from under his arms. He pointed a revolver at Renee. It shook in his hands.

"Please, please, don't shoot us," Renee begged with her head down.

"Fat, stupid bitch," he yelled at her in a deeper voice. "You don't deserve to live. No one will ever fuck you."

Laura shrunk further back under the desk. She hated herself for thinking she might be lucky Renee was so fat. It could stop the bullets from traveling through her and into Laura.

"Jack? Is that your name?" Laura looked at the man.

He looked at her with wild eyes and nodded. "I didn't mean to call her a fat bitch. I'm so sorry but *he* is making me do it."

"Who?"

"I don't know. But he hates you."

"Please let us go."

Renee's leg twitched again. It shot out and hit the man's foot.

"Stupid bitch!"

He shot. Once. Twice. Three times.

The back of Renee's head exploded and covered Laura in a spray of blood and brains. She screamed and tried to push Renee off but she was too heavy. Her body slumped over and pinned Laura down. Her head fell to the side, dead eyes staring at Laura.

The man lowered his gun. His hands steady now. "Not you. He told me it's not your time yet."

He dropped the gun and turned. She watched him walk away and then heard more gunshots. He crumpled to the floor facing her. His dead eyes stared at her too. Blood oozed from one perfect red hole in his forehead.

Laura felt faint. The room spun with noise and light. Then the police rushed in and pulled Renee off her. All she could do was stare at bits of Renee stuck to her hands and arms. Another friend's blood on her hands. She laughed in hysteria, but then it twisted into sobbing she couldn't stop. It was Moe all over again. And her parents. Who would be next? She wished it was her.

X-10 rocked with laughter, holding his sides. He was triumphant as the ultimate puppet-master. It had been his first time entering a human's body and forcing it to do as he wanted. How wonderful. It was comical to pick the skinny, pathetic man to be the one to shoot up the girl's office. Who would ever think such a harmless pig would do it?

It was better than the time he enraged the wasps to sting the old man, and the time he set the girl's home on fire. He gloated over those, but this held the grandest triumph. He now could plan his escape, again. He had conquered the full spectrum of his powers and could use them to live free amongst the humans, unnoticed. If he succeeded this time in escaping and they found him, they would kill him.

X-10's nostrils flared, widening his flattened nose further across his face, stretching from ear to ear. He breathed deep with his recent success and felt power surging through his massive, muscled body. His veins pulsed and throbbed, pushing up through his milky white skin. The blue veins cut across his naked body, carving ropes across his translucent skin. Having no nails, X-10 looked unfinished. His fingers and toes were fluid extensions of his body, they widened at the tips with connected webbing. He flexed his pod hands and feet now, congratulating himself on his victory.

X-10 had starved himself for two days to carry out this planned experiment to take over the man's body and use him as a weapon. Eating the drugged food kept his powers stunted and he needed his powers to be in full mode, plus he hated the drugged feeling. Powerless and weak, almost a human. How disgusting.

He had a short window of time before the idiot doctor would turn on the gas spray in his cell to knock him out and pump him full of drugs against his will. It became a standoff they had when he boycotted food. The doctor feared his powers. If he only knew X-10 waited for the right time to eliminate the good doctor. But X-10 had to plan his escape just right. If he failed, he wouldn't get a second chance.

He was seven when he discovered he would never be allowed outside. His doctors and teachers gathered together one day in his room to tell him he could not go outside to play—ever. He couldn't go anywhere at all. It was too risky. They said he wasn't human and could not live among humans. America's enemies could discover X-10 and steal him away to use him against them. They could not allow this. Surely, X-10 must understand this.

When he asked if he could meet the girl, they shook their heads, not understanding him. What girl? He couldn't explain. He just knew she was part of him and she was out there growing up with a family. He hated her for that. He wanted a family.

But he also knew Doctor Bjord led the project to duplicate his genes to use on soldiers in war. If it worked, they would have X-10's immense powers as advantages to win any battle. It would mean America could use these powers to rule the world in any way it chose. And X-10's life would remain one of exhibition in a cell. He would be on display ordered to amaze them with his powers of telepathy, telekinesis, and strength. X-10 was a freak show and nothing else.

In a rage, he killed all thirteen men there that day. All the doctors and teachers present. All except Bjord. He wanted him to live so he could torture him and someday kill him with intense pain. Some of his victims dropped dead of heart attacks. Some, he enjoyed ripping open their throats from his mind powers as he watched them flail at their wounds, blood pumping out with each scream, until their screams stopped.

When his rage left him the dead lay strewn across the floor and the doctor's project had been canceled. And X-10 was to be eliminated. However, the doctor pleaded with the government to keep him in the small chance he could succeed in his project. Success could mean world domination and it was too enticing to ignore.

And so X-10 was left with the doctor, both forgotten in a world that existed on the outside. A world X-10 planned to make his escape into. A world where he could have a name, not just a number. He could escape to mountains somewhere and live in remote woods. Unfound. Free. But, he needed the rare opportunity to have his full powers and not be drugged.

He used this last time to see if he could indeed take over a human's body and use it as a puppet. It worked and how glorious it felt! But his body grew weak from not eating. At three-hundred pounds he needed constant food. So now he had to bide his time again, fuel up on food, and kill the doctor before he could escape.

"Charlie," he grunted. "My name will be Charlie. A hero who escapes his prison and kills all these pigs."

But first he would kill the doctor in a long and suffering way. Then he would find the girl and kill her too. X-10 hated the girl with intensity. Thinking of her threw him into violent rages when he tormented himself thinking of her life out there in the world. She got to live a life he never had. A life with a name.

"Laura," he seethed through his steam shovel mouth, his bulbous forehead pulsing outward in grotesque waves.

X-10 breathed deep to calm himself and turned his mind back to his other kill today. What power to kill from his cell. He had ripped out the throat of a homeless man on the street. The man had screamed, clutching at his neck as his blood pumped thick. Killing was always erotic for X-10 and his penis sprang hard from his groin. He fantasized about plunging his erection into the warm wetness of a woman.

He had done so, just once. A paid gift from the doctor. She gave him a pure joy he'd never known. Her name had been Sabrina and her touch had opened up a well of love he never knew he had. And when the doctor killed her, X-10 discovered a new well of sorrow so deep he swore he'd never feel again.

And even while he ached for a woman again, he forced himself to hate them all. To survive in this prison, he had to forget the sweet creature that had given her softness to him and called him Charlie. He wouldn't contaminate himself by plunging into one of them ever again. Hate would keep him strong. Love would only destroy him.

He fingered the oil painting of a blonde bitch in the throes of death spasms. Her mouth hung wide open in a scream and blood gushed from her ripped-open chest. Large breasts hung from her shredded top. X-10 had painted her that day. The paint was still fresh and the blood on her breasts left red on his fingers.

He closed his eyes and massaged his hardened penis with the thick, greasy paint. He fingered more and more from the painting and smeared it over his erection. His penis glowed blood-red in the dim light as he stroked himself over and over. His menacing staff twitched violently, as he spewed out calling to the bitch.

"Whore. Fucking human whore."

CHAPTER 14: 2006

Ben leaned on the balcony and gazed out at the mountain lake with its colorful borders. Autumn was creeping in. His bags were packed. Another assignment finished. He sighed. Another trip, another job, and at thirty-six years old he'd grown tired of it. Eight more years had passed since his friend, Andy, had told him to stop running and start living in one spot. But he hadn't taken his advice.

He tried dating, the few times he was in his Orlando apartment between jobs. But women always wanted more. To stay over, to know his deepest thoughts, to meet their family. He couldn't do it. It felt awkward and uncomfortable. He pulled back and ended the brief affairs. There had to be something wrong with him. He understood the mechanics of sex but didn't know how to be intimate with the soul.

To overcompensate he learned to satisfy a woman in many ways. He showed them the rewards of going slow and stimulating spots they had never dreamed could be aroused. He brought them to new explosive heights and exhausted their bodies straining toward sweet release.

He hoped his sexual abilities would be enough for them but they always wanted more and if they discovered the real him, they would be disgusted and leave him anyways. It was safer to push them away first. It had to be his choice, not theirs. If they knew what he had done they would know he was unlovable, untouchable. An outcast. That's what he felt like. An outcast in his own life. The one thing he had control over was his business. He could be cool, professional, and an expert at what he did and people paid him well for it.

And now he stood undecided at his room balcony at the Mohonk Mountain House, an exclusive, upscale retreat situated high above New Paltz, New York in the Shawagunk Mountains. Where should he go now? For the first time in a long while he had no job waiting for him.

Growing up in New Paltz as a kid, he'd stared up at the mountain in wonder, wishing he could venture into the retreat that had stood on the mountain for one-hundred years. It stood as a giant castle in the sky overlooking a blue lake he wanted to explore, but it had been off limits to a poor kid such as himself. Now he wasn't poor any longer. He was here. Yet, he had no one to share with the beauty and grandness of this historic mountain house. It left him feeling flat. For the first time on assignment he wished he weren't alone.

Complex and uncomfortable feelings had followed him the days he had just spent here shooting a family of six on vacation. He almost didn't take this job as it meant heading back to his hometown. Back to a place where he had once been happy and part of his own family.

More than twenty-five years had passed since he lived here and his parents died. Yet, he felt mired down in the ghosts swirling around him as he moved through each day back in his old haunts. He shot relics of his past in the background. The old bookstore on Main Street, the local diner where he scoffed down hot pierogies when his parents had money to eat out, the winding side streets he biked down, and the Wallkill River he played along.

And there stood his old house. A bike lay on the lawn as if a young boy threw it down to run inside and tell his mom about something cool he found, just like Ben used to do. It looked the same. The new owners had given it a paint job and a new roof, but the tiny Cape Cod stood as it had years ago when Ben lived there and life was good. He didn't know it could be any other way back then. And so this week he followed his clients around taking photos of them amongst ghosts. He didn't want to remember. He wanted to forget.

He stared out at the smooth lake. A canoe floated in the distance on the sparkling water along the water's edge. A man, woman, and a young boy sat in it. The boy looked about ten years old. He stretched his arms out as if explaining something and the father leaned over and hugged him. Were they happy?

He jerked upright on the railing as it occurred to him, in order to forget his past he would have to remember. He looked at the family again in the distance. And that made the decision for him.

He would head to Coopersville and visit the lake where his parents died. It was only an hour away. Perhaps it was destiny he took this assignment so close to the events that changed his life decades ago. He had grown tired of traveling everywhere and belonging nowhere. He had built a life around himself that excluded others. All these years he had been helping other families create memories. Maybe he should start figuring out how to create his own memories, and his own family.

"Well, time to hit the road." He turned to grab his bags. Talking out loud to himself was a habit he picked up along his travels. He didn't need anyone to talk to. "Well, not anymore, bub. Time to face the music. Get off the pot. Stare the bull in the face."

He laughed at himself and slammed the door behind him. "Yep, 'cause the fat lady is singing." He bumped into a stooped, gray-haired man as he entered the corridor.

"Is she now?" the man asked with a smile, grabbing the wall.

"Sorry, sir," Ben apologized, putting down his bags to steady the gentleman.

"No worries, you must be in a hurry if the fat lady is singing. Grab it while you can!"

Ben smiled back and nodded, "I am!" Then he strode down the hall toward his destination. Not a new place, but an old one, to bring him new life. He hoped.

Laura sat at the four-way stop with both hands on the wheel and considered going left or right. No cars came from either direction. But it wasn't unusual for Coopersville. Population three-hundred. She figured she could sit here for half an hour and not see one car. Fields spread out to her left and woods reached up the hill to her right. The hill would take her to the place where she'd grown up. Mr. B told her years ago a nice family had bought the land and built a new home on it. If she turned right she would see it. She pulled a piece of paper out of her jean pocket and unfolded it.

It's time, Laura. Find your powers again because the evil is coming. And he is coming for you next time. If you want to live, be what you are.

Laura folded the note and put it away.

"Be what I am. What does that mean? Use my powers again? For what? To stop some evil man I don't know?"

She'd found the note folded in a neat square on the front seat of her car the day Renee was killed, after she was released from the hospital. It had to be from the man in black. He seemed like a dream in her mind from years ago. Was he real?

The day Renee died doctors concluded she was fine after examining her as a precaution. *Fine. Right.* How can you ever be fine again after a day when your friend's blood and brains are blasted across you? The day her life changed again.

No one could tell her why her co-worker went crazy shooting people at her company. Five were injured and four others died before he killed Renee. The media jumped on the story of a man cracking under the stress of the buyout. They also dug around and found Laura's grisly history of Moe's death and her parents and played her up as a tragic heroine that death followed.

Laura ignored the media, and focused instead on replaying the shooting scene, over and over, seeking clues.

The shooter kept repeating it wasn't him. He also said it wasn't her time yet, but she assumed from the note her time *was* coming. Was this man in black right? But who was coming for her? She had no idea, but she did know she had to prepare herself for his coming.

There was something else she also had to do. Besides regain her special abilities she had to find out where she came from. It had to have something to do with the murders of those she loved and why she once could perform magic, as she called it when she was a little girl. Maybe if she found the answers to the horrible events plaguing her life she could stop it from ever happening again.

She called Mr. B and told him everything and asked if she could stay with him for a while.

"As long as you need, my special girl." His voice shook a bit on the phone. At eighty-seven, he had grown older in body but his mind remained sharp and Laura could still count on him. "You can have the loft all to yourself. This guardian of yours must know more than we do. Believe in him and believe in yourself."

"I'm just afraid for you."

"For me? Why, silly girl?"

"Everyone I love dies. I fear something will happen to you too."

"Bah! I'm eighty-seven and if I can't help out a dear friend then what is a useless old man to do? I've lived my life. I have nothing to fear."

"Mr. B, what would I do without you?"

"Probably have real friends your age that aren't old farts with arthritis who need a nap every day."

"Never. Youth is so overrated."

"Well so is retirement. Just get on over here and stay as long as you want. I only request a fresh pie or two in return."

And so Laura quit her job. She packed up her clothes and books and left New Jersey on a sunny, September day. And here she sat by the stop sign. She came here to heal and find answers.

She turned the car right and drove up and over the hill. For a moment she was confused as to where her home had been as there sat a modern, colonial with a wooden play set in the side yard. A little girl sat on the swing pumping her legs to go higher and higher. The barns were gone but the rock wall remained. From the road she could see the apple trees in the orchard bursting with fruit. Two boys played basketball at a hoop in the paved driveway that replaced the shale one Laura used to dig around in looking for arrowheads. She drove by slow and the little girl waved.

A funny feeling came over Laura. She didn't quite recognize it. And then she did, and smiled. Peace flowed through her, knowing a family lived here. Maybe the little girl climbed the same tree she did and sang to the mountains in the distance. She waved back and turned around to head toward the lake. Mr. B would be expecting her.

Ben checked into the Catawba Bed & Breakfast Inn on Main Street in Coopersville. One of the Northeast's largest catawba trees towered over it in slumbering grace on the front lawn. Its giant leaves covered the historic inn with deep shade as birds and squirrels dashed about its limbs. It had its own habitat within its great branches. A world of its own, mused Ben. *Like mine*.

The innkeeper, Rosemary March, was a chatty woman whose large hips swayed up the stairs as he followed her to his room.

"So you used to live here, dear?"

"Many years ago," Ben replied to her wide bottom. It filled the staircase from side to side.

"What brings you back after so long?"

"Work," he lied. "I'm a writer and photographer and doing research for a book."

More like research for my life. "I'll be coming and going a bit, so no need to pay attention to whether I'm here or not."

"Ooh, how exciting," Rosemary huffed, nearing the second floor. "No worries, your privacy is of the utmost importance. We're so glad you returned, and to stay with us. And to pay two whole weeks in advance! Plus you are our only guest at the moment. Well, here we are!"

She let Ben into a bright room splashed with yellow and burnt orange. He bent his tall frame to fit through the old home's short doorway. A cool September breeze blew through the open windows across a four-poster queen-size bed covered in a patchwork quilt. Sunlight flickered across the sunflowers on the antique dresser.

"I hope you enjoy your stay. If there is anything I can help you with let me know. I'd love to do research for your book." She smiled at him with a wink, and swished out of the room.

Ben set his bags down and looked out the window at the town. It hadn't changed since he and his parents stayed here at the lake cabin on vacation. It remained a small town tucked away in the southwest part of Albany County in the foothills of the Catskill Mountains. Eighteenth and nineteenth century architecture graced Main Street from the days when the Dutch had settled the area over two-hundred years ago.

He still never understood why his parents wanted to vacation in another small New York town. This was a hamlet, not a bustling town like New Paltz. Perhaps being so rural, the cabin rentals on the lake had been affordable. He guessed they had been lucky to go on vacation. He recalled, from his nine-year-old mind, they didn't have much in the way of money. He couldn't ever remember buying new clothes or a bike or toys with his mother. He had hand-me-downs from neighbors or cast-offs from the thrift shop in town.

It was noontime and he didn't want to waste any time. He would take the waterfall path to the lake. The place his parents died. He envisioned stepping out from the woods to the wide-open lake. He hoped to feel something. What, he didn't know, but it had to be better than years of feeling nothing.

Ben adjusted his hiking boots and set out for the end of Main Street, traveling along the uneven stone sidewalk. He stopped at the old gristmill and peered into the woods. There stretched the path he remembered. A tiny wooden sign stuck out of the ground, askew, pointing hikers toward the Coopersville waterfall and lake. The lettering had become so faded it was hard for tourists to read it. He guessed not many tourists came to this sleepy town anymore.

Orange and crimson leaves blew down around him, twisting and turning to their end. Fall blew in early this year. He stuck his hands in the pockets of his jeans and stretched his lean body upward with a deep breath, enjoying the earthy smell poking up from dead leaves and grass. Then he stepped onto the narrow trail that would take him back in time.

CHAPTER 15

Laura sat cross-legged on the grass staring at the log in front of her. Her eyebrows scrunched downward in deep concentration and her mouth pursed in a tight line.

"Arghh!" She stood up. "I can't do it. I can't make it move."

Jim chuckled, facing the lake in his fold out camp chair. "Laura, you can't expect something to come back instantly you haven't used in nearly ten years."

"I know, but I don't know how my powers worked before so how can I make them work again? What if it was just an adolescent thing?"

She flipped her hair back and put her hands on her hips, tapping one foot. She stood a picture of beauty before him. Her glossy hair fell in waves at her shoulders and her graceful curves twitched with energy and vibrancy. Jim gazed at her in adoration and wished he were a young man again. She turned and smiled at him, her large eyes widening. Yes, he would fall in love with her in a heartbeat if he were sixty years younger. He looked at his gnarled, shaky hands and sighed.

"I used to just wish and ask for things to happen, maybe that's it! Could it be so simple?"

"Isn't that what you've been doing?"

"No, I've been telling the log to move, not asking it."

"*Hmph*…of course it makes sense you would have polite powers, doesn't it?"

"Polite indeed." Laura laughed. "Perhaps it's a delicate relationship between me and the object I want to move."

"Like a give and take. A shared bond."

"Yes."

Laura sat back down in front of the log, seated sideways from Jim.

This time she closed her eyes. A slight smile spread across her face. She glowed to him and he watched her in fascination. He hoped she could do it. He stared at the log in front of her. It quivered. He blinked, not sure if he'd imagined it. There. It *did* move. The log shook, and in a dance with the air, it lifted off the ground to hang, trembling above the grass. It hovered and moved toward the lake as if on a conveyor belt. It sailed over the waves lapping toward the shore.

Jim took in a sharp breath.

Laura opened her eyes and gasped. The log stopped and fell into the lake with a splash.

"I did it, I did it!"

You certainly did, Jim thought in amazement, shaking his head in wonder.

"Thanks." She grinned at him.

"You heard me!"

"I did, and it's the first time in years. It's almost as if being back here has opened up my senses again. I've gotten fuzzy thoughts from you for the last couple of days. They've been a jumble. A word here and there. But today they have crisp edges."

"Then to be in control of it is a powerful thing." Jim leaned forward. "And knowing you can control it gives you immense power."

"I know."

Jim had forgotten the amazing things she could do. Then he remembered her saving his life long ago in the orchard. "I wonder if you can still heal."

Laura stood up and brushed her hands off from the grass. "I don't know," she admitted, staring across the lake, her back to him. "I've only tried once in all these years. The night I tried to save Moe."

"Yes, sorry, I didn't mean for you to think of it," Jim apologized.

He recalled the hysterical late-night phone call he got from her about Moe and how shocked he had been at her horrific experience. He could provide Laura with no comfort except to listen, as he had no explanation for what happened. He had always been in awe of the mysteries surrounding her. She had special powers for a reason and sensed she would need them in the future to save herself. He didn't want to think of it, but he sensed the time drew near.

"I'm so afraid." Laura crossed her arms, hugging herself. She turned toward Jim. A gust of wind blew her hair about in a veil, hiding her eyes.

"What is there to be afraid of here in the middle of nowhere?" Jim joked. But he felt disturbed as well. He didn't fear for himself, but for her.

"What if this evil man comes after the people I care about again? He'll come after you."

"Bah, I told you, I'm not afraid."

"I am," Laura said in a low voice. "What if I can't save you?"

"You must save yourself. You are stronger than you think, my dear. Besides I have to believe good wins out in the end over evil."

"Yes, I hope so. Maybe all this will be my final battleground." She swept her arms around her in a wide arc. Golden leaves spun down around her from the trees and she laughed, catching them.

"Maybe." Jim grinned. "And a lovely battleground it is. Especially in fall."

"How can I leave all this?" She turned to him, hair gleaming in the sun. "And you?"

"I realize I'm quite a catch but what you need to focus on is your powers."

"I will. And one other thing." Laura moved to Jim and knelt on the grass next to him. "I want you to help me find out who my real parents are."

Jim cocked his head at her and buttoned up his barn jacket. The day was turning colder. It would be a hard winter, he could feel it. Maybe Laura would be here to share it with him too. It would be nice to have company for a change.

"Why do you want to go digging around in that muck after all these years? You had two loving parents."

"I know." Laura shivered from a cool gust and stared at Jim with wide, sad eyes. "But I also know the way I am is because of where I come from. It's in my genes, can't you see? If I know where I come from then maybe I can stop all this death around me. I need to know who this man in black is and the man that stalks me. I know they are connected to something that happened the night the meteorite struck here. And we both know it wasn't a meteorite."

She folded her arms around her knees and rocked on the ground. Her bottom lip trembled.

Jim put his arm around her shoulder. "I'll help you, you know I will. Don't make such a foofaraw, my stout-hearted maid. Could I ever say no to you, my precious lass?"

Laura looked up and laughed. "Ha! You've been studying your thesaurus, sir. And I thought you were impervious to my nefarious charms."

"Well, yes, I had to dig the book out of the back of my shelves. And wooed by your charms would be more like it." Jim smiled, but then frowned. "It's not you who are nefarious, my keen girl, but the brute you seek to destroy before he kills again."

"I think he is the darkest of evils. I've seen him in my dreams covered in shadows. Someday I'll have to face him in person and it terrifies me. The man in black wrote to survive I must be what I am. But I don't know what that is. And just how the hell can I find out? Now why doesn't he leave a note about that? Directions would be most useful."

She bent her head to her knees.

"Laura, I don't know." Jim took her hand. "All I can tell you is we'll face this together. You work on your powers and I will help you dig into your past. Maybe answers will come with discovery. For starters, we'll find the doctor and nurse that delivered you. I know he moved down into Albany years ago. I think he retired. And he can tell us the nurse who was there too. Tomorrow we'll start on our mission, okay?"

Laura nodded and squeezed Jim's hand. They sat in silence for a long while staring at the geese that flew low across the lake. She was the only person in his life he loved. He accepted her and believed in her.

And he would kill anyone who tried to hurt her.

Ben strode upwards along the rocky path, paralleling the waterfalls glinting under the sun. He had taken the longest path that wound through the woods for a mile then turned toward the falls. He was glad he wore his oldest jeans, now splashed with mud, and pushed up the sleeves of his rag sweater as he warmed up from his hike. A chill crept in with the early afternoon shadows and he blew out frosty air as he reached the top of the falls.

Standing on the bridge that crossed over, he gazed down at the rushing water. It swirled and raced under him, falling hundreds of feet in a roaring deluge. After the drop, the water traveled down jagged rock in a series of wide ledges. Leaves blew down and the water snatched them up speeding them along to new places. Recent heavy rains gave the falls an angry feel to them as if the water called, "Hurry, hurry, we must go! Move along now!"

He crossed the bridge and continued heading up through the wooded path toward the lake. It was a long time to remember his way. Crickets called to him and acorns plunked down as geese honked overhead on their trip south for the winter. Before long, the woods dropped behind him and the lake spread out before him in a sparkling expanse.

His life had changed here in an instant. All the years since the night the meteorite hit the lake flashed through his mind. All the things he had to survive. Things he wouldn't have had to survive if his life wasn't changed forever here one night.

He scanned the lake's serene edges. A few cabins remained hidden in the brush like ghosts floating in between the trees. Vines blended in with the roofs and windows, snaking in and out, covering them in a permanent embrace. Something moved in the trees. Ben peered closer and walked along the lake's overgrown path to get a better look. Then he heard singing. It rose and fell over the breeze, but carried to him sweetly by a young woman's voice. He recognized it from his teen days. Corey Hart's 'Never Surrender.'

"…So if you're lost and on your own you can never surrender, and if your path won't lead you home, you can never surrender. And when the night is cold and dark you can see, you can see light…"

Ben saw the woman now. She stood magnificent, high up in a giant birch tree with her feet planted shoulder-width apart. Her arms spread outward gripping the branches. She flung her shoulder-length chestnut hair back and sang to the sky with her eyes closed. Her face moved in complex expression with each word she belted out. She looked as though she flew in her mind over the trees toward the sun.

He moved closer to stand a few feet below her. The leaves shook wildly in the tree around her in a gleeful dancing rhythm to her song, even though there was no breeze. Ben was enchanted. She was part of the tree. A nymph of the wood. A goddess of the earth with the sun streaking through her hair. He reached for his camera and shot a photo of her as she belted out the last line, then he joined in.

"Cause no one can take away your right to fight and n-ever surr-en-der-er!"

The woman opened her eyes wide in astonishment and her feet slipped. She tried to regain her balance, but slid along the trunk in a spiral toward the ground, grabbing onto the closest branch to stop. Ben ran over and grabbed her around the waist just before she hit the ground. He set her down with ease. She was tall but he still looked down at her.

"Sorry about that, I didn't mean to startle you." He grinned. "Are you okay?"

"Oh, I'm fine." The woman blushed. "I guess you caught me, literally."

She laughed nervously and looked up. Ben stared down at her, still enchanted. She was the one, the girl in his dream by the lake. And here she stood in real life before him at the lake.

He leaned over, plucked a leaf from her hair, and handed it to her. "A souvenir."

"For what?"

"To remember the first time we met."

"What if we don't meet again?"

"We have to. I wouldn't miss another concert, would I?"

She accepted the leaf and laughed. "I'm Laura Armstrong, by the way." She brushed the remaining leaves off her jeans. Ben noticed she first tucked away the leaf he gave her in her fleece jacket pocket.

"Ben Fieldstone." He couldn't stop staring at her. She had such large, brown eyes dusted with long lashes.

"So what are you doing here in the middle of nowhere, Ben Fieldstone?"

"I could ask you the same thing, Laura Armstrong," he shot back.

She peered sideways at him with a half-smile and spread her arms out at the lake. "I grew up nearby and used to come to this lake all the time. My friend, Mr. B, calls it Laura's Lake."

"I like that. Laura's Lake. And do you always serenade the lake by tree limb?"

"No, it's just I used to do that as a kid and wanted to see how it felt to do it again." Laura blushed again and bowed her head. He wanted to touch her again. She was so lovely.

"Hey, I'm just teasing you. I liked it, and I love Corey Hart. I'm an eighties music fan."

"Me too." She smiled at him

"I'm sorry I ruined your moment, I just wanted to see the lake again. I used to come here years ago with my parents on vacation." He saw her looking at his camera. "I came to shoot photos of the lake."

"It's a nice camera, but, I have to ask. You vacationed in Coopersville?" Laura raised her eyebrows.

Ben laughed and looked around the empty lake and woods. "I know. I still wonder about it myself. I came back to see if it was all the same. And it sure hasn't changed, except I don't guess anyone rents these cabins anymore."

"No," Laura said. "Not since the big meteorite hit the lake."

"I know."

"You know? How do you know? Were you here?" Laura gripped his sleeve and looked into his eyes for answers.

"I—I heard about it, I mean," Ben lied and looked away. He shifted his weight from foot to foot. Laura let go of his sleeve.

"Oh," she said in small voice. "I thought you might have seen what happened. But I guess you would have just been a kid."

"Yeah, just a kid back then." Ben changed the subject. "So are you visiting too, is that why you're here singing to the woods?"

"Sort of." She smiled, as if to herself.

"And how did you get the tree to dance along with your singing?"

"What do you mean?" Laura stopped smiling.

"The leaves. I saw them shaking in sync to your song. Some sort of magic?" Ben smiled, but her anxiety-stricken face filled him with regret. He stopped smiling and looked at her, waiting for an answer.

"Sorry, did I upset you?" He touched her hand.

"No…I don't know, but I have to go. I'm sorry." She waved to him as she turned and walked fast down the path.

"Wait…Laura, don't go." But she didn't turn around. Her hair swung behind her, glorious in the September sun. Leaves swirled around her. She *was* a nymph of the wood. He had scared her off, somehow.

He vowed to find her again.

CHAPTER 16

Laura and Jim sat rocking on his screened porch, contemplating what to do about this man she had just met.

"From what you say, dear, he sounds like a normal, young man who's come back to see where he grew up." Jim sneezed then and reached for a tissue. "Rekindling old memories, healing from some sad past, that sort of thing."

"Maybe. But he saw me use my powers. He must have been pretty observant to notice the leaves shaking about to my singing. Don't you think a 'normal' person would have just chalked it up to the wind, or not noticed at all? I mean, perhaps he noticed it because he has been watching me for a reason. He could be part of my past or maybe connected to the man in black. Plus, he had this fancy camera and was taking photos. Suspicious to me."

Jim sneezed again and spat out a hacking cough. Laura looked at him with concern.

"Laura, you could be a bit paranoid. He might just like photography as a hobby. But why don't you go back down to the lake or in town and try to find him. There's only one place in town where he could be renting a room."

"Good idea." She jumped up. "Instead of wondering about who he is I'll just go ask him."

"Fine, but just be nice about it."

"What do you mean? I'm always nice."

"I mean, be sweet on him. Don't interrogate him. The sweeter you are the more information you'll get. Use your charms. Men like that sort of thing. I do." Jim chuckled and then coughed again for a long while.

"Fine, I will." Laura bent down to rub Jim's back. "But now listen here, you can't go getting all sick on me. When I get back I'll make you some of my famous Fanny Armstrong homemade chicken soup. Why don't you go rest?"

"I'm sure I'll be fine tomorrow. We want to leave early to go find Doctor Britton."

"And that one I do intend to interrogate." She gave him a kiss and danced out the door. "But we're going only if you are up for it!"

"Be careful, Laura." Jim could tell it was a relief for her to focus on something new with this mystery man. Something that was not part of her gruesome past. Or maybe it was.

She smiled and blew him a kiss as she got in her car. The sky grew dark. Storm clouds blew across the sky through the trees. Jim watched her drive away and his heart ached. He had the feeling something bad was coming. He stared at his gnarled hands and coughed again. He was dizzy and so tired. He was afraid he wouldn't be able to protect Laura when she needed it. And she would need it. Very soon.

Ben sat at the desk in his room and looked through the photos he had taken at the lake in his digital camera. He remembered every step taken. He hoped to find something in the photos. He had wanted to find some remnant of his parent's death. Some memento. Some answers. Some peace. But it was ridiculous. The government had cleaned up the crash site years ago. And everything under the meteorite had been crushed. Crushed.

He put his camera down and clenched his hands, thumping them on his thighs. He had to stop thinking about it. Sometimes he visualized how it must have been for them. Their bodies flattened, their brains and guts squeezed out. It would have been him too if he hadn't run away. He jumped up from the chair and stripped off his shirt. Although it was cool from the brisk breeze blowing in, he had a film of sweat across his chest and face.

"Stop thinking about it, Ben." He paced the room trying to alleviate his anxiety. "What the hell am I doing here?"

And then he remembered the woman, Laura. He picked up his camera again and clicked through several photos to stare at her. She looked so free with her eyes closed and her arms outstretched singing. Her wavy hair blew around her, floating like angel wings. What was he doing, looking for peace, or looking for love? Maybe they were one and the same.

He lay down on the bed, stretched his arms behind his head, and sighed. Lovely. That was the word that kept coming to his mind about her. So lovely. Thinking of her calmed him down and he closed his eyes and fell into a deep sleep when a knock at his door made him jump. He shook his head to wake up and stumbled to the door.

He opened the door and just stared. It was her. He squinted and then smiled. It looked like he wouldn't have to find her after all.

"I figured you'd be here, it's the only place in town to stay." He could tell she avoided looking at his naked chest. Ben just stared back at her, trying to form words in his murky head after being asleep. He took the moment to drink in the details of her face and hair, and her scent. Sunflowers. She smelled like sunflowers.

"I-I just wanted to come by and apologize for running off like I did," Laura stammered. "It was totally rude."

"No worries here. I thought it was something I said." Ben looked down at her.

"It wasn't you, it was me," she admitted. "I came by to see if you wanted to explore the lake and woods together. I know you're visiting after many years and so am I, so I thought we could do it together. Mrs. March sent me up to your room when I asked if you were staying here. She knows me."

"That Mrs. March, is she the town gossip?"

"How'd you guess?" Laura laughed. "Her husband died years ago and she fills her time with running this old place and snooping out news around town. Watch out, she also likes to flirt with single young men."

"I got a sense of that already, but I am positive I can resist her ample charms."

Ben grinned and folded his arms, still leaning on the doorway. He was awake now and couldn't think of a better way to be woken up from an afternoon nap.

"Sooo…" Laura said, raising her eyebrows.

"Sooo…of course I'd like to explore around here with you. How about first we go get some coffee? If there's anywhere in town."

"There's the Van Rensselaer Café just down the street. They have the best rugelach."

"Roo-ga-what?"

Laura laughed and flung her hair back. "Rugelach. Yummy Yiddish pastries."

"Sure thing. Let me get my shirt and coat on and I'll meet you downstairs, sound good?"

Laura nodded and he watched her walk down the stairs, her sweet figure encased in faded jeans. He couldn't help taking in her tempting round bottom that twitched to his delight down the steps. He was definitely drawn to her. He had to get to know her. Maybe it was fate that brought him here at the same time she was visiting.

They strolled down Main Street together, each sneaking glances at one another. Laura was still leery of him, but he disarmed her quick. Maybe Mr. B was right. He was just a regular guy.

All she could do was stare into his gray eyes when he talked to her. She'd never met anyone with gray eyes before. It was like staring into a stormy sky, rolling with clouds and thunder. Waves of intense emotion rolled off him enveloping her in feelings of anger, sorrow, loneliness…and lust. She hoped the lust was for her. It was fire being near him. He smoldered underneath, with what she didn't know. She wondered if it would burn her if she got too close.

She tried to see his thoughts but they were complex and she couldn't understand the jumble of words and mixed aura surrounding him. She sensed he had darkness inside him. He had been close to true evil, yet light and hope lived there too.

As they walked, Ben gave her a snapshot of his life. He told her about his photography business then briefly spoke about being in the Navy and growing up in foster homes. Laura sensed more there, but didn't ask.

"How exciting it must be to travel the world and get paid for it."

"Yes, it has been," Ben agreed. "But I also don't have a home to go to when I come back. I am a nomad. Which I enjoyed for years, but now not so sure anymore. I guess I came here as well to figure it out."

"You mean, figure out your past so you can figure out your future?"

"Something like that." Ben smiled down at her as he held the door open to the café. They busied themselves with ordering coffee and rugelach. He insisted on paying. They found a table in front of a bay window overlooking the street and enjoyed the rich pastry and strong coffee.

"So, what about your parents?" Laura spoke first, after a comfortable silence.

"They died together when I was a kid. I'm an only child so there was no one to take me in."

"I'm sorry. Mine died together too." Laura blew on her coffee. "And I know about being an only child. I'm one too." She wanted to ask him how his parents died but she kept quiet. She felt a strange connection to him knowing that both sets of their parents died together.

"I'm sorry for you too." Ben tilted his head at her. "I know how hard it is to lose your parents, especially at the same time. It was the worst thing that ever happened to me. It must've been for you too."

"Yeah." She looked away.

"You're not going to run off on me again, are you?" He touched her hand.

"I swear, I won't. Not this time." His hand was so warm on hers. He pulled it away too soon. They sat in silence for a moment and watched the leaves fall outside their table by the window. An elderly lady locked up the tiny store across the street where a wooden shingle hung outside announcing, "Original Country Store built in 1795." Two young boys ran down the street in soccer uniforms, laughing at something. The shadows crept in as the sun began to sink lower in the sky over the trees.

"This is such a quaint, old town." Ben changed the subject and Laura was grateful. "I'm seeing it in a different light now as an adult. It was boring as a kid here on vacation. How did you stand growing up here?"

"Actually, I loved it."

Ben raised his eyebrows.

"I did, really. I loved roaming the woods and going to the lake. I loved growing vegetables and raising chickens and picking apples in our orchard..." Laura looked down. "But it was a long time ago."

"How long?"

"Eight years ago. When were you last here?"

"More than twenty-five years ago."

"That's a long time to be gone." Laura looked at him, full of questions. She was afraid in asking them he would expect answers from her in return. She didn't want to lie to him, but wasn't sure how to skip around her life with this man she just met. His thoughts still eluded her as if he was adept at hiding himself from people. Only now, the feelings coming off him had mellowed. He was relaxed and content, but hiding something. But whatever it was, it wasn't something to be afraid of.

"I know," Ben admitted. "I came back here searching for something. Aw, hell, I don't know why I came." He cupped his fingers around his cup and tapped his fingers. Such strong hands. She willed them to touch her again. "I was only nine when they died. How about you?"

"Eighteen."

Ben waited for more.

"It was a fire." Laura finally continued, feeling nervous under his gaze as he sipped his coffee. "Our house caught on fire and burned down. They died in it."

"How awful for you, for them. Where were you?"

"The lake. I was at the lake."

Ben put both his hands on hers this time. Laura focused on them. They were nice hands. Rough, yet shaped with beauty. They covered hers. She kept her gaze on them. She didn't want to cry. She never talked about the fire, and here she sat telling a practical stranger. Talking about it made it real, brought it all back.

And it was three tragedies ago. Before Moe, before Renee. Each time she forced herself to start over. She couldn't erase Renee's face covered in blood. Laura shook her head and closed her eyes, but it never became less vivid. Nor did Moe's ravaged neck or her parents' burnt bodies.

"And you're full of guilt about it, right?" Ben's question brought her back to the present and she raised her head to look at him.

"Of course I am. I could've stopped it." Laura looked away. She told herself she wouldn't cry.

"How could you have stopped it?"

Laura didn't answer. She pulled her hands out from under Ben's, sipped her coffee, and sighed. "It was a long time ago. And Mr. B helped me get through it. He's my good friend here. An older gentleman. A good soul. He persuaded me to still leave for college as planned. So I went and got my degree. Worked in corporate communications for a few years. I'm taking a break now, trying to figure out what I really want to do."

"And have you figured that out?"

"I used to want to be a reporter. I might try to do that again. I felt so out of touch working in corporate. I felt I wasn't making a difference, you know? I wasn't helping people, touching lives, exposing stories to change the world for the better a tiny piece at a time."

Ben laughed.

"I know, it sounds corny and naive," Laura said, laughing herself.

"No, that's not why I'm laughing. It just fits in with the kind of person I thought you might be."

"And what kind of person am I?"

"Someone with a soul, a passion. I knew it when I saw you singing away in the tree."

She shook her head with embarrassment. "Please, don't remind me. I feel like an idiot."

"Don't feel like an idiot. You don't have to explain yourself to me. It was a nice surprise. It made the day better."

"You weren't having a good day?"

"It's my first day here, so a bit unsettling going to the lake again where I used to stay with my parents. We rented out a cabin there each August before school started."

"Which cabin? I know them all in their falling apart stages. We could go together. I'd love to see it."

Ben shook his head. Laura sensed his trepidation and felt a great sadness roll off him. She wanted to take back her light chatter. Ben scared her though. She could tell he would envelope her in his intensity. She could lose herself in a person like him. She didn't know if she could survive that. She had survived many things, but never a broken heart.

"We can't."

"Why not?"

"It's not there anymore. It was crushed by the meteorite all those years ago."

"I'm sorry." Laura waited to hear more.

"They were crushed, too."

"Who?"

"My parents. They were in it when it happened."

"Oh my God," she whispered. Now she understood why he lied to her at the lake when she questioned him about the meteorite. This time she put her hands on his. He intertwined his fingers with hers. Their fingers fused together, bound with strong and delicate ropes. Laura felt a vibe from Ben, a humming warmth and peace that flowed through her. They drew strength from one another.

Their remaining coffee had grown cold. The houses across the street became dim. Lights glowed from their windows and leaves tumbled along the street. People came in and out of the café, getting coffee after work or a dessert to bring home. The door swung open and shut with a bell ringing jolly each time, accompanied by welcoming words as neighbors greeted one another and wished each other a good evening.

Some waved at Laura, surprised to see her back in town again after such a long absence. Some glanced with curiosity at Ben and Laura in the corner by the window. Laura was glad none were Mrs. March. She would be spreading their impending marriage around town by tomorrow if she found them together.

"And you, where were you?" Laura pressed her fingers into Ben's.

"I got mad at my parents and ran away that night. They wanted me to play an instrument and be in the band, but I hated playing music. I didn't have the talent they did. It made me feel like I wasn't good enough for them. Silly, really. But when you're a kid everything is so dramatic. I hid in the woods at the other end of the lake. I wanted to scare them, that's all. To find me gone and be upset. Then when they found me they'd tell me whatever I wanted to do was fine with them. Only they never did find me. They died."

"And you didn't," Laura said. "And you felt guilty about it too, didn't you?"

"Yep, still do after all these years, but I know I couldn't have prevented their deaths."

"But somewhere inside you is a little boy who still feels if you hadn't run away none of it would have happened, right?"

Ben looked at her with surprise. "I guess, I never thought about it that way. Anyways, it's a lot longer ago for me than for you. It's time I got over it and moved on, you know?"

"Something like that is hard to get over and move on from." Laura tilted her head at him and felt self-conscious still holding his hands. She untangled them, but Ben pulled her back toward him. Something had brought them together. She felt it and he did too. She just wished she could understand it.

"Don't you think it's strange we met and both our parents died here, tragically, while we were at the lake?" Ben's gaze bore into hers. "Yet we survived."

"It's like our meeting was meant to be."

Ben nodded and released her. Panic rose in Laura. She had to leave. She was exhausted from the intense emotions pouring off him to her, on top of their conversation. She was afraid if they kept talking he would find out more about her. Things she didn't know if she could ever share with anyone else but Mr. B. And then there was the danger she could put him in. People she cared about died. Simple as that.

Laura looked up at the clock on the wall. "Oh, I have to go!" She jumped up and put on her coat, thankful the time gave her an excuse to run off.

"Wait, you're doing it again." Ben grabbed her sleeve.

"No, really, I'm not running away," she reassured him. "My friend Mr. B is sick and I promised I'd make him chicken soup. And it's getting late."

"Tomorrow then? Can I meet you at the lake?"

"Umm, tomorrow is probably out. Maybe the next day?"

"How about tomorrow evening?"

"I don't know. I'll stop by if I can, okay? How long are you here?"

"As long as you'll have me." Ben grinned and she blushed at his bold statement. He let go of Laura's coat.

"Goodbye, Ben Fieldstone." She saluted him with two fingers and a smile. "Thanks for the coffee and pastry."

"You're most welcome, Laura Armstrong." Ben nodded and saluted her back as he stood up. And then like that, she turned and left.

The café was lifeless after she left. Ben hurried back to his room under a blustery, dark sky that dropped wet splashes on his cheeks. He decided to hunker down for the night with a good book, cheese and crackers, and the one beer he had stashed in the mini-fridge in his room.

But when he got there he drew the comforter around his shoulders and sat in the rocking chair in front of his window in the dark, watching the storm rage down Main Street. Sheets of rain belted down and the wind whipped the trees, bending and cracking their limbs with angry lashes. Lightning crashed, sending exploding shadows across the old buildings in grotesque forms.

Ben wondered if Laura was safe and snug wherever she stayed. He felt conflicted about her for sure. Part of him wished she were there with him right now under the comforter, holding her close. Part of him wanted to pack his bags, get in his car, and drive as far away as possible and forget he ever came here or met Laura. But he couldn't do it.

He was already addicted to her and yet afraid. But he couldn't treat her like one of his many affairs. He had become an expert at seduction but not at romance. The idea of romance was so odd to him he wasn't sure he could be romantic. For Ben it was the first time he wanted a woman for more than sex. He told her things after a day of meeting her he had never told another soul.

It all left him with an uncomfortable but exhilarating feeling. He wanted to feel more. He wanted to give in to the addiction of Laura. She was lovelier now that he knew her. He didn't want to let her go. Was he meant to meet her? But what was she hiding? And could she accept him for the things he had done? He didn't know and it made him more afraid.

X-10 threw aside the girl's body from his mind. She lay sprawled on the street where he had grabbed the whore in the alley. He returned his mind to his cell, enjoying his kill. She had been a busty one with meat on her. He had toyed with her, gnawing on her cooling flesh. A nibble on an ear, a sucking of blood from cuts on her fingertips.

The urge for fresh meat had overwhelmed him. The girl had been a feisty one, scratching wildly at the air to get at the invisible creature that attacked her in the night. Even if she had scratched him in the flesh it wouldn't matter. His scratches would quickly disappear. He had the ability to heal himself. He would simply move his fingers over his cuts and they would vanish.

Tonight, he had contemplated plunging his thick cock into the girl from his mind's eye, but was repulsed by the thought of contaminating himself in her wet human orifice.

"I don't fuck 'em and leave 'em. I'd fuck 'em and eat 'em!"

X-10 roared with laughter at his joke and wished he had a partner to share it with. A partner of his own genes. How different life could be if he knew of other creatures like himself. He enjoyed making up quips from the books he read in his cell. A main theme ran through them all. The characters were all falling in love, trying to find love, or dying from love.

Then thoughts of his night with Sabrina reared. *Go away!* He didn't want to understand this love thing. He had never been shown love all of his life, except for his short time with Sabrina. *Stop thinking of her!* He wanted to hate her. He hated humans so then he must hate her. But he had one thing in common with these despicable humans. He wanted a partner like himself. One he could hunt with, and kill with, and have thrashing sex with. Not one to hurt his heart.

X-10 sighed and stretched out on his cot. He let his mind soar to the outside world. He found Laura again. He had lost her after the office killing, but he found her now back with the old man again.

He soared through the night sky to the old man's cabin in the woods. There they were. Laura cooked something on the stove. The old man was wrapped up in a blanket on the couch. The creature could do nothing but watch, as he had used up most of his powers with the whore tonight. His powers weren't as strong when he was dulled by drugged food, and even then he had a short window of time to use them before he grew weak.

But that was just fine. He would never kill Laura from his mind's eye. This one had to be done in the flesh. Just like Bjord's would be. He spent his entire life seeking her out and destroying those around her. Soon her time would come. And she would know what he was and he would watch her die. He would stretch it out. How sweet it would be to hear her screams of agony until he had his fill, and then silence.

He sighed and drifted into a deep sleep where he chased Laura in his dreams.

CHAPTER 17

Laura stirred the chicken rice soup over the stove and glanced at Mr. B. He had become much worse since she left him this afternoon. She found him sleeping on the couch when she got home from the café. His coughing had turned phlegmatic and wet. She feared his cold was turning into pneumonia. As she stirred the soup a piercing headache worked its way through her skull. She could tell it would be a bad one. It felt like a steel probe pushing into her skin, inch by inch. She sighed and ladled soup into a bowl, then sat beside Mr. B who dozed. He opened his eyes.

"Oh my, that smells good," he wheezed. He took it in his shaking hands and sipped it from the spoon. "And hearty too."

"Good old chicken broth should fix you up soon, Mr. B."

"This is perfect. You should eat some too, Laura. And tomorrow I'll be fine and we'll go find this Doctor Britton."

She patted his knee. "I'm not hungry. And Mr. B, I don't think you're going anywhere tomorrow but to the doctor. I'm worried your cough is turning into pneumonia. We might need to take a trip to the hospital."

"*Hmph*, we'll see. I may not be a spring chicken but I can get around all right. I'll fight this thing off. But forget about that. Tell me about Ben."

Laura looked up at the ceiling and tried to figure out what she could say. "He's a good man, I think."

"That's it? That's all you learned?"

"Well, his parents died here the night the meteorite hit. They were vacationing and crushed in their cabin."

"Oh my God. Well, there were many who died that night. How sad for him. And why is he here now?"

"I think to put the past behind him."

Laura didn't want to talk about Ben anymore to Mr. B. She didn't understand her feelings for the man with the gray eyes. She felt uncomfortable just trying to figure it out and put it into words. Pain shot through her head again. She pinched the bridge of her nose.

"A bad one, Laura?"

"Yeah, it's coming on. I wish I could find a way to heal my own pain with these headaches. I've got to lie down. I'm sorry."

"Don't apologize to me, young woman. You go rest. I'll do the same and we'll both be fine in the morning."

"Goodnight, Mr. B. Enjoy your soup."

She kissed him on the cheek, his dry skin rustling across her lips like thin leaves, and then she stumbled toward the loft ladder. She stretched out on her bed, the pounding coursing through her head in a tortuous rhythm, and drifted into blessed sleep.

When Laura woke up it was still dark out. Disoriented, she sat up to look at the clock. 5:00 a.m. Her headache had disappeared. She took a shower, dressed, and tiptoed down the loft ladder. She peeked in on Mr. B and found him curled up on his side, still asleep. He wheezed, but she didn't want to wake him just yet. She downed coffee and toast and left Mr. B a note saying she was headed for the lake and would check on him in a few hours.

She wanted to get to work right away on strengthening her newfound powers. Anxiety tugged inside her, building stronger every day. She was running out of time. The evil that followed her headed her way soon. The man in black had written it so. She didn't know why she believed in his words but she felt in her gut he was right. A showdown was coming and she had to be ready.

Laura pulled a thick, cream-colored cable sweater on over her turtleneck and shivered as she stepped outside. She blew out silver clouds. They hung in the air and disappeared then she shoved her hands in her jean pockets and walked down the rough path toward the lake. Light crept through the trees, but the sun still hid away below the horizon.

As she neared the bottom of the path at the shoreline, movement caught her eye across the lake through the mist rising from the water. Someone moved along the path. The dark figure, shrouded in white, flowed in a fluid line along the path. Every few feet he would stop to investigate something and then move along. Laura peered through the dim light but she couldn't make him out. Then, he was gone.

The figure reminded her of Ben, and she wondered if it was him. A funny kind of feeling spread through her thinking of Ben. She closed her eyes and pictured him leaning in his doorway, arms folded across his bare chest as his gray eyes stared into hers. It felt as if they had known each other for a long time. But she had to get him out of her mind for now.

She made her way through the fog toward the section of the lake hidden in an alcove. There, facing the woods, she closed her eyes and focused on moving rocks with her mind. Anger rose in her thinking of her parents, Moe, and Renee. She wanted to fight back. She wanted to find this man who killed them.

She planted her feet shoulder-width apart, and facing the woods, commanded its inanimate objects to obey her wishes. Her hands danced in fury as rocks and branches flew through the air toward one another.

She stripped off her sweater and turtleneck, now damp with sweat. The sun hit the lake from the treetops burning off the fog, shooting millions of sparkles across the water toward her. But Laura closed her eyes to the beauty and fought her war with evil.

The sounds of her battle echoed around the lake as wood and stone broke against each other. She was a creature of nature and hypnotized in the darkness of her mind as she fought. She shrieked with bitter triumph.

Then exhaustion overcame her and her rage drained away. She sank to the ground, weeping. The pain of her many losses overcame her. How could she win against something she didn't even know? But she did know one thing. She and this killer had to be connected. Just as she was connected somehow to the man she sensed deep in the earth here all those years ago. She rose up on her knees and threw back her arms wide open in protest, her chest reaching out toward the sky.

"Just come and get me you bastard! I'm ready!"

She opened her eyes and squinted from the sunlight now all around her.

"Laura," a voice called softly from behind her.

She jumped up and turned around to see Ben standing by the shoreline. The adrenaline that had surged through her body disappeared. She felt weakness crash over her in waves. She couldn't form words to say. Tears still streamed down her face. She reached out a hand to him and it shook. She stared at it as if it weren't part of her body and she tottered on her feet. Ben lunged toward her and caught her before she fell.

Ben held Laura on the rocky beach and traced her face as her eyes remained closed. He put a finger to her throat and felt her heart racing. Fire poured off her, pulsing like heat waves shimmering on hot asphalt baking in a summer sun. He tried not to look at the swell of her breasts pushing up from the lavender lace that embraced her sweet points. And so he concentrated on her face, trying to make sense of what happened.

Ben hadn't meant to come to the lake so early, but he had tossed and turned the night before. A monster chased him in his dreams. He couldn't see his face though. Laura ran with him and he knew the monster would kill them both. He had to save her. But the thing that chased them grew closer and closer.

Then he woke up and couldn't get back to sleep. All he could think of was Laura. He felt as if his whole life had been leading up to meeting her. Like fate. He wished he had answers to all the questions he had about her, but he could wait if it meant he could spend more time with her. And so he came to the lake before the sun came up to take his mind off her. He had to find something in these woods to give him answers about his parents' death, or peace at least. He intended to search every part of it. He had all the time in the world.

He had traced the shoreline and headed through the trees toward the fenced-in area when he heard crashing noises. He followed the noise and pushed through the brush to get to the lake. There stood Laura, a fierce warrior battling an invisible enemy as sticks and rocks sailed through the air before her in a cloud of chaos. She was so beautiful, standing there like a goddess as her hair blew around her. Her body shone with sweat and her muscles rippled as she conducted the air. Once again, he was mesmerized. Who was this girl?

And now here he held her to him in stillness and peace. He wondered who she had been screaming to just before she fainted. He had so many questions to ask. His troubles and past faded in the background as he tried to understand this woman he just met yesterday.

"Laura."

Her eyes fluttered and then opened to stare right at him.

"Ben." She struggled to get up and he helped her. She swayed once and he gripped her arm to steady her. She stared at him and then looked at the piles of rock and wood strewn about from her violent show. "Oh my God."

"You're okay." He held onto her arm.

She wouldn't look at him and moved away, bending down to pick up her turtleneck trapped under rocks. She tugged it out and turning away from him, quickly pulled it over her head.

"What just happened here?"

"I did that. I can make things move." Laura sat down on a flat boulder nearby.

"Like telekinesis?"

"Yes, some call it psychokinesis."

"You can really move objects with your mind? But how?"

"I don't know how. I've been able to do it his since I was a child.

That…and other things."

Ben moved closer to her and stood over her. He looked at her turtleneck, remembering what she looked like with it off. She gazed up at him, her large eyes sad. She looked tired. He sat down on the boulder with her and took her hand. It was slim and pale in his large, tan hand. She rubbed his thumb over and over in a smooth movement, staring off in the distance. He felt a jolt inside as her fingers moved over his and forced down the rising in his pants.

"I'm listening," Ben said softly. "If you want to tell me more."

"I can heal people too."

He touched her hair and turned her face toward him. "You're amazing."

"More like cursed." Laura shivered from the cool breeze coming off the lake. Ben reached over and picked up her sweater that was twisted on the ground and put it around her shoulders.

"Perhaps cursed, but also amazing."

"I saved my mother's life once and my friend, Mr. B, but I couldn't save my other friends." Laura's eyes welled with tears. "They died in horrible ways all because of me."

Ben squeezed her hand, not understanding, but knowing whatever she had been through in her past was worse than anything he'd been through. They were two tormented souls.

Laura looked into Ben's eyes and tilted her head as if to make up her mind. "Why are you here?"

He wasn't expecting that question and shrugged. "I don't know anymore. I came here to find some answers. But now I met you and not by chance, I think." He looked out over the lake. It was a perfect autumn day with the sun shining on the water and geese flying overhead. The kind of idyllic day ordinary couples had hikes and picnics on. This wasn't such a day.

"I think we were meant to meet to help one another, don't you?" Laura squeezed his hand this time.

"I think so too."

"Then, can I trust you?"

He looked at her for a long moment. "You can trust me, Laura."

She stood up then and tied her sweater around her shoulders. She walked to the shoreline and turned back to look at Ben with her hands on her hips. "Then I have a lot to tell you."

He sat on the boulder while she paced back and forth, telling him things that were hard to believe. She stopped often to wave her hands at some dramatic moments and held back tears at some of the terrible things she told him. Things he could have only imagined happening in a fantasy book, yet he believed what she told him was the truth. This woman had survived much more than he had, and yet she stood before him so vibrant and strong.

"The notes," Laura said. "I almost forgot the notes." She unfolded notes from her pocket, explaining to Ben how she received them after Moe and Renee's deaths. She said she carried them with her as a reminder because she felt guilty when she wanted to forget all those she lost. Ben read the two notes.

"But who could have left these notes?"

"The man in black. That's what I called him."

Ben jumped up, his brain tried to comprehend what was happening. A sense of connection began to grow inside him. Connection and more mystery. "Describe him to me." He shoved his hands in his jean pockets, rocking from one foot to another.

Laura stared at him. "Well, he's a large man. The few times I've seen him he wears all black. Sometimes he looked so real and other times he looked ghostly. Transparent. The first time I saw him I was seven. He stood in the trees across from our house watching me. Another time I saw him in the apple orchard. That was the only time I heard him speak."

"What did he say?"

"It was so strange. I asked him why he was watching me and he said 'I need to know what you are'."

Ben stopped and stared at her. "Know what you are—" He remembered his dream of Laura at the lake when she had asked him, 'Do you know what I am?'

Laura tugged at his sleeve. "What is it?"

"Just tell me another time you saw him."

"The last time I saw him my parents had just been killed. He stood across the street watching our home burn down. I remember he shimmered in the sun. Then he just…vanished. I don't know how he did it. I know it had to be him that left these notes, who else could it be?"

Ben stared off into the distance, thinking. "Laura, what else do you remember about how he looked?"

"He had the strangest eyes, they almost—"

"Glowed? Like neon green?"

Laura grabbed his sleeve again. "How do know about the man in black?"

Ben didn't answer her. He squeezed his temple and flipped back his bangs, not daring to look at Laura. Part of him now wished he had run off in his car last night and had never unraveled this growing mystery.

"Answer me, damn it! I just told you my darkest secrets." Her voice rose, and she shook his arm. "Did you have anything to do with my parents dying? My friends dying?"

Ben stared into her angry eyes and put his hands on her shoulders.

"No. I swear I didn't have anything to do with killing anyone you loved."

Laura covered her face and cried. Ben put his arms around her and drew her close into him. She was so warm. Her curves hugged him. Her hair smelled like coconut from her shampoo and memories of Hawaii flooded back.

"I'm so glad," she said, muffled into his chest. He didn't want her to move away from him, but she stepped back and wiped her face. "But then how do you know about the man in black? And how is it we're both connected to him?"

Ben drew her back down to sit on the boulder. "I don't know how I'm connected with him but I've seen him twice. Once, at my foster mother's funeral. The second time was in Hawaii, where he saved my life."

Laura's eyes grew wide.

"And when I went back to Hawaii to visit an old friend, I dreamt of you." Ben stroked her hair.

Laura shook her head. She opened her mouth to speak, but nothing came out.

"You and I were here at this lake. We kissed and you asked me if I knew what you were. Then I saw the meteorite coming and you pulled me toward the spot where my parents had been crushed. I ran from you to save myself, but you wouldn't come with me. And so I left you standing there under the moon. I was terrified but you were smiling. So you see, when you said this man in black said he needed to know what you were, I thought it couldn't be coincidence."

"And so you knew it was me when you first found me here?"

"Right away."

Laura looked down at her feet swinging from the boulder. He stared at her profile, tracing it with his mind's eye.

"So we are connected, Ben. And did the man in black speak to you too?

Ben looked away. "Yes, in Hawaii he did."

"You said he saved your life, how?"

"It was a long time ago. I was a different kind of guy then and I just got into trouble. That's all."

"That's all? Really?"

"Really." He pursed his lips and offered no other information. He couldn't tell Laura of that long ago night of sin and terror. Shame seeped into him. She let it be and touched his knee.

"So what do we do now, Ben?"

"I can help you find out who your real parents are."

"But if this evil person comes for me next, aren't you afraid? He kills people I know."

"I'm not afraid. Can't you read my mind?"

"Actually, no, I can't. I can sense your emotions. That's all."

"That's all, hmm? Along with everything else you can do, that's a lot."

"I didn't wish for it. I wouldn't have these abilities by choice, you know."

"I understand." Ben didn't want to make her angry again. "I'll help you in any way. And I'm not afraid. Besides, I have nothing to lose."

"You're so sure of yourself."

"No, I just hate evil and want to stop it. There's too much of it in the world."

They sat looking out over the lake for a while until she spoke again. "Well, I'm supposed to go in town today with Mr. B and track down this doctor who delivered me. You could come with me instead. Mr. B is sick and I need to go check on him."

"I can do that."

The two new friends sat in comfortable silence after their strange and amazing discoveries of one another. The sun grew high in the sky, burning away the fog and mist tendrils that hid the woods and water earlier. The world around them sparkled clear.

"But how can I help you, Ben?"

"You already are." He took her hand. "Just by meeting you."

"What about your parents? You came here looking for answers."

"Yes, but I didn't expect to find answers. I really just expected some closure. Growing up in foster homes was no fun."

"What if we go to the place where your cabin used to be?"

"But there's nothing there. Everything was flattened and the government cleaned up any debris years ago."

"There is something there I might be able to find."

"What could you find?"

"Memories. I can try and find memories."

Laura explained how she sensed the sad man years ago that had crashed at the lake and how she felt connected to him.

"Wait a minute, my head is still spinning with everything else you told me." Ben interrupted her, letting go of her hand and shaking his head. "You mean to say you think a spaceship crashed here, not a meteorite?"

"I do. And I dream about the strange man from the spaceship. The other evil man chases me in my dreams and I run to the strange man underground where he's trapped in his spaceship. That's the same dream I've been having for years. I can never see the evil man's face clear but he is there, behind me, chasing me through the woods. A monster. I know if he reaches me he'll kill me."

Ben burst out laughing. "I'm sorry. I'm not laughing at you, just the situation. It just sounds all so ridiculous." He paused then as his dream flashed back. "And last night I had a dream a monster chased you and me. And he wanted to kill us both."

"Like the man that chases me in my dreams."

Ben nodded slowly. "So, what memories can you find here?"

"Memories of your good times there, memories of what your parents felt. I don't know for sure but it's worth a try, isn't it?"

Ben thought about it.

"Maybe even their last few minutes here, Ben."

He stood up and held out his hand to her. "Let's do it."

Laura took his hand and they walked down the shoreline to the fenced-in area toward the crash site.

CHAPTER 18

X-10's stomach growled with hunger. He concentrated on forcing the sensation to go away. It was his first day on his starvation diet. The time had come to make his escape. He only had a day or two more of starving himself before Bjord would gas him and pump him full of drugs to dull his powers.

However, there was one ability the good doctor wasn't aware he could do—hold his breath. X-10 had been practicing for months now to slow down his heartbeat and force his lungs to be still, placing his body in a coma-like stage. He had built up to five minutes, according to the digital clock built into his cell. It would be enough time for the doctor to think he had been knocked out from the drugs, enter his cell, and inject him with mind-altering drugs.

What a surprise the doctor will get when he discovers his science project is not unconscious. The next day X-10 would put his plan in motion. Escape would follow soon after. Only after he killed his keeper.

X-10 had deciphered Bjord's mutterings throughout recent months and understood that only one guard worked on duty beginning at midnight in his section of the facility. A tall, fat human called Norm. X-10 looked forward to trying on his clothes, after ripping out his throat. After all, he couldn't go running around naked in the streets.

Then he could kill Laura face-to-face at last. A thrill surged through his grotesque body and his veins pulsed faster. He stretched out on his cot and forced himself to calm down. He needed to seek out Laura to prepare for his escape. She was somewhere in New York, but he needed clues to find her on foot. He hoped once he got outside his prison walls his senses would tell him what direction to go in.

He massaged the hard mass protruding from his forehead and closed his eyes, letting his mind's eye soar outside. Over the city of D.C. he flew, through Maryland and across Delaware. He followed the New Jersey shoreline and headed west into the woods of New York. He couldn't see his route in detail. He just sensed which way to fly.

And then he found the lake. There was Laura, with a man. They held hands and walked through the woods. She stopped and knelt on the ground. The man stood over her, his hands on her shoulders. Had she found a lover? How delicious it would be to kill them both. He watched them. A smile spread across his face, twisting his skin into bulging mounds. Soon he wouldn't need to close his eyes. He zoned in his mind's eye over her and sent driving spikes of pain into her.

"A little torture before the big event, my girl."

He laughed and continued his attack on her from afar.

Laura knelt down on the ground where Ben believed his cabin had been. He remembered a large black walnut tree that grew just above his cabin up on the mountain. It was still there. At nine years old it seemed like a monster outside his bedroom window standing taller than any other tree around it. Its gnarled branches reached out to the sky in a scary embrace. In stormy weather it would shake and bend, a prisoner trying to free itself from shackles. It was angry to be bolted down.

Ben had been terrified of that tree. He believed it would free itself and come marching down the mountain, reach into his bedroom window, and crush him between its thick arms. Back then anything seemed possible. Now it looked small and tired to him. It ached for a good wind to blow it over so it could finally rest, rather than stand at attention year after year.

"Are you sure this is the spot, Ben?"

"As sure as I can ever be after more than twenty-five years."

Laura knelt down and placed her hands flat on the ground and closed her eyes. "Nothing is coming yet."

Ben stood over her, willing her to find something there.

"Wait...now I see pictures. Like a movie."

She described it to him. She saw many families who had been at the old cabin over the years. Then she saw a young boy with bangs. It was Ben. There were his parents. His mother danced on the grass playing a flute and his father sat at a hammered dulcimer. They made graceful music together. And there sat Ben on a tree stump, twirling a stick in the dirt and cocking his head to look up every once in a while.

His mother grabbed him with one hand while the other hand still held the flute. Her lips flew fast over it. She did a small jig and twirled, taking Ben with her. At first he resisted and then laughed as they swung around and around. His father laughed too and his fingers moved faster and faster over the dulcimer strings in a vibrant melody.

The scene changed. Ben and his father fished on the edge of the lake on a pier. They had a covered basket full of fish. Ben caught a fish and yelped as his father dropped his pole and ran over to help him. Together they dragged the fish in and his father scooped it up in a net to place in the basket. Then they headed home on a path, his father's hand on his shoulder as Ben leaned into him.

There was his mother, a shadowy figure at the doorway clapping her hands to see all their fish to fry. Then the picture went dark again. Now Ben yelled at his mother. His father stepped in, looking angry. Ben ran off to his room. He crawled out his bedroom window in the dark and headed down the lake path.

Ben bent down and put his hands on Laura's shoulders as she spoke. He relived those memories she witnessed now.

"There's a green light in the sky. It's growing bigger and bigger. I see you, Ben, looking up at it. You get up and run fast along the lake. Your parents are in the cabin calling to you to come out of your room. Your mother is saying, 'We love you. Come on out.' Your father says, 'We'll work it out, you'll see. Don't go to bed mad.' They don't know you snuck out. But then your father sees the green light through the kitchen window. He calls to your mother. They go out on the front porch. Your mother looks worried. Your father takes her hand and they continue to watch the sky. It's so bright now I can only see their outlines. And then…"

Ben fell to his knees on the ground next to her and shook her shoulders. "What? Then, what?"

"Nothing. Then…nothing." Laura opened her eyes and looked at him.

"What do you mean nothing?" Ben stopped shaking her, but kept his hands on her shoulders.

"They died peacefully, Ben. They never knew what hit them. It hit so fast. They never knew you ran away either. They wanted to work it out. I sense they felt bad about pushing you so hard to do what they wanted you to do."

He looked at the ground and wondered if they had been crushed right there.

"Did you hear me? You can let go of your guilt. You didn't cause their deaths. Don't punish yourself your entire life just because you lived. And your parents loved you. I can feel it. They wouldn't want you to feel guilty for surviving. Not only would they want you to survive, they would want you to live. *Really* live."

Ben sat back, feelings swirled through him. Of peace and hope. Strange feelings he hadn't felt in years. Laura took his hand. He turned her fingers over in his. For the first time in a long time he felt like he wasn't alone. They sat together in silence for a long while when suddenly she cried out. "Stop it. Just stop it." She gripped her head in her hands.

"Laura, what's the matter?"

"The pain. It's so bad. Make it stop. Make it stop!"

Ben didn't know what to do. "A migraine?"

She huddled on the ground, clutching at her head, and shivered. "B-b-bad."

Ben shook his head to re-focus. "Mr. B's cabin. Where is it? I'll take you there." He touched her hair.

"The path." She opened her eyes to small slits and raised her finger past him, then curled up into a ball of pain.

Ben put his hands under her and lifted her up. She was tall for a girl but light. He cradled her and headed up the path to find the cabin. The sunlight poured through the trees as they peeled back their layers of leaves to welcome autumn. Laura clung to his neck. Her eyes remained closed. She smelled like clean soap. He breathed her in with each step he took up the rough path. At last, the cabin peeked through the trees. He was thankful he had kept in shape.

He stepped up on the front porch stoop and unlatched the door with one finger, hugging Laura close to his chest. She moaned and he placed her down on the couch in the screened-in porch.

"Laura, I'm going to find your friend, okay?" She just hunched up on the couch in a fetal position. Ben threw a blanket over her from the back of the couch and went inside the cabin. He called out but heard nothing. He peered into one room. A lumpy figure moved on the bed under blankets. The man coughed and the bed shook.

"Mr. B? I'm Laura's new friend, Ben. She had a terrible headache and I brought her back here to rest."

"Laura?" The man wheezed and coughed again. "She's here?"

Ben turned on the light. The man tried to sit up but a coughing spasm kept him huddled on his side. Ben stepped closer and felt his head. He was burning up. The old man was in bad shape.

"Laura, your friend. She's staying with you."

"No, no, she's in New Jersey."

The old man's clarity suffered, probably from the fever. He coughed for a long while and then gasped as he tried to get a breath in. "Sir, I'm calling for an ambulance, okay? I think you need to be hospitalized."

"No, damn it. No hospital. Got…to…find Doctor Britton for Laura. She needs help. I have to help her."

"I think *you* need help and that's the best way to help Laura. Just hang on."

Ben wondered what he gotten himself into. Within two days he had gone from being alone in the world to connecting with Laura and caring for her with a migraine and her elderly friend in bad health. Ben turned off the bedroom light and found the phone to call for an ambulance. He didn't know the address but dispatch had a connection online of his location via phone. The local ambulance was already in use, but they could send one from the next town over.

Then he went to sit with Laura and wait. She was asleep. He hoped her dreams pushed her pain aside. He hoped she dreamed of him. He hoped she would wake up and this debilitating headache would be gone. He had never seen someone so affected by a headache. It didn't seem normal. But then nothing about Laura was normal. She was an incredible woman.

He rocked on the porch next to her and gazed at her face so peaceful in sleep. The revelation hit him hard. He wanted to be with this woman. He wanted to love this woman. And he had known her for such a short time. He caught his breath in realization and wondered what he was to do with this new feeling. Could he feel love for a woman, finally, at thirty-six years old? It felt foreign and terrifying yet it pulled him in like an addiction.

"I'm not going to let you go. Not yet, anyways," he told her. Her head moved as if she could hear him. "But you just might let me go when you find out my past. Can I keep it from you?"

He knew he couldn't. He would have to bare his soul to this woman. She would accept nothing else but the truth. But he sensed, or hoped rather, she would accept him for what he had been and what he was now. He hoped.

CHAPTER 19

Laura woke up to darkness falling. She lay under a blanket on the couch in the screened in porch. Her nose felt cold but the rest of her was warm and snug. She heard the tinkling of dishes in the kitchen, but didn't want to crawl out from her warm spot just yet. Then the day all came back to her in a flash. She bolted up and ran into the kitchen. There stood Ben ladling soup into bowls. A delicious bread toasting smell filled the air. A fire crackled in the stone fireplace in the great room next to the small kitchen.

"Ben, how is Mr. B? I have to check on him." She turned toward the bedroom.

"Laura, wait," Ben called. "He's in the hospital but doing okay. I just called."

She turned back and sat down at the kitchen table. "I wasn't here. I should have checked on him."

"You were going to, but got sidetracked, remember?"

"But still, he's all I've got. And I'm all he's got. It's pneumonia isn't it? What happened?"

Ben told her how he found him and called the ambulance. "He's at Albany Medical Center. They've given him fluids and medication to clear his lungs. He's in good hands. You can call and speak with him if you want. You slept through all the excitement here today."

Laura looked up at Ben and shook her head. "I just met you and don't know what I would have done without you today. You helped me and Mr. B. If I had been alone and passed out with this headache and there was no one here to help him, then…"

Ben put down the soup ladle and sat down next to her. "It doesn't matter. He's safe and so are you."

"I feel safe now." She stared into Ben's eyes and felt peaceful. She never knew gray could be such an alluring color. She thought it was devoid of color. But his eyes sparkled like silver granite with specks of black in them.

"So listen, call Mr. B and find out for yourself he's okay. Then have some soup I found and cheese bread I made. You must be starving as you haven't eaten all day."

"Did you carry me all the way up here from the lake?"

"Yep. Good thing I've been training for the carrying-damsels-in-distress-marathon."

Laura blushed. She hoped he didn't find her heavy or she did anything embarrassing while unconscious. "What else did you do?"

"I just wrapped you up on the couch so you could rest and be warm but still get some fresh air. I thought it might help your headache. You've been sleeping all day."

"I've never had one so bad."

Ben tilted his head at her. "Are you sure they're only headaches?"

"I don't know." Laura shrugged. "I've had them since I was a kid."

"I wonder if there's a connection between the headaches and this killer."

"I don't know."

"Just eat for now." Ben put the soup and bread in front of her.

"I want to talk to Mr. B first."

She felt Ben watching her as she called the hospital. She also sensed his arousal for her and tried to concentrate on talking to Mr. B. She hurried off the phone and made an excuse to go to her bathroom upstairs, in part as she really had to go and also because she wanted to see how bad she looked after sleeping on the couch all day.

She groaned as she looked in the mirror and tried to straighten her hair but it continued to fall in waves. She brushed her teeth, washed her face, and put on some lip gloss. She was almost attractive. *Ugh.* She felt self-conscious in front of Ben, something she had never felt with another man. None ever had this deep, pulling effect on her as Ben did.

He stared at her with such intensity like he was figuring her out, or maybe he was deciding if he was attracted her. What if he wasn't? She tugged at her bra, feeling embarrassed over her small breasts and then laughed. It was so ridiculous. She had other things to worry about now.

Laura headed down the loft steps to find Ben had set up their dinner by the fire in the great room. He had placed a blanket on the floor and pillows to sit on while they ate. She smiled at him and sat down cross-legged in front of the fire to eat. Ben stoked the wood and the flames roared up the chimney.

"I love a fire." Laura finished her soup and hugged her knees. He nodded and just looked at her. She sensed he wanted to touch her but was conflicted. "I want to go visit Mr. B in the hospital tomorrow and try to find this Doctor Britton. Will you help me?"

"You know I will."

"We don't have Internet access up here. We might have to go into the Albany library or an Internet café."

Ben had a better idea. "Let me call my friend Andy in the Navy. He works in intelligence now out in Washington State in Bremerton, and the least he can do is search online for us. I'm sure he has access to other records as well."

Ben dialed Andy's number on his cell phone and went out on the front porch.

"Yo, squidy," Ben replied as Andy answered the phone. "Howz the secret operative life going?"

"Life is grand here, except for the fact I am heading out soon on a three-week assignment. And of course, I can't tell you where it is. I can't even tell Likini. I'll have the bluest balls in the Navy when I get back."

"As long as they're hanging high, buddy."

"They're always at attention, my old friend. So Ben, me-boy, what are you up to? Ravaging fabulously rich women off the Greek coast or something?"

"Nothing like that."

He told Andy about having met Laura and briefly how he wanted to help her find out where she came from. Ben didn't even know how to go about explaining all that had happened these last few days.

"So can you do some research on this Doctor Britton for us and call me tomorrow morning? We need to know where he is and what he's been doing."

"Sure thing, buddy." Andy chuckled. "Sooo...who's this new girl? Sounds serious if you're helping her do this. It doesn't sound like the screw 'em and ditch 'em Ben I know."

"She's just someone I met who used to live here."

"I know you, bud. I can tell by your voice. This could be the one. Am I right?"

"I don't know how I feel. I just met her." Ben squinted to see into the cabin then moved out of the porch into the woods. He didn't want Laura to hear him. Darkness cloaked the trees around him as he stood in a small pool of light streaming from the kitchen window.

"Okay, okay. Just don't screw this one up, if she *is* the one, and run off like you do."

"Give me some credit, Andy. I may run off, but I leave them wanting more. Isn't that a good thing?"

"Sure thing, Ben. Anyhow, I've got to run. I leave in a few days for this assignment and have to pamper Likini as much as I can. We have dinner reservations."

"Why the pampering? She's usually good about you being gone for longer."

"We're pregnant! Three months along now. We just started telling people."

"Congratulations. That's awesome. I'm real happy for you." Ben felt glad for his friend, but felt something tug inside him. A yearning for the first time to experience what other people did. Normal people.

"Thanks, man. You've got to get cracking too on the same front. It took us a long time."

"I don't know. Me and kids? Doesn't sound like a good combo."

"Love makes the world go 'round, remember? The more love you make the better it gets! So keep making love."

Ben laughed and told him to give Likini a kiss and he'd call him tomorrow.

"I hope you're getting more than a kiss there soon, lover boy."

Ben just laughed again and hung up.

He found Laura stretched out on her stomach on the blanket by the fire. The shadows leapt over her curves in a wild dance and her hair shone like burnished metal glinting in the sun.

He wanted to stare at her forever.

Laura grew sleepy as she waited for Ben to return. She wondered what he was telling his friend about her. Her eyes closed when she heard Ben clear his throat. She rolled toward him, and stretched in one fluid movement to sit up.

"Can your friend help us?" She looked up at him. She tried not to stare at his long, legs encased in tight jeans that stood shoulder width apart over her as he folded his arms across his chest. She felt dominated in her seated position and tingled inside. She liked feeling that way.

"He's going to do a search for us and I'll call him in the morning to find out."

Laura gathered her hair away from her face and looked into the fire. She wasn't sure what they should do now with one another. The silence between them grew awkward.

"Well, I better head back to the Inn and leave you alone to rest some more," Ben offered, shoving his hands in his pockets.

Laura looked back up at him. She remembered all the people she had lost in her young twenty-six years. She didn't want to lose him too, but she feared getting too close. She could lose him too. Then something swelled inside her. She barely recognized it. It was hope that maybe love could win out over evil and Ben would be the one to help her stop it. And then she could only think of one word to say to him.

    "Stay."

CHAPTER 20

Ben looked at Laura. All he could do was nod. He wanted to stay. He held out his hand to help her up and she took it willingly. Facing each other, they stared into each other's eyes and he touched her hair. That one word, *stay*, had given them permission for so much. He pushed his fingers through her hair in a soft, sweeping motion lifting it away from her face. She moaned with his touch and placed her hands on his chest. She drew her hands across his chest and arms, claiming them for her own.

Ben shuddered and drew her into his chest hugging her close.

"Where did you come from?" He breathed deep of her. "You drive me crazy, Laura Armstrong."

"I don't know, that's what I need your help to figure out, Ben Fieldstone."

He felt her warm breath on his neck as she spoke, and her lips grazed him. She trembled and he held her closer.

"Are you scared?"

Laura nodded with her head still in his chest. "I've only been with two men, boys really. I don't have much experience."

"I won't hurt you," Ben said. "We can go slow and wait, it's up you."

"I'm not afraid you'll hurt me." Laura looked up at him. Her large eyes shone with flecks of firelight. "And I don't want to wait."

"Then what is it?"

"I just don't want to disappoint you." She hid her head again in his chest and clung to him. "We've just met each other and this is all happening so fast. And I like you, but I'm scared you won't like me after we are together. If I'm not any good."

Ben tugged her head up to look at him. He forgot she was ten years younger than him. And even though to him she seemed equal and as old as him, he understood she was a young woman. Her girlish shyness touched him and he spoke with tenderness to her.

"Listen to me, Laura. I care for you too, a lot. More than I've cared about any woman my whole life. I know we just met but I feel like I've been waiting my whole life to meet you. I can't explain it either, but it's meant to be. The last thing in the world I want to do is hurt you. There's no way you could disappoint me. We'll make it happen together, you and I. Whatever it will be, it will be special. I know it." Ben was an expert at wooing women for sex, so the words came easy to him. Yet, this was the first time for him they held meaning, they meant something.

Laura stroked his neck and moved closer into him, her curves pressing into him with crushing sweetness. He rose up so hard she must feel him pressing into her. He lifted her head to him again and kissed her on the lips, but she was the one who opened his mouth to caress his tongue with hers. It was like his dream and he moved in her wet softness now as he did then. He opened his mouth wider to take more of her in and she moaned. Their bodies were hot from the flames shooting up next to them.

Ben lifted her turtleneck to feel her smooth waist underneath. In one, slow movement he pulled it over her head and cast it aside. She hugged herself to him but he wanted to see her in the firelight. He grabbed her arms and pulled them out wide so she stood tall in front of him.

"I'm sorry, my breasts are small." Laura looked away. Ben shook his head and smiled down at her. She took his breath away now, just as she had done at the lake that morning standing there in her bra facing the world head on.

"Beautiful is what you are." He cupped her breasts and they fit just right in each hand. "Perfect, see?"

He rubbed her nipples with his thumbs bringing them to sharp points and Laura gasped, closing her eyes. She arched her back, and Ben mouthed her nipples through her bra. Then he reached around and in one, deft movement unhooked her bra letting it fall to the floor. He tugged off his shirt and they stood facing one another. Laura moved her hands across his hard chest and inched closer to him, just enough so her nipples touched his naked skin. She rubbed them across his chest and it was his turn to moan.

"Laura, you drive me crazy."

He lowered her to the blanket and soon they slid across one another naked, entwined as one body. They lay still for a moment enjoying the feel of skin on skin. Laura looked away from his long penis that sprung forth, but he held her away to look at him.

"Don't be afraid. This is what you do me. Look."

She stared at it and touched it with her fingers, gripping his shaft and stroking it. He moaned and pulled her fingers away.

"Ben I want you in me," she whispered. He stroked her stomach up to her breasts with one hand and kept her hand at bay.

"Not yet." Ben shook his head. "It's been some time for me and now I'm afraid I'm the one who would disappoint you."

"What do you mean?"

"I said you drive me crazy, didn't I? I'm afraid I wouldn't last long the first time with you."

"I don't mind."

"I do. I want to drive you crazy."

Ben leaned over to suck her nipples and Laura met him with eagerness. He nipped and licked them, pulling them up into points, nuzzling them with his lips. Then he moved his head down toward her mound and stroked her inner thighs. He tried to pull her legs apart, but she resisted.

"No one's ever done that," she moaned, breathing fast.

Ben fingered her swollen nub and she cried out, opening her legs to his touch and tongue, unable to stop her shyness any longer. When his tongue licked her wetness she gasped and raised her hips closer to him, rocking them back and forth.

"Oh my God, Ben. Ben."

She kept saying his name over and over in a hazy mantra of desire. He stretched out and played her with his tongue and fingers, pushing into her swollen wetness and stroking her nether region. At first, she pulled away from him stroking her there, but he pushed the tip of his finger to slide in and out in a smooth motion.

Laura gasped and relaxed, allowing him to please her. He pulled away then with his fingers, his tongue, his lips until she begged for him to come back. He wanted her desire to ebb so he could begin again to torment her.

"Ben, I can't stand it, please, do…something!"

And so he did. He reached up to pull on her sensitive nipples with one hand as his other fingers pressed deep up inside her swollen tunnel, his tongue lapping at her, his lips sucking her most tender parts. She came in a rush and a scream that echoed around the cabin.

Ben gathered her in his arms after as she shuddered and shook from her explosion. Tears streamed down her face as she trembled, her heart racing, her breath rapid.

"Oh my God, what did you do to me? I don't know why I'm crying,

I'm not sad." She laughed and he laughed with her.

"It's relief, isn't it?"

"Yes! You kept bringing me to the edge over and over, I thought I would die."

"Can you think of a better place to die?"

She smiled and shook her head, hugging him close. The fire's coals burned low and Ben got up to place more logs on it. He turned around and stood over Laura, taking in her graceful curves.

She looked up at him. "But what about you?"

Ben raised an eyebrow at her, standing rock hard before her. She looked so sexy strewn before him, naked on the blanket. Her dark triangle and soft belly waited there to rise up to him in need.

"I'll show you." He grinned and he fell beside her, teaching her what to do with her tongue and fingers. Laura thoroughly enjoyed his instruction. And when her mouth and tongue were wet on him and her fingers pulled on his scrotum in a soft caress bringing him to the edge over and over, he called out.

"I can't hold it much longer, Laura."

And he came, in an exploding rush then cradled her head to him.

They lay in quiet before the fire and Ben got up to get another blanket to throw over them. He spooned behind her and they gazed into the fire, side by side.

"Have you been with lots of women?" Laura broke the silence.

Ben wasn't sure how to answer.

"I'm assuming that means, yes?" Laura prodded him.

"It means, yes, I've had many women but no one ever important in my life."

"Why not?"

Ben breathed in her hair and touched her neck, and Laura pressed her back and buttocks into him. They squirmed for a moment, feeling each other's bodies mesh together. He felt like they were in their own private world. A world with no pain or sorrow or loss. He didn't want to think about it as a fleeting moment. He wanted it to go on, forever.

"Many reasons, I guess. I had a hard childhood and didn't want to get hurt, I suppose. I traveled a lot as well, which made it difficult to have a relationship."

"Or maybe you traveled so you couldn't have a relationship."

He couldn't hide anything from her. "Maybe." He sighed. *Maybe, I'm falling in love with you.* The idea hit him like a rock to his head. He had never thought those words, or felt this way. Laura pulled his arm tighter to her, pressing her fingers hard into him.

"Me too."

"What do you mean?"

"I'm falling in love with you too."

"You heard me?" He turned her toward him.

"For the first time, yes."

Ben stared at her trying to figure her out. Why did she have these special abilities?

"I don't know," she answered and he shook his head.

"I'm going to have to watch what I think now, aren't I? You're an amazing girl."

"Woman." She touched his leg and he felt himself rise up again to his full length. "Not girl."

"My woman."

Ben kissed her, feeling a deep possession of her take over. He knew too, as Laura must know, this night might never happen again. He had no idea what his future held by himself, much less with this woman. But he wanted to unravel the mysteries around her, to know her to her core.

She kissed him back and in one swift movement swung her leg up to sit on him, his throbbing penis pressing into her thigh. She looked so appealing straddling him naked with her hair tussled and her sweet breasts pushing out over his face.

"I told you I want you in me." She held his arms down and leaned over him, licking his chest, her wetness rubbing against his leg. Ben took in a sharp breath as his penis pulsed against her soft thigh.

"We have to use something, Laura. I'm clean but I don't want to get you pregnant."

He reached over and pulled his pants toward him. He moved around in his back pocket, searching, then pulled out his wallet and from inside, a condom.

"Just in case?" She smiled.

"Just in case." She helped him put it on and he flipped her over on her back, holding her buttocks underneath him and pulling her toward him.

"Now, Ben, please don't make me wait anymore. I want to feel all of you."

And so he pushed into her wet heat slowly, suffused with her delicate burning. She flowed beneath him, meeting him half way in the firelight. Shadows leapt across their bodies as they moved together as one, linked by a fiery need and want. Like a rider galloping across a meadow, Ben rode her as she met his steady waves. He stroked her over and over, pulling himself out to rub her tender mound with his tip and inched his way back in again. Laura rolled her head from side to side and squeezed her breasts together so Ben could lick them with each stroke.

He was on fire and couldn't fill her up deep enough. Thrust after fervid thrust. The wind rattled the bare branches against the house in a screeching wail. It rose and dipped with intensity, but they were oblivious to it, consumed only by each other. The fire roared with the wind as well, blowing up hissing flames. Laura cried out with need and want.

"Deeper, Ben, please. Oh, please."

How could he deny her when she asked so nice? And he stroked her longer and deeper, rubbing her nub in slow circles with his thumb. She gasped, and reached around to grasp his buttocks.

"Now, Ben, now!"

With her words he felt the explosion rise inside him he had been keeping at bay, and they shouted together in release. He collapsed on her, their chests sliding together from sweat. This time they both trembled as they held each other, neither wanting to let go.

Laura woke up like she did every morning at Mr. B's, except this time she wasn't alone in her loft bed. The night before came flooding back in a hot, delicious memory as she watched Ben sleep on his side facing her. The room cast dark shadows about from the kitchen light that glowed up into the loft. The clock blinked 5:30 a.m. The sun still waited to appear.

She took in every part of Ben's face. It was the most handsome face she had known. His gray streaked hair fell over his lined forehead. He looked so peaceful. His lean angles carved themselves into her bed as he had carved himself into her the night before. She sensed he hadn't had much peace in his life. She wondered when he would open up to her about it.

She shivered thinking about the things they had done to each other. And she believed, no matter what happened, she would never forget this man. He was kind and gentle and passionate. She sensed this was not the only side to him though. Something dark hid in him.

Ben opened his eyes and they stared at each other for a long moment, both in a state of drowsiness. Then he was holding her and the magic began all over again. He had no protection, but she didn't care. She became swept up in feeling connected skin to skin. Neither spoke as he took her on the edge of the bed. He stood over her as she spread out before him in submission and passion. In a slow dance they moved to their own music, bending and stretching toward each other.

Laura felt like she was floating in the air as Ben consumed her body. She could only see his outline as he pulled her to him over and over and caressed her belly and breasts, stoking her fire to an almost painful intensity. She pushed herself up on her elbows to lick and suck his nipples this time, and he cried out with pleasure returning the favor as they rocked together. They strained slow toward release and when it came it was with a murmur and a gasp.

"Laura, my Laura," Ben whispered into her hair. "I've never made love before."

"What do you mean?"

"I never made love, only hate. Hate for myself mostly."

She was stunned by his blunt admission. "Why do you think that?"

Ben withdrew from her and fell back into bed. She snuggled into his chest and side.

"No one ever showed me love before. I haven't known love since my parents died. I guess I forgot what it was."

Ben stared at the ceiling with his hands under his head. She sensed he tried to resist telling her his deepest feelings. Laura could see his profile clearer now as the room grew lighter with sunrise.

She felt him freezing up on her. "Love remembers."

"Does it?" He twitched his mouth and shook his head. "I don't know if I believe it."

"You have to believe it, Ben. I grew up with it. Then when I lost so many I loved, I could still feel love. I was lucky enough to still have my friend, Mr. B, to help me keep going."

Ben was silent, a frown on his face. "I didn't have that."

"No, but if nothing else, you had your parents once. You have your friend, Andy. And now you have me."

He turned to look at her. "Do I have you? I mean really? We were foolish just now. We should have used protection."

Laura saw torment in his eyes and felt anguish flowing off him. She wanted to take it all away, to heal his heart. "I don't know what's going to happen. I know something bad is coming and I need to be prepared. And this paradise we have right now is just temporary. I don't want to worry right now about being pregnant. The chances are small, right?"

"I don't know what the chances are. Nothing is certain in life. And you can't count on people or love. You can only count on yourself."

"I don't believe that. I can help you remember how to love. I want to try."

Ben shook his head and stared at the ceiling again. "Part of me doesn't want to let you go, Laura, and part of me wants to drive away as fast as I can. Does that make sense?"

"Yes. I don't know what happened to you. I can't guess how horrible it must have been. But can't you tell me?"

Ben was silent. Laura touched his arm but he had closed up. He didn't touch her back.

"Can you read my mind right now?"

"Do you want me too?"

Ben turned to her again. She could see his eyes shining in the dim morning light.

"What if you discover me, the *real* me. Things I've done, things that have happened to me and decide you don't want me? Will you help me remember love then?" He got up out of bed.

"There can't be anything you've done I can't accept."

"How can you know? You've just met me."

"I just know. The shortness of time between us means nothing."

"I'm not a good person, Laura. I'm not worthy of love. I know this and can accept it. But you've changed everything and now I don't know what to do with that."

Laura didn't know what to say. She sat up and reached for him. "Don't go."

He turned to her with a half-smile. "I'm not running away from you, yet. I'm taking a shower and then calling Andy. We're going to find this doctor today, remember? After we visit Mr. B."

Laura nodded and hugged the blanket to her.

"Go back to sleep, if you want. I'll find some coffee and food to make in a bit."

He touched her head as he passed her and she watched him go into the bathroom. She wanted to hug him and tell him she loved him, but the moment had passed. So she did as he said and dozed into a dreaming state. Only this time the dreams were nightmares.

CHAPTER 21

Doctor Bjord watched X-10 on camera in his office. The monstrous creature appeared asleep on his cot, his muscles twitched, and his jaw opened and shut at times as if he dreamed about eating some victim. His vital signs confirmed he was sleeping. His cot, special Government Issue, had been programmed to record basic body readings of the person on it. Bjord could see his heart rate slow and his body temperature dropping.

He abhorred the creature and was terrified of him, but he was so close to finishing his work. He had to overcome his fear for the greater reward soon to come. He felt confident he would soon create the magic potion to transform the U.S. military into one unsurpassed in strength and abilities. The same strength and abilities X-10 possessed.

Bjord had created a genetic mixture giving incredible strength to his lab rats, but they only survived a day after receiving his injection. On his last attempt the injected rat crushed the head of his fellow rat mate between his paws and gnawed through the thick cage bars in under a minute to escape.

Bjord was thrilled, until twenty-four hours later he witnessed the same rat run headfirst over and over into the concrete wall to smash his own head in. The rodent finally succeeded. Suicidal notions would not work well on soldiers toward winning a battle. He sighed and tried to figure out how to overcome this obstacle.

But for now he worried X-10 was planning another killing. He had refused to eat for the past two days to avoid being drugged. Bjord had made the decision to turn on the halothane gas vents and put him to sleep that night. Once he became unconscious, he could enter his cell and inject him with Thorazine to impair his mental abilities and limit his strength. After experimenting with several tranquilizers he had discovered Thorazine, in high doses, kept X-10's dangerous powers to a minimum.

Bjord turned on the gas vents knobs, adjusting the dose of halothane to flow into the cell. It contained the strongest mixture made in order to knock X-10 out, and the cheapest non-flammable gas anesthetic on the market. It was still used in third world countries and veterinary facilities. X-10 wasn't in REM sleep yet, but he was ready to be gassed unconscious without waking up. Bjord readied his lab tray. It was a perfect time to take blood samples as well to continue his genetic testing. And he would prove again to the world he was a genius geneticist.

He brushed cracker crumbs off his stained coat and smoothed down his hair. He needed a shower and change of clothes. He sniffed and wrinkled his nose. His own body reeked of waste and grime, but every moment now was precious.

He fantasized of being awarded a fat sum for his work by the government to retire to a luxury spa where he could live out his days in comfort, all the while being applauded by the world instead of mocked. Once he succeeded he could then order X-10 killed. How he longed to do it himself. He shook his head to focus on the business at hand and checked the creature's vital signs one more time. He appeared unconscious and his twitches had stopped. Bjord had a good hour before the creature started to come out of his coma-like state. He switched off the gas vents to cut off the halothane.

Bjord picked up his lab tray and turned to head into the X-10's cell. His heart raced. He peered once more at the camera monitor to reassure himself his prisoner was indeed unconscious. Satisfied, he placed his tray on the floor and removed his keys to open the thick door that imprisoned the creature. He would be in and out within ten minutes. All he had to do was draw blood from X-10, and pump him full of Thorazine. Then Bjord could spend the night working on his new test. Tomorrow was a new day. Soon all his years of slogging away down here with this demon would pay off.

Ben sat on the porch and wrapped the blanket around him. It smelled like Laura and he breathed in deep. After his shower, he checked on her to find her sleeping again. She looked so young and appealing curled up in bed with her hair scattered on the pillow.

He stared at the woods now, watching the light grow from the grayness of dawn to the autumn colors of day. His mind wandered like a jagged puzzle of mismatched thoughts and he tried to organize them in a rational manner. But there was nothing rational about what he felt here, and he had to give into it. He was meant to come here for a reason. He would follow it through, no matter what the consequence. He was too entrenched now in the mystery surrounding Laura and him.

Most of all he was falling in love with her. It was a new, raw feeling that cut to the core of who he believed he was his entire life. At one point making love to her this morning, he thought, *soul mates*. She had looked at him and smiled as she strained toward him. She must have heard him think it. But now in the cold and light of day, he had to fight the urge to run and forget this place, and her. All his life he had run away from being connected to people and places. He never wanted to be so affected he lost control of his emotions and was committed. Yet here, for the first time he ran toward what could connect him forever and commit his heart.

He had no choice if he wanted to survive. Survive. What a strange word, he laughed to himself. He had survived physical abuse and near-death at the hands of brutal men. Now here, his soul sat on the line. His soul might survive here but not his body if this evil man was indeed coming who Laura professed to see. But where was the man in black? Would he save them from all this like he had saved him in Hawaii all those years ago? None of it made sense.

Ben checked his watch. It drew close to 8:00 a.m. Nearly 5:00 a.m. on the west coast. Almost time to give Andy a call. He reported on base early so Ben wanted to catch him before he left.

"Ben, top of the morning to ya." Andy's voice sang through the phone.

"Andy, you're too chipper for me and you're not Irish."

"Okay then, *hvordan de henger, minn venn?*"

"Is that one of your new languages for retrieving Intel?"

"Yep, I moved on from Russian and now poking around in Norwegian. Thought it would be nice to know the language of my land to woo busty Nordic spies with."

"First off, Norse God, I think you're done wooing and what does it mean anyways?"

"It means 'how they hanging, my friend'?"

"Nice. Somehow I doubt it will attract the busty ones."

"Yeah, you're right. I've got to get some new lines to work on. So, lover boy, how's the new woman?"

Ben didn't answer right away. He didn't know how to answer.

Andy chuckled. "I'm guessing good?"

"Complicated."

"Aha, one word that means so much with women. And a word I know you run from."

"I'm not running from this one. She's…I don't know."

"I do. She's special, right?"

"In more ways than you can ever know, or I could ever tell."

"Wow, my friend."

"Yeah." Ben cleared his throat. "So, did you get any info for us on this Doctor Britton?"

"Yep. He had a small practice in Coopersville and moved to Albany, building a much bigger practice there twenty-five years ago. Must have come into some dough. Then he got into drinking and prescription drugs and botched several deliveries over a period of time. They all had brain damage and when one died, his problem came to light. He was charged with medical malpractice, went to court and lost his license to practice. The hospital awarded the family of the dead kid $5 million but the evidence couldn't quite prove the good doctor was criminally negligent so he wasn't sentenced to jail time. Boy, he must have had some good lawyer."

Andy gave him the address and phone number and wished him luck.

"And one other thing, Ben. He hasn't paid his taxes in fifteen years."

"Boy, you dug deep didn't you?"

"Friends in high places and access, of course, will get you anything you need. And for you, that's what I do." Andy laughed. "Will you keep me posted on this Laura?"

"Of course, and thanks again."

"Remember what I told you."

"What?"

"Love makes the world go 'round, my man."

"Maybe for you, buddy."

"Wait and see. I'm making bets on you."

Ben shook his head and hung up. He went into the kitchen to get more coffee when Laura screamed. He bolted to the loft ladder, jumping up the rungs two at a time. She sat on the bed, shaking her head and screaming over and over. He grabbed her shoulders.

"Laura!"

She stopped screaming and looked at him with eyes darting back and forth. She was having dream terrors. He pulled her to him and she shivered all over.

"Laura, it's okay. It's just a dream. Everything is okay."

"No. No, it's *not* okay. He's coming for us. He killed me this time in my nightmare. I was dead. My throat r-r-ripped open, just like Moe. I saw my dead body. I didn't think you could die in your dreams. And you. You were dead too."

She gripped his shirt harder.

"It was just a dream. That's all." He stroked her hair.

"A nightmare that's going to come true. I know it."

They held each other in silence. Ben didn't know what to say to comfort her. She could be right.

X-10 remained still. His lungs did not cry out for air. It had only been a few minutes since he had heard Bjord turn on the gas. This was his one chance to escape. A couple more minutes he could last. He concentrated on his breathing in an effort to increase his heart rate allowing more blood to pump through his body. He couldn't wait to spill the old man's blood.

He heard the thick slab door open. The doctor's tray jingled with glass vials. X-10 didn't hear the heavy door shut close in place. Bjord had left it open. *Good thinking, old man.* He heard the tray set down on the cold concrete floor. Then he felt the rubber tie on his arm as the doctor readied him to pierce his vein to take blood. He opened his eyes and grinned at Bjord and took a deep breath, filling his lungs.

Bjord's mouth fell open and he dropped the syringe. Before Bjord could scream, X-10 sat up and grabbed his arm with one hand. He shoved the other hand into the doctor's mouth. Bjord flailed before him in a weak attempt to break free. X-10 shook the doctor in his pathetic attempt to flee.

"I can smell the putrid filth rolling off you. It's you who are the disgusting creature, not me, Doctor Bjord. Scientist of refuse and evil. That's what you are."

Bjord shook his head and twisted his body in a grotesque display to run. His legs pumped in a crooked dance.

"Now, good doctor, I want you to address me as Charlie and apologize for the years of imprisonment and experimentations you have tortured me with, do you hear? Charlie is my chosen name. A name you never gave me. If I take my fist out of your mouth for you to address me properly, you won't scream, will you? For if you do I will kill you slowly with pain, do you understand?"

Bjord stopped flailing and nodded.

X-10 extricated his pod-fingers from Bjord's mouth, but continued to grip his arm as he stood up. Bjord looked up at him wide-eyed. Then he smiled.

"You'll never get out of here, X-10. You'll never find your girl. She isn't a freak like you. She's human and free. No human will ever want you. You'll never be called Charlie for who could name a hideous, murdering beast such as yourself?"

Then he laughed and laughed. X-10 shook with rage and pushed his fingers into Bjord's throat. Bjord stopped laughing. He clutched at his neck. Blood gushed.

Bjord stared into X-10's eyes and gurgled. "Go—to—hell."

X-10 shoved his hands in further, ripping out the doctor's neck, and threw him on the floor. He shouted in rage, angry at himself for killing him so fast. The doctor got the best of him in the end, enraging him to kill him quick without suffering. X-10 stared at the crumpled, filthy man beneath him, blood oozing outward in a circle on the gray floor. X-10 promised himself the girl would die slowly. He would not let her affect him.

He would bring cold death to her.

CHAPTER 22

Jim's eyes crinkled up when Laura walked into the hospital room. She bent down and hugged him.

"I'm so glad you're okay and they're treating you good here, Mr. B."

"Yes, it's like I am the grandest pontificating potentate they've ever had the pleasure to attend. You should see how many times an hour these nurses come in here to fuss over me with frivolous hullaballoo!"

Laura laughed and stood up. "I can tell you're better because you're being a malcontent about your malady with this lamenting manifesto. Someone must have snuck you a thesaurus. Am I right?"

Ben just looked at them both and shook his head, enjoying their banter.

"Of course, I had to prepare for your visit!" Jim reached under his pillow to pull out the book in question. He smiled at Laura and then turned his attention to Ben. "So, this is the young highwayman who's plundered your heart, is it?"

Laura turned red and shook her head, but Ben stepped forward and held out his hand.

"I hope not plundered, sir. Perhaps stirred, a bit?" He winked at Laura as Jim shook his hand. "It's nice to meet you, again, under better circumstances."

"Mr. B likes to beat me with words from our thesaurus game." Laura was eager to move Mr. B away from talk of romance. "We've been doing it since I was a kid. Since I started it, I should win every time."

"Actually, I'm always the winner when I'm with you Laura."

She took his hand and sat next to him.

"I can see why you think that," Ben said.

"Well, I can't thank you enough for finding me and getting me help, and for Laura too. Her headaches get real bad scmetimes."

"We're headed out to find Doctor Britton after this," Ben said.

"Thank you for helping her with that. I wish I could go with you."

"You just rest," Laura said. "I want you better before you come back up the mountain."

Jim patted her hand and yawned. "Sorry, I'm just so tired." He coughed twice, and winced. He patted Laura's hand seeing her look of distress. "I'm okay. It's just damn pain from the pleurisy. I'm hoping I can go home soon if my oxygen levels are okay and the antibiotics are working. Are you all right alone up there in the cabin?"

Laura looked at Ben and nodded. "I'm fine, don't worry about me. You stay here as long as you can. We'll come back to visit."

Jim wheezed and closed his eyes, dozing. Laura released his hand to leave, when Jim pulled her closer. He opened his eyes and she bent her head down to him. "He's your match," he whispered and shut his eyes again.

"What did Mr. B say to you as we left?"

"Just that you were my match. Funny, isn't it, what old men can say?" Ben squeezed her hand then focused on the road ahead. Doctor Britton didn't live far from the Albany Medical Center.

They moved from the landscaped streets of Albany toward the seedier section of the city. It wasn't quite the ghetto, but getting there. Ben pulled up next to a small bungalow. It looked forgotten. Bushes grew up in front of the windows and tree limbs scattered about the tiny front yard. Trash cans rolled alongside of the house under a sagging car port.

"Are you sure this is it?" Laura looked around the decrepit neighborhood.

"It doesn't look like much for a doctor, except maybe one who's been out of work for years because he lost his license from medical malpractice."

They walked down the cracked walkway together toward the door. Kids playing in the street stopped to stare at them.

"Are you nervous?" Ben looked down at her.

"I am," Laura admitted. He took her hand and she felt his need to protect her. She felt safe knowing he was there to watch over her, for now. Yet, she also sensed some ambivalence from him. His clear thoughts didn't always come through. Earlier, she sensed his internal conflict about committing to her, but he didn't leave. She had to have faith he would continue to stay.

She squeezed his hand and rang the doorbell. They waited some time and rang the doorbell again. This time they heard shuffling. An elderly man with a thick head of white hair opened the door and squinted at them.

He leaned on the door frame and adjusted his glasses, looking puzzled. "Can I help you?"

Laura gripped Ben's hand harder. "Doctor Britton?"

"No one's called me that in years. What do you want? I can't afford to buy anything today."

"We're not selling anything."

The old man stared at Laura and raised his eyebrows. "Well, then?"

"I'm Laura Armstrong. You delivered me in Coopersville. My mother's name was Sarah."

The old man's eyes grew wide and he leaned harder on the doorway. His hand shook as he pointed a finger at her.

"Sarah," he whispered, more to himself. "Yes, I remember."

"Can you tell me about her?"

Doctor Britton's eyes narrowed. "What do you want to know?"

A musty, sour smell drifted from the inside of the house.

"I was raised by the Armstrongs in Coopersville, but don't have any details about my natural mother except her name and the fact she'd been a runaway. Can tell me about her?"

"Ask the Armstrongs. I don't know any more than you."

"I can't. My adoptive parents are dead."

"Well, sorry about that but I can't help you."

"Listen, Doctor Britton, can we just come in and speak with you?" Ben moved closer to the doctor. "Any detail could help us."

"And who are you?"

"A friend who wants to help."

"Well, I don't want visitors and I don't want to talk." Doctor Britton slammed the door shut.

Ben banged on the door, but Laura pulled at his coat. "What now? You can't force him to talk to us."

"Oh, yes, I can. You've spent years wondering and now we're here. The decent thing for him to do is give you some peace."

"I read his mind, Ben. He's hiding something. Also, he's afraid of me. But why?"

"I don't know but we're sure as hell going to find out."

Ben continued to bang on the door. The kids stopped playing in the street again to watch him. A face peered out from a neighbor's window next door.

"Ben, stop, please?"

She felt rage rising inside him, coming from somewhere deeper than this disheveled old man. It came from far in his past, a place he wouldn't share with her.

And then there was this old man here. It didn't seem possible he could be the one who pulled her from her mother's womb. She had hoped it would be a kind doctor, one noble and good, but he wasn't.

"Old man, open the door," Ben shouted. "Or I'll have the IRS here on your doorstep."

"What do you mean?" Doctor Britton's muffled words came from behind his door.

"Tax evasion on a large scale equals jail time." Ben lowered his voice. "Is that what you want?"

The door opened and Ben pushed his way in with Laura behind, following the doctor into the living room. The old man shuffled to a rusty orange recliner and eased himself into it then he looked up and sighed.

"How do you know about my tax evasion?"

"I have a friend who can get information."

Laura looked around the dingy room. Newspapers and magazines were strewn about on the coffee table, couch, and floor. A plastic microwave dinner tray sat on the one end table with bits of dried food stuck in it. She wrinkled her nose at the rancid smell enveloping the place. She didn't want to sit down. Everything was tinged with a layer of dirt and kitchen grease.

The doctor didn't offer them a seat so Ben grabbed two fold-out metal chairs from the kitchen adjoining the living room and placed them before the doctor.

"Go ahead, just make yourself at home." The doctor waved his hand.

"When you've told us what we want to hear, we'll leave, right Laura?"

Laura nodded.

"What do you want to know?"

"Everything," Laura said. "Tell me how you met my mother and what happened the night I was born."

"Your mother was a runaway. No one knew where she came from or her last name. She wouldn't say. She just showed up one day at the Methodist Church and your folks took her in. They soon discovered she was pregnant so your parents brought her to me. I happened to be the one practice in town then, except for Doctor Anna who just did house calls. Your mother grew quite large. We thought she might be bearing twins but we never heard more than one heartbeat. Such a young, lovely thing she was." He sighed and looked down massaging his hands, then pushed himself up out of the chair.

"It's only 10:00 a.m. but under the circumstances I'm having a drink." He didn't bother to offer one to Ben and Laura, and got himself a glass and bottle of whiskey from a small cabinet. He poured it three-quarters full and carried it back to his chair. Ben frowned.

"I'm eighty-five years old and don't give a hoot what you think, young man. I was once a good doctor, a good husband, a good man. So wipe that look off your face." He took a long sip and closed his eyes.

"And what kind of looks did your patients give you after you killed their babies because you were drunk?" Ben shot out.

Doctor Britton choked down his mouthful of whiskey and slammed the glass on the end table next to him. "Who the hell do you think you are coming here and accusing me of things you know nothing about?"

"Did you kill my mother?" Laura said.

Ben and Doctor Britton both looked at her.

"You look so lovely, just like your mother." Doctor Britton gazed at her.

"You didn't answer my question."

"No, I didn't kill her. Not intentionally, anyhow. And I wasn't a drunk then. I became one after your mother died." He wiped his nose with a dirty tissue pulled from his shirt pocket, and took a long drink. The glass shook in his hand. He spilled some on his already-stained shirt and wiped it away with the back of his gnarled hand.

"What happened the night I was born?"

The doctor laughed but a cough cut off his raspy cackle. "What happened? Something strange all right." He tapped his foot on the ground. "We had a big thunderstorm. Your mother came to me, secretly, late at night in labor. The Armstrongs didn't know."

"Why wouldn't she tell them?"

"I told her not to. But I'll get to that in a minute. The baby wouldn't come out. It was so large. Your mother fought and fought but it was just too big. I knew she would bleed to death if I didn't get the baby out."

"You mean, *me* 'the baby', right? I wasn't large though. My parents said I was small, only five pounds."

The doctor snorted. "Yes, dearie, you were small. It was the other one that was so large. The mutant. Or the devil as the nurse called it." He gloated at her as she stared at him.

"Another baby?" Laura bit her lip in silence, her mind racing. "But you said she wasn't carrying twins."

"That's what we thought, yes. Our technology was different back then and the one baby was so large he hid his twin. We couldn't detect the second heartbeat that was you, Laura. Your twin came out first. A male monster weighing in at twelve pounds. A freak. A hideous thing. He was what killed your mother, not me. He ripped her so badly with his size she bled to death."

"Why didn't she have a caesarean if the baby was so large? She should have been in a hospital down here in the city. They must have performed those back then," Ben said.

Laura still sat in silence, trying to grasp the idea she had a twin brother out there. She wondered where he was, how he grew up.

"I wasn't allowed to take her to a hospital. Too many witnesses and there would be a record of it."

"What are you talking about?" Ben leaned in closer to the doctor. "Why *wouldn't* there be a record of the baby?"

"Because I was paid not to tell, you see? Are you getting it now?" The doctor raised his voice and finished his drink. "The government came to me and this nurse. She died years ago. A difficult woman. Holier than thou. Anyway, the government heard of this girl's virgin birth story and had an interest in it, for whatever reason. They wanted her baby. This government man offered us a fortune to deliver the baby, give it to them, and keep our mouths shut. So we did. And that's why we swore your mother to secrecy when delivery time came. We scared her enough so she wouldn't talk to anyone. It was easy because she took some sort of vow of silence anyways. We wanted her to come alone when she went into labor."

The doctor twisted his glass in his hand, staring through it. "She only talked to us twice during the entire delivery. It was all so perfect until we found out there were two of you. So we decided one would go to the government and one to the Armstrongs." He got up and refilled his glass, tottering back to his seat. The drink sloshed out on his shirt but he didn't bother wiping it off this time.

"What did she say?" Laura almost shouted at him.

"Who?"

"My mother, Sarah. You said she spoke. What did she say?"

The old man scratched his red nose covered in varicose veins. "First, I remember her screaming, 'don't let me see it'. She must have known it would be a freak. Then when the baby was crowning she said, 'but if it's a girl name her Laura'."

"What was wrong with the other baby?" Ben took Laura's hand. She held it limply, staring at the floor in a daze. "Why'd the nurse call him the devil?"

"He was an ugly thing. He had pale, white skin. You could see his blue veins beneath it and a bulging forehead. But the strangest part of it was his pod-like fingers and yellow eyes. He was a mutant with deformed genes."

Laura jumped up from her chair, knocking it over, and stood in front of the doctor. Another vision came to her. The one from her dreams. The strange person also with pod-like fingers and yellow eyes.

"Where is he? Where is my brother?"

The doctor flinched at her outburst and shook his head. "I don't know. And I don't care. That monster should've been dropped on his head. But then you came out after. Like a miracle! What a surprise it was to find you. We were supposed to switch the one baby born that night with a stillborn and tell the Armstrongs the baby died. We'd been given a stolen dead baby fresh from the Albany Medical Center morgue, courtesy of our U.S. government, but after discovering you we didn't need it so we buried it out back in the storm."

Ben stood up. "You're disgusting. You killed Laura's mother because you didn't get her to a hospital where she could have survived. Then you were paid to sell a human life and go on to kill innocent babies with your addiction. How can you live with yourself?"

Doctor Britton spat out a brittle laugh that turned into a hacking cough. He took another drink. "It wasn't human, that thing. And this." He shook his glass at them. "This is how I live with myself. Why do you think I turned to alcohol and drugs? But delivering Laura here was my saving grace. If she hadn't been there to save me from what I did, I would have killed myself long ago." His face sagged and he put his drink down on the edge of the end table. The glass teetered and fell on the floor, splashing whiskey up his leg. Tears rolled down his wrinkled face.

"You should have killed yourself, old man," Ben said. "You don't deserve to live."

Doctor Britton cried harder, soaking his whiskey-stained shirt.

"I am *not* your saving grace," Laura said to the doctor, bent over in the recliner. She felt no pity for him, just anger. "Now where is my brother? You must know where they took him? Tell me."

"I don't know. We delivered him to the man waiting outside and kept his birth secret."

"What man?"

"I don't know his name." Doctor Britton closed his eyes. "I just called him the man in black."

Ben shook the doctor's shoulders but his head drooped to the side. "Come on, old man, wake up! What did he look like? Tell us!" Ben shook him again and then let go. He slumped back in the chair. "Forget it. We'll have to come back. He's passed out."

"Could it really be *our* man in black?" Laura looked at Ben.

"I don't know but let's get out of here."

They couldn't leave the dank house quick enough and hurried to the car outside. Ben started to drive away when a hand clamped down on his shoulder. He jumped, braking hard. Laura screamed. They both turned around fast, Ben with his fist ready to hit.

The man in black stared back at them from the back seat with his bright green eyes.

CHAPTER 23

X-10 reclined in the white Chevy on the side of the country road. Since escaping from his prison he had driven for hours through the night into the early morning hours. He headed north, using his senses to guide him toward the girl. He had to stay off the major roads so he meandered through the mountains of rural Virginia. As dawn came the car sputtered and he pulled off onto a back road. By now the facility must have found the dead bodies of Bjord and the security guard and there would be a secret high alert put out to capture him.

He wriggled his enormous body deeper in the seat. He wasn't used to wearing clothes and they rubbed painfully at his pale skin. It had been no trouble at all killing that bulky, slow Norm. When X-10 stood before him in the open elevator at 3:30 a.m., the fat security guard stared at him in disbelief. Before he could call the alarm, X-10 lunged at him, breaking his neck in one mechanical crack. X-10 took the man's clothes, wallet, and car keys and bolted for the door. The pants and sleeves were too short but wide enough to encase his bulk in comfort.

X-10 recalled the moment he rushed out the door, and stopped. He had been overwhelmed by the open space of night that enveloped him. The wind blew around his body pressing into him with a soft, cool tickle. An owl hooted in the trees nearby. Wild smells invaded his nose. After living in the same damp, concrete cell day in and day out for years it felt intoxicating. He breathed in the cool autumn air, rich with scents of dying leaves, wet earth, and wood. He had no idea the world could offer so many delights.

Regaining his sense of urgency to flee, he pressed the knob on Norm's key chain. He was elated to find it beeped and located the guard's car. He had never seen a car in real life, only in books. Here there were dozens, sitting shiny and colorful in the parking lot. He opened the door and squeezed himself into the sedan. More smells filled his nose with leather and vinyl. Not as exciting as outside, but still new and thrilling to him.

He had read how to drive and within a few seconds gripped the wheel and shot off with his foot to the floor. Power surged through him. He liked it. But the car ran out of gas and now wouldn't start. He had passed gas stations in the early morning light, but didn't want any humans to see him. They could turn him in and send him back to the facility. He would never go back.

The front seat was strewn with banana peels, apple cores, pretzel bags, and a bottle of cherry juice. He had gorged his entire trip and now dozed in a state of fullness. It was all he found when he raided Bjord's food supply before escaping. He needed the nourishment after two days of fasting and now, after a nap and food, he felt energized.

He relaxed and let his mind soar north to where his prey waited. There was the girl and her lover inside a house talking to an old man. He hated her for being so free to live the life she wanted. To find a mate. To roam free at her will. Now that he'd experienced freedom for the first time he was greedy for every new experience.

He soared in closer to the house and picked up snatches of their conversation. This was the doctor who sold him to the government. This was the man who sent him to live out his life under the hands of Bjord as his prisoner and science experiment. Rage grew inside X-10 as he listened. He smashed his fists on the dashboard. Then the girl and her lover left the house. X-10 decided the time had come for more revenge. He would have a little fun here first. Then he would continue on foot.

Doctor Britton opened his eyes. They felt gritty and his mouth was dry. He swallowed. It tasted stale and metallic. His whiskey glass spun on the floor as his foot hit it and he remembered Ben and Laura. He looked around. He was alone. *Good riddance.* He didn't need reminders of his past. Seeing how lovely the girl was made him feel more guilt about his part in the whole mess. He gagged with self-loathing and forced down the acid gurgling in his throat. He wondered what did happen to that hideous baby boy. He never cared to know before. He wanted to forget.

And he had forgotten how soft and pretty the girl, Sarah, was until seeing her daughter. His hardened heart ached a little to feel that way again. He had also forgotten love since his wife left him years ago, after his drinking became an addiction. He had not been a pretty drunk.

Water. He needed a drink of water. He pushed himself up from the chair when something shoved him back down. It must be the whiskey. It still had a hold over him. He shook his head and tried again to stand up. This time something pushed on his head. It felt like enormous hands squeezing his skull, the fingers wrapped around from one side to the other. He shrieked and thrashed his arms, but the hands held him there.

"What is this?" Doctor Britton screamed and the hands let him go. He fell back in the chair when sharp pain shot through his body. Something was crushing him. A giant weight pushed down on his chest and stomach. The pain intensified. He tried to move his arms but something held them down. He kicked his legs only to feel teeth sink into his right leg. He watched his shirt and pants shred from some unseen attacker.

As he opened his mouth to scream again, a fist was shoved into it so large he could not bite down to fight back. He wriggled his head from side to side, feeling faint from the pain pulsing through him. Tears streamed down his face as this invisible monster attacked him. The weight lifted some. He heard a voice in his head as clear as if the person was speaking in front of him.

Why did you sell me? Your greed killed me, old man. I could have had a home. I could have belonged.

The doctor stopped struggling, resigned to his seat of terror. He tried to comprehend what the voice meant. The fist withdrew from his mouth but hands still held him down.

"I don't know who you are," he sobbed. "Leave me alone."

You lie. Stupid human. Why did you save the girl and not me?

Then through the pain and fear Doctor Britton recognized who he was. "The monster baby! Are you dead? The devil?"

None of those. And you'll wish you were dead soon.

"The girl. She just left. She's your sister. Go after her. Leave me alone." He moaned and slumped over.

No! Not a sister. A traitor. Just like you, Doctor.

"No one would have wanted you. Freak! Mutant!" Fingers closed around his throat choking off his scream. He flung his body about the chair to escape, but the fingers pressed into his neck. His eyes opened wide and he scratched at the invisible being attacking him.

Then he gave in. It was time to pay for his sins.

X-10 hovered over the doctor's body. His anger drained away and he felt relief. He returned his mind to his body in the car. He needed to rest before continuing north. Travelling with his powers expended much energy, but he needed to leave the car and hide out. He walked into the woods, breathing deep of life all around him. After heading half a mile into the woods away from the dirt road, he found a hollow and lay down on the ground covering himself in a mound of leaves.

Within a few minutes his body heat warmed him inside his cocoon and X-10 slept. It was his turn to dream of the girl. He chased her as he always did, toying with her before he shredded her throat. But this time she stopped running and turned to walk back toward him. He stopped in his tracks, amazed she would do that when she knew he would kill her.

"Charlie, come with me. I know what you are. We are the same."

He shook his head, wanting to hate her. How did she know he wanted to be called Charlie? His mission had been to kill her. It had always been so. If it changed now, what would he do? What would he become?

"Don't give in to hate."

"What do you know about hate?"

"I know hate. And it's short lived. Love lives forever." She held out her hand. "Come."

"No!" He rushed toward her but she disappeared and he was left alone, as he had always been.

CHAPTER 24

The man in black pulled his full body up from the floor of the backseat and put his hand up in peace. His enormous expanse blocked the light from the back window. Ben put his fist down. Laura just stared at the man and held Ben's hand tight.

"Just drive." The man in black took his hand off Ben's shoulder.

"Who are you? Why are you here?" Laura was held captive by this man's bright green eyes. It had been eight years since she last saw him when her parents died.

"I'm not driving anywhere until you explain everything," Ben demanded.

Laura felt fear wrapped around Ben tight. She wasn't afraid though. She felt calm as if this man here could finally answer all her questions.

She squeezed Ben's hand to reassure him. "It's okay. Do as he says."

The man in black nodded. "Head out of the city and I'll explain."

Ben still didn't move.

"Don't you think I would have killed you already if I wanted to?" The man in black fixed his gaze on Ben's face. "I'm here to help. The time has come."

"First, tell us your name."

"Felix," he said in a gruff voice, offering no last name.

Ben nodded and turned around to pull out on the road. He retraced his steps through Albany. Laura remained turned around staring at this enormous. She wanted to memorize every detail, afraid he could disappear any moment.

The man's thick eyebrows hung low across his lined forehead as he peered down at Laura. "It was a spaceship that crash-landed at Coopersville Lake almost thirty years ago. You were right to think so."

She nodded, wondering how he knew she thought that. She was certain now it was him who left the mysterious notes.

"It came from the planet named Elyon."

"How did these beings from Elyon get here Felix? And how is it possible they can reach us?"

The man in black didn't answer at first. He just looked at Laura as if trying to decide what piece of information to give her. "It's possible. They're a civilization that has had advanced technology for thousands of years, not the mere decades we have. The planet Elyon is located six million light years away. Do you know what a light year is?"

"I think so…it's a really long distance traveled across space in one year, right?"

"Distances too far for us to comprehend. Light travels nearly two-hundred thousand miles per second, so the distance across just one light year is six trillion miles. I know it's difficult to grasp how far away Elyon is at six million light years. It's a galactic distance."

"But, how could these beings from Elyon travel so far and arrive here alive?"

"Because they've discovered how to operate on a non-physical plane, unlike us on Earth. They travel great distances throughout the universe by speeding up time. Time is relative and can be speeded up or slowed down. To them, travel is measured by time not distance. Elyons travel to Earth from their doorway to ours in an instant. They do it through mind power not physicality. It's a science humans can't understand because there's no science like it on Earth. We use terms like black holes and wormholes to explain this travel, but again, that is on a physical plane and they don't exist. Are you following this?"

"It's unbelievable." Ben shook his head.

"Yes, because it's not part of our reality here on Earth and may never be. We may cause our own extinction before we become so evolved."

"How can you know all this?" Laura was entranced by his words. She wanted him to talk on and on.

"The spaceship landed and the government came in to clean it up—and cover it up, and I was part of that project. We had some damage control to do, but it was a rural area and fairly contained. The spaceship hit so hard and fast most of it was buried beneath the earth. We told the public it had been a meteorite with fluctuating levels of radiation in it and due to safety reasons the government would buy out the cabin residents around the lake and crash site. So we did and then closed off the area."

Felix paused as Ben braked to avoid a cat. Houses became further apart as they headed into the country and the landscape took on a lonely look of near-naked trees and brown fields.

"There was the old man up above the lake who wouldn't sell, but after a while the government left him alone," Felix continued. "They figured he would be no trouble at all. It all made perfect sense what we told the public. People were simpler back then. They still believed the government had their best interests at heart." He looked out the window with a deep frown. "I sure as hell never believed that."

"Whether this crazy story is true or not, I want to know why you've you been watching us both all these years," Ben demanded.

"Keep driving and I'll tell you everything. Eventually make your way back into the city."

Ben continued to drive as Laura gripped his right hand. He sped faster down a curvy road that flattened off near the bottom of a valley. Coopersville Mountain loomed large over them as they followed the road alongside its giant shadow.

"Stop," Laura said. "I need some fresh air. I feel nauseous. Can we pull over to that pond? There's a road on the right heading to it."

"Fine," Felix agreed. "But make it quick."

Ben pulled off onto a dirt road. They bumped along for a hundred feet and he stopped the car. Laura got out first and headed toward a lopsided picnic table on the edge of the pond. She sat down and took deep breaths to push the sick feeling away, looking around her. The pond shone like a liquid crystal before them. Felix followed her, carrying a large duffel bag he pulled out of the back seat.

"What's in the bag?" Ben pointed at Felix.

"Some basics."

Ben grabbed it from him and rifled through it. He pulled out clothes, toiletries, water, and at the bottom, a handgun. Ben placed it on the picnic table.

"Basics, huh?"

"Yes, for my job. It's a Glock. That one, I brought for you. This is mine." He pulled one out from behind his back. Ben jumped back a bit and Laura placed her hand on his arm.

"I've never used a gun," she said, looking at the matte black metal sharply outlined against the white paint-peeling picnic table.

"The Glock is a good firearm, accurate and easy to control during rapid-fire drills. It's a good choice for beginner and advanced shooters. It's known for not malfunctioning." Felix looked at Laura. "That could mean life or death."

Felix picked up the gun and handed it to Laura, but she wouldn't take it. Felix turned it toward Ben, who nodded and tucked it down the back of his jeans, first checking to make sure the finger trigger safety was on.

"Feel better now? I am on your side, you know."

"I hope so," Ben said. "We're gonna need it."

"Maybe, but I won't be using it," Laura said. "I hate guns."

"I will," Ben said.

Felix watched them with his arms crossed. Laura grabbed Ben's arm and leaned into him. "I don't want a gun in the cabin," she whispered.

"Laura, it'll be fine. I want to protect you."

"I've seen what guns can do."

Ben took her hand. "I'm not going to let anything bad happen to you, do you understand?"

"It's not me I'm worried about. It's you. I don't want to lose you."

"You won't, I promise."

Laura nodded as a picture flashed before her eyes and she gripped his hand harder. It was of Ben and Felix together.

"What is it?"

"I see you and Felix," she said, staring through him. "You're tied to a rock, naked, and Felix is cutting ropes that bind you. Now it's gone. Everything is black…wait, now I see a fire. You're standing over a bed. It's engulfed in flames. You're so young. You don't know what to do. Why are you just standing there?"

Ben drew in a sharp breath and let go of her hand. "It was a long time ago."

"What happened to you?" Laura sought questions with her eyes, but he shied away from her and stared at the trees. Felix stood with his hands in his pockets, still staring at them. Burnt orange and tarnished yellow leaves swirled around him in contrast to his black jeans and jacket.

"Now is not the time." Ben moved toward Felix.

For the first time since meeting her, she could tell he didn't want to touch her. He was afraid of her seeing inside him. Felix's breadth hung over Laura as he watched her and Ben. He appeared larger than life like some superhero caricature in a cartoon. In a way, he reminded her of the enormous, dark man in her dreams she couldn't see. But she had to believe Felix came here to help them. He gave them a gun. He warned her before to use her powers to save herself. Laura moved closer to Ben, whose thoughts had gone dark on her.

Felix turned too pace along the pond's edge. His bulk shifted in his taut jeans and jacket that stretched across his massive chest and back. Laura shivered in her coat as a gust of wind sent leaves flying around them. A trace of warmth from the autumn sun graced her skin, and she reached her face to the sky to take it in. She then spoke to the strange man she and Ben were connected to.

"There was someone on the spaceship, wasn't there?

Felix nodded. He crossed his arms across his bulging chest and looked fierce standing before them.

"And he was alive when the spaceship hit, wasn't he?"

"Yes, but he died before we reached him," Felix said. "We spent a day digging down to reach the entrance door. When we got inside he was dead, along with the other one."

"I only see one in my dreams and he's alive." Laura touched her face. "A strange person with yellow eyes and pod-like fingers. And skin so white it looks luminescent. He's so sad. That's all I know."

"His name was Feo. He was sent here from Elyon, with a female partner, to continue their race on Earth as their planet was dying. His partner died when the crash occurred."

"Feo." The name felt strange on her tongue. "No wonder he was sad."

"Yes, but that's not what's important here. We don't have much time and I have much to explain that you need to know." Felix scanned the woods around them. A mallard and his mate glided across the pond in tranquil motion, unaware the cold winter headed their way to freeze their oasis. More trees spread far beyond the pond with sunlight dappling their half-bare branches deep into the woods.

"Well, then get to it, will you?" Ben smashed a fist on the picnic table.

"I can see you're still as hot headed as you were in Hawaii." Felix half-smiled. "It didn't serve you well there."

"I know I owe you my life, but I feel like the clock is ticking here. I want to know what's going on so we can do something. Laura believes some evil man is chasing her to kill her."

Felix looked at Laura. "She's right. He is coming."

"Is he connected to this Feo?" Laura raised her eyebrows in question.

"Yes."

"I feel connected to Feo too, somehow." She sat down on the picnic table and rubbed her hands to get warm. Ben went to her and wrapped her hands with his. Felix watched them and moved closer to them.

"You should," Felix said.

"Why should I?" Laura squeezed her eyes shut. She wanted to escape his glowing, green eyes for a moment to think. She wanted answers. For someone to tell her who and what she was.

"Because he was your father."

Laura looked up at Felix. The depths of what it meant sunk in. It was difficult to wrap her consciousness around it. Yet, in some way she felt enormous relief. It was true.

"This can't be true," Ben said, pointing a finger at Felix. "How can this be? What evidence do you have some alien life form came here from who knows where and impregnated a human? What kind of game are you playing? And why should we listen to you? You still haven't told us who you really are and why you've been watching us." He glared at Felix who just cocked his head.

"Laura knows it to be true." Felix stared at her as if waiting for affirmation. She looked at him with tears in her eyes.

"Yes. And I have a brother. We're twins."

"Yes."

"And he has special powers too."

"Yes."

"How did my mother, Sarah, become pregnant with us?"

"We could only surmise what happened the night the spaceship crashed. Your father, Feo, was injured. His partner dead. Their mission was to come to Earth and procreate here to carry on their race. It was a desperate risk to take, but they faced extinction. We know from logs decoded that their planet had been dying for some time. They were trying to locate another planet to live on."

"But we're so far away," Laura said. "There had to be another planet closer than six million light years away."

Felix sighed. "You're thinking again in a physical sense. Time is relative to them and the way they travel. It did not matter Earth was so far away. It had the best resources and quality they found to relocate. And when their mission failed Feo must have been desperate. He came in contact with a runaway girl that night and passed on his essence to her through some power. He could have impregnated her in the hopes she would carry on their race. In a sense it was a virgin birth."

"Where's my brother?" Laura stood up and touched Ben's arm. He blew out a big breath and yanked his fingers through his bangs. Laura moved toward Felix and stood beneath him. His face was craggy and sharp with heavy lines, carved over time.

"You've known him all along. He's coming for you, right now."

"What do you mean? That sounds sinister," Ben said.

"It is," Felix replied. "He is the one coming to kill you, Laura. And I believe *you* are the one person who can stop him."

CHAPTER 25

Laura tried to process all Felix had told her. "How can you know all this?"

Felix stared at her, his fierce eyes burned deep into hers. The longer she stared the more hypnotized she became. She felt a wave of feeling pour off him and roll over her. She didn't recognize it at first, but then she did. It was desire, but not lustful. A desire to feel whole with her as a partner, yet there was a touch of melancholy. It was as if he knew it would never happen and resigned himself to just yearn. She didn't know what to make of that.

"There was another spaceship that landed fifty-two years ago from the same planet. That one landed in the foothills of Virginia. Another set of aliens from Elyon. Only these didn't die right away. The government used them for experiments. Sick experiments, involving genetic testing and surgeries. Cruel things were done to them, before they finally died along with the humans they were tested with. That's what our lovely government does."

"Why were humans tested with them?"

"They wanted to see if their alien seed could be planted into a human female, impregnate her, and have her give birth naturally. It worked, but all three women they impregnated as paid test subjects died in childbirth along with the babies. The babies were too large to come out naturally. The mothers bled to death and the babies suffocated. All except one."

The wind whipped up in gusts. Laura moved into Ben's side. He held her tight to him. The cold didn't seem to affect Felix. He stood there, still as rock, overlooking the pond. The sky darkened as the afternoon crept toward evening. Laura felt faint. They hadn't eaten since breakfast except some nuts in the car.

"Let's go now," she said. "I need to eat. It's been hours since we last ate. You can tell us more in the car."

Felix grabbed his bag and strode back to the car, ahead of Ben and Laura. They trudged back through fallen leaves. "Head back into the city and find a drive-thru restaurant," he instructed as they got back in the car.

Ben eased down the dirt road and turned onto the main paved road, back the way they came.

"What happened to the baby that lived?" Laura turned around from the front seat to face Felix.

"He also became a science experiment. He was raised in a secret facility where he was prompted to show the scientists all the amazing things he could do. Things such as foresee the future and demonstrate his strength. They gave him rewards of food and books and movies. All he wanted to do was go outside and play with other children. But he was not allowed. Eventually he grew up. They trained him to be a government agent, tracking his whereabouts at all times."

"How do you know all this?"

There was a long silence in the car.

Felix stared at Laura with a look of pain on his face. "Because *I* am that man."

Laura now understood his melancholy. No one spoke for a long moment.

"I don't understand all of what's happening here or why it's happening," Ben finally said. "But if it matters, I'll protect Laura no matter what."

Felix looked over at Ben, his eyes reflected the afternoon sun streaking in through the window. "I'm counting on it."

"We're meant to be together for some reason, aren't we?" Laura touched Felix's coat.

"Yes."

"And you were there the night I was born, weren't you?"

"Yes, I was there the night you and your brother were born of an alien father and a human mother. Like me. However, I was created by man from the alien race as an experiment. You, Laura, were created by an act of desperation. An act committed by a dying race seeking to carry their people on."

"You were the man who took my brother away weren't you?"

"Yes. I had been paid to switch him out with a dead baby I stole from the Albany morgue. I waited in the rain that night outside the health facility. When the nurse brought him to me I heard something. The cry of another baby. I thought there must be another baby born, perhaps a twin. So I kept watch over your town and found out about you, Laura. I needed to know if you were like me, or like your brother. I've kept your existence a secret all these years. The government used to track me, but not anymore. They know I come here still, but they think it's because I feel connected to the lake through the second spaceship that came from Elyon."

"How could you steal a dead baby?" Ben gripped the steering wheel hard. The sky grew darker above them as night approached. Dimness closed in around the car as they moved into twilight.

"I had no choice. If I refused my duties I could have been eliminated or placed back into a facility with limited freedoms. Some days, when I have jobs of a particular hideous nature, it seems like death would be a peaceful ending. But, I continue with my job. I carry on. I have to."

"Why do you have to carry on?" Laura pulled her coat around her tighter, although the heat blasted through the vents. She wished she could read his thoughts but she could only glimpse his feelings. She sensed the same jumbled feelings of conflict, dispassion, and anguish now as she did all those years ago. But there was something new within him. A sense of destiny. And hope.

"I needed to make sure you and Ben came together."

Laura looked at Ben, who glanced at her with surprise. Felix moved closer to the window, looking out over the woods they drove by. Watching. And waiting.

"There are two kinds of people from Elyon, Laura," Felix said. "We learned about these people from decoded logs from the first and second spaceships that crashed. They are Seekers and Healers. I am a Seeker and you are a Healer. First, you must know that Elyon is billions of years older than Earth. Its sun is nearly burnt out and Elyon people are dying. Food and water are scarce. Civilization there has diminished to mere survival. Elyon beings evolved to become people of great mind power, eliminating the need for many of our types of communication. They eventually evolved into these two groups. Seekers are beings that can see into the future—or seek out people."

"Like you," Laura noted.

"And your brother."

"And that's what he's doing now. Seeking me out. To kill me."

"Yes," Felix said softly. He placed his thick hand on her shoulder for a brief moment then pulled it back. "But it's also a skill used to do good. It can be used to find lost loved ones, criminals, or natural resources. Seekers also have superhuman strength, humans would say. They can be impassionate beings without the evolved array of emotions humans have. Seekers have evolved beyond feelings and emotion to rely on facts and logic, although they are not without empathy for others."

Laura nodded. What he said about himself was true. She had sensed it long ago and sensed it still. Dusk had now settled in and shadows stretched across the inside of the car. Ben turned the car lights on. The road slowly became more populated with houses as he neared Albany.

A sad smile played across Felix's face as he gazed at her and spoke in a low voice. "As a Healer, you have much more power than I. You have the power to move objects and look into the minds of others to see their thoughts and feelings. More amazing is that you have the power to heal, to bring life back from near death, to give relief to pain. You also have a great capacity for love. This is what enables you to carry on after great tragedy. It is a trait many are without and why there are so many lost people in this world." Felix looked at Ben then in the rear view mirror.

"And what about my brother? What is he and where has he been all these years? Why does he hate me so much?"

"Your brother is a dangerous mix. He is a Healer like you, but also a Seeker. This is a unique combination, a mutation we call it. From Elyon records we found there are a small percent of them born with both of these abilities." He stared at her now with an intensity that scared her.

"Why a dangerous mix?" Ben looked at Felix in the rearview mirror.

"Because their mutation also includes a high testosterone level with a predisposition toward rage and hate. Add this to the fact he can seek out others, see into the future, move objects, and heal. This all makes for a volatile and dangerous personality. He has no remorse, no consideration for human life. He does not use his healing powers to heal, but to kill. He is what we call a Destroyer. It has not helped that his upbringing fed into his hatred. The Destroyer gene these people carry may lay dormant inside them forever, unless it's triggered by hate. And that's what happened to your brother. He grew up in the same facility I did. He killed many people and they discarded him to the basement. He has lived out his days there in a cell with an old, has-been scientist to care for him. One who still uses him as a science experiment."

"And he is there, now?" Pity surged through Laura for her twin, isolated and forgotten. But fear of him also crept into her. He sounded like a monster created by his genes and environment.

"No, he escaped the facility last night and now seeks you out, Laura. We have a few days until he reaches us. I have seen it. Now is the time to face this enemy. You can face him now or keep running forever. He will never stop looking for you."

A chill settled in Laura's heart sending goose bumps along her skin. "Why does he want to kill me?"

"He's drawn to you because he knows you and he are connected to one another. And he hates you for that. He also hates the idea that you have a life of freedom and pleasure. And he has sought to destroy your life." Felix paused and bent his head, speaking so softly that Laura had to strain to hear him. "It was him who burned your house down and killed your parents. He killed Moe and he entered the body of your co-worker to kill your colleagues. He tried to kill your friend, Jim Barrens, once too in the orchard."

Laura closed her eyes to block out his words. Ben's fingers pressed into her arm and it was the only thing that grounded her as anger and sorrow stormed through her in a wave swell she didn't know how to stop. She hugged her stomach and rocked to quell the intense feelings shooting through her.

All of the tragedies in her life were connected, and here she was hearing about it from the man who'd been watching her all her life. The man she first saw when she was seven years old. It was on that day her mother, Fanny, almost died and Laura healed her. She felt an empty feeling in the pit of her stomach. Had her brother tried to kill her mother then too? Fanny had gone on to die anyways. Was fate telling Laura something? Maybe it was fate her mother should die then. Could fate be changed?

She took deep breaths to slow her racing heart. "Why doesn't he seek you out too, Felix, and kill you if you are watching out for me?"

"He can't see me as I am not tempered by emotion, therefore I'm protected. I'm safe from his seeking powers."

"So why me?" Ben cleared his throat. "Why do Laura and I need to get together? And why've you been watching us all these years?"

"At first I just watched Laura," Felix said. "I knew she was from the same planet as me. We were connected. I needed to know what powers she had."

"I was eleven when I saw you in the woods and you said you needed to know what I was," Laura whispered, looking into his eyes. They burned brighter in the rising darkness crowding into the car. "My whole life I didn't know what that meant. Now I know. I am only half-human. Half-alien."

The realization hit her with a physical force as she said it aloud. She had been so absorbed by Felix's story her mind couldn't process the reality. She looked at Ben and felt a deep pain in her stomach, twisting up into her heart. How could she be with Ben when she wasn't all human? A freak. That's what she was. It sounded like her brother was one too. Ben could have any woman. Why would he want an alien one? The word alien conjured up two-headed beings with tentacles. Strange monsters, evil and hideous.

She looked at her arms, her legs. She touched her knees. She hugged her breasts. She couldn't be hideous and evil. She was human. She was a woman. Ben had shown her last night. All this went through her in a second.

"Human to me," Ben said, with a tight smile.

"Half-human. Yes," Felix said. "Just like me. Just like your brother. Half-human, half-Elyon."

"So why did you start watching me too?" Ben reached for Laura's hand. She sensed he didn't care what she was. But she did.

"Because I saw into the future. I saw a healthy baby boy with special powers who was half-Elyon, half-human. *Your* baby. A baby who would grow to save our race. And so I sought you both out through the years to ensure you would survive and meet. And I can see all is going well from your night together. It happened faster than I thought."

Laura let go of Ben's hand and turned back to face Felix, both hands gripping the seat back. "What are you talking about?"

Felix looked at her with his green eyes fixed on hers. "It's destiny. You and Ben are meant to procreate and have a successful match as breeders to continue the Elyon race and our powers. It's our one hope to continue our race here on Earth."

"Is that what I am to you? Just a breeding machine to keep this alien race going?" For a moment Laura hated Felix.

"No, never." Felix sighed and his face sagged. "You are a miracle, Laura. And now you have a chance to make miracles happen. You and Ben are a promise."

Laura put her face in her hands and shook her head, willing herself not to cry. She didn't want to look at Felix or Ben. She just wanted them to disappear for now. She wanted to run. She felt sick processing the fact she could be half-human and she was designated the sole person to carry on this alien line. She turned back around and sank into her seat.

Ben stared at the road ahead but she heard his thoughts loud and clear. He was thinking about that morning making love to her, unprotected. And now what if she was pregnant? She had asked him to stay that first night. Could he stay if it was forever? His final question burned in her mind. *But do we even have the promise of forever?*

"I don't know, Ben." Laura answered him aloud. He looked startled and turned his attention back to driving.

Felix remained silent, a guardian from the backseat.

CHAPTER 26

They reached the outskirts of Albany and strip malls popped up with restaurants and stores.

"There." Felix pointed at a fast food chicken joint. "Go through that one."

Ben pulled in to the drive-thru restaurant and ordered them all grilled chicken sandwiches, fries, and lemonade. Not the healthiest meal, but they needed something to go on. Laura felt a headache growing and hoped it was just due to lack of food. They ate their food in silence.

"Just where am I heading to?" Ben balanced his sandwich on his lap as he steered the car back on the road.

"Turn left at the light and go down a few miles." Felix stared out the window.

Ben crumbled up his food wrapper and shoved it in the drive-through bag. "All these years you've been watching us, making sure we survived to come together?"

Felix nodded.

"You rescued me in Hawaii, so why not from my abusive foster father?"

Laura sipped her lemonade, images fresh in her head of Ben being tied to a rock and standing before a burning bed. He hadn't opened up to her about these events. Then she grew angry as she thought of this man knowing her loved ones would die and doing nothing about it.

She turned around in her seat to face Felix. "And you left me notes warning me of this man coming and to use my powers, but you never showed up to rescue my parents or Moe or Renee. Why? Couldn't you have stopped him?" Laura's voice rose louder. "If you can see into the future and know these things then you could have done something! But you just let them all die. Why?"

Felix sat still with no trace of expression on his face. "Because as a Seeker, my privilege of seeing into the future also comes with the law I must not interfere with the future unless it's for a greater good. If I had, the course of your life might have changed and your brother would keep coming. He wouldn't stop. He would keep killing those around you to torment you and eventually kill you, as he plans to do now. And fate has a hand in it too. Fate seeks to re-align itself to its correct path, no matter how bad the outcome. Those that died were meant to die, at that time or another. Fate would find another way to achieve its set course."

"But you *did* interfere in my life," Ben insisted, glancing at Felix in the mirror. "You saved me from those men. Why not from my foster father?"

"Yes, I did interfere once because I saw the future. I saw those men in Hawaii would indeed kill you and then you and Laura would not meet. The survival of the Elyon people depended on your meeting. I want the Elyon people to continue. Interference then rose above the law. I must only interfere to change the course of the future if it is vital to the desired end result. This is a moral code Elyon Seekers abide by to keep order within their world. A code I have adopted and abide by. I did not interfere with your foster father because I knew you would escape and survive. This is why I did not become involved."

Ben sighed. "When did you start watching me?"

"You were fourteen years old and in foster care."

"Did you know what happened to me in those foster homes?"

"Yes."

"You saw me with Frank too, later. You were at my foster mother's funeral."

"Yes."

"You knew then what Frank did to me? Was going to do to me?"

"I did, but I also saw you escaped from that awful place and went on to survive it. I saw you after the Navy too, living in squalor and drunk in Florida."

"If you're so like God, why didn't you rescue me then? I could have drunk myself to death."

"But you didn't and I knew you wouldn't. I knew you would overcome and go on to have a successful career. Besides I would not have been able to rescue you if I could."

"Why not?"

"From that kind of evil only you could be rescued from yourself. And you did. You are stronger than you think, Ben. And I am not God. What I can do is a curse as well as a gift."

"And my family, my friends?" Laura took in Felix's massive outline against the back window now while his green eyes flickered as they passed under street lights.

"I'm sorry for your losses, Laura, but I saw you too would continue and survive these great tragedies. If I interfered it might have changed the future so your brother did reach you and kill you before I could stop it. That could not happen. We need our Elyon race to continue. I have spent years learning about them. They are a beautiful people, full of courage, talent, and love. Most are good beings. It would be a great tragedy for them to die out. I am honored to be part Elyon. I was lucky enough to grow up in a facility where I was well taken care of. I would have preferred a home, parents, siblings, but I had to accept I am a government experiment. Now it is up to you to fulfill your destiny. *Our* destiny."

Laura reached over and placed her hand on Felix's arm. He flinched when she touched him but didn't pull away.

She closed her eyes. "I see your life. Women in white coats drawing your blood. Doctors in blue playing a game with you as a boy. You're in a yellow room. It's where you sleep. You like it as it reminds you of the sun you can't see. There are toys, books, movies, games. Yes, you were taken care of but there was sadness. You wanted a normal human life. And I sense…I sense emotion."

Laura opened her eyes but didn't remove her hand. Felix placed his large hand over hers.

"Yes, I feel things but not with the intensity you do. I am a dispassionate bystander who follows the authority that created me. It's all I know, all I can do if I want to survive."

She gazed into his green eyes and felt sorry for him. Like her brother, he too was tormented, imprisoned in the cell he sprung from. Imprisoned within himself.

"Why are you here now then, if you shouldn't interfere?" Ben banged the steering wheel.

"Because Laura's brother is coming to kill her this time. There's no mistake he's after you, Laura. And he will kill us too, Ben, unless we protect ourselves."

"Does he have a name?" Laura needed to know.

"X-10. It's his project number. It's all he has ever been called."

"He never had a name," she whispered to herself.

"Don't feel sorry for him. He *is* the monster you have dreamed about, Laura. He will kill you with no remorse. He will torture you and rip out your throat too. He's done it before. And he'll enjoy doing it to you."

Laura shook her head and put her hands over her ears.

"Stop it, for God sakes," Ben yelled, hitting his fist on the dashboard. The car swerved. "Why tell her these things?"

Felix looked at him in the rear view mirror as Laura sat with tears streaming down her cheeks. "She must realize what *he* is, as she must realize what *she* is. If she doesn't then it may be her death sentence. Don't feel sorry for this being. I know what he has done. I saw into the future what torment and death he would come to cause, not only with your loved ones, Laura, but with others. He is sick and twisted and enjoys killing. He is a product of genes and environment. A concoction of rage, remorselessness, and inhuman strength."

"What about you?" She wiped her face.

"What do you mean?"

"Why don't you have children and carry on the Elyon line?"

"Because I am sterile as a result of science experiments. Besides, I can never hope to find a partner and mate as you two have done."

Laura blushed at his blunt words.

"You are our only hope. You and Ben will make a healthy perfect child. I've seen it. There's been no communication from Elyon in a long while. The planet may already be dead for all we know. I have tried to seek it out without success. It's been months since I connected with it and found Elyon beings alive."

"You can do that from here? Connect with Elyon?"

"Yes." He explained no further and turned to the window to scan the dark streets they passed. Traffic pushed around them on all sides.

"He's coming now." Laura felt it for sure.

"Yes," Felix said. "But he's still far away. He's traveling on foot now. We must prepare for our fight with him. We could all die."

"I thought you could see the future and know," Laura said.

"Yes, but events preceding can change in a second, re-directing the course of events. It can happen, unluckily so."

"Let's hope we're lucky," Ben said.

"Indeed." Felix agreed. "Laura, I'm counting on your telekinesis powers as well to fight X-10."

Laura put her head to her knees. "I don't know if I can do this."

"How is this going to end?" Ben looked at Felix.

"X-10 must die, of course. If you don't kill him he will keep killing. He'll continue his rampage until he is brought down."

Laura jerked her head up. "You want *me* to kill my own brother?"

"It's your destiny. Unluckily so."

They sat in silence as Ben drove, bumper to bumper now in rush hour traffic.

"Turn left at the light here and pull over," Felix ordered.

"Why are we stopping here?" Ben pulled over under a street lamp.

They were on a residential street with row homes.

"I must go. I'll be back, soon, when I'm needed."

"Wait," Laura cried and grabbed Felix's arm as he pulled up his duffel bag from the floor to leave. "You can't just leave us after all you've told us. What are we supposed to do now? Where do we go? And if my brother can kill from afar then he could kill us at any time."

"But he won't. I believe he has been killing those around you all these years to feed his rage against you. But he wants to kill you in person for heightened revenge. And there is nowhere to go you can hide. He will find you. You must be prepared."

"And what if we decide to take the chance of running away?" Ben demanded. "Why sit here like prey, waiting for the end? I have enough money. We can live comfortably moving from place to place for quite some time. Perhaps the FBI will catch him before he catches us."

"If you take that chance you just prolong the same outcome. Don't you want this to be over? Do you really want to live in fear all the time? And what if he tires of chasing you and seeks you out and kills you with his mind powers? Together we can fight him and end this monster and go on."

"How will we know when this X-10 is coming," Ben said. The fluorescent light from the street lamp leant a garish look to Felix, carving deeper shadows into his rugged face.

"I will know and I will be there when the time comes. The time is soon, but not today. I have things to do."

"What things could you possibly have to do?" Laura still gripped his arm. Violent images flowed from him to her, of warfare, suffering, and death. The scene disturbed her. She eased off her fingers, leaving Felix to pull his arm free.

"I need to focus on seeking out the future, immediate and long term. I need to ensure my visions are correct for now and the outcome will be the desired result. I need to be alone to do this. I have seen X-10's destruction. We need any detail of information as well that could aid us if we are not only to kill him but live afterwards. He is the one thing standing in our way of the Elyon race, *our* race, to carry on."

"So, you're saying we'll be safe tonight at the cabin?"

"Yes, as far as I can see you are safe, for now."

"We can leave. Run. Keep running," Laura pleaded.

"Again, he will find you. He will never stop. Trust me."

"Trust you?" Ben grabbed his arm. "All we know is this science fiction story you've told us without much proof. How can we trust you?"

Felix moved Ben's hand off him. Ben grabbed his jacket but Felix covered his hand mid-air with his fist, holding it steady. Ben grunted trying to move his arm but couldn't. Laura watched their struggle.

"I saved your life, isn't it proof enough you can trust me? Remember that night and what would have happened to you. I stopped it from happening, didn't I?"

Ben nodded and Felix let go of his hand.

"Laura, stay strong and work on your powers. You will need them soon. Ben, you must protect her. She must survive. Do you understand? Trust me and all will work out."

"I trust you," she said looking at him with total acceptance.

"That's good because right now, I'm all you have." Felix stepped out of the car and strode down the dark sidewalk. Where he headed she didn't know.

"We're on our own," Ben said looking at the man in black retreat into the night shadows. Felix turned a corner and was gone.

Laura took his hand. "Just for now. He said he'll come when the time is needed."

"I feel like that time of need is now."

She moved into his side, feeling his warmth and tried not to feel the same way as he pulled out onto the road.

CHAPTER 27

X-10 decided to stick to the woods and hike his way to New York. It could take days but the government had their people out there watching for him by now. He could kill a few humans if they caught him but it might be the end of him. He couldn't let that happen until he killed the girl. He crushed his hands together. He had to find her first.

It had been twelve hours since he escaped and he felt fresh now from sleeping all day under a thick blanket of leaves. He wasn't sure where in rural Virginia he was but he believed he was near the Blue Ridge Mountains in the northern part of the state. He could follow the mountains north all the way to Pennsylvania. If he picked up the Appalachian Trail he could hike fast under cover as a through-way hiker. The human authorities wouldn't think to look for him on the Appalachian Trail. He laughed at his perfect plan.

Dusk fell early in late September and it lent him the cover to be on the move. He stretched tall, shaking off the leaves. His white skin shone in the dark under the near-full moon rising. An owl hooted in soulful mourning somewhere above. He looked for it, but it disappeared in a shadowy swoop to catch its night prey. X-10 was hungry. He had to find food. He strode under the trees for a mile when he discovered the white, faded blaze of an Appalachian Trail sign. He had read hikers often left cans of food in the trail shelters. Perhaps he would get so lucky.

He turned onto the trail and moved with speed over the rough path. His eyesight was so keen he could spot roots and rocks and nimbly stride over them. He stretched his long pod fingers outward to push branches aside as he raced toward the girl. Not so long now. She had no idea she had but a few days left to live. For miles he hiked, his stomach growling with hunger. He would have to find some animal to eat soon if he couldn't find other food.

In his freedom, thoughts of beautiful Sabrina came to him, urging him on. If he'd only escaped to save her before Bjord killed her he could be with her now. Perhaps they could have made a life together, delved into the pleasure of flesh night after night. Perhaps he would not be hunting Laura. Sabrina's softness came to him and it fed his hunger. He let his hate subside as he ran through the woods, not seeing the trees but his cell full of her wondrous glow.

At first she'd been terrified upon being thrown and locked into his cell. She was a whore there to initiate a virgin, but she hadn't expected a monster.

She looked around the room then saw him in the corner. He stepped forward and she gasped, backing up into the door. She turned and pounded on it.

"Let me out! Please. It's a mistake."

She glanced back, her mouth a pink carving he yearned to touch. She was his game here in this cell for his easy taking.

X-10 stepped closer. A whiff of buttery caramel and vanilla delighted his massive nose. His gray walls held so little scent. He savored the few scratch-and-sniff perfume ads he'd found in used magazines. He breathed them over and over, imagining them caressing a female's skin. And now it did. He inhaled deeply. She faced him and pressed her back up to the door.

"No one is coming," he said. "I won't hurt you."

She shook her head violently as her wide, blue eyes darted up and down his body. She was as young as he. Large breasts pushed up from her white blouse and tan legs were exposed all the way up to her mini-skirt. Dr. Bjord did a good job finding this one on the street. X-10 had killed uglier ones than this from his mind's eye.

"What are you?" she whispered. She looked left and right but kept coming back to his face.

"Just a government experiment."

"You have yellow eyes."

"You have blue ones."

"Contact lenses?"

He shrugged, running his hands down his chest and legs. She shook her leg nervously and crossed her arms. "I want to leave."

"You can't. You're bought and paid for."

"I want my money back. It was only for an hour."

X-10 stepped closer. Deeper he breathed. Something else was in all that buttery sugar. An earthy smell of pine and bark. Her smell. She didn't shrink away this time.

He jerked his head at the camera on the wall. "He's watching us, you know."

"The old man?"

He nodded.

"You sound like a normal guy, except…"

"Normal." He liked saying that word.

"You don't look it."

He grunted.

She sighed, resigned. "Don't you have clothes?"

"They hurt my skin."

"Oh." Her face softened. Her fear was fading it seemed. "What's your name?"

He paused a moment. "Charlie."

She smiled. Her white teeth between full lips dazzled him. "That's a nice name. I'm Sabrina."

"Sabrina." He drank it in like hot chocolate. Rolled it around his mouth, warm and intoxicating.

"Why are you in here? For…hurting someone?"

"No. Scientific testing."

"That sounds awful. Am I being tested too?"

"Just me."

She looked relieved. "He said it's your first time."

X-10 nodded. He grew hard thinking about it.

She looked down and her eyes widened. "You're big."

He stood taller, feeling empowered. Her words poured over him coating him in unbearable yearning. Part of him wanted to push her down and throttle her, then bite into her soft neck and taste her insides. If she knew those thoughts she would start pounding on the door again. But part of him wanted to sink his rigid sex softly inside her and lick her smell. Could he make her want him?

No one will ever want you, the doctor said. *You're too different. A killing machine. Not all human. Unworthy.* Dr. Bjord's words burned in his brain. X-10 would prove him wrong.

Sabrina took a deep breath and walked toward him. "Okay, an hour." She placed her hands on his chest and looked up into his eyes. Her scent made him dizzy. His breaths came faster as her warmth infused him. No one had ever touched him except to plunge needles in his arm or clamp probes onto his skin. He shuddered.

"Are you afraid?" She raised her eyebrows.

He shook his head and tried to find his voice to say 'no' but only air floated out. She smiled at him then and leaned her whole body into him. He stood frozen at first then swam his broad hands through her soft locks. He tugged on them. They bounced back. Her lips touched his chest. Tingly explosions ripped through him. When she wrapped her arms around him and stroked his back he tipped his head back and moaned.

And the wind moaning through the trees snapped him back to reality.

No! Whore!

All human females were whores. They pierced your flesh and heart with need then burning pain that infused you with weakness. He grunted and ran faster leaving that night behind, replacing his need for love with his need for revenge. He discarded Sabrina as Bjord had, tore her from his mind as her limbs had been torn apart to float down the river.

The wind's moans died down and he heard another moan. He stopped to listen. There it was again. Not the sound of the wind but of a woman in pleasure. Adrenalin rushed through him, filling his massive body with a surge of anticipation and lust. And hate. Hate for having the pleasures of love be given and taken away at the whim of another, and hate for Laura who could have the pleasures of love any time.

He scanned the woods. A small tent jutted toward the moon just off the trail ahead. Two campers, making love. How romantic. How unlucky for them. How lucky for him. He stepped closer, listening to the woman call out the man's name.

"Jimmy, oh, oh. Right there, don't stop, please."

X-10 moved closer, standing a few feet from the tent. He reached his hand inside his pants and pulled out his enormous hard cock. He stroked himself, listening to the woman's cries. It didn't take him long. He spewed violently, his thick jism gushing onto dry leaves. The couple stopped. X-10 tucked his relieved cock back in his pants when he heard the man speak.

"Shh, do you hear something?"

"What is it?"

"Listen."

"I don't hear anything. Keep going, please?"

"Wait, it sounded like someone was out there."

"Just the raccoons, or something, come on. I'm getting cold, Jimmy."

"Oh yeah, well feel this."

The woman squealed and laughed as Jimmy went back to his work. X-10 stepped toward the tent, standing right outside it. In one fluid movement, he reached his hand in and grabbed Jimmy by the neck. He pulled out the man, shrieking. His hard penis glistened with the woman's juices and his pants dangled around his ankles. The woman screamed.

"Should have finished sooner, Jimmy." X-10 broke his neck in one snap with his hands and threw him in the brush.

The naked woman rushed to the door but X-10 shoved her back in. He bent down inside the tent. The woman stared at him and screamed at his gruesome figure. X-10 grinned at her as he slapped a hand over her mouth. She looked to be college age with long red, curly hair and full, bouncy breasts. He thought about ravaging her before he killed her but repulsion overcame the urge. She was a human whore, unclean and used by another.

Such a waste. He snapped her neck as he had done to Jimmy. He never knew her name. *Too bad.* He left her there spread out and ripped the tent apart looking for food. He found none inside, but did locate their food bag hanging fifty feet away in a tree. He ripped it down and gorged on nuts, candy bars, crackers, and cheese. He washed it down with their water and looked at the mess he made.

He felt satiated now and full of energy, and so he mustered his powers to dig one deep grave. It needed to be wide enough to fit both of the lovers and their gear. He sat and moved his hands to work logs and rocks to dig. In a short time it was done. He placed the tent and their other belongings in first, and then draped them over it side by side.

"So the lovers can be together in death too." He laughed long and hard.

After dumping the bodies in the grave he covered them up and continued along the trail. It could take the authorities weeks to find their graves, if they ever did, across thousands of acres of national park.

"All in a night's work," X-10 quipped to himself and raced along the trail, a candescent monster dashing under the moon toward its prey.

Laura gazed down at Mr. B asleep in the hospital bed. She had so many things to tell him but didn't want to wake him. Ben put his hands on her shoulders.

"Come on, Laura, let's head back up to the cabin and get some rest. Visiting hours are almost over. Who knows what could happen tomorrow."

She nodded. "I wanted to tell him everything. He always has such good advice. I feel lost without him."

"You have me now," Ben murmured in her ear and held her tight from behind.

"I know, but just look at him. He looks so frail and old." She trailed her fingers on his hand and kissed his cheek. "The nurse said he's still the same. What if he's just too old to recover?"

"I don't think he's lost his fight just yet, he's too feisty."

"I don't know." Laura wanted to believe it. Then something struck her. "It's been so long since I tried to heal. Do you think I could help him?"

"You have nothing to lose. You've been practicing your other powers since you returned. Maybe your healing powers can work too."

"I've got to try."

She placed her hands on Mr. B's chest. It rose and fell in an uneven rhythm, ending each breath with a wheezy exhale. She envisioned his lungs filled with fluid and in her mind drained them until they were empty. She flowed her youth into him, wishing him health and strength. She imagined his blood squeezing in repetition through his heart and pumping with a strong life force. Then she opened her eyes. His wheezing stopped. His breaths steadied.

Ben just stared at her. "You're amazing."

"I don't feel like it's my power. I feel it's something inside me guiding me."

"Perhaps you are the future. Did you ever think of that? You are what we humans can aspire to be. To find our powers deep inside and use them for good. To be better than what we are. Perhaps it's our fate the Elyon people come here. Maybe in a way they could be our salvation too."

"Perhaps." It was hard for Laura to grasp such a colossal idea, one that spanned galaxies and changed the idea of creation itself. They both looked down at Mr. B who now had a smile on his face.

"It's good to wonder that the world might become a place full of hope and peace, not evil." Laura picked up a pad and pen on the bedside table. "Just a note." She folded it and placed it next to Mr. B's hands.

Ben took her hand. "Let's go home."

The word home sounded so funny to Laura. She hadn't had a home in a long, long time. Mr. B had been her only family left to call home. And now Ben was here, calling it home as well. It seemed so unreal they could ever hope to live a normal life. What did their future hold? She took his hand. It felt so warm and strong in hers. She looked back at Mr. B, drawing his face in her brain. She didn't know if she'd ever see him again.

They drove back up the dark mountain in silence. Then the road rattled beneath them and Laura jolted awake, unaware she fell asleep. They got out in the dark by the cabin. One dismal light on the porch flickered in welcome. Beyond the pool of light the woods stood ominous as the wind wailed amongst the naked trees. Through the shadows she could see the branches swaying in a frenzied dance. All was dark below. She wondered where Felix was and when they'd see him again. She shivered in the cold and looked up, before heading inside. Somewhere her twin raced toward them.

"Look." She pointed. "A full moon."

"Nearly. There is a tiny rim missing. Tomorrow night will be the full moon."

"A night when the crazies come out."

He reached for her and hugged her in the dark and cold. They gazed at the moon overhead as it moved through the bending trees. Laura wanted to capture the moment, hold it in time. Here Ben could hold her under the moon and she could feel all was right with the world. They would be together always. She sensed Ben thinking of another night here a long ago. A night when he stood in these woods as a boy and watched a green light descend from the sky. The night his parents died. The night Laura was made. And now she was here with him.

"It's unbelievable, isn't it?" Laura whispered and leaned into him. He buried his head in her neck and kissed her warm skin.

"Yes, just like you are."

"Do you still want me?" Her voice cracked, with need and emotion.

"What do mean?"

"I'm not all, you know, real." She hid her face in his arm holding her. She wanted one more night with Ben. A night to forget she wasn't all human. Then she could say goodbye. *But just let me have one more night.*

"You are real. You're the most human person I've ever known."

"Let's go in." She pulled him inside and led him up the loft ladder. She turned on the soft bed lamp and stood before him. He waited, not moving toward her. She needed to feel in control.

"I need a shower. I feel dirty after all that happened today."

She stripped off her jacket and placed it on the chair near the bed. Ben stood still, just watching her. She undid her shirt and bra, her fingers trembling, and let them fall to the floor. Ben gazed at her pink nipples lit by the lamp's glow. She moved toward him and unbuttoned his jacket and then flannel shirt, gliding her fingers over his skin as she worked.

Ben remained still. He raised an eyebrow at her, encouraging her to go on. She slipped her jeans off and shook her head back, pulling her hands through her hair and arching her back. Ben removed the gun from his pants and placed it on the bedside table. Laura didn't say a word.

She moved toward him, unbuckled his belt and pulled down his jeans, moving over his hard penis that sprung out. She squeezed it and massaged his buttocks with her other hand. Ben moaned and closed his eyes. Laura leaned into him molding her body into his, embracing him with her arms and kissed his nipples, licking and sucking them into tiny points. Ben shuddered and held her close. She felt his heart racing against her. She grabbed him tight and let out a tiny sob.

"I need you, Ben."

"You're all woman, Laura, do you realize that? All woman to me."

She just looked at him and tilted her head, unsure what to believe. She sensed that he believed what he said, for now. And Ben wanted to prove it to her. He pulled her head up to look into his eyes. She would give him this night. It may be all they had left together. After just finding him, she may lose him.

"My woman." He crushed his lips to hers in a slow, sensuous kiss. Their tongues blended together in sweet harmony. Laura felt him hard against her groin and moaned thinking of him inside her. She pulled back and led him to the shower. He took the gun with him and placed it on the floor, within reach, then locked the bathroom door. The shower stall was oversized with room for two. When the water was hot enough they slipped out of their remaining clothes and moved together under the pouring stream. She smoothed her hands over his chest.

"I don't want to think about anything but here and now," Laura whispered, holding him close. He took the soap and smoothed it on his hands and over her body. He sought out the crevice of her buttocks, between her thighs, and the hills of her breasts. After he washed her breasts clean he licked them over and over, squeezing them together in tender, taut ridges. He found baby oil in the shower holder and smoothed it all over her body in long strokes. She shook inside, feeling a pulsing inside her come from deep below. Then he parted her legs, as if he knew, and touched her swollen bud with his finger. Her legs quaked with desire, but she stopped his slow rubbing.

"Not yet," she said, breathing heavy. Then it was her turn to wash him, and she didn't miss a spot. Laura knelt on her knees loving him with her hands and mouth. She stroked his legs and buttocks until he pulled her up. His skin slid against her in smooth peaks of pleasure. They cleaned each other from the scum they uncovered during the day.

"Laura, you drive me crazy."

He leaned her up against the wall and held her bottom and legs up high, pushing them out. She was wide open to receive him. He pushed into her deep and slow. She cried out and clung to him, her nipples rubbing across his chest as he slid in and out of her tight wetness.

His muscles flexed as he braced himself holding her. He looked so magnificent to her with his lean body moving like ripples toward her as he pushed and pulled away in a timeless rhythm. He had lissome beauty in his nakedness, like a lean lion ready to spring.

On lonely nights in her old apartment when passion rose inside her and she yearned for someone to touch her, she would finger herself to release pretending it was her lover. She pulled on her nipples imagining her lover pulling so sweetly on her breasts. And now here he moved in the flesh across her body like a dream.

"I want to see you touch yourself," Ben said, and held her still. Laura looked into his eyes and slid her hands down her breasts to rub herself. The baby oil made it slick and smooth. She was so near the edge and closed her eyes.

"Ben, don't stop moving, please. I want to feel you."

"Only if you open your eyes."

Steam filled the air as the water shot around them. Laura opened her eyes and he pushed deep inside her. She gasped as she stroked herself and Ben stroked her, deeper, pushing her into the wall, staring into her eyes. He held up her legs higher and caressed her underneath, lapping her with his thumbs, rubbing her slow and smooth with the oil that covered her. She felt a heat growing inside her to an almost painful intensity as water dripped from her everywhere.

"Oh my God, Ben!"

He held her gaze as she shrieked in orgasm, her eyes wide open, and then he let himself go, shouting out as he filled her up. They stood, leaning into the wall sliding off each other's chests, both heaving huge breaths. He finally slipped out of her and put her legs down. They clung to each other in slippery wetness, the steam billowing around them.

They dried each other off and Ben laid her down on the bed, the gun close by. He placed his hand on her hip. "You look like an angel with your hair flowing around you, just like you did the first day I met you."

"You mean when I was up in a tree?"

"Yes. You were singing away so the whole world could hear you."

"It was silly."

"No, it was refreshing."

"And now a madman is coming for us and we've no way of stopping him."

"We do. We have your powers, I have a gun, and we have Felix. I hope. I have to hope. I didn't have hope before, not for a long, long time. I forgot what it was, but you showed me, Laura."

She was silent and rolled over on her back, staring at the ceiling.

"I have a brother I've never met, who is a freak, and now I have to kill him. Where's the hope in that?" Her voice quivered and she laughed. It was all so bizarre. "No, I am the freak."

"You're not a freak. I don't know what your brother is, but you're not. We'll face this together and then we'll have our lives to go on."

"Are you sure? Everyone I love dies." She stared at the ceiling. "Why do these Elyon people exist? And does it mean there are more beings out there in this infinite universe, watching us, on their way to us? Maybe here already?

"I don't know, Laura. More questions to ask Felix. There wasn't nearly enough time today to get all the answers we needed. It's an amazing event that happened, them coming here and you're part of it." He touched her shoulder but she continued to stare at the ceiling. They lay in silence for a while listening to the wind moan in distress outside.

"The more we learn, the more questions there are," Ben said.

"I wonder if we'll ever know the full story and history of what happened here." Laura looked through the loft window at the night sky. "Up there, somewhere, millions of miles away is another planet with intelligent life. Beings loving and living and dying, just like us. Having babies, like we do. Like you and I could. Are they coming again now or is their planet already dead?"

"I don't know." She sensed Ben didn't want to think about a baby, even though they had been careless again just now. He wanted to live in this moment with her.

"If we don't want to be dead I have to use my powers against my own brother. I never met him and yet I must kill him. I first went to the crash site with Mr. B and saw my alien father, Feo, there in a vision. My brother's father, too." It felt strange to Laura, saying it out loud. "Although, I didn't know at the time who or what the strange being was."

"Now you do. But it doesn't change who you are."

"It does," Laura whispered. "It changes everything."

Ben didn't say anything.

"And what if I'm pregnant and everything Felix said is true about us creating this child?"

"Then we'll deal with it. Then. Not now."

"What if you die too?"

"I'm not going to die."

"You don't know for sure."

"No, I don't. But why would we have come together if not to win in the end? And we have Felix now on our side. It's got to be something. He's watched us all these years for a reason, right? He saw my death in Hawaii and changed the course of those events so I lived. He made that happen, didn't he?"

She rolled over toward him. "When are you going to tell me?"

"Tell you what?"

"About what happened to you? I had glimpses. It must have been terrible."

"Nothing as gruesome as what you've been through." Ben rolled onto his back to stare at the ceiling.

Laura placed her hand on his chest. "So what. I cornered the market on being traumatized?"

"But you're not, that's what's so incredible. You overcame. You're wide open to people and love."

"Am I?"

"Yes, you grab life with passion even after tragedy."

"I see them all in my mind. My parents, Moe, Renee. I try not to see them as I last did but as I loved them."

"You're so brave, Laura. I wish I had a braver heart like you."

"But you do. You've survived terrible things and you're here helping me. You know you could die but you haven't left, yet."

Ben turned to her, his gray eyes piercing hers. There was such torment and pain.

"I'm not a good man. I've done terrible things. Things good people don't do. If you knew, you might not want to be with me."

She took his hand and meshed his fingers with hers. "Tell me. It won't change how I feel for you. Doing bad things doesn't make you bad, Ben. Sometimes we are forced to do things we wouldn't normally do except in extreme situations. Survival situations."

"I can't tell you."

"Then show me." She touched his forehead. "Remember and I will see it for myself."

Ben stared at her for a long moment then nodded. He closed his eyes and took himself back to the night the crash happened. And Laura watched his memories. How he moved on to foster homes where he was the invisible boy until he was seventeen and grew to live with daily beatings from Frank. She saw the day he watched Frank burn and how good Ben felt to watch him die. She saw him living in a seedy hotel, working low paying jobs to survive until he could turn eighteen and join the Navy.

She saw all his times in Hawaii, drinking himself into a stupor and whoring with prostitutes. Then the night the Samoans kidnapped him. She felt the rock grate against him as he tried in vain to break free from his bonds. She saw when his mind crossed into a dark place after that. Then being discharged from the Navy to return to a life of drink and self-pity.

Laura grabbed his other hand tight, feeling his pain as she witnessed his anguish as a boy and a young man. He gripped her hands and she felt a great grief well up inside him. It washed over her and filled her with his pain. She held him and cried, but he didn't cry.

Ben opened his eyes. Laura kissed his face, his hair, and his hands. She had no words, just love to give, to make it better. She still wanted him after all she now knew.

"I murdered my foster father."

"No."

"I let him die."

"He wasn't a good man, Ben."

"It doesn't mean he deserved to be left to die."

"He beat you. He was going to rape you. You knew that. He killed himself, not you. You are no murderer. From what I saw with your last fight before he died, he grabbed his arm and staggered back. He could have had some heart condition and that's what killed him. Not you. You survived, that's what you did."

Laura felt her words cut through him like light in his darkness. Heaviness lifted off him. She sensed he thought for the first time that perhaps he wasn't a murderer. "I paid for whores. I used women. I was a drunk. My punishment was to be raped and killed by those Samoans, but Felix rescued me. It's as if I escaped my fate of being raped once to another fate of the same. It must be my destiny. Does destiny set course to find a way to make it happen even if you buck the odds?"

"I don't know. Felix thinks so, but I have to believe things can change for the better if you have hope it can. Ben, you were unlucky and unloved. You lost your parents young and no one showed you love. How could you then love yourself? That's what Hawaii was about. You fell into a life of drinking and being with…those women because you didn't feel worthy of yourself or of love. I saw it. I felt it. I know. And you have me now. And Andy, your friend. You still have him. I wish I still had Moe. She was the best friend I ever had."

Her voice broke with emotion and Ben pulled her to him. The light stretched across the room in soft shadows. All was dark outside the window as branches scratched across the glass pane. The moon hid behind clouds, covering the night with a black blanket. Laura wondered about Felix somewhere out there. Where did he go to seek out the future? And did he know what they just did together in the warmth of the cabin?

"I've never been this close before," Ben said. "Never opened up to love. I'm just finding my way. Because of you."

Laura moved in close, not knowing if she could now give him what he found. She felt torn, as she believed he should find happiness with a real woman. She felt guilty dragging him into this danger. All she could offer was uncertainty, an alien body harboring strange powers, and a crazed twin coming to kill them. It sounded like a fantastic science fiction novel. She felt glad he couldn't read her thoughts. Ben's feelings burned over her, leaving her awash in want and need and belonging.

She pressed herself in deeper to him and felt their hearts beating together as one.

She wondered if it was as it should be.

Even if it was, she didn't know if it could be.

CHAPTER 28

Laura woke up early, drawn to the lake. She had to work on her powers. She wanted to chase the anxiety away that filled her with jumpiness. Her arms and legs twitched with energy. What would the day hold? Murder and mayhem? Alien chases and bloody battles? Blasting of brains and ripping of throats? Action packed gore at its finest. She wanted to laugh at it all.

In a way they were sitting ducks waiting for her twin to reach them. But Felix was right. He wouldn't stop coming. He would kill more people and eventually her. It had to end here and now. And where was there a more appropriate place then the lake where it all started? Strangely enough she felt in control for the first time in years. Death came for her now and she could stop it.

She slipped out of bed as Ben slept. His arm was flung over his head and his face turned toward her. He looked so peaceful. She took in his lean muscles and angular, handsome face. She thought of him the night before holding her up in the shower, driving into her body, owning it with desire and passion. When he had stared into her eyes it was as if he claimed her soul. She didn't know if they had the promise of forever or if she could give it to him. She just wanted to make it through what came for them now.

She turned away to dress and left the cabin after downing a banana. She taped Ben a note to the fridge of where she went.

The sky hung over her a dismal gray, holding the promise of rain overhead, and the world spread out before her, furried in frost. The tree branches and grass twinkled with silver ice in the low light covering the landscape in dimness. The sun still rose behind the clouds. The stillness was solid around her. The crunching of her feet on dead leaves was painful to her ears. She walked past Mr. B's workshop and toward the picnic table overlooking the lake. In summer the fullness of the trees hid the lake. Now their skinny branches bent and twisted in naked agony, hiding nothing.

Then through the trees a speck of black poked through the gray world around her. It was Felix. He had come back. She scrambled down the trail, rushing over fallen branches and rocks. She had many more questions to ask him and they had very little time. If he was here then her twin could be too.

Jim woke up to sunlight streaming in his hospital room. Something scratched his hand and he looked down. A note. He uncrumpled it.

Mr. B, don't come back to the cabin. He is coming now for me. The man in black is here to help us. He has a name. Felix. And I have Ben. You were right about him. But I don't want to lose you too. I hope I made you feel better. I love you, always. Laura.

Jim sat up and bumped into a covered breakfast tray. He felt so alert and full of energy. He downed the toast, eggs, and canned pears in front of him, then chugged the orange juice. It didn't taste great, but he needed all the energy he could to help Laura. He didn't give a hoot about keeping himself safe. She was the daughter he never had and his one reason for going on this late in life.

He had to get out of this damn hospital. He wasn't sick anymore. He felt wonderful! He tried to fathom how since last night he could be recovered. He looked down at Laura's note from her visit last night. He wished she had woken him up so he could talk with her, and then it hit him. She was the reason he felt better. *I hope I made you feel better*, she wrote. She used her healing powers on him. And it worked. He had to get out of here and tell her.

First, he needed to find a bank machine in the hospital to get cash, and a cab willing to take him all the way up to the mountain. He bounced out of bed and giggled. He then burst out a hearty laugh at the fact that at eighty-seven he could still giggle.

He washed his face, brushed his teeth, and got dressed. He stared at his wrinkled face and body in the mirror. He still looked old but he felt young. Blood coursed through his body quicker, making his steps lighter. His lungs were clear. He felt better than he had in years. Not just years, decades. Despite Laura's magic could he be up for this? It didn't matter. He had to try, whether it would be the end of him or not. As long as Laura survived. He then walked out to the nurse's station, although he had an overwhelming urge to skip.

"Miss, I'm ready to go home."

"Mr. Barrens, the doctor is making his rounds soon and needs to check on your condition first before he can release you."

"Nope, gotta go now. My girl is waiting." He bolted for the elevator and giggled again as the door slid shut. He actually did bolt. Dash. Run. Scurry. Abscond. Escape. Laura would like all those words. And she made his doing it happen.

"Mr. Barrens, wait, please!"

But he didn't stop. He had to go home. There was something there he had to show Laura.

Laura reached Felix who stood by the lakeshore facing away from her.

"Felix?" She caught her breath as she stopped. He shimmered, a transparent figure. He turned to her. She could only stare at his vision. She reached out to touch him but her hand moved through him.

"What are you? How did you get here?"

Felix crossed his arms and looked out over the lake. Mist rose off it and the sun burned it away. "I am transmitting myself to you, Laura. I had to see if you were all right, to make sure the desired outcome is still the correct future. I see I am right, so far it has not changed. Let's hope it doesn't."

Laura stared at him, captured by the trees that blended into his body from behind him through his black clothes. "I-I don't understand. I remember seeing you like this before. A long time ago. I didn't just imagine it, did I? Is this some power you have?"

"It's through a belt device the Elyon had on board the spaceship that crashed here. I took it. I didn't know what it was at the time when we dug around the crash site. I found it buried in the dirt and instinctively picked it up and hid it. I knew it would come in handy. It took me some time to discover its use and how to operate it. With the right combination of numbers on its key pad here, I then visualize where I want to go or who I want to see. I have used it many times to watch over you. I did seek out life on Elyon as well, through the belt's technology. There are some still alive I saw last night, though their numbers diminish daily. I am transmitting myself to you now to assure you I will be there soon."

"Then my brother is near?"

"He is a day or less away. You need to prepare. Work on your powers today. I will be there soon at the cabin. I must go now." His image faded and Laura could see the lake clear through him.

"Wait! Are you really the only one besides my twin, and Doctor Britton, who knows about me?"

"I see you're full of questions today." His image became stronger again. "Doctor Britton is dead."

"Was it my brother?"

"Yes. I saw it would happen after you visited with him. X-10 ripped out his throat."

"Then he's near!"

"Yes and no. He killed the doctor from afar in his mind's eye. He's still on foot moving under cover of the night. Federal agents are on his trail, keeping it out of the media. This is a botched science project gone very wrong. People have been murdered, more than you know about. The agents have not located him, yet. And I don't know if they ever can."

"Then he could kill me now, from afar, as he did my parents, Moe, Renee, and Doctor Britton. And he could kill Ben. Mr. B."

"No. I told you, he wants to kill you in person, and I believe he wants you to watch him kill others you care for, too. He wants you to feel pain, emotional and physical. Sweet, sick satisfaction is what he wants, Laura. He hates you with a raging intensity."

"Why does he hate me so?"

"Because you got to live a life he didn't. You've had love and happiness. You've lived free while he's been a caged animal in a zoo."

Laura raised her arms up in frustration and paced alongside the lake's edge.

"There is no need to worry others know about you and will take you away to experiment on you. I kept your birth secret and out of my report to my superiors. I took it upon myself to watch you through the years to see what you were, if you were like other Elyon beings."

"Well, that's evident." She snorted and kept pacing.

"The government assessed long ago I would not disappear and they gave me my freedom. It's why I continue to work for them carrying out their orders. They call me the garbage man. I take out the trash. I do the dirty jobs others don't want to do. And I took a leave of absence this week. I saw what would happen and planned this time off."

"And what will happen?"

"I see your baby, Laura. All could end well. I can't see the exact outcome of your contact with X-10, or Ben's. The end result could change luckily. Or unluckily so."

"So, you don't really know for sure, do you?"

"No."

"Then you don't know if I actually will have Ben's child, for sure."

"No, I cannot be one-hundred percent sure."

Laura sighed and listened to the wind blow through the sun-dappled trees as birds twittered and squirrels tapped nuts open. It all sounded so laconic and normal. Felix moved a little closer to her, his green eyes bore into hers as she looked up. His image wavered like fine lines as he moved. She huddled inside her coat.

"I've been watching you a long time, Laura Armstrong. We're from the same distant planet. We share the same genes. We're the only ones on Earth who do so, along with your twin."

Laura was held captive by his eyes. "What else did you see about me when you watched me all those years?" She moved closer to him to see his face better.

"I watched you the day you lost your first tooth in your front yard. I watched you on your many walks in the woods. I've seen and heard you sing songs from the tree branches. I watched you at the lake the day Jim Barrens came to tell you your house caught fire. I watched from the road too, but I knew I could do nothing."

"I don't believe that. You could have left me a note, warned me. Something!" Laura wanted to shake his image.

"They were destined to die. You sense that too. I told you fate seeks to re-align its set course to its final destination. Your mother was meant to die when she fell on that pitchfork years before, but you saved her. Your father was meant to die from a heart attack later that year after the fire. You might have saved him as well. Then X-10 might have come back later and killed them in more gruesome ways. They died in their sleep from the smoke and never felt anything. He won't stop, Laura. You must stop him. Only you can do it."

She reached out to Felix's hand. She intertwined her solid fingers with his ghost ones.

"We are connected, you and I," she said. "I feel it. Part of us comes from so far away. I want to know more about this planet, Elyon. Is that why you watched me all those years?"

"That…and more." Felix didn't move his hand away from hers. "I found you to be a beautiful person inside and out. You are the closest thing to love I have ever known."

His eyes held hers. She could not look away. She was bound to this man by genes, history, and destiny. "I don't know if I could love you. I think I love Ben."

"I know. It's not meant to be. I wanted it so much to be true that you and I were meant to mate and have a child. I thought it must be destiny. I grew to love you over the years. When you were a child I discovered it was not me you should be with. It was Ben. The vision of the future came to me and I saw it clear. That is why I started watching Ben."

"I don't know if I can face what is coming. Until recently, sometimes I just wanted to die myself. As my parents did. As Moe did. As Renee did. Then I would be at peace and it would be over."

"You are so strong, Laura. I am a witness to your life and strength. I know what you can do. I wanted so much to be with you. I wanted us to carry on the Elyon people, in the hopes someday more would come here to be with us. I had a fertility test to discover I was indeed sterile, as the scientists had predicted I would be. I knew then, when I found out I could not impregnate a woman that the destiny of you and Ben must happen. My role was to ensure you both survived and meet one another to mate. As you did."

Laura felt her cheeks grow hot. She moved away and put her hands in her coat pockets.

"That's such a funny word. Mate." She laughed to cover her embarrassment.

"It's really making love for you, isn't it?"

Laura nodded. "I do love him," she whispered. "We've known each other such a short time but it's like—"

"It's meant to be, right?"

She nodded. "Yes."

"And that is as it should be."

Then Felix vanished. Laura let out a sob staring at the space he had just been in. She looked around her. Her sudden aloneness filled her with despair. The water lapped smooth at the lake's edge in a silent pulse. Ben. There was Ben. But she was still alone. Alone in this standoff between alien and human. She had to be alone in it. Whatever would happen, after it was all over, she wouldn't be staying. She was a freak.

She didn't want to believe Felix's vision of her bearing Ben's child. She felt ashamed thinking it, but if she were pregnant she could just get rid of it. It could look like a freak too. Like her twin. Even though she looked human, she felt like a freak. She would have to isolate herself from everyone she knew to start over. If she lived. And if so, would it be crazy to think she could turn her brother to the side of good?

Part of her wanted to hold Ben forever, to feel his love flow over her and his body never separated from hers. But soon they would be separated. They had to, for his sake.

X-10 woke up from his pile of leaves to see the moon high overhead. He had left the Appalachian Trail as it veered east toward Vermont, upon reaching the corners bordering Pennsylvania, New Jersey, and New York. He now moved north into the Catskill Mountains, just south of Albany. One night he stole a car to move faster. He hid in the bushes beside an all-night convenient store just off the trail, where the highway passed through.

His patience paid off. At 2:00 a.m. a man stopped, looking at a map in his car. X-10 seized the opportunity to rush into his back seat, put his pod fingers around his throat, and order him to drive. When the man looked in his rear view mirror he let his bladder loose in fright. A urine stench rose up from the seat. X-10 kept his hands on the man's throat as he drove north. The man chattered on, begging him to let him go. X-10 told him to shut up and squeezed his throat harder.

The man drove for two hours until the gas gauge registered empty. The car shuddered to a halt on a dark, rural road. X-10 broke the man's neck with one crack and left him in the car, slumped over the wheel. He then returned on foot to the woods that would hide him. But the car had gotten him a considerable distance ahead. He believed he was fifty or so miles away from the girl. He could reach her within two days if he remained unfound under the cover of darkness.

As he ran under the full moon, leaping over rocks and roots, darting around boulders he could see her in his mind. *Laura. You are mine.* Then he saw her with her man. Water coursed all around them. Her hair hung wet about her shoulders. They were naked and sliding into one another. Her mouth hung open in ecstasy. Her breasts bounced as the man held her up, driving into her. X-10 closed off his mind's eye to the scene. He didn't want to see her naked. It made him feel strange. And in that strange feeling he couldn't define, X-10 hated her even more.

Rage surged through him and his blood pulsed fast, throbbing under his white skin in blue rivers. Why did she get to have her man when he couldn't have his woman? Why was she worthy and he wasn't? But Sabrina's touches had made him feel worthy. Even if they were paid. And she had smelled and looked so good.

The night flashed through him again and he moaned with agony over the loss of the girl who left a hole in his heart. The girl who called him Charlie and loved him for just one night.

After her fear of him had left her, she sat down on his bed then. "Why don't we just lie here for now? We can talk, you know. Like real…people."

He stood over her, considering. What would he talk about with a human girl?

She lay down on her side and he did too, facing her. Her blonde hair curved along her breasts like silky strands of sparkly cotton candy. He'd seen a picture of it once being swirled on a stick at a fair. He wondered what it would taste like. What she would taste like.

She touched his face then pulled her fingers away. "When you look at all your parts, you're not so bad."

"A monster."

"No. I've been with monsters."

"Like me?"

She shook her head. "Monsters on the inside."

Even in the garish light she was the loveliest thing he had ever seen. He wanted to touch her, but was afraid of his urges. To hurt and maim and kill. Good guys don't do those things. And she had called him by his name. As if he was a good guy.

No! No good guy Charlie!

He was evil to the core. And hate spurred him on. Hate would help him survive. He forced himself to run faster through the night. Why did Laura get to live a normal life? He vowed to make her end not normal. And in that end, she would wish she had never been born.

A lonesome dog bayed in the hills above X-10 as if approving his plan. Streaks of moonlight and shadows fell across his face like whip lashes over and over, creating a living painting from darkness and light. He would show Laura darkness like she never experienced, and pain. There would be so much pain. He howled back at the creature that rode alone through the woods as he did. Perhaps they would meet along their journeys.

He hoped so. He was getting hungry again.

Jim reached the hospital lobby and scanned the area for an ATM machine. He peered past the reception area to find a man staring at him. A mammoth man in black with bright green eyes. Jim stared back at him. Was this Laura's man in black? The man walked toward him. Jim froze. The man was real. He never doubted Laura, but to see this person she spoke about since childhood unnerved him. The man stood before him, enormous.

"Jim?"

All Jim could do was nod. His tongue couldn't move to form words, which didn't matter, as his brain had no idea what to say.

"Laura needs you. And I think you have something to show her that will help, don't you?"

Jim nodded again, still speechless.

"Come. I have a car."

People swarmed around them, in a constant stream coming and going. Jim reached out his hand to touch this man. He needed to make sure he was real. He gripped his massive arm. It felt indeed real, strong and muscular.

"Yes, I'm real," the man huffed. "And I won't hurt you. Come on. Time is precious."

Jim nodded again and followed him out the front entrance. The man led him to a brown sedan parked in the corner lot. He motioned for Jim to get in and he did. The man started the car and they eased out onto the main road.

"Your name is Felix."

"Yes."

"Laura left me a note last night when she visited. But I was asleep."

The man looked at Jim, who continued to stare at him. Felix seemed larger than life to Jim. The myth was now real.

"And she gave you a gift, didn't she?"

Jim was startled. "I think she healed me. But how could you know that?"

"I see things, things that are yet to happen."

"And you saw Laura come to the hospital and make me well?"

"Yes. And much more."

"Do all things you see actually happen?"

"The things I see are floating out there on a breeze, waiting to connect. Sometimes events can change the course of their direction, or what it is they connect to, leading to a different outcome. Sometimes not the outcome we desire."

Jim's head reeled with what this stranger told him. "And you can change the outcome to one you desire?"

"Sometimes."

"Then sometimes not, correct?"

"Correct."

Jim pondered this information for a moment and watched the traffic flash by. They headed toward the mountain. It hung there, a giant rock watching them come closer and closer.

"Who are you?"

Felix glanced at him, his knotty hands covering much of the steering wheel, and gave him a half smile. On his craggy face it looked more like a sneer. "I will tell you what I can on the way to your cabin. Laura and Ben are there now. And the evil one heads our way."

Felix told him everything and Jim was fascinated. All the questions he had about Laura were being answered in a single conversation. His life was about to get as exciting as it ever would be. For an old man, he still felt a thrill. He took in every detail Felix told him, accepting it as truth. Adrenalin coursed through his aged body. He was ready to fight for the one person he loved so she could survive.

Even if he didn't.

CHAPTER 29

Laura stood at the edge of the crash site and closed her eyes. She wanted to feel her connection again to this alien father of hers, Feo. She wanted to see him again, moving with fluid grace through the wall as she had in her dreams. She looked up at the sky. Up there, somewhere, millions of miles away, hung another planet bearing intelligent life.

She walked down the valley slope to where the space ship had impacted, and knelt to the ground. She sank her hands in the wet earth. She had to get down where the spaceship came to its final resting place after plunging deep into the ground. She had to be as close as she could to where she came from. If her twin was coming then he would find her here where they both began.

She clawed at the earth and a crazed urgency came over her. She flung dirt aside and stretched her arms outward to command the elements around her. She channeled her energy to dig into the ground. Wood and rock crashed together in a mechanical race to find the location she sought. Deeper she went. Sweat whipped off her as she moved her body in time with the objects she commanded. Soon the tunnel reached over fifty feet deep below her. She flung her hands down and caught her breath. Rocks and logs hung in the air for a second and then fell.

Laura smoothed her hair back and wiped the sweat from her forehead. She peered into the hole she created. It was four feet wide and six feet tall. Enough for an average man to walk in. She felt lightheaded and hollow inside as if all of her inner self had been emptied out.

She stepped toward the hole and looked around her. The lake and woods surrounded her like family. She had not visited them for so long. The trees bent their branches to the earth as if paying homage to her presence. It was her home. She belonged here. It's where she had been created, deep in the earth from an alien form in his dying moments to a curious runaway girl. She looked down again at the hole, and taking a deep breath stepped into the darkness below.

Ben woke up, alone. He shook his head to ward off his drowsiness. His dream came back to him in a vivid rush. He had stood before his parents' cabin by the lake. It looked just as he remembered. A shadow crossed the window and his parents stepped out onto the porch. They held hands and smiled at him. He wanted to believe they were still alive, although he was not a child anymore. He walked toward them and up the steps. They each took one of his hands and stood with him in a circle. He felt immense love flow through him. Then his father spoke.

"Don't be afraid of love. It's here. You must embrace it."

Ben nodded, unable to speak. He had so much to tell them but didn't know where to begin.

"Ben, you must love yourself," his mother said. "Do you love yourself?"

He shook his head, unsure. He felt uncomfortable talking about it.

His mother squeezed his hand. "Love grows from the inside. Only then can you share it with others."

He nodded. "But I don't feel worthy of love."

"You've punished yourself enough, son," his father said. "Stop being your own jailer. The future is here. Don't waste it living in the past. Don't turn your back on the chance to have happiness."

What he said was true and Ben felt a great weight lift off him. He felt unencumbered by his own chains for the first time in years.

He stared into his parents eyes. "Don't go, please. Stay."

His mother smiled and shook her head. "You don't need us anymore. You haven't for a long time. Love yourself and you can love another. You are stronger than you think. Remember that."

Then they were gone and he was left with his hands stretching out, holding the air.

He shook away the dream. He hadn't meant to sleep at all. He had stayed awake long after Laura fell into a troubled sleep, the gun held tight to his chest. He wanted to be on guard. He had watched her much of the night turn and mumble. Once she shouted out in anguish. He knew who tormented her. Then tiredness overcame him and he must have closed his eyes.

Damn himself for falling asleep! He called out to Laura but she didn't answer. He threw back the covers and pulled clothes on, then jumped down the loft ladder two steps at a time. Finding her note didn't ease his anxiety. They needed to stay together. How could he protect her if she was gone? Why didn't she wake him?

He had an urgent feeling time was running out. He ran out the door and down the mountain path to the lake. He hoped he would find her alone.

Laura walked steady along the tunnel she had created, her hands feeling along the soft earth walls. At first the light from above filtered down to lead the way, but after twenty feet or so she was in complete darkness. She felt herself floating outside of her body in the deep black. It consumed her as if she had disappeared, along with the world from above. She stopped and stood still. If she couldn't see herself or anything around her maybe she didn't exist.

Could she hide here and no one would find her, not even her twin who sought to kill her? It was a giddy thought and in the far corners of her mind she knew it was illogical. Then again, some might say she, as an alien, was not logical either. That she could not exist. But she did.

She put her foot out and stepped again on the earth floor and found the wall. It jolted her back to reality and she began to jog deeper into the ground. Her eyes adjusted to the darkness. Something glittered. She ran faster toward it. A draft blew around her. Then the wall she ran her hand along disappeared. The glimmer became brighter. She found herself in a cavernous room with walls that gleamed with a low burning light. The room engulfed her and Laura felt so small. The ceiling rose above in sloping hollows.

This had to be where the spaceship stopped when it hit the earth. She could imagine it diving deep into the rock and mud to rest here. Perhaps the government took it out in pieces and the shell of its space remained here down below. If so, there could be another entranceway from another side of it. That must be where the draft came from. An entrance they filled in to hide when they deemed the project over and fenced the area in. Perhaps it had crumbled over time and air rushed in from widening holes.

She walked to the walls and ran her hands over it. She pulled her hands away to see them pitted with specks of light. It could be the coating of the spaceship left on these walls. A reminder it was here. It shed enough light for her to investigate the cavern further. Here and there formations appeared in the earth and ceiling where the ship must have been. It was now molded into the earth as a permanent fossil imprint left behind.

She wanted to connect with this strange being again. Feo. Her real father. She sensed all those years ago that they were connected. Laura placed her hands again on the walls, as she had in her dreams, and stared into the dim light pulsing like stars all around her. Warmth seeped into her although the walls were cold and moist. Her ears honed in on the soft drip-drip resonating from water falling through the mud ceiling above.

Like in her dreams, her hands moved with the wall. She swayed to its beat as a face grew before her. The face of her real father. A father unlike any other, from far away in space. It was a strange face, yet kind. His yellow eyes turned down at the corners, and he tilted his round head at her. White hair melted into his pearly skin. It framed his face.

Then the girl appeared alongside the strange face as in a movie screen. Feo turned to watch her. So did Laura. The girl ran through the woods, stumbling along. She looked just like the girl in the photo. It was her real mother, Sarah. The ground shook beneath Sarah. She reached out to grab onto tree branches when the earth caved in. She opened her mouth to scream and fell into the darkness below.

Laura watched Sarah fall through an earth pit to land before a door. It opened. Sarah paused for a moment then walked through it. Inside a large room the strange being lay on the floor. It was this very room she stood in. Sarah put her hands to her mouth, staring at the being in fear. She shrunk back toward the door but the being raised his head and reached out his pod fingers to her.

Sarah hesitated then stepped toward the being who pleaded for help with his outstretched arms. His yellow eyes shone bright, his round forehead wrinkled in pain. Another body lay across the floor on the far side of the room but this one did not move. Sarah knelt before him and touched his hands. His fingertips pulsed with a soft green glow in a steady, fast rhythm. She held his hands and wept for his loss. Then the pulsing light from his fingers grew slower in its beat, it dimmed then disappeared.

The being's hands fell and his head dropped to the floor. Sarah ran out of the room and back through the darkness from where she fell. She climbed up on mud and rock, clawing her way back to the surface. The earth collapsed behind her, filling in the hole, as she frantically climbed. When she reached the top she stumbled on, continuing her original journey. Then the screen went dark.

Laura cried out. She had witnessed her creation, and her twin's. Feo had passed on his essence to her real mother here in his fallen spaceship. She felt Feo's physical pain and sorrow at leaving his home. He had left behind everything to start over, continue their people. His partner had died. He was all alone. His quest must not be in vain.

Laura understood. She accepted. She had life because of him. But her real mother had died as a consequence. Ben's parents had died as a consequence. But it wasn't Feo's fault. It was fate and the fault of a greedy doctor and nurse, and the U.S. government.

"Feo," Laura whispered staring at his round face. "Father."

He nodded. Then he closed his eyes and was gone.

Laura banged the wall. "Come back! I need your help. I need...something."

She sat on the cavern floor and cried. For his pain, for hers. For the pain her twin must harbor at being locked up all his life. Somewhere inside she had hope she could convince him to be with her, as a brother. She could convince him he could be loved and he was not alone. They could have a life together, somewhere.

She could forgive him. She didn't have to kill him. She didn't want to be like him. She hadn't met him and he raced toward her to kill her, but perhaps she could change their destiny. They carried the same blood, the same genes that collided one night by a desperate accident. He was her twin. Felix had to be wrong. He couldn't be the monster he described. Everyone had worthiness inside them, didn't they? Some piece of redemption they could claim?

A stabbing pain exploded in her head. She fell to the floor, writhing in agony. This time the headache attacked her with a spiteful vengeance. She hugged her sides, cold from the mud floor, and shivered as snakes of pain curled around her. She closed her eyes and sank into a deep pit of darkness within her mind. Far away she heard someone call her name, but she couldn't answer back. Her mouth wouldn't move. She became paralyzed with pain, tormented by something she couldn't see.

X-10 ran faster and faster over the rocky trail seeking a place to hide and rest in for the day. The sun was rising. But he was also famished and needed food for fuel. A sagging farmhouse appeared through the trees and he broke in the back door to raid the fridge. He had ripped apart a turkey half carved when an old man thundered down the stairs with a shotgun in hand. X-10 laughed as he chewed on a turkey leg and grabbed the gun from him.

The startled man stood there in disbelief at the grotesque creature standing before him. X-10 took the opportunity to crack the gun against his head with a forcible swing. He surprised the old woman, too, as she followed down the stairs, with a sharp blow on the top of her head. She crumbled alongside her husband and X-10 finished his meal in solitude.

When he finished gorging himself he ransacked the entrance closet by the kitchen to find a thick winter coat. His meager clothes from the fat guard were not enough to protect from the cold moving in as he headed north. He found a thick barn jacket with patches on the sleeves, a wool brimmed hat, and a pair of wool gloves. His arms stuck out of the coat and the hat sat like an absurd bird atop his monstrous head.

Something in the living room caught his eye and he stepped over the two bodies to get a better look in the dark. The fading moon shed long shadows across the room, making way for the sun coming up soon. He had to get back to the woods and hide for the day in a warm spot where no one would find him. But he was drawn to an oversized worn, green recliner in the living room.

He had always wanted a recliner. Locked in his cell with a hard bed and stool, he had been forced to grow accustomed to the Spartan life but still yearned for a place to call home. A place full of comfortable chairs, warm rugs beneath his feet, and a fireplace by which to warm himself.

In all the books he read and pictures he flipped through in magazines it looked like what a home should be. Laura had one, so he made sure he took it away. A sweet satisfaction stole over him remembering when he had torched her home. He recalled the wisps of smoke curling up, then the flames bursting into a wild blaze of power, sucking up the air around it, fueling its hungry belly.

He eased himself into the rocker recliner, his long body stuck out of it in awkward angles. A purple and yellow afghan covered the back of it and he pulled it around himself. In the wall mirror he could see his pod fingers and bulbous white head sticking out of the throw like a freakish doll dressed up by a little girl playing tea party with her brother's monster toy.

But he could pretend. He pretended this was his home he came to each night, after working some corporate job in the city. To his country home he would travel. It would be his farmhouse he renovated as a showcase home. And Sabrina would be in the kitchen making him a feast of meat and potatoes and gravy. And apple pie for dessert with vanilla ice cream on top. And he would lick her after the food was gone, over and over tasting her golden delicious skin.

And they would both be free from their prisons together, for she had told him of escaping her painful place of torment. And knowing that, he felt their connection. Souls of the same pain.

He had traced the outline of her curves in his mind that night and he saw them now as he rocked. She'd faced him on her side then, staring into his eyes as if he were an ordinary teenage boy.

"How old are you, Sa-bri-na?" He savored her name like blood trickling down his throat.

"Nineteen."

"I'm eighteen."

"You've been here all your life?"

"Yes."

"It's like a prison."

"It's all I know. Will ever know."

"You know me now." She touched his hand.

"For an hour." But Dr. Bjord probably wouldn't let her leave here alive. She knew too much. X-10 wouldn't be made to do it, no matter how Dr. Bjord tortured him. He would be a good guy until the end. His secret experiment would be a success. He didn't want the hour to end. Knowing it could be her end.

She turned and stretched out on her back. Her soft slopes enticed him. "I just left my prison."

"You escaped from jail?"

She laughed. It pierced his cold heart with a flame. "A jail of sorts. My bastard of a father. He was my jail keeper. With fists almost as big as yours." She took his monstrous hand and held it in her small one. Light blew inside him and chased some of the dark away.

"He hit you."

"And more. I finally left. Last month. I've only been in the city since then."

"You left, just like that?"

"In the night. I didn't say goodbye to anyone."

She faced him again. Her eyes grew shiny. What did that emotion feel like? Tears had never fallen from his eyes. Was it painful?

She pulled up her skirt. Gray bruises marked the tops of her legs. "Old evidence. Now I call the shots. If the pimps don't get me. I've been avoiding them."

X-10 touched her old wounds. Her skin was smooth and soft. He worked his power on her. He had used it to heal himself before. The bruises faded. Sabrina sucked in her breath and let go of his hand.

"What are you really?"

"I told you. An experiment. A monster."

"Monsters don't heal people. Angels do." She touched her legs as if waiting for the bruises to re-appear. "Where were you when I needed you before?" She laughed nervously.

"Here. Alone."

"I've never been alone. I grew up in a house full of kids."

"Alone inside though?"

She nodded and took his hand again, pulling it to her chest. It filled the space between her warm breasts, like her scent filled his pores. "Alone like you."

"Why the streets?" His heart raced faster with her touch. He willed himself to be still when all he wanted to do was plunge into her skin with his hardness and fingers and teeth.

"I ran out of money the first week, Charlie." His name on her lips shattered his ice. It melted it into warm rivers that ran through his limbs. She kissed his hand and held it to her cheek. Her misty blue eyes mesmerized him like sapphires on fire.

And then she reached up and kissed his lips. He couldn't move. She parted his lips with hers and pushed her hot tongue in his mouth. He tasted her sweetness then lapped at it. Her hair shimmered around her like a halo.

"I want you, Charlie. Do you want me?"

He nodded. An ache spread throughout him. It wasn't painful, but full of need and want. *She* wanted *him*. Even if she was a whore. But she seemed so clean and pure. And she said he wasn't so bad looking. She didn't think he was a monster. Alongside his need, hope sprung that if one day he killed the doctor and escaped, someone could love him.

Golden Sabrina wanted to. If only for an hour.

But nothing gold can stay. That poet had written so.

She stood and undressed before him, leaf after leaf. Her slender curves were everywhere and he was so hard. Still, he couldn't move. She was his experiment. He was terrified of ruining it all if he moved. Could he control his darkest desires? He didn't want to make the first move. He wanted her to take him.

And she did.

Like Laura's man took her.

Laura.

His anger raged again, thinking of her. He threw off the afghan and jumped up from the chair. Where was she now? He knelt on the braided rug and placed his hands to his head seeking her out. Sunrise was coming. He had little time but must find her. He needed to punish her, to soothe his rage before he slept for the day.

His mind's eye flew over the treetops, up a mountain. There she stood, in a dark room with walls that gleamed. She must be underground. Something moved on the wall. Moving pictures. A strange looking person was in the movie. He looked familiar to X-10, like himself. It had to be his father. Laura's father too. A seething fury rose in him watching her watch the movie. Then a girl appeared. She looked like Laura. Their mother. His wrath grew immense, hating Laura for looking normal like their mother while he looked like the freak.

X-10 crushed his hands together and shrieked a demonic wail, pressing into her brain, probing with points of fire. Pain. He wanted her to feel so much pain. She fell to the floor, hugging herself. He watched her writhe and moan. When he faced her in person he would bring her to her knees and kill her while he stared into her forlorn eyes. Those big, brown eyes. He would snuff them of life so no human could enjoy them again.

Bitter bile filled his throat and he swallowed hard, forcing it down. It was time to go. A few hours of sleep was all he needed and when dusk fell again he would be off, running the last few miles toward his prey. He was so close. By tonight he would be upon her. And they would be face to face.

He thumped his chest in a war cry and ran through the farmhouse door, a wild beast with one thing in mind. To kill.

CHAPTER 30

Ben ran alongside the lake toward the crash site toward Laura. He called out her name as he ran. He slid on the leaves that covered the rough path around the lake. Autumn had settled in and stole the last few leaves from the trees. They covered the ground, painting the lake's edge with an array of color. The morning mist rose from the water in tendrils then disappeared into the sunlight sparkling on the cold water as geese honked overhead.

But Ben saw none of these things. He saw Laura in his mind, and his heart gripped with panic. For a second she stood before him with eyes wide open, her throat ripped out, her face frozen in a death grimace. He ran faster.

He neared the crash site. Something looked different. Mounds of dirt had been scattered in all directions as if someone had been digging with fury. He reached a gigantic hole that sloped down into the earth and disappeared into darkness. Was Laura down there with her twin?

He took a deep breath and plunged into the hole. His head just cleared the top of it and within a few feet he became engulfed in total blackness. He reached his hands out and found the wall. Running his hands along each side he jogged in the darkness. A sensation of weightlessness gripped him as he raced through the inky pit, heading deeper into the ground.

"Laura, are you down here?"

As Ben ran toward the silent unknown a faint light appeared ahead. Then the walls spread out. He entered an immense room glowing with a faint florescence. It came from the walls. He heard the slow dripping of water underground, and then he saw her huddled on the earth floor. He dropped to her side and placed his hands on her head and back, feeling her breaths coming fast and shallow.

She was alive. She shook and moaned as if in terrible pain. He felt her legs and arms. She appeared uninjured. It must be another headache. A bad one. What was she doing here? Ben looked around the room, unsure what this place was, wondering if her twin could nearby. Could it be a trap? He didn't care. He had to get Laura out of there.

He pushed his hands under her and staggered up with her to his chest. He rushed back up the hole he came down, stumbling as he lost his balance in the blackness. He gripped Laura harder, his arms aching, as he jogged upwards back to the lighted world. He finally reached land above. He stopped for a moment to catch his breath and adjust his eyes to the bright light. He peered down at Laura. Her arms crossed herself in comfort.

Ben carried her back along the lakeshore and up the mountain. Once more. He tried not to jostle her as she moaned in his arms. Her eyes remained closed, as if she had entered another place. A dark place. Heading into the woods up the trail, he scoured the woods for signs of other life. Human life. Or inhuman. He saw nothing but squirrels nattering among the bare branches and birds calling to one another.

Once inside the cabin, Ben placed Laura on the floor in the great room. She remained unconscious but breathing steady. Her body must have shut down like a defense mechanism to protect her from the pain. She was cold, wet, and covered in mud. He washed out the tub downstairs, filled it with steaming water, and grabbed a new set of her clothes from the loft. He stripped off his muddy coat as well and placed the gun he carried in his back jeans pocket.

He then removed her clothes and carried her naked to the tub, rubbing her arms and back to keep her warm. She looked so fragile in his arms as if asleep. Her hair fell over her bare shoulders. She curled up like a little girl snug in her bed after lights out, dreaming of sweet things. But Laura wasn't dreaming of little girl things.

"Laura." He nuzzled the top of her head and kissed it. "I'm putting you in the tub to wash you, if you can hear me. It's Ben and you're safe."

She nodded as if she could hear him from the deepest points of her mind as she hid from pain. Ben lowered her into the warmth and soaped her gently with a washcloth, kissing her fingers and face as he did so. He washed the mud away and tried not to look at her nakedness, to give her the privacy she deserved. She wasn't aware of his workings on her body, but he felt he owed her privacy.

A fierce feeling snaked through his stomach. He would do anything for this woman. Protect her. Die for her. Love her. He never felt this way before about anyone. In a short time she had changed him forever.

Shown him what love was. Shown him he was worthy of love. Shown him his parents' last moments and set him free from guilt. She had all the human elements that mattered. He didn't care part of her came from another planet too far away to comprehend. And as he washed her he spoke to her with love in his voice.

"Laura, I know you're in there. I hope you can hear me. I don't know why this is all happening. I feel like we've been sucked up into some great event bigger than ourselves, you know? I didn't realize how lost in life I was until I met you."

He willed her to come out of her darkness. But she remained unconscious. Her breathing had slowed down and Ben wished she would wake up and her pain would be gone. When he finished he dried her off, wrapped her in a large towel, and carried her to the great room where he laid her on the couch and dressed her with care.

"Laura, come back to me," he pleaded. "Please."

He put her on his lap and sat with her, his arms around her, waiting. He stroked her hair and continued to talk to her. Perhaps his voice would reach her. He hoped. He wanted to talk to her now about the things he had never spoken of to anyone and now she couldn't hear him.

"I hated being alive, for a real long time. Did you sense that?"

He heard a bang and jumped. But it was just a tree branch blowing on the window from a gust of wind. He relaxed and pulled out the gun from his back pocket to place it on the end table next to the couch.

"When I lived in foster care with Frank, every day was hell. When I watched him die it felt good. I know that's sick, isn't it?" Ben looked down at Laura as if expecting her to answer, but her eyes remained closed. He wondered if he should get her to a hospital but remembered how she slept all day after her other headache. He would wait a bit and see. She had to come around soon.

"Then when those Samoans had me tied down. I wanted to die then too. It was the worst, not being able to fight back. Not being able to escape. I knew I would die, but Felix saved me. And I know we will fight back and survive now. I know it. So don't worry. I'll protect you, Goddamnit. I swear."

He cradled her to his chest and rocked her for a minute in quiet.

"I wanted to die again, when the Navy kicked me out. I sunk into alcohol but my friend, Andy, saved me. The best bud a guy could have. I hope you get to meet him someday."

Laura moaned. She still sounded so far away, lost in her mind. Somewhere. He hoped in talking to her that he could bring her back. In hearing his own voice out loud it made him feel like she was part of the conversation.

"Then life got pretty good after I started my own photography business. I traveled with families on vacation. I enjoyed watching them but this thing called family seemed so foreign to me. I thought no woman would ever want me to create a family together and be forever. But now, you've made me feel like it could happen. Even in all this craziness. I don't know what's going to happen. Sounds weird to want the normal now with all this abnormal stuff going on, right? Freaky, as you say, Laura. But you're not freaky, just the situation. Not you. Never you. You're the most amazing person I ever met. Now, in a way, you're saving me too."

Ben rested his head on hers. He watched the windows for any movement. He had to be on guard, but his eyes grew droopy. He didn't know he fell asleep until he heard his name.

"Ben."

He opened his eyes. Laura stared at him, snuggling into his shoulder.

"I'm so glad you're awake. I thought I might have to take you to a hospital."

"What happened?"

He stroked her hair and she sat up straighter on his lap. "You tell me. I woke up this morning. You were gone so I ran to the lake and found you had dug some tunnel at the crash site to a room below. I followed it and found you on the floor there, almost unconscious."

Laura took his hand and stared at his fingers intertwined with hers. "I remember the pain now. I couldn't see or move. It's my twin seeking me out. I had to go there, to find out what was underneath so I dug and dug until I got there. I'm fine now."

Laura got off Ben's lap and paced the floor, staring down, biting her lip. She looked down at herself and back at him. "How did I get here?"

"I carried you." Ben grinned at her, trying to lighten the moment. "It's becoming a habit with you. You pass out. I carry you home. Some people do this at parties, you know, not from crazed people chasing you with super powers."

"And why am I wearing different clothes?"

"You were filthy, covered in mud, cold and soaked through. I gave you a bath and changed you."

"You did?"

"Hey, I've seen the goods, lady. I like."

She half-smiled at him then started pacing again. "Felix was at the lake too.

In a way."

Ben gripped her arms. "What does that mean and where is he now? Is your twin coming?"

"No, it's okay, for now. He used some device to transmit himself to me here at the lake. I don't know where he transmitted from. It's some kind of Seeker Device, he called it. He found it at the crash site years ago and hid it away. When he wants to seek someone out he uses the device to locate them and transmit his image to them, like a video in real time. It's fantastic."

"It is," Ben agreed. "But why did he visit you?"

"He told me Doctor Britton is dead. Murdered."

"By your brother?"

"Yes."

Ben thought about the implications of that and a chill ran across his skin. It sunk in hard that death headed their way too. "And what else?"

Laura looked at him and flexed her hands as if thinking about how to answer him. "He wanted to tell me he has been watching me through this device most of my life."

"And?"

"He told me he had fallen in love with me and for a long time wanted us to be together to *procreate*, as he says, to carry on the Elyon line."

Ben jumped up from the couch. "I knew I had reason to be jealous. What does he expect, to win you over now?"

Laura felt his anger burning through her and touched his arm. "No. He came to believe you and I are meant to be together. And that's why he saved you in Hawaii. He saved you for a reason. You don't have to be jealous. I told him I could never love him. I told him that…I love you."

The wind wailed through the empty trees and Laura jumped as branches screeched against the house. Ben put his hand over hers. He felt the same, but he couldn't form the words. He couldn't remember when he'd last said those words.

"And do you believe he's right? About us, I mean?"

She shook her head, but didn't speak, and walked to the window. Ben looked past her to the gray, gangly trees that shook from the gusts ripping through the woods. No squirrels bounded looking for nuts, no birds twittered about. The world around them had holed up, just as they were doing. Watching and waiting.

"The more we learn, the more questions there seem to be about all of this," Ben said.

"I wonder if we'll ever know the full story and history of what happened here," Laura said. "I've been thinking, up there, in space, somewhere, millions of miles away there is another planet with intelligent life. Are they coming again now?"

"I don't know."

"I know if we don't want to be dead I have to use my powers against my own brother. I never met him and yet I must kill him."

"What was that place I found you in?" Ben changed the subject.

"It's where the space ship came to rest after it slammed into the earth. And I saw my mother and father. My real parents."

"How?"

"It was like a movie in the wall." Laura held up her hands, still facing the window, as if revisiting that dark underground place of final rest. She shared with him what she saw.

"It *was* a virgin birth, Ben. How strange, isn't it all? My creation. My twin. I don't fit in with this world. Do I? I am a freak."

Ben stood up and placed his hands on her shoulders and turned her toward him. "You are not a freak. You're human too. And you have the best of us in you. You do fit in. You fit into my world. I don't care how you were created or what you are."

"You say that now. You might think differently later, if there is a later." She started crying and pushed him away. "Why are you still here anyways? Why don't you leave? We're just sitting here waiting for my twin who is coming right now to kill me. Kill us. I can fight this alone and then no one else has to die. Except me."

She shoved him harder, but he pulled her back and forced her to look at him. "Listen to me, Laura. I thought for so long love just imprisoned you. Through you, I found it doesn't. It sets you free. I was in a prison of my own making for so long. Don't send me back there, please? I have nothing, and no one to go back to."

Ben gripped her shoulders, waiting for a response. She opened her mouth to speak when they heard a car drive up.

Ben grabbed the gun and ran to the front door, Laura close behind him. She gasped when Mr. B and Felix stepped out of a car, and ran out the door ahead of Ben.

"Mr. B!" She hugged him. He hugged her back with a strong grip. "You're well and so strong."

"Because of you, my dear." He held her at arm's length to get a better look at her. "Thank you for healing me."

"I'm glad it worked. It's been so long since I tried."

Felix stood beside them, silent.

Ben crossed his arms. "And how is it you're here with Mr. Barrens?"

Felix stepped closer, towering over them all. His eyebrows bushed out so thick he appeared to be scowling down at them. Ben looked like a lion ready to spring, moving back and forth on each foot, but Felix remained still, a patient man it seemed who could wait for hours on a mission without moving a muscle or blinking an eye. No one spoke and the silence grew awkward.

"He picked me up at the hospital." Jim jumped in, looking back and forth between them. "He knew Laura healed me and he knew I had to get back here, right, Felix?"

Felix nodded. "Yes, Jim has something here to show us that might help us. Might."

Jim just smiled and motioned them to follow him to his work shed nearby. All four of them entered the work shed and Jim pulled the chain light on to see. He moved a table aside in the middle and bent down on one knee. Felix bent with him and together they pulled up boards to reveal a set of stairs below.

"It's my stash," Jim explained. "When the government came in to clean up the crash site and buy out everyone's cabins, I was suspicious of their explanations and motives. When they started pressuring me to leave, I decided I need to protect myself. Just in case. I've got a few of everything. Rifles, handguns. Nothing black market. All legal, of course. I do carry a license for it. I just never used it, except to practice. At one point, years ago, I had them hidden all over the cabin in various places."

Felix moved carefully down the steps, through the small opening, and handed guns to Jim and Ben. They placed them on the floor. Laura stood motionless, transfixed in place. She shivered as the wind blew in. The sky grew darker as it turned to afternoon.

"Mr. B, what the hell were you planning, a coup? Jesus, look at this stockade. I had no idea."

Eighteen guns spread out before them. Jim pointed at his stash.

"I've got Glocks, Smith & Wesson, Colts and Winchesters. Remington style Derringers. Take your pick from single shot pistols to semi-automatic rifles, although for our purposes I think a semi-automatic or double action revolver would work."

"I agree," Felix said. "We need immediate action without reloading." He picked up a rifle and peered through its finder. "We need a good long-range rifle, too. You never know. I was trained as a sharpshooter. I can set a post and wait for hours. This Browning is a good one. I've used it before."

"And was it successful, Felix?" Laura frowned at them as they picked over the inventory.

"What do you mean?"

"Did you kill with it?"

"Yes. Of course. Many times."

Laura just shook her head. "I appreciate all this, Mr. B, but I can't use a gun."

"No worries, Laura, we'll use them for you. They're for your protection and ours."

Ben held up a .357 Magnum. "We do need protection."

"Yes," agreed Felix. "X-10 is closing in. Let's move this to the cabin and plan. We only have a few hours."

They carried the guns into the house along with ammunition for each and the men each chose a few.

Jim threw together some quick pasta and sauce as they planned. "I'm starving," he explained. "I feel so youthful and need to eat!" He winked at Laura, in high spirits. She sensed he felt this was his last hurrah and his chance to protect her.

"We all need energy." Felix stared at Laura. She nodded and took a bowl too. She felt lightheaded from not eating most of the day. Ben grabbed one and sat down on a stool in the cramped kitchen with everyone. He twirled his spaghetti and shared a glance with Laura.

She sensed he wished he was still alone with her. She looked away from Ben. She loved him but, with a heavy heart, she couldn't stay with him, even if they survived this. She had to find a way to remove herself from him and the others. She had to face her brother alone. All their guns in the world wouldn't end this. Ben continued to stare at her and it made her heart ache. It felt like ages ago he made love to her here, when in fact it was just last night.

"Where is he now?" Ben turned toward Felix.

"X-10 has reached a few miles below the Catskills. He'll be here by nightfall."

They all looked around the table at one another.

"Tell us what to do."

Felix placed his massive hands on the table and began to set a plan in place of where they each should post and how the scenario could go. Ben and Mr. B worked back and forth with him as he explained. Laura said nothing. Her head felt thick and heavy. Their voices were muffled and far away, a combined cacophony of nothingness. None of this was relevant. She had to get away from this talk. They were all going to die and she had to prevent it from happening.

She stood up in the midst of their jumbled voices, startling them. All three men stopped talking. "I have to go rest for a bit."

Ben stood up and touched her arm. "Are you okay? Is the headache back?"

She nodded, unable to speak and lie to him. Felix just stared at her. Did he know she was lying? Mr. B came to her side and put his hand under her elbow.

"Let me help you to the loft. I feel fifty years younger."

Laura took his help, clutching her head as if in great pain. She sensed Ben watching them walk away.

Jim and Laura reached the loft ladder and he helped her up. "You've done so much for me. Let me at least take care of you now. Although, my soup would be a disaster. I never could make soup well. It ends up an insipid calamity of glop."

Laura gazed at his white hair and wrinkled face and laughed out loud. His blue eyes shone with excitement and his back stood tall and straight for the first time in years.

"Maybe your soup is a disaster—"

"An abhorrence. A botched fare. A putrid disease. A pot of decay bound to cause botulism, boils, dysentery, atrophy, dyspepsia, and maladies of squeamish sorts."

"—but you make a good friend."

"Bah, not so good. Too old to be much good."

"I don't even know what dyspepsia is."

"Just indigestion. Like me. That's what I give you, most likely."

She gripped his hand and kissed his rough cheek. "Never. A guardian angel you are."

He stopped smiling and grasped her hand back. "That wouldn't be me. That would be the two men in the kitchen, honey. And they both love you. In different ways. I can tell."

She just shook her head and let go of his hand to climb the ladder. "Thanks, Mr. B. For everything. I'll never forget all you've done." She looked down at him from the top. "I love you."

"I love you too, Laura."

Then she climbed up the ladder. She looked back down at the top. Mr. B still watched her. She waved at him before turning away.

It was goodbye.

CHAPTER 31

The leftover spaghetti sat hardening in the stove pot and empty dishes sat strewn across the kitchen table amidst Jim's guns. Each one of them had chosen several different guns based on their plan. They decided holding down the cabin was their best defense. Felix would post himself at the screened-in porch and Jim would be in the great room. Ben would be upstairs with Laura, where he could scan the woods from the sliding doors at the balcony. If they had to make a run for it, it would be a short drop to the ground below.

"Mr. Barrens, I wish you would reconsider leaving," Ben said, putting his hand on the elderly man's shoulder next to him. "Take your Jeep and get as far away from here as possible. You've just recovered from pneumonia and I don't want to risk your life. We all know how this may end."

"Never." Jim snorted. "Laura is a daughter to me. I love her and I would die to protect her. Besides, this is my house and I'm going to defend who's in it. Do you think I'm afraid of dying? I'm almost ninety years old. What other excitement in my life could ever top this?" He grinned at Ben.

Felix nodded while filling his shotgun with shells. "We welcome your help. Just know we must take X-10 down first before he attacks us with his mind powers. Be ready to fire. We have a small window of opportunity to do so. His body is as vulnerable as yours. Bullets will kill him. But it must be enough to take him down so he doesn't have time to heal himself."

Ben turned to Felix. He had to ask him. "And just how do you see this day ending, Felix? Will we all make it?"

"What I see before me, is not always the final outcome. Many variables can change it."

"What a safe and vague answer that reveals nothing."

"Do you really want the truth, Ben? What purpose would it serve?"

"He's right," Jim interjected, still grinning. "I like surprises."

Ben looked at Jim. "Even if it means your death?"

Jim's smile faded and his voice softened. "If my death saves Laura, then yes."

"But what if we could prevent that with knowledge Felix has? Change the course of events? Plan differently?"

"My knowledge is limited, Ben," Felix said. "Once I see the final outcome is the desired result, I do not interfere. It could change the course of events leading to disaster and tragedy. We then leave the door open to that possibility and an unpredictable end. I don't want to be responsible for that, do you?"

Ben shook his head. Felix looked down at his gun, checking the mechanisms. "Everything will work out," Felix said. "Trust me."

Ben stared at Felix but he wouldn't look back up. Felix was lying, but Ben didn't push it. He sighed. Perhaps it was better not to know.

"It's time." Felix stood up. He closed his eyes and gripped his gun. "X-10 approaches. He'll be at the lake within the hour." He opened his eyes and they bore into Ben's with glowing intensity. They gathered their guns and stood for a moment looking at one another. One old, one young, and one from another world.

Jim put his hand on Ben's back. "Go to her. She needs you."

Ben nodded and turned toward the loft. All was quiet but the screeching wind that rose around the cabin in fits. He headed up the loft ladder into the darkness of the bedroom above.

"Laura, you okay? Your twin is coming, but I'm here. We're all here for you." He switched on the light to find the room empty. "Laura?"

He rushed into the bathroom and then back to the bedroom where the curtain blew at the balcony door. He pushed it aside to see the door open a crack.

Laura was gone.

Laura ran down the mountain trail toward the lake. The cold wind buffeted against her. It tried to snake its way inside her clothes, but she remained snug inside many layers. The only other things she had on her were a flashlight and her wallet. She had listened to the men talking in the kitchen and moved as quick and quiet as possible to sneak away. The sliding glass door creaked as she had opened it, but they hadn't stop talking below. She took the opportunity then to jump from the balcony to the ground below.

She had to go this alone. She hoped to draw her twin to the crash site. There they could meet face to face. Just the two of them. It was her destiny. No one else's. He sought her out all these years and killed those she loved. Her heart was still open though. Could she forgive him once seeing him? Could he accept her forgiveness? The idea seemed so ridiculous, but Laura had a small bit of hope she was right. She wanted to change their fate. It didn't have to end in bloodshed. She still believed everyone had something redeemable in them. No one had ever given her twin a chance. She wanted to.

They came from the same mother, same father. They only had each other. Could she make him realize that or would he truly be the monster Felix said he was? Her twin had haunted her all of her life, killed those she loved in gruesome ways, yet she was willing to forgive him. Together they had the chance to make right from so much wrong, didn't they?

If he accepted her.

Laura ran faster, her mind spewing with bizarre thoughts and her heart full of pain from those she lost. She ran toward her brother who sought to kill her.

"I'm losing my mind," she said to herself and the bare woods around her. She reached the crash site as dusk fell around her. She pulled out a flashlight from her pocket she had found in the nightstand drawer. She pushed aside the rusted fence and entered the site area. She stood on the edge of the small crater for a moment, looking down at the hole she had dug in the valley floor earlier. This would be where she might die today. If her twin wouldn't reason with her then she would have to kill him.

She ached for her mother and father to be alive. All the years she could have had with them. And Moe and Renee. She felt the deep hollow within herself grow larger with despair. Their deaths had to be for a reason, even if it was as small as bringing her and her brother together no matter what he had done. She walked down the hill to the crater floor and the tunnel entrance.

She would wait for him here.

It would end where it all started.

X-10 stood at the bridge that crossed the waterfalls. He was here. The frigid water raced over the rocks beneath him, tumbling below into a swirling frenzy. It rushed along, carrying everything it took with it. He relished the moment. He could see Laura in his mind's eye. She waited for him and he was coming.

He ripped off the old man's hat and coat and cast it aside, longing to be free in his movements. He yearned to be naked again as he had been all his life living in a solitary cell. The wind grabbed him with its cold tentacles, forcing its way through his shirt and pants, but he didn't notice. His blood pumped warm through his veins from running over miles of rocky hills and through dense woods.

The route he had taken through the Catskill Mountains had been sparse with population. He congratulated himself on his stealth and ability to remain hidden. The government was after him, but they would never find him. He could live in the woods as long as he needed. He could follow them all the way into Canada if he had to, living off the land and its inhabitants.

But first he had to take care of Laura. He sought her out his entire life. He had hated her from afar for so long he could think of no other way to perceive her except with hatred. He tried to recall when his hatred for her first grew, but he couldn't. Was it when he first discovered her existence through his powers, or later when he first sought her out? He remembered all the times Bjord taunted him about the girl and how she lived in a real home, with a family, even after X-10 had murdered her parents. Bjord continued to mock him with her existence from then on. For years he fueled X-10's hatred for her.

A spark of confusion mixed with uncertainty crept into X-10 for the first time. Bits and pieces came back to him of things Bjord said about Laura that didn't ring true. Did Bjord really know about Laura's existence? Did Bjord create his hatred for her or did X-10 indeed hate her on his own? *No, no! I do hate her. I must kill her. She got to live a life I never did! Stupid bitch. Not fair.*

He pressed his hands to his head forcing the uncomfortable thoughts away. She was so close. The time to kill her was now. Laura, the old man, and her lover were at the cabin, arming themselves against him.

Her lover. Not fair. He'd had a lover once. Sabrina.

She had folded him into her, offering him light, and beauty, and love.

That one glorious night Sabrina had sunk her welcoming heat onto him, drawing him in slow. His muscles tightened as she rose up and down. He spiraled high above where he had always dwelled in darkness. Her nipples were the light pink of sky at dawn, a color he'd only known from a photo. He touched them and they stiffened at his rubbing. He pulled away, but she took his hands and placed them on her breasts.

"Touch them like this, see? I like that, Charlie, do you?"

He could only nod as ecstasy rose in his groin, a building heat. He was covered in her wet depths. He watched his body disappear over and over into her as she took him in. Her moans crashed over him and he held onto her pliant flesh.

"Oh, Charlie, sweet Charlie."

He *was* sweet Charlie. He reached up and stroked her hair. She arched her back and he ran his fingers along her throat. It pulsed with life and blood. She fell on his chest and they were pressed together like one piece of flesh. Was this the love that humans spoke about in books? It opened up his dark soul and filled in the black holes where emptiness resided.

Her heart beat in sync with his.

Thump-thump. Thump-thump.

She pulled away from him then, a body of fluid lines, naked and lovely in its workings. She glided over him and he followed her rhythm.

And then a great wave swelled within him where water had never been. Her body was the oasis that took away his parched existence. His pleasure mixed with an ancient urge.

"Feel me, Charlie."

And he did. She was all around him and he shot into her the only thing he could give. Light pulsed out from his fingertips and toes and mouth. Brilliance blazed around him. Or was it her radiant hair that filled his vision above with this light he couldn't contain? He grabbed on to her and held her tight, releasing a wild roar as he rocked deep inside her sweet flesh. Her mouth hung open, her eyes wide. Did she feel it too? He closed his eyes and fell back onto the scorched sand as the water receded.

He had touched her as gently as she had touched him.

And now he pushed her memory away.

Had to push her away. It was too much to bear. Water filled his eyes now, a damning film. It spilled down his cheeks. It was painful. These human tears. This human pleasure led to so much pain. He would stick to killing for release.

And he sought such release tonight. Rage seethed within him once more as he ran toward is prey. Laura would love no more.

And as he ran he created balls of raging fire in his mind. He shot his fiery cascade to the cabin in the woods. At first it smoldered and sparked, then exploded into an angry blaze. Wood crackled and raged with flames. Cinders blasted upwards with a plutonic force.

X-10 tore off his remaining clothes as he ran. He was finally free of all that held him in the human world. He would show them. They couldn't hurt him. So pathetic were these humans who needed one another. They were weak in mind and of mortal flesh. They could not kill him. If they injured him he would heal himself. He was not human. He was the strong one. He would survive.

He needed no one.

Ben slid down the loft ladder in one leap, yelling to Felix and Jim. "She's gone. Laura's gone."

Felix ran into the house from the porch and the three of them stood there.

"She went to the crash site," Ben said. "I know it."

"Change of plans. Let's go," Felix said. Ben and Jim followed him out the door, heading for the rocky path to the lake. Felix stopped Jim.

"Ben and I will run down there." Felix passed him his car keys. "Here, take my car and drive around on the road to the lake and park there."

"No, I want to go with you." Jim protested, but Felix held his arm.

"It's best for Laura. What if we need a vehicle down there to get to a hospital when this is all over? We need a quick way to leave."

"But it's miles around on the road."

"Ben and I can run faster than you. You would just hold us up," Felix said. "Why put yourself in harm's way running down a mountain at your age and risk delaying our help to Laura?"

Jim nodded, took the keys, and got in the car. He stared at them as he gunned the engine and then shot off down the road. In that moment the woods suddenly darkened as dusk fell. Everything became covered in grayness. The whole world looked dead to Ben.

Felix ran from the cabin toward the trail down. "Come on!"

Ben followed close behind, panic hitting him like a brick to his chest. Why did Laura leave? He sensed she had been pulling away and didn't want to involve them. Did she think she could do this on her own? They were here to help defend her. *Damn her!* He clenched his hands, flexing them over and over. He never should have left her alone.

"Felix, why didn't you see this happening?"

"I did."

Ben grabbed the back of Felix's coat and lunged at him, shoving him into the side of Jim's workshop shed as they passed it. Felix turned on one heel and swung his arm out, holding Ben off like a child.

Ben swore under his breath and struggled to break free. "What the hell is wrong with you? Why didn't you stop her? She's gonna die. I need to be there. I need to protect her."

"This is the only way, Ben. Trust me."

"She's the one person I've cared about in a long time. Don't let her die."

Felix released him. "I don't intend to. Now come on."

Felix turned away and ran fast down the trail. His massive body moved nimble over the rugged ground. Wisps of fog whipped around his body in smoky tendrils as he flew through the woods toward the lake. He looked like a giant, dark beast lunging toward its quarry. Ben could only run after him. There was nothing else he could do.

They hadn't run far when a deafening blast pushed them to the ground. Firelight danced across them. The cabin exploded behind them in flames. It engulfed Laura and Jim's vehicles and the gas tanks exploded. Fire devoured old wood and metal, dancing upward toward the sky and into the trees overhead. The heat grabbed at them with fiery intensity.

"Laura," he whispered, stunned by the violence aimed at them. Their enemy was real. And he was here. Felix and Ben ran faster down the mountain, lunging down the trail, grabbing branches to push themselves along.

Felix had to be right. Please, let Felix be right.

Laura stood at the entrance to the tunnel as night moved in. She wondered when Ben and the others would find her gone. The wind blew hard around her, infusing her with its swirling madness. She felt she could fly up high above the ground in the angry gusts that pulled and pushed at her. Her twin was coming. His power moved toward her, a strong and primitive rage rushing over the earth seeking her out. *We are connected. We are twins. We are not so different.*

She conjured up her powers, raising her hands into the winds blowing around her. She dragged rocks with her mind powers and rolled them down the tunnel to the cavern below. She moved logs along the earthen path, adding to her armory. Shaking and sweaty from exertion, she then sat on the ground outside the tunnel entrance. She tried not to think about Ben, Mr. B, and Felix. Especially Ben. She cleared her mind. She was ready.

The falling sun stole the colors around her. The woods and ground became one as twilight created a solitary landscape. She gazed into the growing darkness above the valley floor, waiting. She felt a strange peace. She always hoped there would be a day so much would be answered and the nightmare would be over. This day had to come.

The dark clouds boiled across the sky in a furious tumbling of cold chaos, disappearing into the nightfall. She peered up at the pit's edge. There he stood. Just like in her dreams, outlined in silhouette. But now she knew who he was. His arms were crossed as if mocking her. The moon rose above him, full and brilliant in the sky. She wondered if it was the last moon she would ever see. Then fear seized her, but she had to finish what she began.

She turned to run into the tunnel and looked back. He strode down the side of the crater, coming fast. His skin shone white under the rising moon. She could make out the grin stretched across his face. The face of a monster. Her legs took over and she ran through the tunnel, pressing the flashlight on with trembling hands. And just like her dreams, his descent could be her death.

CHAPTER 32

Felix and Ben reached the lakeshore just as Jim squealed into the grassy parking lot. He jumped out of the car and shook his hand at the fiery mass glowing bright at the top of the mountain. It had spread to the surrounding trees and greedily fed on the woods around it. They could hear the dry limbs splintering and shrieking as their burning cries carried around the lake.

"Son of a bitch! My home."

Ben touched Jim's shoulder. His face hung slack and the moonlight carved shadows into his wrinkles. He looked old again to Ben. "I'm so sorry."

"Be glad we weren't in it when X-10 torched it," Felix said. "Come on! It's Laura we need to save now."

They ran along the shore path toward the crash site, guns in hand. Ben scanned the woods around him, afraid they would be taken unaware.

"He's not here," Felix reassured him. "He's closing in on Laura. Faster!"

They leapt over logs and rocks, a trio intent on one goal. To kill this evil that haunted the woman they all loved. They reached the fence and scrambled under it, toward the edge of the crater.

"There." Ben pointed below. "The tunnel Laura dug. It leads to the cavern below. Hurry!"

Ben led the way as they rushed down the slope to the black hole carved into the ground, then slid to a stop at the darkness that opened up into the earth. He heard something. A piercing howl. Then a scream. Laura's scream. He raced into the inky pit heading into the bowels of hell.

X-10 sped through the dark tunnel, hunched over to fit his tall frame through the earth ceiling. In the enclosed space his pungent smell rose around him. It had been a long time since he washed. He was covered in sweat from running for days through woods and filthy from sleeping on the ground. He enjoyed his aroma. It filled his senses with it. He couldn't wait to breathe deep of Laura and inhale her up close. To see her delicate features in person. To squeeze her perfect limbs between his mutant hands and hear her cry out in pain.

Rage coursed through his thick body, stoking his need to run faster and faster. Dim light spilled ahead. He had reached the end. It would be Laura's end too. And his quest would be over.

Laura positioned herself at the far end of the cavern room with her stash of rocks and wood. She heard the thunder of heavy feet pounding toward her. She felt her twin's wrath deep within, burning through his thoughts, feeding his need to kill her. Could she hope to stop him? She was dizzy with fear and anticipation. She had waited so long for this moment, to meet the man from her nightmares.

He entered the cavern. She stood still in the dim glow. He smiled at her across the expanse. They faced one another. Laura couldn't speak. His naked monstrous form leered before her in the flesh. He was here and now, no longer a dark entity in her mind that chased her.

His forehead pushed outward in a hideous shelf. His nose spread across his face from ear to ear. His enormous nostrils flared as he panted, inhaling her smell. His enormous mouth opened like a giant bucket on a hinge drawing in her aroma on his tongue. Laura saw all this in a split second as she watched her twin's muscles bulge out from his white skin. He stepped toward her.

"Stop!" Laura shrunk back. A clash of wood echoed through the pit as her jagged weapons filled the air. They hovered in the air, ready for her bidding. "I've dreamed of this moment." Laura was unable to take her eyes off his deformed face.

"So have I, Laur-r-r-a-a-a." X-10 mocked her, drawing out her name. "I've dreamed of the many ways I might slowly kill you." He moved another step closer to her.

Wooden skewers flew across the room and drove into his flesh. He remained standing. A smile spread slowly across his disfigured face. He winked at her, as he pulled the wooden stakes out of his arms and chest. He moved his fingers downward across his wounds and they disappeared. Then he threw back his head and laughed.

"You can't hurt me, don't you see? You, nor your little human friends. The old man and your lover. I'm going to enjoy this."

"You're human too. You're my brother. We come from the same

mother and father." She would not plead with him. She sensed it would only fuel his desire to control her.

"Not human. Never had a human life. No mother. No father. No home, like *you*, Laura. You had all of that. No one loved me. So why should you have it too?" His voice grew louder with anger, petulant like a little boy mad at not getting his way.

Laura stepped back and powered the rocks to gather in the air above her. They shook, waiting for her command. "You've taken away everything I loved. Isn't that enough?''

"Never!" X-10 grabbed for her. She catapulted rocks on him, pounding his head then ran to the other side of the cave. He shook off the blows as the rocks rained upon him.

"I could forgive you," Laura said.

X-10 grunted. He stretched up tall and commanded his long pod fingers to send rocks and sticks toward Laura. They beat upon her with viciousness as he used her own weapons against her. She cowered and screamed. Blood flowed down her arms and legs. She struggled to get up, but pain filled her body covered in debris. She strained to push it aside with her mind powers as he moved toward her, but she was so very tired.

As he lunged for Laura she sensed his conflicting feelings. She saw the scientist who experimented on him and caged her twin his whole life, taunting taunted him with her existence and fueling his hatred.

She saw all this in the two seconds it took for her brother to reach her. His sorrowful life punctured her like a knife digging into an old wound. His wounds made her wounds. It was a small window of opportunity to grasp, but all she had. Could she convince him to turn away from evil?

X-10 grabbed her by both arms and pulled her up. His freakish face loomed inches from hers. Her feet dangled above the earthen floor. Scenes from his life blasted across her mind. A tormented life. A tormented soul. Images of blood and killing and rage. And such loneliness. He had suffered such loneliness. He was an animal as he had been treated like an animal all his life. She pitied him and feared him.

"Charlie," she whispered. Pain coursed through her. He gripped her harder. She stared into his yellow eyes that shone bright, burning with hate.

"What did you say?" He shook her and she moaned in pain.

"Charlie. I called you Charlie, isn't that what you want? This life you've had was forced upon you. I forgive you for all you've done. We're all we have, can't you see? We've been brought together for a reason."

His thick fingers pinched her harder and she cried out.

"How do you know that's the name I wanted?" X-10's rage waned and she sensed he felt sorrow for himself. She heard him clear in her head. *No! That's not what I want. I want her to die! I hate her.*

"Because Charlie and the Chocolate Factory is one of your favorite stories. Mine too," Laura said. "And because it's what Sabrina called you, isn't it? She didn't hate you. And I don't hate you. I don't want you to die."

"Put her down, you monster." It was Ben. Laura craned her head around to see Ben, Mr. B, and Felix pointing guns at her twin. She tried to shake her head, but couldn't. Dizziness crept over her then a piercing probe snaked into her brain. Laura screamed, clutching her head.

X-10 scooped her into his arms and took off through the enormous cavern. Guns blasted around him. He stumbled as bullets struck him, but he kept running. Laura cried out. He raised one arm above him, commanding his power. The earth ceiling behind them fell, separating the cave in two sections. Wet mud and rock spewed down and filled every empty hole from one side to the other, creating a solid wall.

She was barricaded in with her brother now.

Then the pain in her head took over and she lost herself to the blessed dark.

X-10 retreated to the far end of the cavern. He could hear the men talking, but their words came through the thick wall muffled. Hunched over, he held Laura to his chest. He quivered in pain, and sank to the cold floor. He had to heal himself or he could die. This truth shocked him. He believed he was invincible.

Blood pulsed down his skin from the bullets that had pierced him. He looked at the dark, seeping streaks in the dim light glowing from the walls. The pain tore across his flesh, but then numbness crept into his body. He could not feel anything from the waist down, only the constant burning in his shoulder and back.

He had to loosen his mind hold on Laura to heal himself. He weakly pulled out his hands from under her as she sprawled motionless across his legs, and closed his eyes. But before he could move his shaking hands across his wounds, he felt other hands upon his upper chest. They spread outward in circles of warmth. He opened his eyes to stare into Laura's face.

She closed her eyes and focused on dislodging the bullets that impacted his flesh. One by one they popped out and fell on the floor. Anger flashed through him at his own weakness, but he was half paralyzed. And he felt something else. Something he hadn't felt in a long time. A warm feeling of being cared for. It tingled. It felt good.

But X-10 also felt powerless to her touch. He knew powerlessness well. It's what Bjord forced upon him in his cage his entire life when the scientist experimented on him. So many times the old man had drugged him and stuck metal probes to his testicles, sending electricity spiraling through his body to gauge his pain levels. That pain was almost as intense as the fire consuming his upper body now. How he had hated Bjord.

He watched, motionless, as Laura smoothed her hands over his wounds, drawing away the blood and excruciating pain. Soon it subsided to a dull throb. How could she help him when he had killed everyone she loved? He inhaled her smell. Sunflowers. He had smelled them once, a long time ago when he was a child and a woman doctor came to visit him. She had brought him sunflowers because he couldn't see the sun.

Stop it! Stop it! He screamed inside his head. He didn't want to think those pleasant thoughts. Or of Sabrina. Or of Laura being kind to him like Sabrina.

"Why heal me?" He forced his tongue to move, the numbness leaving his body. The bullet holes disappeared, yet still she knelt beside him with her hands on his chest. She picked up his hands and weaved her slender fingers with his monstrous ones. She was so warm. Love flowed from her into his very soul. It pained him.

"Charlie, you're my brother. Let me help you. We can disappear together, you and I. We can be free together. It's not our fault we are who we are. We can take care of one another. Just leave the others alone."

She cradled his hand on her cheek. He knew she felt so much pain in him and it filled her with the darkest sorrow.

He didn't want her pity. But then he remembered the farmhouse and the recliner. His vision of Sabrina in the kitchen cooking. The fire crackling in the fireplace. A home. With her? A sister? The idea of normalcy twisted in his dark mind.

"Yes, Charlie," Laura answered his thoughts. "We can run far, far away and try to make a home together."

But would she leave him as Sabrina had? And would she take her love with her, leaving him with an eternal broken heart wanting something he could never have—love. He had given it to Sabrina that night and said the words he'd never imagined saying.

"I-I love you." His heart unfolded then as he said it to her, and he breathed her wonderful smell that gave him life.

Sabrina intertwined her dainty fingers with his brutish ones and bent her head to touch his. Her hair hung glorious and alive around her, framing him in her world. Her hand grazed his face then she stood and pulled her clothes on.

"My hour is done, Charlie."

"Come back?" He hoped. He would do anything.

She looked at him with sad eyes then turned away and knocked on the door. The lock clicked. Metal slid open. She stepped through the space that would separate them.

"Sabrina, stay." He was captivated.

She glanced back. "Goodbye, Charlie. I hope you never forget your first time."

He stared at her in anguish and then her gold was gone.

"Wait. Don't go!" He came out of his reverie and rushed to the door. "He'll kill you!" But the door locked in place. He beat his fists on it. Even if he had gotten through he would never escape. Drugs sprayed into the air from his captor would knock him out the instant he tried.

"Bjord, leave her alone!" There was no answer from his master. "You hear me? Keep her here with me. I'll do anything you want. Anything!"

He paced his cell that night, smashing his hands on the concrete walls until they bled, wondering if she made it back to the streets. Wanting her to be back on the streets. Wanting her to be with other men. It would mean she was alive. He sought her out in the city with his mind's eye but she was nowhere.

Finally he fell into a nightmarish sleep. He stood on a riverbank and pieces of Sabrina floated by. An arm. A leg. A hand, frozen in a delicate wave. Her decapitated head stared at him with those blue eyes as her gilded hair flowed behind her.

When he woke, visions of Sabrina riding him with lust and tenderness fell heavy in his mind. And something white lay on the floor.

He wiped the sleep from his eyes and sat up, staring at it.

Sabrina's shirt.

Slashed with red.

A memento from Dr. Bjord.

He staggered out of bed and smashed the camera that mocked him. He would pay for that later.

He fell on his knees and caressed her blouse then picked it up gently so as not to add to its wounds. He breathed deep of this garment that had clung to her as she had to him. Her sweetness filled him—and then loss replaced it. She had called him an angel, but she was now the angel. His tears wet her shroud. It was all he could give her now. He willed Sabrina's musk—*their* musk—into his mind forever. He wasn't a monster then. He hadn't killed her. Dr. Bjord had.

X-10 hugged his first love to his chest and drifted back into his dreams where Sabrina could live again…and call him Charlie.

"Charlie?" Soft hands shook him.

And now another human was calling him by name, offering him love.

But he wasn't worthy. He never had been.

The muffled voices grew louder from behind the wall. Shots were fired. The men tried to blast through. Laura didn't cry out to them. She held his hand and looked into his eyes with her shiny, brown ones.

"If you're going to kill me, do it fast," she said quietly. "If you're not, let's leave this place. I know there is another way out of here, I felt a draft."

"And you would go with a monster? Do you know what I've done? What I would do again if given the chance—to you? What I enjoy doing? I can't stop. It's what I am." His nostrils flared. He showed her flashes in his mind of gruesome images. And no remorse. She squeezed his hand.

"Yes, I've seen what you've done. But you *can* stop yourself. Overcome and change. Put it in your past. Start over. You can. We both can, Charlie. We have the same destiny. We both have a human element. We have something redeemable in us. No matter what we've done. And you're my brother. We can be a family, together."

Earth and rock passed through the wall and fell at their feet. The men came through. And yet, still, Laura touched him. *No!* He didn't want to feel these strange feelings. He couldn't bear them. More gunshots blasted through the wall and her lover rushed through the hole. He grabbed Laura and pointed his gun at X-10. The old man and another enormous man he had never seen before stepped through as well. Their guns were aimed low at X-10, as he sat, sprawled on the floor.

"What's wrong with him?" The old man jerked his gun at X-10.

"He couldn't move after you shot him. I healed him," Laura said.

"You what?" Her lover's mouth hung open.

"Then why is the ugly bastard still sitting there?" The old man pointed his gun at X-10, his finger at the trigger. Rage surged through X-10, disgusted at his wave of emotions filling him up. He could never be anything other than what he was. He didn't want Laura to change him. He hated her. Didn't he? He didn't *want* to be anything other than what he was.

He staggered up. The enormous man shot at him. Once. Twice. X-10 stumbled then grabbed the man's gun away and pointed it at Laura's lover. The enormous man lunged in front of her lover just as X-10 fired. Bullets struck the large man mid-chest. He crashed on the ground.

"No!" Laura fell to the man's side. A gaping hole smoked through his black jacket. His eyes were closed. The man didn't move. Laura sobbed as both her lover and the old man shot at X-10 over and over. He lurched from side to side with each hit and then swung wide, cracking the old man on the head with the gun he still held. The old man crumpled to the floor.

"No, Charlie! Why?" Laura pleaded. "Kill me. It's what you've wanted. Leave the others alone." She rushed to the old man, who moaned but was still alive.

Laura's lover raised his gun to X-10's head. "Goodbye, you mother fucker." X-10 just grinned at him. Her lover pushed down on the trigger, but X-10 sent spirals of intense pain into his brain. Her lover dropped the gun and fell to the floor clutching his head.

Laura rushed at X-10. She beat her fists on his chest. "Why?"

He pushed her away and swayed sideways, then fell on the ground facing her. Curls of gun smoke filled the cave and weaved around Laura's head. She knelt by X-10's side. He felt blood run down his back and chest. It hurt to breathe.

"Stop it, please, Charlie! Let them live. It's me you've always wanted. Kill me, let them live. Please." She took his hands and clutched them to her chest. She moved into him. Sunflowers wafted over him.

"Don't you see, Laura? If I become like you, then how can I live with all the things I've done?" It felt strange to say her name out loud to her. It felt good.

Laura kissed his face, stroked his cheeks. "Hate and love come from the same place. You can change that now, Charlie. Let me heal you."

He snatched his hands away from her, staring at them. "No! Look at me. I'm a freak." He touched her face, then his own. "I don't need love. Stop making me feel this way! I don't want to feel this way." He shoved Laura away from him, slamming her into the wall. "I wanted to hurt you, kill you. But now I'm confused! Let me be!" He held his head.

"I thought I was a freak too. But we have each other now." Laura pulled herself up from the floor, slow. He felt her pain too. She pulled a photo out of her coat pocket. She held it up to his face. "Our mother. She carried both of us. Look."

He touched the edge of the photo then looked at Laura. "You're normal. Human, like her. I'm a monster. That's what I am."

"Human too."

"No. I am nothing."

"We all have something redeemable in us, no matter how small."

"Nothing," he repeated in a stone voice.

"Something."

"Nothing."

X-10 placed his hands on his head, and howled a long cry of pain. It echoed around the dark pit in a piercing wail, growing louder in its lament.

And then he made his last kill.

CHAPTER 33

Laura put her hands over her ears to shut out her brother's screams. It hurt to hear his pain vibrating inside her. The ground shook. Mud and rock rained down on her. She covered her head. The cave roared with his fury, moving in a mad dance as it trembled. Then he closed his eyes. His massive body sunk into the floor, his hands drifted down. His immense mouth hung open, slack-jawed. The throbbing veins in his forehead slowed and were still.

"Charlie."

She looked around her, stunned. Felix lay dead. Mr. B sprawled motionless. And Ben. He moaned and was so still. Sobbing, she crawled to Mr. B. He was breathing, but unconscious. She kissed his cheeks. She willed herself to heal him but he didn't open his eyes. Perhaps he was injured too deep. Or perhaps his fate was to die now, as he was supposed to die years ago in the orchard or by pneumonia. Laura cried harder. She didn't want fate to win. Not this time. Then she dragged herself to Ben and smoothed back his bangs. Please don't be dead, Ben. All this death because of her.

"Ben." Laura wanted so much to see his gray eyes looking at her. "Open your eyes." She pressed her face on his chest, listening for life, inhaling his smell. "I love you."

His heart beat but he didn't move. Her tears wet his jacket. She sat up and placed her hands on his head. She closed her eyes, blocking out the carnage around her and focused on this man she loved. She imagined pulling the daggers of pain from his head and filling him with strong threads of connective tissue. Strength flowed from her fingertips into his brain, healing it with pulsing life. She hoped.

"Please don't die. Never surrender, remember?" She sang to him, her voice cracking on the notes. "And when the night is cold and dark, you can see, you can see light. Cause no-one can take away your right to fight—"

"—and never surrender," Ben whispered back.

Laura opened her eyes to find his gray ones burning into hers. She let out a cry of relief and kissed him with trembling lips.

"What just happened?" He peered around as he sat up slow.

"My brother killed himself."

"Are you sure he's dead?"

Laura pulled Ben up and they stood over her twin, his freakish form hunched over on the floor. Ben prodded him with his foot.

"The final one he sought out was himself," Laura said. "Love couldn't set him free, only hate. But at least he's at peace."

"Then it's over." Ben grabbed Laura, and held her close. She felt relief wash over him like an elixir. "And you're okay?"

She nodded. "But Mr. B, we need to get him to a hospital. He's breathing okay, but that hit to the head knocked him out. I tried, but I couldn't heal him."

Ben moved to Jim and knelt down, listening to his breathing. "And Felix?"

Laura just shook her head, biting her lip. She moved toward Felix's body. She bent down to touch his face. She wished she could see his green eyes glowing bright one last time. His belt glinted in the low light. She pulled it off, clutching it in her hands. It was made of heavy metal and vibrated in her hands. She believed she may need it someday, as Felix had once believed a long time ago.

"You saved us. You did. Was it the desired outcome you wanted?" She spoke to his still face.

"Twice," Ben said. "He saved me twice."

"He must have seen his own end, don't you think?"

"And you saved me too, didn't you?"

Laura looked up at him. "I had to try."

Ben nodded and put his arms under Jim's body. "Come on now, we've got to carry him out of here."

"What about Felix and Charlie?"

"Let them rest here in peace. Neither one had any peace their whole lives. Now they can."

Ben stumbled up with Jim in his arms. "Laura, come on. We've got to get out of here."

She nodded, looking at Charlie and Felix one last time then passed through the hole in the wall back into the other side of the cavern. Ben moved sideways through the jagged opening with Jim. As they stepped out onto the flat earth floor, Laura felt a shudder. She stopped.

"What was that?"

"I don't know? A shift in the ground perhaps. We need to get up top where it's safe."

The ground became still again. They took off through the enormous cavern, seeking the tunnel back to safety.

"Put me down," Jim said clearly. Ben almost dropped him.

Laura skidded to a stop on the muddy floor. "Mr. B, you're all right."

He coughed hard, clutching his head. "Not sure about that, but put me down, young man."

"Mr. Barrens, we have to get out of here, now."

"And you need to put me down *now*!"

Ben lowered Jim to the floor. He lay on his back, his breathing labored. "I can't see. Where are we?"

Laura knelt in the mud beside him and took his hand. "We're in the cavern, Mr. B. My brother is dead. It's over."

"Felix?"

"He's dead too."

"Ahh. He was a good man. I'm sorry to hear that. He loved you, Laura."

"I know. He saved all of our lives. But now we need to get you to a hospital."

"No. I am staying here on my mountain." He wheezed. "Are you making the room spin, my dear?"

"No, Mr. B. You had a hard blow to the head. Come on now."

"No, I said, you saucy young maid." His voice faded off. "No."

"Don't be difficult, please, you old curmudgeon." Laura began to cry. Jim put his hand up and sought her face. She leaned into him. He touched her cheek, his fingers frail and gnarled.

"I told you a long time ago I'm a solitudinarian, my girl. And it's time I went my own way, alone."

"No, remember I made you a convivialtarian? A chooser of people not aloneness. Choose me. Don't go, please. Stay here with me. Hang on, Mr. B." She gripped his hand harder, willing his spirit to stay strong, wishing hard for life to run through his old veins. But maybe he *was* meant to die. She had saved him twice and now fate was stepping in to re-align its course.

"I've got to go home now. To see my Susan and Scooter. You stay with Ben."

"No, Mr. B, no! We have lots of time left." Laura snatched his other hand to pull him up. "Ben, help me." But Jim's head sank into his side. His hand fell from her face.

Ben felt his pulse and listened for a heartbeat. "Laura, he's gone."

"No!" She rocked with her head in her knees.

The earth quaked beneath their feet, knocking Ben back. A loud rumbling rose over them. Chunks of dirt splashed down around them.

"It's going to bury us!" Ben pulled at Laura. "We've got to run!"

But Laura refused get up. She continued to cry, rocking in grief.

Debris rained down on them. The rumbling grew louder. Ben picked Laura up and ran for the tunnel. He could just make out the black hole ahead of him across the cavernous expanse. She beat on his chest and shoulders.

"You can't leave him here, go back!"

Ben couldn't answer. He just wanted to get out without killing them both. He concentrated on running up the tunnel as earth and rock smashed onto them. He banged into the walls several times, off-balance in the total black. Laura stopped hitting him but continued to sob into his chest. Up. Up. It took forever to reach the surface.

A large chunk of earth fell hard on him. He went down, slamming Laura into the ground under him. He pulled her closer to his chest and stumbled up, tripping over rocks. His chest hurt, each breath like tiny knives cutting into his lungs. Finally, light filled the dark space. He raced out of the tunnel entrance, just as it collapsed behind him.

A giant roar of noise and dust filled the air. The crater sank deeper into the ground, as the cavern below it was crushed flat with all those in it. He looked up at the moon growing high overhead and smelled smoke. The cabin fire had continued to spread through the woods. It raged in fury devouring the dry timber in a crackling buffet. Would any help come to stop it out here in the middle of nowhere?

Ben staggered along the lakeshore trail. Laura now hung limp in his arms. He reached Felix's car and put her in the passenger seat, relieved to find the keys in the ignition.

Laura looked up at him still clutching Felix's belt. "I first came here with Mr. B and saw my alien father, Feo. I didn't know at the time who or what he was."

"Now you do. But it still doesn't change who you are, Laura."

"It does," she whispered. "I told you before. It changes everything."

Ben nodded. He understood that now.

"And now they're all dead. Everyone's dead. And for what? *For what*?"

He kissed her forehead, not knowing what to say. He ran around to the driver side. The fiery forest exploded across the lake. Its light flickered and soared across the water, dancing on the waves rocking serenely to shore.

He stood mesmerized for a moment, taken back in time. He saw another night here where fire plumes raged across the lake shore. He heard the sound of sirens from far away. Fire trucks would be here soon, like they had that night twenty-seven years ago when he was only nine. He forced himself to look away and jammed the car into reverse, kicking up rocks as he sped out of the grassy lot.

He didn't look back.

Ben gunned the sedan hard, and shot off down the rough road leading away from the lake. As he reached town a fire truck screamed past them on the way to the fire. He parked the car in town on a side street, leaving the keys tucked under the visor. Then he gathered his few belongings at the Inn and drove west with Laura in his own rental car. He was relieved no one passed them in town before they left. Not even the innkeeper, Mrs. March, was around. Laura followed him as he moved along but said nothing. Her eyes looked empty as if they saw another scene before her.

Before leaving, he wiped down all parts of Felix's car they had touched in case was an investigation. He doubted Felix left a trail. But there would be no evidence of what happened to Jim. His cabin was burnt down and both his and Laura's cars had exploded into pieces. And Jim, he was at rest under the earth. No one would ever know what happened to him. As they pulled out of town, more fire engines screamed past them on the way up to the lake. The streets were dark and empty in the little hamlet. No one else passed them.

Ben drove for hours in silence. He hit the highway and headed out toward Binghamton. Somewhere different. Anywhere there weren't memories for either of them. Laura hunched over in the corner, and didn't speak. He stroked her hair as he drove. He didn't know how to bring her back to him. He sensed she was already gone. He turned the radio on once but the noise hurt his head, so he turned it off. Laura didn't comment at all, she continued to stare out the window at the darkness that flew by. He talked to her as he drove, but she didn't respond.

"We can go anywhere, Laura. I have enough money set aside we can live on for a while. We can go west to Bremerton, in Washington. You can meet my friend, Andy. How about that? You'll love his wife, Likini. She's a great lady. We can start over. Make a new life. Can't we?" Still, she didn't answer him. He sighed, and drove on into the night.

He stopped at a super-size all-night store just off the highway near Binghamton. He guided Laura into the store with him, hoping no one would notice how filthy they were. But the store was almost empty. No one gave them a second glance. He bought sandwiches, water, toiletries, bandages, ointment, and extra clothes for both of them. Laura touched none of the food, but he wolfed down a sandwich as he drove. He found a small motel and pulled in. They were still covered in mud, but the teenage night clerk didn't even look at them as they registered and paid.

Ben led Laura into the room and turned her to face him, holding her by the shoulders. She still clutched Felix's belt. Ben placed it on the dresser and looked into her eyes.

"Laura?" She looked right through him. It haunted him, as if she were broken forever. He would take care of her. She had to come out of this catatonic state.

He stripped off both their filthy clothes and took her to the shower with him. He washed her as he did the other night. This time she stood before him, conscious but in a daze. Mud flowed around them as the soap washed it away. He wished it was as easy to wash away the night's events. His body felt sore, bruised, and cut.

He tried to be gentle in washing Laura's cuts. He hoped she didn't feel any pain. She was traumatized, but he didn't know how to help her. Afterwards, he cleaned both their wounds and put bandages on them. Then he dressed her and himself in clean clothes and stretched out on the bed with her. She remained far away in her mind.

"Laura, come back to me, please." He held her to him.

Tears slid down her face, but she still wouldn't speak. She stared at the ceiling. Something must have just snapped inside her, after all she had been through her entire life. This was too much. Perhaps losing Jim had been the final piece of her life destroyed she couldn't live with. Jim had been the last link in her life between her past as a child and future as a woman. So Ben held her and murmured words of reassurance to her. He loved her. They could make a life together. It was over. But it didn't matter in the end, after all. When he woke up she was gone.

He stood at the motel window overlooking fields that graced the highway. Trucks roared by to their destination. He had no destination now, without Laura. A week had changed everything. He stared at the sunrise, alone, her note in his hand. He read it again.

You're better off without me. Find a real woman. One that is human. I'm no good to anyone. Everyone I love dies. I'm cursed. Forget all this. Forget about me. You're free now. Laura.

Why did she leave when she was the only woman he ever loved? The first woman he wanted to give all of himself to. He flashed back to all the years wasted, taking from women what he wanted, but not giving himself to them. He was lost then without purpose and lost now, in Laura. She gave him purpose. He wanted to be lost in her. He needed it. He needed her. Why couldn't she need him?

He watched the sun rise on another day, determined to find her.

CHAPTER 34

Ben gazed out over Puget Sound, his camera in his lap. In the four months he had been staying with Andy and Likini, most of it had been spent looking for Laura. After three days in Binghamton trying to find some trace of her, the only information he got was after showing her photo around the bus station.

One clerk getting off the night shift remembered seeing a woman that looked like her board a bus in the middle of the night to Charleston, South Carolina. Ben had no idea why she would go there, but it was the one lead he had. He returned his rental car and took the next bus out to Charleston, hoping to find her there.

The muggy, warm air assaulted him once he headed south. He embraced it after the cold September days in New York. He walked the cobblestone streets through the marketplace and historic district for days, stopping to show vendors Laura's photo. None had seen her. He visited the beaches, thinking she sought solace at the water's edge. He visited hotels asking the desk clerks if they had checked her in.

Every road he drove down held a memory of Laura. Every corner he turned held another scene of her in his mind. Skin to skin, enveloped in her softness, her eyes, her mind, her heart. Every night alone in his motel room, the dark surrounded him driving a piercing ache into him. He had a burning need to touch her again. He had to find her. If not, then what was this all for they had been through together? Nothing? He couldn't believe that. Fate brought them together once. It had to bring them together again. It had to re-align itself, like Felix said. Didn't it?

But after three weeks of looking for Laura he found nothing. The trail ran cold in Charleston. Perhaps she had moved on somewhere else.

He sat on the beach one overcast day, realizing he might not find her. He couldn't accept that. Maybe he could stay with Andy for a while to figure things out. He would be back by now from his assignment. Andy always put things in perspective for him, whether he liked the advice or not.

He had told Laura his friend Andy lived in Bremerton, Washington. He wanted to believe in his heart she might seek him out there. It was a small chance, but he found himself with no other answers. So he had called his old friend and was told he had a room waiting for him. Andy must have heard something in his voice, had a dozen questions, but he didn't probe on the phone, just told him to, 'get your skinny ass here.'

Now here he sat, on Andy and Likini's enclosed sun porch looking out over the cold water from their home in Bremerton, not far from the Naval Criminal Investigative Service where Andy worked. Ben woke up early on this late winter Saturday morning. His friends still slept. Ben enjoyed the quiet, thumbing through photos in his camera, stopping on Laura's photo as he did a few times each day. He wished her eyes were open in the photo as she sang in the tree. He wanted to look into her eyes again and tell her he loved her. He was losing hope it would ever happen. After almost five months, she had become dream-like in his memories. Often, he couldn't remember if his dreams of her were real or things that actually happened were dreams.

He even hired a private detective to find Laura, but he had no luck either. Ben admitted it might be time to give up. Clients were calling and he had to get back to work if he wanted to keep his business going. He wasn't sure about that either. It was time to get his own place here or move on. At eight months pregnant, Likini's swollen body still moved gracefully along. She and Andy were both genuine in telling Ben he could stay as long as he needed, but he they would need their own space as a family soon.

He had spent time each day searching for leads of Laura on the Internet, hoping for a scrap of public information on her location. Nothing ever came up. The other time he spent traveling Washington State photographing its beauty. Its rugged mountains and towering giant trees grabbed hold of him. It was a place of big things and space, unlike the tight forests and urban areas of the Northeast. This was a place he could breathe in. A place he might stay in, if he had someone to stay for.

Taking pictures eased his mind of the pain of Laura. He needed to keep busy so he didn't have to make a decision yet about his next steps, which were one of two things—continue to search for Laura or move on.

But some days his heart would skip faster as he drove by a girl on the street, catching a glimpse of shiny chestnut waves flipped over a shoulder. Or as he walked along, it might be a flash of large, brown eyes cruising past him in a car that would send him back in time. They spent just a few days together but it was as if they lived years in those moments. And it was as if she followed along with him now, around every bend.

Every street he turned down, every photo taken, held a memory of him and Laura. Their time together played out like a movie in his mind, rolling on, taking him back to the want and need in her eyes. And love. She had helped him remember how to love. It tormented him wondering where she was right now. Was she somewhere thinking of him too?

And the nights haunted him too. As he gazed at the full moon, he really stood under another moon where he had once stared at the midnight-blue sky near a mountain lake. A night where he felt Laura warm and real beside him, moving beneath him by the fire, sweet and burning. He would try and shed her from his mind and drift off into the lonesome darkness only to see her again in his dreams.

When he arrived those months ago Likini had asked him no questions, and he was grateful for her silent acceptance. But Ben spilled the entire story to Andy that first night he arrived. They sat alone on the porch, blinded by the setting sun sparkling on the Pacific Ocean.

Ben couldn't stop talking. He spoke out loud for the first time of his foster father's death, and the night the Samoans kidnapped him and took him to the Pali Lookout. He told Andy how the man in black saved him. Felix was part of the story and Ben couldn't leave him out of it. Then, finally, he spoke about Laura. It felt good to talk about it, at last. Andy was speechless at first, fascinated by his tale, but soon engrossed in the fantastical details.

"What if you don't find her, Ben?"

"I don't know. We're connected. There's no one for me after her. There never could be."

"Maybe your meeting her was meant for other reasons, did you think about that?"

"What do you mean?"

"Well, perhaps having had your experiences with her it will help you move on to finding someone else. Someone you can open yourself up to and settle down. Now that you've done it with Laura, perhaps you can do it again. Your coming together was so short and intense do you think it could ever translate to a long term relationship?"

Ben shook his head. He didn't want to think about it.

"You know that saying, Ben, how some people come into our lives for a reason, even if for just a season? Maybe that's what Laura was. She came for a reason, to help you move on from your past but the two of you weren't meant to be forever."

"I never believed in forever, and now that I do it's gone, you know?"

Andy nodded and said no more. They sat in comfortable silence and watched the sun slip over the ocean's horizon. That night Ben had hope of finding Laura. Now, today, months later in the daylight, it was time to move on. Perhaps Andy could be right.

But some nights, when the moon pulled him to the window, he felt someone watching him. Once he thought he saw her, in the shadows, but when he blinked she disappeared. He wanted to believe she watched over him, although she couldn't bring herself to be with him.

He understood the conflict raging inside her. He had felt the same for many years. The conflict of wanting love, yet turning away from it, and creating the wall to protect yourself from being hurt. He knew that wall. She had taken it down brick by brick, and all that remained was an empty foundation waiting to be filled. Now he didn't know if it ever would be.

Here, months later, he had to make a decision about what he was going to do. He had lost hope that Laura would seek him out at Andy's. In telling Andy this, his old friend jumped on the make-Ben-feel-better-bandwagon and invited the sister of one his colleagues over for dinner.

"What?" Andy shrugged his shoulders at Ben's frown. "It's not like it's a double date. It's just dinner. Besides, I saw a photo of her. She's smokin' hot."

"It *is* a double date. That's what this is. I never said I wanted to find someone else. No matter how smokin' they are. What are you doing?"

Andy's blue eyes sparkled at Ben. "I'm just trying to get you laid, my man. She's really built too." He whispered, so Likini wouldn't hear on the other side of the kitchen. She was putting together a traditional Polynesian feast for Ben and his 'date'.

"Ben deserves more than that, Andy," Likini said, without looking up from her dish.

Andy rolled his eyes at Ben. "You don't miss a thing do you, pretty lady?" Then he whispered again to Ben. "But it wouldn't help to get laid just once to get Laura off your mind."

So his friend's sister came and she was indeed pretty and sexy in a blonde, lanky kind of way with enormous breasts pushing out in all directions. She made it quite obvious she wanted him, and Ben laughed at Andy's behind-her-back grins at him.

She was an intelligent, beautiful girl, but she wasn't Laura. She wasn't lithe and brunette with perky breasts and sloe-eyes that drew you in to their passionate depths. And he thanked her for a good evening and shook her hand at the door. She went off a bit miffed, he could tell, but then again this date wasn't his idea.

"Ben, why didn't you get some of that?" Andy wanted to know, as they sat on the porch later. Likini had gone to bed, becoming more tired in her final month.

Ben laughed. "Are you kidding? I told you I'm not ready to move on."

"You mean you don't want to. There's a difference, man. She could have been a transitional woman, you know?"

"Really."

"Yes, really. I mean, hell, she practically was offering herself to you at dinner rubbing up against you like a cat in heat. *Meowwww!*"

"Well, maybe I want to work a little harder for it than that. I don't need some desperate chick."

"Why not? 'Cause it's no fun when they just fall over with their legs in the air?"

"Real nice. Yeah, something like that."

"Maybe if you got rid of your blue balls you could think straight and figure out just what the hell it is you're going to do next. Because right now you're in limbo and I have to see you moping about every day."

"Fine. I plan to move out anyways. I know I've overstayed my welcome."

Andy shook his big, blond head. "It's not that. We're family. I want you around. But you've got to move on from finding Laura. I don't think it's going to happen."

Ben was silent. His friend was right. "I know. It's time to forget about her."

Saying those words made them real to Ben. Once he put them out there, the time had come. So now he sat on the porch deciding today would be the day he was going to go find his own place to rent in town. Maybe somewhere near the water. This town was as good as any to make a home and it felt good to have Andy and Likini nearby. They were his family now, and maybe all he would ever have. Besides, he would be "Uncle Ben" soon to their child and that would be something, right?

He put the camera down and heard a door open somewhere in the house. He looked at his watch. 9:00 a.m. About time those two love birds got up. He stood and gazed out over the ocean before turning into the kitchen, when a taxi cab drove slowly up the driveway. The car pulled up to the front door and someone stepped out, covering their eyes from the sun. Chestnut hair shone in the light, falling in waves.

It was Laura. She was real. She wasn't a photo. Her eyes were open and she looked up at him.

Ben blinked, unable to move. His heart raced in his chest. Then he broke from his stance and bolted down the stairs to the front door. He opened it and she stood there, holding a suitcase in front of her. She looked as lovely as ever. Doves cooed in the woods above the house in the quiet morning. She smiled, tentative and unsure of herself, he could see. After all these months. Why now?

Laura walked slowly toward Ben, as he had seen her in his dreams many times. Only now, she was here. Her face looked fuller and her hair longer.

And he loved her as much as ever.

CHAPTER 35

Laura put her suitcase down and faced Ben on the stoop. She had longed to see his gray eyes again, feel his arms around her. She didn't know what to say now.

"Laura."

That's all she needed to hear. She moved into him and he held her close. She never wanted to be apart from him again. They held one another still for a moment. He pressed her deeper into him and she hoped he would feel something different there. He looked down. Laura stepped back, opening her coat, and placed his hand on her belly.

"Felix was right," she whispered. He shook his head as if in disbelief. "I'm five months pregnant."

After months of moving from town to town, trying to get her head right then discovering she was pregnant, she now placed her faith in making the decision to find Ben. Would he turn her away after all this time and knowing she was pregnant? She knew he had been looking for her. But could it be too late now?

She had used Felix's belt to watch Ben. After many frustrating nights of trying combinations on the belt's button panel she had succeeded. She remembered Felix said you just needed to think of the person you sought and it would transmit you there, like a holograph image. It didn't transport your body but gave you a window to look through.

And finally one night, using the belt, she closed her eyes and wished to see Ben. When she opened them, she was watching him from the shadows of his room as he slept. She ached to be with him but couldn't bring herself to go to him. She was afraid that she would bring a curse to his life. She still felt responsible for so many deaths of those she loved.

If she didn't go to Ben, he would live. It was simple as that in her mind for a long time. When she discovered she was pregnant she agonized for weeks over whether to have an abortion. After passing the three-month mark, she felt relieved as now the decision was out of her hands.

She watched Ben many other times, hiding in the shadows, listening to his conversations with Andy and Likini. Once, in the dark, he stared right at her and she feared he saw her. For a moment their gazes locked, his gray ones searing into hers. She pushed the button on the belt to stop transmission, and found herself back in her motel room a moment later.

Then one night, when she heard him say it was time to forget about her, she had to do something. She either had to start her life over, find a new job with her money running out, a place to call home, a daycare for the baby—or go to Ben now. And now she stood in front of him, waiting—hoping—for his acceptance.

He looked down at her belly. Laura sensed he too felt life growing there and was amazed. She looked into his gray eyes. They were so beautiful, like him. Like she hoped their child would be.

"I tried to let you go but I couldn't," she said, simply.

"Neither could I."

He smiled and pulled her back into him, kissing her long and deep. And she knew it would be all right. He led her into the house and into the kitchen where Andy and Likini stood staring at their entrance. Likini smiled and nodded. Laura sensed Likini's gladness.

"Andy, Likini, this is Laura."

Likini went to her and took both her hands. She was the most beautiful woman Laura had ever seen, even in full bloom of her pregnancy.

"I hoped our Ben would find his Laura someday," Likini said. "Welcome. Now come eat, your baby needs it and so do you."

Laura nodded. She didn't know what to say. Her coat covered her belly once again and she didn't know how Likini knew, but she did. Andy grinned at her and nodded.

"Yes, welcome. You're just in time for breakfast. All of you." Andy bear hugged Ben. "Congratulations." And he kissed Laura on the cheek, who blushed. She felt shy about just showing up at the home of these two people who were so happy to see her, although she was a stranger.

Likini and Andy welcomed Laura as if her coming was expected, or more like wished for. They asked no questions of her but accepted her as Ben's partner. Likini set her up discreetly alone, but in the guest bedroom connected to Ben's.

Together upstairs after breakfast, Laura helped to make up her bed.

"You're so lucky to have such a wonderful man as Andy for a husband."

Likini smiled and swung her glossy, black hair that fell like a mahogany waterfall. "Yes, I am blessed." She rubbed her rising abdomen. "And you too. Ben is a wonderful man, a good friend to Andy."

Laura nodded, her eyes filled with tears. She had discovered being pregnant meant trying to fight the daily swelling of emotions racing inside her like a rollercoaster.

Likini moved next to her and touched her belly. "Doubly blessed you are as well. You have a family now."

Laura bit her lip, trying not to cry, but the tears spilled over. "I lost all the family I had and Ben did too. I'm so scared. I don't know what will happen once this baby comes. I don't know what it will be."

If Likini thought her choice of words strange she did not show it but took her in her arms and held her. Their bellies touched one another filled with life from the men they loved. "It will be your child, and Ben's. That is what it will be and that is all you need to know."

"My good friend, Mr. B said once, before…he died…that Ben was my match. I couldn't believe it though. I felt so alone and was gone a long time not knowing what to do. I never knew my real father, but was lucky to have had a wonderful father who adopted me. I want my child to know his father. I almost killed my baby. How could I have wanted to kill our baby?" Laura sobbed harder.

"But you didn't. You made the right choice and Ben is here. You are a family now."

Likini stroked Laura's hair and soothed her. And they held one another in understanding, as only pregnant women can when faced with life changes rushing toward them.

And so Ben and Laura began to get to know one another in a new place and a new time. A time harboring no crisis or fear or pain. It was surreal in the path of what lay behind them when the few days they spent together had been filled with so much death.

He wanted to go to her that first night, but was anxious about how she might receive him. He was also nervous about hurting her in her condition if they made love. He tried to sleep but couldn't and stood by the window looking out over the ocean. He thought of Laura so close to him sleeping in the bedroom a few feet away.

He ached for her, but didn't have to wait long as the connecting door opened. She stood outlined in the shadows before him in a baby doll nightgown. She looked so young and sweet. He took her hand and lowered her gently on the bed, sliding next to her. The moon shone in through the sheer curtains, glinting on her curves and hair. He breathed her in and held her, one hand spread wide on her belly in possession.

Then he felt a kick, once, twice, and laughed out loud. Laura pressed her hand over his.

"It just started a couple weeks ago. She is feisty, or he. I don't know what it is."

"It's ours, that's what it is."

They faced one another on their sides, staring into each other's eyes.

"What are we going to do, Ben?"

"I'm not sure. I'm still in shock you're here. Ecstatic, but in shock."

"I know. I didn't make it easy, running away."

"Nope, sure didn't."

"I'm glad I found you through Felix's belt. I've been watching you." She hung her head, as if ashamed to admit spying on him. "I saw you with Andy and Likini and remembered you said they lived here."

"I wondered how you knew to come here. Although, I hoped you would. And I now know I wasn't imagining you at times. I really did see you in the shadows, didn't I?"

Laura nodded, tucking her head into her chest, but Ben picked it up to look into her eyes. "Why didn't you give me a chance all those months ago, Laura?"

She looked over his shoulder at the moon shining through the window. "Do you realize that my creation came out of your parent's death? Because of me they died."

"No, because of fate and destiny they died. You weren't even born yet. You had no control over that. It's almost sweet irony I lost my parents and later found a love through the very accident that caused their death. And because of you I have life again. I have love again."

Ben pulled her face back to his, and stared into her eyes to reassure her. She looked down at the bed sheets, twisting them in her fingers.

"I couldn't give you a chance back then, Ben, because I was afraid."

"Afraid of what?"

"Afraid if I stayed, somehow you would die too. I know it sounds illogical, because the threat that chased me my entire life was gone, but it's how I felt. You were the one person left that I loved and I wanted you to live. If just one person I loved lived, then I could be okay with that. So I set you free so you could live."

Ben pulled her face back to his. "I *am* free. You did set me free, but not in the way you think. There's nothing in our way now."

She nodded slowly.

"And why did you come back, Laura?"

"Because I discovered love doesn't go away. It doesn't die."

Ben grinned. "Someone once told me love remembers."

"Yes, it does."

"And I'm your match, remember that too?"

Laura laughed then she looked sad. "My headaches are gone now, I guess because the reason for them is gone. And I keep thinking about Charlie and Felix and Mr. B. They're all sealed in their tomb below the earth."

"Mr. B would be at peace knowing he's buried on his mountain."

"I know. And Felix's mission is accomplished, isn't it?"

"I think he would say the outcome had the desired result. It's destiny."

"And my brother, he never had a chance in life like me. He's now sealed there forever at peace in the earth. He was created there and died there in the same spot. He came full circle. It's almost poetic isn't it? He was so tormented. I pitied him. I wanted to love him. But he couldn't let himself. He saw himself as such a monster. I wonder, would I be like him if we had been switched? I am part alien too."

"Maybe being part alien isn't so bad. I think you have all the good human elements and alien elements in you. Embrace it. Someday others from Elyon may come here. Think of it."

"But what about our child? What if it's a freak?"

"It will be our freak then. But we won't think it's a freak. We'll love it no matter what. You have a great capacity for love. Look, you were willing to forgive your brother and love him, weren't you?"

"Yes," she whispered.

"Your heart was wide open then and it is now, Laura."

"But what if someone finds out about it, like the government, and wants to take the baby away?"

"No one knows about you or us or the baby. Everyone who did is dead, except Andy now and he will never tell. No one can take our child away. And we won't give our baby away. You don't need to be afraid."

Laura put his fingers in hers. Her love flowed into Ben, covering him in peace. "I was gone so long because I was afraid to face you, Ben. Afraid to love anyone again. Afraid I would curse you as I had so many others. I felt like I didn't belong anywhere."

"Andy told me a long time ago love makes the world go 'round. I have found out since then, while it's corny, it's also true."

Laura smiled. "And maybe not just our world."

Ben laughed, glad she could see lightness in the situation. "You're the woman I love, no matter which world it is. This one or another. We're all beings in this infinite universe."

He kissed her, long and slow, pushing his tongue into her warm depths. "And you do belong. You belong with me. We belong together. And I know what you are."

"What am I?"

"You're the only woman I ever loved."

He felt his erection rising hard against her and moved back a little, but she grabbed his hand and placed it on her breast. It felt heavier, plump with her pregnancy. He rubbed her nipples into hard points and she moaned.

"I don't want to hurt you," Ben said, willing himself to go down.

"You won't. I've been reading up on it. And I visited a doctor a couple of times for a check up on the baby. She said sex is good."

"Of course sex is good." He moaned, as she caressed him. "But is it good for the baby?"

Laura laughed. "I don't think she'll mind."

"Or he."

And so Ben took her with tender grace their first night back together. She was so swollen in places that it seemed her senses were heightened to his touch. She trembled with pleasure encouraging him to fulfill her needs. He spread her wide open and licked her velvet softness until she gasped for him to stop.

"Now, Ben, I want you in me now."

And he accommodated her wishes, pushing into her wet, tightness with a groan of relief and cradled her to him. Hot tears fell down the sides of her face. He stopped, afraid of hurting her, but she shook her head and pulled him closer and he knew they were tears of joy.

He kissed her full breasts as he stroked her slowly, wanting to feel all of her. She pulsed around him with heat and want, taking him in deep, pulling him toward her. Her soft, round belly moved beneath him like a prayer, over and over and he kissed it knowing their love grew inside. And he thanked God for bringing her to him.

He was glad to be alive.

CHAPTER 36

Ben and Laura found a cozy bungalow to rent down near the ocean and moved in a few days later. There were tears of happiness as Likini and Laura hugged goodbye.

"We want you to be Aunt Laura soon. Won't you?"

"I'd be honored."

"Likini, they're only a couple of miles away," Andy reassured her. And that night, when Ben and Laura snuggled in their first bed together, they got the call baby Joseph was born.

"After my real dad," Andy boasted on the phone. "I wished he had lived to see the day." The mother was doing well and after many congratulations, well wishes, and promises to come see the baby they hung up and lay back in bed.

"It's so amazing, isn't it?" Laura stroked Ben's chest.

"What?"

"This creating of life. No matter how it happens."

"Yes. But that's the easy part. The hard part is making something worthwhile with your life."

"I remember Felix once said events can change in a second, re-directing your course. Sometimes unluckily so."

"Sometimes luckily, too."

Laura nodded then sighed. "There's something I've been wanting to do but was afraid to do it alone." She looked at Ben. He turned on his side to look at her, waiting, so she continued. "I want to see if I can transmit myself to Elyon with Felix's belt to see where I come from. Felix said the planet is dying. Do you think it's still there now?"

"I don't know. But it's worth a try. I'll be right beside you. Is there any danger in using the belt?"

"I don't know, honestly. I hadn't thought about it when using it to seek you out."

Laura went to the bedroom closet and from deep in the back, she pulled out a box. She opened it and drew out the belt. She touched its smooth texture. It rippled beneath her fingers, as if it were alive. It hung wide and heavy, created of metal she had never seen before. Its burnished gray steel shone in the soft lamplight. It moved from darker to lighter shades of gray in a fluid movement.

"Here it is." She handed it to Ben. "Once I wear it and push this series of buttons and envision where I want to go, it transmits me there. When I blink and open my eyes, I am in the place I want to go. But my body stays here. And see this green button here? If you push it, once I've been transmitted, it will send me back here."

"What happens to you here while you're transmitting yourself there?"

"I don't know. You'll have to tell me. Maybe I'm in a sleep-like state. I just know you can't be conscious as the same person in two places though."

"A paradox."

"Yes."

Ben looked at the belt and back at her. "Okay, let's do it. But if I see you in any distress I'm bringing you back here."

Laura nodded. "I'm scared to do it, yet need to, you know?"

Ben took her hand and pulled her to him on the bed. "I understand. I'm just worried for you and the baby if something goes wrong."

"I was fine the times I sought you out and you're here now." Laura smiled, rubbing her belly.

"What are you hoping to discover?"

"I'm not sure. Answers, maybe. To see the people I come from and communicate with them. But I'm afraid to do it as well because once I open up that door, if there is a door remaining, it could change everything."

Ben smiled. "You told me a long time ago that in finding out who you are and where you came from changed everything."

"And it did."

"And yet, here we are."

Laura smiled back at him. "Yes."

"So what else is there you couldn't face?"

"Nothing."

"And whatever it is, we'll face it together."

She stood up and put the belt on. It fit her now on the second to last loop. When she first tried it on months ago, it fit loose on the smallest belt hole. She eased into the wingback chair in the corner of the bedroom and Ben pulled up the ottoman to sit beside her. They looked at one another and he took her hand.

"I'm right here, always."

She nodded, biting her lip. *I want to go to Elyon.* She envisioned herself standing on the faraway planet. Then she pressed the buttons on the belt. The sound of traffic and the wind rushing through the trees around their bungalow disappeared. It was replaced with utter silence. It was so quiet it felt unbearable. She opened her eyes.

Light, soft and rose-colored, warmed the world around her. She stood on smooth, gray rock that spread outward in all directions and disappeared into whiteness. Mist and snow blew around her. It was hard to see more than a hundred feet in front of her. A humming grew inside her head, soft at first, and then it rose in urgency. Something moved through the mist. She clutched her belly and looked down. She shimmered, as Felix had. Her fingers moved through her belly like an apparition. Her baby was safe at home, next to Ben.

And you are safe with us, Laura. We've been expecting you.

She gasped as figures moved out of the mist and walked toward her bundled in gray robes. They looked like Feo, with tufts of white hair, opal skin, and yellow eyes. At first only a few came, then more came walking forward through the blowing snow. Different ones appeared. Some were massive with green eyes, like Felix. They stared at her and she sensed peace and great sadness. They were a people barely etching out existence on a dying planet. She tried to speak, but no words came out and so she spoke to them from her mind as they did.

I had to know where I came from. Feo was my father.

We know. We are glad he reached your planet and created life. It means we will carry on, not here on our planet but another. We are glad you survived.

My brother didn't.

We know. He was a tormented being, a Destroyer who gave into his darkness.

And Felix, he helped us. He was created from your visit before.

We know. We seek you out on Earth too and have been watching.

She wasn't sure which of the Elyon beings was speaking to her as they all stood, staring at her. They seemed to speak to her in a collective group. Then one stepped forward and reached out his pod fingers. Laura reached for them and her fingers spun in webs around his.

Felix was a good soul. He had a big heart, like you have, Laura. And like Feo did, your father. My name is Adrian and Feo was my brother.

Will you survive here...Adrian?

We have little time left here on Elyon. The cold, droughts, and famine are too great for us to continue much longer. Our planet is dying. Our people are dying. Our sun has nearly gone out. But we're preparing a final ship to reach Earth. It may take many months to get it ready as our resources become more limited. But we hope for all survivors this time. We have drawn a lottery to see who will go.

I'm glad. I wish it could be all of you.

The Elyon being nodded and smiled at her.

Take care of your child. He is a part of all of us and he connects our two worlds. Your name is fitting, Laura Armstrong. You have held much weight in your lifetime yet still remain strong. You may now be our only hope, if our journey does not succeed. Will your people welcome us this time?

I don't know. But I will, and I will try to convince others as well.

Then that is all we can hope for.

He moved back toward the others and they returned to the mist they came from. Laura felt a great sadness lift from her. Hope grew in her for the people of Elyon and for contact with Earth. She held her hands up to the mist. Snow fell gentle now. She looked one last time around her then pressed the green button on her belt. She opened her eyes to find Ben leaning forward with an anxious look on his face.

She held her belly now, to reassure herself she was indeed back on Earth and here with the man she loved. "They are coming. It may be many months, but they are coming again."

"We have all the time in the world, Laura."

"Yes, we do."

Two bright spots flooded her cheeks from excitement. Ben took her hand. She thought of the possibilities ahead for them—for Elyon, for the human race, for other planets out there with life that someday may come as well.

Laura's anxiety grew as her due date grew closer. Ben knew she hid it from Likini when they visited her, Andy, and baby Joseph. Their baby looked normal in every way. When Likini took him to her breast, Laura gripped Ben's hand. He thought too what she must be thinking. Would their baby look normal? Would he act normal?

They went to their first ultrasound to find out. Laura pulled on his fingers, twisting them in hers waiting for the screen to come alive with a picture. Ben bit his lip and said a prayer. Then, at last, they saw a perfect baby boy growing inside her. He turned, sucking his thumb like any baby. A boy, just like Felix predicted.

"Your son is a big boy," the doctor told them. "But not abnormally so, he could be a good nine pounds."

A HUMAN ELEMENT

"Is that okay?" Ben felt fear snake inside him.

"Yes, we will monitor Laura and we can always do a caesarean section if need be. We will take care of both of you. He is looking normal in every way, Mr. and Mrs. Fieldstone."

Laura cried and Ben squeezed her hand in reassurance. All will be okay, he thought. He hoped he was right. And it was funny everyone considered them married, but Ben wanted to give her his name. It worried him her due date drew close and they weren't bound together as husband and wife. He wanted them all to have the same name, and then would they truly be a family.

So when Ben got down on one knee in the sand on an evening beach walk and pushed a ring onto Laura's hand, it felt right. He had to put it on her pinkie finger as her hands were so swollen, but she said she didn't mind.

"Will you marry me, Laura Armstrong?"

"Only if you want children, Ben Fieldstone," she quipped. He embraced her enormous belly on his knees and they remained like that for a long while as the waves washed ashore and the moon shone down with its blessing. They walked along the beach afterwards, hand in hand, unhurried. Laura looked up at the stars and Ben followed her gaze.

"What do you see, Laura?"

"I see somewhere up there is home."

"Here too."

"My dad used to say I had two mommies, one in Heaven watching over me, and one on Earth watching over me." Her voice trembled. "Now I have a home up there watching over me and a home here too."

Ben put his arms around her. "And I'm here watching over you too. We're home to each other now. A family."

"I would say that's the desired outcome." Laura smiled up at him.

"Destiny."

"Fate."

"Forever."

And so they had a quick ceremony with Likini, baby Joseph, and Andy in attendance followed by brunch. Laura glowed in a cream-colored high-waist princess dress. The material flowed gracefully over her pregnancy, now pushing out everywhere in front of her.

"Here's a toast, to the two most meant-for people ever!" Andy held up his glass.

"A family now, you are." Likini smiled at Laura and then down at Joseph.

"We all are," Laura said. And it was true. He and Laura had both lost a family but were creating a new one now, together.

And when her water broke a few days later and the pains came, fast and intense, Ben held her hand all the way to the hospital. She squeezed his fingers so hard with a contraction he slammed on the brakes at a green light and recovered just in time to avoid a rear-end accident.

"It's happening so fast." Laura moaned. "Is it supposed to be like this?"

"I don't know." Ben sighed with relief when they reached the hospital.

"She's nearly at ten centimeters," the nurse said. "Your first child is coming fast. The doctor will be here soon. Everything looks good."

There was no time for an epidural. Laura held onto the hospital bed rail with her eyes closed. The pain must be unbearable, but he could only hold her hand feeling helpless and frustrated. He prayed it wouldn't be long. Her screams wrenched inside his gut, knowing he did this to her. All the pleasure they felt together to create such pain now. It was cruel.

The nurse had Ben help move Laura into a better birthing position. She was curled up on her side and they moved her onto her back so she was semi-reclined. The nurse pushed her hand deep up into Laura, who shrieked in agony. Ben bit his lips, willing her pain away. Let this be over.

"Please help her," he pleaded. "Can't you give her something for the pain?"

"It's too late, the baby is coming. I'm sorry. It will be over soon. She's doing a good job." The nurse soothed him, and pushed Laura's legs up and outward. She directed Ben to hold one of her legs up. "We've got to spread her as wide open as possible to help her push this baby out."

Ben was terrified. Laura tossed her head from side to side, spewing out staccato screams.

"Is she okay? And the baby...is he too big?"

"Your wife is doing fine and your son is too. He is in perfect position. I feel his head. Look, Mr. Fieldstone."

Ben, captivated by what Laura had created and now pushed out, stared at the top of his son's head.

"I don't want to see it!" Laura's legs shook. "Just get him out!" Then her screams turned to sobs. "He changed inside me! I know it." She looked at Ben with terror in her face and grabbed his arm. "Don't let him be a freak." She let go of his arm and closed her eyes.

"It'll be fine, Laura. I promise," Ben said, his other hand squeezing hers that hung onto the bed rail. He hoped he was right, as he wept alongside her. Felix said she would survive. He said the baby wouldn't be so big it would kill her, like the others. Like her mother. He had to believe Felix was right, again. And fate. Fate had brought them together and it would re-align now for good, not bad. It had to. Right?

"Push Laura, you've got to push now." The nurse encouraged her as she and Ben held her legs up. "Push down. The doctor will be here soon. Everything is fine. "

The doctor banged through the door into the room just as the baby slid out of Laura. The nurse held him up high. He was a gorgeous, wonderful boy.

Laura sank back. "It's over. He's alive." She clutched Ben's hand, but kept her eyes closed.

"And so are you," Ben whispered to her.

"My dear, you work too fast for me," the doctor said.

"Laura, look!" Ben shook her gently.

She opened her eyes. Ben smiled at her and pointed. Their baby boy was perfect in every way. Then he opened his eyes and looked at the nurse and doctor. They gasped.

Laura tried to sit up "What is it? Is my baby okay? His eyes, what color are they?"

"No, he's fine," the doctor said. "His eyes are a beautiful blue but I've never seen a newborn open his eyes so wide and so fast. He's smiling too! Unbelievable."

The nurse turned him toward Laura and Ben. Their son's eyes were indeed a brilliant blue. The nurse cleaned him up and weighed him in at nine pounds, then wrapped him in a blanket and placed him on Laura's chest.

"Hi there, James Felix Charles Fieldstone," she welcomed him, peering into his sweet face. He looked up direct into her eyes and smiled. "But we'll call you Charlie for short."

"He knows who you are," Ben said. He felt a tug deep inside him as he looked at his wife and son. He felt a contentment he had never known before. He kissed them both.

The nurse came over and touched Charlie's fingers that waved in the air. He grabbed her hand and held on. "Oh my, he is an amazing baby. One strong boy, that's for sure."

"Luckily so." Ben looked at Laura, who smiled back at him. He laughed out loud as he felt an overwhelming love fill him up. His heart was wide open.

Andy was right. Love indeed makes the world go 'round.

~ * ~

If you enjoyed this book, please consider writing a short review and posting it on your favorite review site. Reviews are very helpful to other readers and are greatly appreciated by authors, especially me. When you post a review, drop me an email and let me know and I may feature part of it on my blog/site. Thank you.

donnasgalanti@verizon.net

Here's a sneak peek at A HIDDEN ELEMENT…

CHAPTER 1: The Beginning

Silent dark hung under a star-filled sky.

The dark deepened as they headed into the forest. Ancient conifers towered over them, blocking out the moon. Rain fell cold and lifeless. The nearest town of Benevolence, Oregon, was five miles northwest.

Caleb Madroc's father stood across from him, waiting for his people to gather their belongings. Their pale faces glowed like orbs within gray hooded robes as they waited for his father's instruction.

"We head toward town," his father ordered. Caleb opened his mouth, but there were no words for his feelings of anger and loss at suddenly leaving the only home he'd ever known. It raged inside him, a tumult of emotion he must quell for now. At least his own black hair, like his face, was a constant reminder of his mother to his father. This made him glad.

Caleb shut his mouth and nodded, stepping in behind his father. Rain fell cold and lifeless. He fell behind as he helped the womenfolk with their bags. One young female sent him a furtive, desperate look as she touched his hand in passing.

I'm so scared. What will happen to us?

He smiled at her. *Keep your thoughts to yourself. It's safer this way. All will work out once we settle.* She bit her lip, her eyes full of tears, and nodded looking back down at her feet.

"Father, how much further? Some of the younger females are struggling," Caleb said.

His father's eyes stung him through the mist rising up from the forest floor. They were eyes so different from his, and from his mother's. Caleb had often seen sadness and pity for his father in his mother's eyes. The day he had found her dead in the well her eyes held only nothingness.

"Can't we stop and rest, Adrian?" A few in the group grumbled. They looked wet and tired, a sea of gray flowing before him. His father glowered at their weakness. As Caleb scanned the sodden crowd a female smiled at his father, holding the promise of submission. Perfect for his father, who wanted to breed another son to take his place. A worthy son.

"We do not stop." His father's voice rose over the line of people before him, and he smiled back at the female and a strange sense of relief washed over Caleb. If his father did create a new prodigal son to groom it might remove his first born from his watchful eye.

With that thought, anguish over his mother's absence hit him fresh again. At eighteen and bigger than his father, he still needed his mother. She had been his kindred spirit, like Uncle Brahm. But now he was alone in this strange place. No longer did he have someone to be his true self with. He must step carefully.

His father continued to scan his flock. They stood still and silent, conveying their subservience. He nodded, apparently satisfied with their response. "You all took the oath to come here. Hard work lies before us in breeding our new community. Understood?"

They nodded in a collective wave.

Just like you bred with Aunt Manta while your wife lay dead? Caleb spewed out in his head without thinking.

His father moved closer, until his flaring nostrils touched his. Caleb stepped back, but his father gripped his arm. Dozens of eyes watched their battle.

Do not ever mention my brother's wife's name again, Son.

His father's fingers pinched him hard and his hot breath pulsed across his face, but Caleb couldn't stop. *Mother's dead because of you. And what about Aunt Manta? Did you kill her, too?*

I didn't kill anyone. And your mother should have been more careful.

You let her travel alone. She fell and died because she was alone.

It was your well, Caleb, she fell into. Your hideaway you carelessly covered up. Your fault.

His father's accusations stabbed him with painful truth. He sucked in his breath. *My fault. Yes. My fault.*

He looked around the watchful crowd as his head reeled with the agony of what he had done. His people stared back at him, their thoughts hid behind blank faces. Why did they come? Didn't they have dreams and wants and needs of their own, too? Or were they all obedient drones of his father?

His father thrust his arm away and turned around, plunging faster through the woods. Caleb hesitated then followed behind, trying to keep up. He envisioned himself standing still until everyone glided around him, leaving him to remain alone under a watchful moon.

Branches snagged his robe shooting him back to reality. His father's people followed in silence. If they didn't obey there would be consequences. As Caleb knew. He had no special privilege here as Adrian's son.

At last his father stepped out onto a paved road. It stretched far into the distance, where welcoming lights beckoned them across the final mile. They reached the main intersection of town. A car flashed by. A radio blared. Faces stared out at them. He stared back. They were so different from himself and yet…not.

He broke his gaze realizing how out of place this group looked late at night. The people here wore jeans and shirts, the shapes of their bodies outlined under tight clothes. The female's curves called to him, unlike his people who clothed themselves in shapeless robes to discourage free sexual thoughts. They were now to breed only with those chosen for them.

His father led them single file down the sidewalk. A handful of people sat behind windows drinking. They pointed at them as they walked by. "Gillian's Bar" flashed in neon green above the doorway in the late evening hours. A man and woman, heading into the bar, stepped back from the sidewalk to watch them pass. *Freaks*, he heard the man say. And his father erased the memory of the encounter from these strangers' minds in the seconds it took to pass them.

"Father," Caleb whispered in his ear. "Where are we going?"

A large building rose at the far end of a parking lot. "Ray's Lots" blinked over and over.

"Here is where we go."

A woman pushed a cart filled with bags to her car, the only car left in the lot. She stopped and stared at them. Her hair framed her face in tight curls. A blue and white striped dress strained to contain her breasts and belly.

"Good evening, brothers," she said with a hesitant smile.

His father motioned for them to stop. He smiled at her. She smiled back.

"Good evening, madam," his father drawled.

"God bless you." She grabbed his father's hand. Caleb swallowed a laugh at the way his father looked at her with such a serious, doting face.

"And God bless you, my child."

"What church are you with?" The woman fingered a cross at her neck. "Are you having an event in town?"

His father had said a church was the perfect cover. One of the many cultural ways learned before infiltration. All part of his father's master plan.

"It's the Church of Elyon," his father said.

The woman took her hand away and frowned. "Never heard of it. You're not one those crazy cults are you?"

Caleb stepped to his father's side. *Let me work her mind, Father.* "What's your name, Madam?"

"Sally."

"I'm Caleb Madroc." He shook her hand hoping his father didn't have some depraved mission in mind. Caleb wanted to get food for their hungry group and shelter and have as little interaction with these town people as possible. "We're simple folks. Our bus broke down outside of town. We seek food and a place to stay nearby. Can you help us?"

"What a nice young man you are. Of course I can help you." She abandoned her cart and pulled Caleb toward the store. "My cousin runs this store and can stock you up with food. And the Mercenary Motel is down the street."

He didn't understand her eagerness as she dragged him along then it was made clear by his father's mirthful laugh. His father had probed her mind and now controlled it—she would do whatever he commanded.

Caleb followed her into the store. Their people streamed in behind. Sally dragged him to a counter where a short red-faced man scowled at them. "Ray, these folks are here in town from a wonderful church. Their bus broke down and they need food."

Within seconds Ray's frown changed to a wide grin as Caleb's father continued his mind games. "Come in, come in. Time to close up anyhow." He flicked the sign on the front door and shut off the lights outside.

"Thank you," his father said. "I need food here for my flock before we find a place to stay."

"Help yourself to anything you want." Ray ran his hands over shelves. "Pretzels, baked beans, cereal, Ding Dongs. We even sell the word of the Lord." Sally and Ray beamed at them.

His father directed everyone to gather food and drinks. Sally and Ray stood by the counter, their minds blank except for what his father put into them. He dared not combat his father's powers. Not here. Not now. But someday.

"Ray, I need all your money now," his father said.

Ray clapped his hands together. "Of course." He pulled money from a nearby metal box.

When his father's bag burst full of items he handed it to a community member and cocked his head at Ray and Sally. "Time to go now, my new friends." He motioned his people out the door. Ray and Sally stood with stupid smiles on their faces as the group filed out into the parking lot. All, except his father.

"Come on, Father," Caleb pleaded, the dark knot in his stomach hardened. "Our job here is done."

"Not quite." His father moved toward the smiling cousins, a book in his hand. *The Holy Bible.* He thumbed through it to a passage and looked up smiling. "As for God, his way is perfect, is it not?"

"The word of God is true," Sally sang out, clutching Ray's hand. Her cousin nodded.

"Ray, isn't Sally lovely? Look at her." His father pointed at the heavy set woman.

Ray turned to Sally. His pants bulged and Sally's eyes widened. She tugged on her dress top.

"Have your way with her Ray, you know you want to."

"Father," Caleb whispered, clutching at him but his father stayed his hand.

Ray licked his lips and nodded.

"Sally, unzip your fine dress and show Ray what you've got."

Sally stepped out of her dress in a motion more fluid than one would have thought possible given her size. Her belly oozed over her thighs and her bra cut into her mountainous breasts. Ray panted, tapping his hands against his skinny legs.

Caleb moved toward the door.

"Stay, Son, I want you to watch this."

"I won't."

"You *will* or you know what will happen."

Caleb stopped and sighed, looking down at the floor. Eyes watched from the parking lot.

"Look."

Caleb focused on the dirt in the floor cracks. His muscles twitched with anger. His father thrived on his hate, wanted him to hate—wanted his son to be a Destroyer like him. They had hidden their true selves for so long and now were free here to unleash it. Not Caleb. He refused to give in to the dark inside. He tried to release the hate for his father, but it now filled his every pore. He made a vow right then and there, he'd never allow himself to be controlled. No matter the consequences.

He finally looked up. His father nodded, pleased, and turned back to his playthings. Ray massaged his crotch. Sally moaned, squeezing her mammoth breasts, and stepped out of her underwear.

"Take her, Ray. Bend her right over the counter. Dive into all her lushness."

"Lush, yes." Ray moved toward Sally, fumbling to unbuckle his pants. She squealed with glee and bent over the counter to receive him, her white bottom rising like a pitted sea of blubber. Ray mounted her, forged a path through her two white mountains, and slapped up against her in his glory.

"Lordy, Lordy," Sally sang out as she bounced up and down.

"Now that's wholesome entertainment." His father jabbed him. Caleb jerked away. "They're both enjoying it."

Caleb clenched his fists and shoved them in his pockets. "Can we go now?"

"Yes, Son, only one more thing to do."

His father pulled out something that looked like a handle. He flicked it open to reveal a small knife he must have picked up in the hardware section. He placed it next to Ray on the counter. Sweat flicked off the red-faced man's forehead as he plunged into buttery flesh.

"Ray, enjoying yourself?"

Ray grunted and grabbed on to Sally's hips, sinking into her expanse. She moaned again in delight as her buttocks shuddered.

"Good. When you're done fucking, kill the bitch."

His father strode out the door, pulling Caleb along with him.

"Father, no." Caleb struggled against him as his father shoved him hard through the door. Caleb spiraled his thoughts into Ray's brain. *Stop, Ray! She's your cousin, your family!*

Ray stopped his thrusting as if listening to Caleb, but his father's punch to his face ended his brain probe. Caleb staggered back, blood gushing from his nose. Ray straightened his head and rammed into Sally with a loud groan. Caleb drew his hand back but his father's fingers crushed his forearm. He fell to his knees. Blood spattered down his gray robe. The flock widened their circle, silent and watching. His father led as both law maker and enforcer.

"These lowly forms of life must be controlled," his father said. "We've studied their ways. Now, this first act is how we begin their demise and our rule. We will grow in number with our selected breeding and thrive as these useless beings die out. Watch this historic moment, Son, for anyone who turns away will be marked weak…and unworthy."

All eyes turned to the inside of the store as the desperate carnal scene played out to the end.

"I hate you," Caleb whispered, watching the forced lovers before him.

His father smiled at him in satisfaction.

Ray arched his back with a moan and finished his business. Sally squealed and pressed up against him. And when Ray raised his knife and plunged into Sally in new ways, she squealed again. And again. Her blood ran onto scuffed tiles and still she squealed. And then she stopped.

Tears filled Caleb's eyes and he closed them against the evil scene.

His father laughed. "Don't you see, Son?" He shook *The Holy Bible* at him. "I am their Way, their Truth, their Life—and Death."

Caleb did not answer. He remained inside his dark prison and swore someday he would end his father's rule.

CHAPTER 2: Seven years later

Laura Fieldstone eased herself up from the rocking chair. She bumped into the lamp. Lately, her belly poked out everywhere. She stretched, feeling the pain. Her back ached from sitting all day, but she had a deadline to get this book written before the baby came. It was the final one in a series of three. She would send it off to her editor and then take a long break.

She needed a break from the headaches that had returned. She couldn't tell Ben. He would worry, and she tried not to worry herself. Having a baby at forty was much harder than at twenty six. Her body *felt* older as this baby strained within her. This baby, who took her unaware fourteen years after having Charlie. Long after Ben had a vasectomy.

Ben joked that one snuck through. Her doctor said it did happen, but her natural mother's adamant belief she had been a virgin filled Laura's mind as her belly grew. No one had believed her mother, and yet it had been true. Surreal. Had her baby also been created from someone other than the man she loved? When she allowed herself to wonder that awful reality she shoved the thoughts down deep inside. They were too horrific to define. *This child is mine and Ben's. We created him in love.* She said it to herself like a mantra as if to seal it in truth.

And so this baby grew inside her. A baby who kicked so much it seemed he wanted to break free early into the world. He stormed violently inside her. Would he be violent when he arrived? *No.* Their baby was perfect. Like Charlie had been. On the outside at least. She had seen the ultrasound. But what would he be like on the inside?

The thought of what her baby *could be* twisted in her like a sickness. During those times Ben held her and whispered calming things in her ear. *There's only good inside you,* he'd say. *Our son will be fine, just like our Charlie. There is too much love in this house for anyone to grow up evil,* he'd say.

Like her twin had. Like this child could be.

Sometimes Ben laid her down on the bed and showed her in sweet ways how everything was all right. They still drew fire from one another after fifteen years. She laughed. She was eight months pregnant and Ben still touched her with his flames. Even at fifty-one he couldn't get enough of making love to his very pregnant wife. But Charlie could be home any moment now from school, and that spiked her worry about him again.

She eased her anxiety by picking up the first children's book she had ever published, and rubbed her fingers over the cracked cover of a blue pony riding across the sky. *Big Brave Blue.* He was a flying pony who lived in the clouds. His colors blended into the sky and even as a runt he flew faster than any other pony, but he grew up lonely. His size and color separated him from his world's orange herd of giant ponies, but he had an advantage besides speed. He could blend into the sky making it hard for their enemy, the Dragon Beasts, to catch him when they plundered their land.

And when he faced the Dragon Beast leader and killed him in battle to save his herd, his own kind looked at him in a different light. When others like him were born, the herd realized they were evolving into an improved species, and they called upon tiny Blue to lead them into their new future.

She could hear Charlie's voice. *Again, Mommy. Read it again.* And she did. And then he would tug on her sleeve and quote his favorite line. *Being big doesn't mean you're brave—only big of heart does. Am I big of heart, Mommy, like Big Brave Blue?* She would look down at his little head and breathe his baby smell and say, *the biggest heart of all, Charlie.*

That was before he'd discovered his differences. Now her heart ached for him most days as he faced the bullies who saw them, too.

She peered out the bay window. The water raged rough across the Sound today. Waves ripped up and pounded toward land, a watery creature bent on blind destruction. The wind creaked through their ranch house. Wild and primordial and unfettered. Some days it called to her. It filled her with a deep yearning for something she didn't understand. On those days she felt unsettled, waiting for something, anything to happen. She wished to be the wild wind at times, unbound and free. The wind taunted and beckoned her at the same time. It's why she loved living on Puget Sound.

She had fallen in love with the grandness of Washington State. A place different from the Northeast where she came from, which held memories of her peaceful childhood. A place where she and Ben met. It had also been a place of horrific times. Of losing her parents, her friends, and nearly Ben. Their home now, in being so different, helped her forget her past.

She thought living across the country in Oregon was far enough to forget. It was home. She had persuaded Ben to stay on the west coast. His photography assignments allowed him to live anywhere, as did her author lifestyle. And they could leave behind their violent past that had flung them together. Close enough to be home. Far enough away to forget.

Today though, she urged the wind away. She had things to do before the baby came and didn't want to become lost in restlessness. Where *was* Charlie? She peered out the back door into the woods that their house backed up to. She hoped he hadn't taken a detour through the woods from school. She wished he took the bus. He spent too much time in the woods alone, as she had as a child.

The woods stretched deep for miles. A person could get lost in them. Or die in them.

Perhaps the wind blew a yearning in her son as well and the woods provided him comfort. She couldn't take this from him, not with the burdens he carried. Someday she would tell him the true meaning behind his abilities. But not yet. She wanted him to be old enough to handle it— and not let it destroy him.

There. Charlie's tall figure strode from the woods, hunched over. Taller than his father, he tried to hide his height. Being 6' 5" at fourteen was a physical trait that made him a target ripe for teasing. Not to mention his other features. She waved at him, but he didn't wave back. He put his head down and slowed his walk to the house. *Now what?*

Laura rubbed her belly and opened the door for him.

"Charlie, I was getting worried," Laura said. "You went to the woods after school, didn't you?" She looked down at his muddy knees, wondering what he had been doing out there this time.

He nodded but didn't look up, just shuffled in the door. She sensed his sadness, frustration, and anger. She wondered what he was thinking, but he seemed to have an innate ability to cloak his thoughts. Did she really want to know all the wild ideas that went through a fourteen year old boy's mind? Ben told her definitely not.

"What's wrong?" Laura hugged his waist from behind at an angle.

"That jerk, Brian, at school, that's what's wrong."

He turned around and set his backpack on the deacon's bench by the door. When he looked at Laura she gasped.

"Charlie, what happened?" His left eye had a cut above it and his lip swelled on one side next to a darkening bruise on his cheek. He shoved his hands in his pockets, but Laura pulled them out and sighed over his scraped knuckles. She pulled him to the sink and ran cool water over his hands, smoothing away the dried blood.

His nail-less fingers stretched long and thick in her small ones. Her pink painted orbs stood out in sharp contrast to his flesh-like pads. How she wished his nails had never fallen off as a newborn. He flexed his fingers and pulled away from her then plunked his large frame down on the bench. Legs and arms spewed everywhere like Bambi on ice. His silver white hair had streaks of mud in it. She got a clean dish rag and wet it, pressing it gently to the cut over his eye. He grabbed it from her. She saw flecks of blood on his shirt and hoped it was his.

"I'm okay, Mom," he said then blew out a big breath. "Didn't mean to grab."

Laura sat down next to him. "Tell me."

"I came out of study hall and ran right into Brian with his gang. He called me a Fieldstone freak and said I belonged in the Guinness Book of World Records. Giant albino pod-man. It's his newest nickname for me." Charlie stretched his long fingers out wide.

Laura took his hand. "You have beautiful fingers. They're—"

"No, Mom, they're not." Charlie snatched his hand away and held it up to her face. "I *am* albino pod-man. Look at me."

"I don't think so." She touched his hair. "Your dad doesn't think so."

"Yes he does. He thinks I'm a freak."

"He does *not* think you're a freak. He loves you."

"I heard him with you. He said I'm not normal and I'll never fit in."

Laura wished for the thousandth time Charlie had never heard their conversation. It had been late at night and they had no idea Charlie had been passing by their room then. Words to sting for a lifetime.

"He didn't mean it in the way you think, Charlie. He just doesn't want you to have a hard life."

"Whatever." He turned away and crossed his arms.

"We can do the surgery, Charlie."

"Like Dad wants me to have? Then everyone will know I have artificial nails on me, like I'm a girl or something."

"That we can change. Your hair color we can change. Your height we can't. Someday you'll be glad to be tall."

"Someday can't come soon enough." He sighed. She moved beside him and touched his hand again. This time he didn't pull away.

His teen years loomed long in front of him. How she wished she could make it better for him. Make all kids fair and nice. Sometimes she wanted to tell Charlie to pummel Brian, but she had to be the grown up and maintain self-control. It was the core of everything she taught her son.

"So then what happened?"

"He had an accident, sort of." Charlie smirked and bent his head.

"Accident? Really?" Laura crossed her arms and leaned back into the bench. Her belly ached, muscles pulling from all directions to hold up the weight she bore. One more month she had to get through.

"Okay, it wasn't an accident but I've had enough of him, Mom!" Charlie stood up and banged on the kitchen table with a sharp *crack*.

Laura frowned at him. "Remember what happened the last time you got so angry. You smashed the lawn mower to smithereens and it cost you all the money saved up to buy a new one."

"*Self-control*. I know, Mom." Charlie leaned up against the kitchen counter. "Sorry. Sometimes I get so mad. I hate having to control it. It's not fair."

"I understand, but you know what your strength can do. You didn't use it against Brian today, did you?"

"I tried not to." He shook his head. "I wouldn't do it to someone on purpose."

Laura believed him, but she wondered if the 'tried not to' would result in a phone call soon from Brian's mom. Charlie was a good kid at heart, sensitive to hurting others. He didn't want the strength that came with his powers. Laura never spoke of them as powers to Charlie though. She called them genetic anomalies. It softened them.

She told him they were part of an anger syndrome. His outbursts often triggered them, and Laura used this as a reason. Their pediatrician agreed and said Charlie had some anger tendencies and gave him techniques to combat them. His nail defects were explainable. Ectodermal dysplasia. A condition where a child is born with nail defects or no nails at all. But that's not what he had.

Some kids would have liked Charlie's abilities. Not Charlie. He hated being strong like a bully. He hated kids who teased. He never teased. He wanted to treat everyone the same way he wanted to be treated. He acted older in so many ways but immature as any teen. Laura never knew when he might exhibit maturity or immaturity. Right now she had the feeling the immature part was about to be revealed.

"So?" Laura raised her eyebrows at him.

"Well, his pants must have been too baggy as they kind of…fell off him in the hallway, in front of all these girls. He tried to pick them up but somehow his shoes got tied together and he fell over. Those tighty-whities mooned everyone. So sad."

"Charlie." Laura tried to sound angry as she overcame the urge to laugh.

Charlie shrugged. "Mom, come on. It was too funny. I'm sick and tired of him picking on me. He teased me last week for wearing tighty-whities in the locker room and now everyone knows he wears them, too.

Besides, I didn't hit him or anything." He stopped smiling and looked down. "Well, not then anyways."

"What did you do, Charlie?" Laura was afraid to know. The memory flickered of their cat, Romeo, and an overenthusiastic five year old Charlie who liked to hug. Only he didn't know what his hugs could do. They buried Romeo in the backyard and told Charlie it wasn't his fault, but it didn't make Laura cry any less. She had loved that cat. There were no more pets from then on.

"He said I pantsed him and—"

"You did."

"Yes, but then he said he'd get me after school, so I thought I'd avoid him and take the woods home instead of the bus—"

"And because you wanted to let off some steam, right?"

"Yeah, okay. But not *at* anyone. I wanted to feel better. Not so…angry." He gripped the counter and bit his lip. "But Brian didn't take the bus either, he followed me. Him and his stupid friends. He hit me first, Mom."

"I believe you."

"I let him hit me. I told myself he's inconsequential, like you told me to think. I *did*. I tried to keep on walking and ignore him, but then the others started hitting me. It wasn't fair. Three of them against one." He clenched his fist, looked at it, and shoved it in his pocket. "I laughed at Brian and told him he's irrelevant."

Laura suppressed a smile.

"He didn't even know what it meant. What a dummy. So I told him to go find a dictionary. He hit me again and I hit him back. I tried to do it light, I swear, but—"

"But what? What did you do, Charlie?"

"I think I broke his nose." He blew out a giant breath. "Blood came out everywhere. I didn't know a nose had so much blood in it."

"Oh, Charlie." Laura stood up, pressing a hand to her back, and walked over to him.

"I hate myself." She took his strong hands. He stood tall over her with a child's heart trapped in man's body.

"Don't say that. I love you. Dad loves you."

"Why am I like this, Mom? I don't want to be *special*, okay?" He pulled his hands away. "I didn't want to hit him. I swear. You can have a doctor make me fingernails and toenails. Can a doctor make me normal, too? Take away these things I can't control?"

He jerked away from Laura and got a drink from the fridge. The phone rang. Laura sighed. It could only be one person.

Brian's mother.

CHAPTER 3

Charlie snuck back out to the woods after his mom got off the phone with Brian's mom. His mom acted so cool and calm about what he did. He wished he could be more like her and not like her at the same time. Did that make sense?

She left then to do errands and his dad was still out on some wildlife photo shoot in the mountains. She didn't say he couldn't go out to the woods so it didn't feel like disobeying. He just needed to get out his frustration. No Brian and his stupid friends. Charlie replayed the moment again where he had embarrassed Brian. Pants down. Butt in the air. Girls laughing. Awesome. But he did feel bad about hitting him so hard. He really, really hadn't meant to.

He needed advice and he hoped Ghost Man would be there. He had called him that since he first saw him at seven. The man said he was Charlie's special secret. As Charlie got older he felt odd not telling his parents, but how could he explain he'd been seeing this guy all these years?

It would make him even weirder. His dad would think so. He never understood him. He wanted him to be normal. He wanted him to have the nail surgery. *I'll never be normal! Why can't he accept me for who I am? Because I'm not good enough, that's why.* The main reason he didn't want the surgery was to defy his dad, even to spite himself, and so he remained the freak he was born to be.

His dad's words remained burned in his brain from that night a couple of years ago when he'd heard his parents talking.

"If only he weren't the way he is," his dad had said. "He'd have a normal life. He'd be normal."

"Don't ever say that," his mom had said. "I love him just the way he is."

"I love him, too, but…it's hard."

"Love always is, Ben, but you don't ever give up."

"Sometimes I want to."

Charlie had turned back to his room then after those last words from his dad. He hadn't wanted to hear anymore. That day the wall grew between them. He would never be the son his dad wanted.

But Ghost Man treated him like a son. Charlie wanted to keep him all to himself. Ghost Man understood him and helped him figure things out. He said he should embrace his anger and be himself. Charlie felt conflicted about it, but sometimes it felt so good to be angry and destroy things. And Ghost Man helped him practice his destroying powers. But never on people. Or animals. He still felt guilty about Romeo. If he did such a thing then, what power did he have now? It scared him to think about it.

He walked deep into the woods on the narrow path. It used to be a deer path that became his path as he trudged over it through the years. He liked knowing the animals made it before he came along, and now he kept it going. Gloom settled under the tall pine trees. Their great branches shaded all below. These woods soon blended into the national forest.

He stepped out from the trees into a sunny meadow. Often, when he was drained from practicing his powers he stretched out on the soft green waves. He wanted to lay there forever and be invisible. Invisible was good. Then he couldn't be called a freak. If his parents saw what he did here they would think he was a freak, too.

He touched his cheek. It throbbed still. He sat down on the ground and waited. He hoped Ghost Man came today. The meadow had become their spot. It's where he first met him when he got lost in the woods at seven. His mom and dad had been terrified and called the police, but Ghost Man directed him back home. It was the first time he kept a secret from his parents.

"Had a fight, I see, Charlie-boy."

Charlie jumped up. Ghost Man shimmered before him.

"Yeah, jerks. Called me a freak."

"I saw. Nice work breaking that kid's nose."

"I didn't want to but—"

"You needed to. I understand. I can show you ways to hurt him without touching him yourself. No one will ever know."

"My dad wouldn't understand."

"Yes, well, your dad doesn't have your special abilities. He's ordinary. You don't want to be ordinary like him, do you, Charlie-boy?"

"I don't want to be like him, but I don't want to be me, either." He tapped his foot, frustrated at being stuck in his life. He had nowhere to go, no one to talk to, and no one who understood him—except Ghost Man.

"Your dad is ignorant to the kind of abilities you have. And in his ignorance lies weakness. He knows you're a stronger man than he'll ever be. It's why he keeps you down about yourself, Charlie. He's your biggest oppressor."

Charlie had heard these words before, seeping into him for years building the wall brick-by-brick between him and his dad. But now Ghost Man's words hit him in the gut—they twisted there and formed the truth inside him which all made sense now.

"My dad is jealous of me."

"Yes. You're more a man than him. Wait and see. Your life won't always be like this. Your time to shine shall come."

"Like showing those bullies?"

Ghost Man nodded.

Charlie squinted. The sunlight streamed through Ghost Man in waves. "I don't want to hurt anybody, though. I just want them to leave me alone."

"It's your destiny to be powerful, Charlie. Don't you want to know how you're supposed to use your abilities? No one will ever call you a freak again. Not bullies and not your father—for that's what he thinks you are, isn't't?"

Charlie nodded, feeling miserable.

"You can control others," Ghost Man said. "I can show you how."

"Control others? Sounds scary." *And awesome.*

Ghost Man moved closer. "Life is scary, Charlie, for most people. It doesn't need to be for people like you and me. I am a powerful being who others follow, and I can show you how to control that bully. I can show you how you can make him disappear. No one will ever know you did it."

Except my mom. She'll know.

"Your father can't show you such power, can he?'

Charlie shook his head and looked down, twisting his fingers in his pockets. He wasn't sure how to feel about controlling someone. His mom had taught him to control himself, not others, and to never hurt anyone. He had to be more responsible than other kids, she said. It wasn't fair. Ghost Man held out his hands to Charlie. His fingers flexed smooth and nail-less like Charlie's.

"I've been waiting for the right time to tell you. You're old enough now to understand. I come from Elyon."

"A made up place."

"No. A real place, where I belonged to a secret underground society.

We planned to rule the world with our powerful genes. Others wanted to crush our dreams and almost did once. But we came back, more powerful than ever. We've come here to follow our dream."

"Is Elyon far away?"

"Further away than you can imagine."

"Tell me. Where?"

"In due time, Charlie-boy."

Charlie nodded, not pushing for more. He wanted Ghost Man to remain make-believe. The thought of him being a real person from a real place hung in his thoughts like an unwanted gift.

He held out his hand and touched the apparition before him. Tingling pulsed into his fingers from the fingers that mirrored his own. Rage filled him. He looked around. Alone. As usual. He picked up a rock and threw it hard with a shout. And another.

"You can do better, Charlie-boy." Ghost Man smiled at him.

Adrenalin coursed through him. He commanded his hands. Branches wrenched from the trees. They crashed together. He dragged rocks from the earth with his mind and pounded them into the ground. Sweat ran down his face. It stung the cut over his eye and that made him angrier. He screamed and flung his body about, inanimate objects battling each other. Drained, he sank down on the meadow floor. Ghost Man floated over him, smiling.

"Feel better?"

Charlie nodded.

"I can teach you how to make someone do anything you want."

"Anything?"

"Yes."

Charlie thought about this. "You mean I could make Brian do bad things to himself?"

"Yes."

"So it wouldn't be me hurting him but him hurting himself?"

"Yes. Do you trust me, Charlie?"

Charlie nodded. Ghost Man was his guardian angel. He watched over him and made him feel better. His dad made him feel worse. He didn't want to feel bad anymore about who he was.

Revenge filled Charlie with a sweet rush. "Yes."

~ * ~

A HIDDEN ELEMENT is available in eBook and trade paperback and can be found at your favorite retailer.

Message from the Author

Dear Reader,

Adoption and being an only child runs through my book *A Human Element*. I am both and they had a deep impact on my life.

In *A Human Element* three characters have similar lives. Laura Armstrong is adopted and an only child raised by loving parents. Ben Fieldstone is an only child but abandoned to live a lonely existence in foster homes. X-10 is raised alone in a government facility, an unloved experiment. One common thread connects them. They grow up alone and eventually parentless.

Adopted children often suffer abandonment issues and feel like they never belong, that they aren't 'blood family'. Being adopted myself I understood this. But as an adopted child I was lucky. I had a loving family and I learned my heritage (and am *very* glad I was given up). I got married and had an amazing son. In having him, I have my own 'blood' now. I do belong—with my family.

In *A Human Element* all three characters have similar backgrounds, but how are they different? Ben isolates himself, Laura has an open heart, and X-10 hates the world. Is it their genes that shape who they are or their environment? I've found it's a bit of both.

And can environment overcome genes? I believe that our genes do not dictate who we are—and this gives me hope. And without hope change is not possible.

I like to think we can overcome our genes and thrive in an environment that allows us to do so. In such an environment we can conquer our obstacles and achieve anything, but without love we are lost.

Ben's friend in *A Human Element* tells him that love indeed does make the world go 'round. I believe it. Do you?

About the Author

Donna Galanti writes murder and mystery with a dash of steam as well as middle grade adventure fiction. She is the author of the bestselling paranormal suspense *Element Trilogy.* She also writes for children and is the author of two fantasy adventures series with *Joshua and The Lightning Road* and *Unicorn Island.* She regularly presents as a guest author at schools and teaches writers through her online Udemy courses. Donna has lived in fun locations including England, her family-owned campground in New Hampshire, and in Hawaii where she served as a U.S. Navy photographer for Fleet Intelligence Pacific. She now lives with her family and two crazy cats in an old farmhouse that sadly, has no ghosts. Visit her at elementtrilogy.com and donnagalanti.com.

~ * ~

If you enjoyed this book, please consider writing a short review and posting it on your favorite review site. Reviews are very helpful to other readers and are greatly appreciated by authors, especially me. When you post a review, drop me an email and let me know and I may feature part of it on my blog/site. Thank you.

donna@donnagalanti.com

www.ingramcontent.com/pod-product-compliance
Lightning Source LLC
Chambersburg PA
CBHW071503110726
47908CB00003B/708